# A Year in the Château

## Sarah Long

ZAFFRE

First published in Great Britain in 2020 by
ZAFFRE
80–81 Wimpole St, London W1G 9RE

Copyright © Sarah Long, 2020

A CIP catalogue record for this book is
available from the British Library.

ISBN: 978–1–78576–476–9

*Also available as an ebook*

1 3 5 7 9 10 8 6 4 2

Typeset by IDSUK (Data Connection) Ltd
Printed and bound in Great Britain by Clays Ltd, Elcograf S.p.A.

Zaffre is an imprint of Bonnier Books UK
www.bonnierbooks.co.uk

*For my dad, Ron Long*

# Part One

# Winter

# CHAPTER ONE

A dull night in January is the best time to start again. Just when you think the days will never get longer and you feel the heavy girdle of Christmas excess wrapped around your middle as you lie on the sofa and wonder if you can be bothered to get up to make a cup of tea.

Nicola pulled the rug over her knees – the central heating only really kicked in when Dominic came back from the office – grabbed her phone and decided she'd play one more round of Ruzzle. She'd never thought of herself as having an addictive personality but she loved the adrenaline hit of forming words against the clock.

Thirty-seven games later, she heard a key in the door and guiltily slipped her phone into her pocket, picking up the improving book with no narrative drive that was abandoned on the coffee table. Ruzzle was sneaky like that, the way it hooked you in, so anyone with time on their hands and a reasonable vocabulary could easily waste an entire afternoon. Still, at least it wasn't Candy Crush. She had deleted that after one too many nights spent in its thrall.

Dominic put his head around the door, stern-faced in his reflective jacket and bicycle helmet.

'You look cosy,' he said, managing to make it sound judge-mental. 'I need a drink – do you want one?'

'Bit early for me. And you can take your helmet off now, you're not in enemy territory.'

'Says you. You've no idea what it's like out there, tucked up on your snug sofa. I'm going to get changed, then we need to talk.'

He pulled the door shut behind him; it was important to keep the heat in, now Nicola only had her pension to rely on, as he liked to remind her. Albeit a doctor's pension, beyond the wild-est dreams of anyone in the private sector, as he also liked to remind her. Like most GPs, she had taken early retirement – you only had to do the maths to see why. The reduction in income seemed worth it for the sake of no more sleepless nights over how her most fragile patients were doing. No more passing over the tissue box as she sent people she'd treated for years for tests she knew would bring no good news. No more worried patients burdening her with minor ailments or their own latest theory on what Google said was wrong with them.

Dom said they needed to talk – that sounded heavy. She pulled her phone out of her pocket. Might as well fit in another game before whatever it was. A two-minute window to calm the mind and put her opponent, bigmouth69, back in her box.

'Sorry for being grumpy,' said Dominic, reappearing in jeans and the grey jumper she had bought him for Christmas to complement what she affectionately called his Nigel Havers bouffant. 'I just had such a shit day.'

He sat down beside her and lifted her feet onto his lap.

Nicola pressed pause – no point giving the round away – and gave him her attention.

'Poor you. I remember how that feels.'

In her case, a shit day might have resulted in someone's death – a missed diagnosis, a failure of judgement. But she never played the moral superiority card; every job had its own pressures.

'Which is why I said we need to talk.' He jumped up and made his way to the fridge. 'Is it late enough for you now?'

'Go on then.'

He filled two glasses with their favourite Chablis premier cru and moved briskly back towards her. Cock of the walk; she loved his energy. Even tired after a long day, and thirty-five years older than when they'd met, he still made her smile.

'So, you're not leaving me?'

'What?'

'When you said, "we need to talk". That's what people say when they're about to end their relationship.'

'Not my style. If that's what you've decided, there's nothing to talk about, is there? And anyway, nothing could be further from my mind! Here's to you, my darling, and to many more years of our loving union. *Prost!*'

He raised a toast, leaning over in mock earnestness to make exaggerated eye contact, the way a German friend had taught them years ago. She responded by staring solemnly into his face, before dissolving into laughter.

'That's enough of that nonsense,' she said. 'Don't keep me in suspense. What is this serious thing we need to talk about?'

'Bullshit jobs,' said Dom, as if this was perfectly self-explanatory.

'Excuse me?'

'Someone wrote a book about it. Half the population work in jobs that are entirely pointless and fail to make the world a better place. I've just realised that mine is one of them.'

Nicola had been of this opinion for many years, but had so far managed to keep it to herself.

'But I thought you were a great believer in the value of Change Management,' she said.

'I've changed my mind. What could be more pointless than sticking your nose into how people run their businesses and telling them you know better? And now I've lost faith in my profession, I can't go on. They'll see through me soon enough and I've got to jump before I'm pushed. A man has his dignity. How about we finally get around to that gap year we used to talk about?'

Nicola frowned. First he was telling her he was throwing in the towel and then he wanted them to take a 'gap year'! Both prospects were unappealing.

'What gap year?' she asked. 'Are we eighteen again?'

'You know we've always discussed it. When we – sorry, when I – decide I've really had it with work, we would pack a rucksack and see the world.'

'Have we? Sounds pretty ghastly to me.'

She had an unwelcome vision of them waiting for a bus in some dusty country, followed by a twelve-hour bumpy ride before checking into a hostel where you shared a bathroom with entitled young travellers, probably suffering from dysentery.

'What's brought this on?'

He squeezed her leg and took a glug of wine.

'All that jostling. The upcoming thrusters biting at my heels. I know it's always been this way – the old guard getting supplanted by the new hires – but what I really can't swallow is the fact they hide their ambition in the guise of something called "wellbeing in the workplace". The latest suggestion in my 360 appraisal was some bloke thirty years younger than me recommending I take a step down for the sake of "work–life balance". I wish they'd just say they've got their eyes on my corner office and they want me out of it. Why can't they just grow a pair of balls?'

'I hope you didn't use that expression.'

'Of course not.'

'When you say gap year, do you really mean gap year or are you thinking about early retirement?'

'I hate that word!'

'Retirement? I love it. Look at me and my many hobbies. What about that stool I just re-upholstered? My morning Zumba classes, my midweek visits to nurseries to stock the garden? I couldn't do that when I was chained to the surgery.'

'It's so final! There's no way I'm going to shuffle off on a cruise with a bunch of coffin dodgers. You know they keep a morgue on the ships, don't you? For when a retired CEO has a heart attack after all that fine dining. They call it Operation Rising Star. I read about it.'

'Hello! Just because you stop working doesn't mean you have to go on a cruise.'

'I'm only talking about a break. Not the end of my useful working life.'

'Call me a prophet of doom but I think if you leave this job, you won't necessarily breeze into another one. Look at Will.'

Will was Dominic's best friend who had made a midlife stand by walking away from his partnership in a law firm, only to find that the grass wasn't greener on the other side. After retraining as a life coach, he became enraged at his clients' unrealistic expectations. What did they expect – happiness served up on a silver platter? He wasn't a bloody miracle worker! He'd made attempts to go back to his old job but soon found out that nobody was interested in an expensive old lawyer. He was dead meat, to the poorly disguised disappointment of his young wife, Fizz. Her silver fox had rather lost his gleam.

'I'll cross that bridge when I get to it. Anyway, what do you think?'

He finished his wine and beamed at her, full of enthusiasm.

Nicola tried not to be a wet blanket; she hated always being the sensible one, but she couldn't help it if she was a realist.

'What do I think about a gap year? I think I'm too old for hostels.'

'Don't be so middle-aged! Remember when we trekked through Thailand and you sat on the elephant's head? You loved it.'

'Not sure my joints could take that anymore. I remember it well, though; I wore my floral patterned shorts.'

'Oh yes, I forgot about those! I haven't seen you wearing them lately.'

'There's a reason for that,' said Nicola. 'I read somewhere that no woman over fifty should be seen dead in shorts.'

'Nonsense, you've got fabulous legs. Don't let some vacuous magazine tell you what you can and cannot wear.'

'Ah, you're lovely,' said Nicola, blowing him a kiss. 'My loyal and biased husband.'

'I mean it. You haven't changed a bit. Forget the hostels, though, we'll do an upscale version. Stay in decent hotels.'

This sounded more appealing. A carefully mapped-out tour of India, being chauffeured to the Taj Mahal at dawn where Dom could take the obligatory photo of her looking lonely on the Princess Diana bench. They could post it on Instagram and enjoy being envied. But then it would be back for a lie-down and dinner for two before moving on to the next destination with all the other tourists dutifully ticking off items on their bucket list.

'I don't know, really. There's a terrible sense of being processed, don't you think? Are we ready to be Saga-insured seniors in sunhats spending their kids' inheritance playing at going off the beaten track?'

'Don't be so negative! Would you rather lie on that sofa playing Ruzzle for the rest of your life?'

Nicola guiltily switched her phone off.

'I like playing Ruzzle because at least I'm using my brain. Also, I can see those places on telly or read about them – I don't actually need to be there.'

'Well, it's a good job you don't work in the travel business. What a dismal perspective you have.'

'No I haven't! I'm like Dr Johnson's *Rasselas*. He left the Happy Valley to go round the world looking for happiness, then realised it was pointless, he was better off staying at home.'

'With your pipe and slippers.'

'Better than a rucksack and espadrilles. And having to listen to dreary travellers' tales. Machu Picchu – you can keep it.'

'Come on, where is your soul? Let's have a top-up and I'll fix dinner. Who's in?'

'Maddie's at John's tonight, and Gus is out at some event. We never went to "events" when we were their age, did we? We managed to be more specific about where we were going.'

Like many parents of adult offspring, they had failed to eject their young from the family home and lived parallel lives alongside them, witnessing their daily dramas while making sure the fridge was fully stocked. They were like benevolent older flatmates who didn't get in on the action. Although it was beginning to wear a bit thin.

Dominic peered into the fridge for inspiration and took out some tuna steaks.

'Let's have these with a black bean salad, as for once we're not feeding the five thousand. Any chance of them moving out any time soon?'

'Don't be silly.'

'Nothing silly about hoping your grown-up children might finally be ready to stand on their own two feet. You've made it too easy for them, putting food on the table and a roof over their snowflake heads.'

'We've got the space, and you know how expensive it is to rent in London.'

'That's the thing. If only we lived somewhere less convenient . . .'

He stopped in his tracks and turned to her.

'Of course! It's obvious, isn't it? That's what we should do! I can't believe I didn't think of it before.'

He abandoned his preparations and rushed over to sit beside her.

'You are right, it's ridiculous for me to carry on working just to feed the mortgage and my undeserving kids when we're sitting on a fat piece of equity. Let's downsize to the country! Let's grow chillies in a greenhouse and be vibrant third-agers!'

Nicola could see he was excited because he was now wielding an imaginary cricket bat, which was his way of expressing pure joy. He had done it when she agreed to marry him, and when Maddie had got into university, and when Arsenal had made it to the cup final.

'Calm down,' she said. 'One minute you're taking me on the hippie trail – but only for a gap year, because you're far too young to think about retiring – and now you're pushing us out to grass so you can wear a fleece and nurse your seedlings.'

'Exactly – *that's* the way decisions evolve. There's no need to stay in London once my wage slave days are over.'

'Wrong! There are many reasons to stay in London.'

'Give me just one. And don't say the theatre.'

'I was just about to say the theatre.'

'The last time we went was nine months ago and you agreed it was two hours of your life you'd never get back and that was a hundred quid down the drain.'

'True, it was a bit shouty. And the time before that was a stultifying period piece. I only managed to stay awake by admiring their dresses.'

'There you go, then.'

'There's always stuff to do in the city. Museums.'

'Which you never visit.'

'But I know they are there if the urge takes me.'

'Overruled.'

'It is true that I'd like to live somewhere you don't get ex-cons knocking on the door to sell you dusters at an extortionate rate.'

She thought of a card she kept in her bedside cabinet that Dom had sent her soon after they met. It was a romantic Victorian painting of a garden with flowers spilling out over a path leading up to the front door of a stone cottage. Inside he had written a one-line message – 'Our future home?' – because that was what happiness had looked like to them then, even if they had ended up in a terraced house in Clapham.

'It makes so much sense,' said Dominic, pacing the room as his plans took shape. 'Think what we could get in exchange for this house. And there is one huge advantage: it would mean the kids would finally have to fly the nest!'

Of course. The children. Their rooms were still stuffed with paraphernalia from their schooldays, teenage posters curling on the walls. The single beds had long been replaced with guest-friendly IKEA doubles, but otherwise their dens remained intact, cocoons from which, surely, they would one day emerge.

'It's a bit brutal, don't you think? It might be kinder – more organic – to wait until they're ready. Let them fly the nest rather than shaking them out.'

But even as she spoke the words, Nicola was coming round to the idea. A nugget of excitement was growing inside her as she imagined them skipping off to a bucolic retreat with nothing to worry about except picking the runner beans before they went to seed. It had never happened, the country cottage; common sense prevailed and they remained in London because neither of them wanted to become a grey-faced commuter ghoul. To compensate, they made weekend visits to obscure nurseries, loading up with rare plants and bags of compost to bring them on in the thin city soil, creating a tribute to Gertrude Jekyll in the narrow strip behind their townhouse.

'We could actually plant a proper six-feet-deep border,' she said.

'We could! And a massive lavender hedge to nourish the bees, because obviously we'll install hives to harvest our own honey. Grow our own vegetables and make chutney, too.'

'I'll get a copper preserving pan and make jam to tide us through the winter months.'

She thought for a moment about long, dark nights. Curtains drawn at 3 p.m. Staring at endless pots of jam with only the two of them to eat them. They didn't even like jam, really. It was a chilling prospect. And in the country, no one can hear you scream.

'You don't think it might get a bit lonely?'

'Of course not! You'll have me, what more do you want?'

He wrapped his arms around her in a tight bear hug. Even after all these years, she still loved the way that made her feel, the certainty that everything was going to be just fine.

'Anyway, the kids could come and stay,' he said. 'We'd have weekend parties, invite all our friends. It would be a riot! You love mass catering, you always say so.'

He jumped to his feet and went over to light the gas beneath the griddle pan. She watched him bustling round the kitchen, moving with the same youthful alacrity as their son. Whenever she heard one of them running up the stairs, she could never tell whether it was Dom or Gus; they had the same tread and the habit of singing under their breath.

'Slow down,' she said, 'let's be rational here. It's too easy to run away from everything you have. You hear about it all the time, people upping sticks, then finding they miss their old life, their friends . . .'

Her friends, there was the rub. You could talk all you like about the attractions of city life, but the whole point of staying put was having your friends on hand, the people you had loved for years, who were there for you to have fun with at the drop of a hat. Unless . . .

A fantastic idea had just presented itself.

She rushed over to join him by the cooker.

'Dom. I have just had the most brilliant brainwave! We don't have to do this on our own.'

'What do you mean?'

Now it was her turn to pace the room.

'Do you remember, years ago, when we were on that day trip to Sussex with Beth and Simon, and we broke into the grounds of that ruined stately home? We came up with a brilliant scheme. We said that when we were old, we should buy a big house and move in together, with all our friends. A kind of retirement party home, the opposite of nuclear coupledom. That's what we should do!'

Dominic frowned. 'Move in with Beth and Simon? I'm not sure . . .'

Beth and Simon were their official best friends, but she could tell by the look on Dom's face that didn't mean he wanted them to live together.

'No point in finally getting rid of your children, only to find yourself saddled with a different, fake form of family,' he muttered.

'Not just them. We'd get the others in on it, too. Doug and Mary. Leo, of course. And Will, though that young wife of his might have other ideas. I'm sure we could persuade them. A dream of communal living – we'd all have our private quarters, of course, but it would be fantastic!'

She could see him processing the idea, thinking his way through her list of their dearest friends. To her delight, his face was lighting up as he absorbed the possibilities.

'I see . . . yes, I do see. Forget the sensibly sized village house, we could go properly grand. A wing each! I'm not sure Dougie would be on my dream list of housemates, but I agree we'd have to have Mary. Maybe we could get somewhere with a gatehouse and Doug could park himself there at a safe distance with his scholarly files. Do you know, I think you're right. It would be fantastic!'

And that was it. In one evening, they had conjured up a plan for the rest of their lives. Sailing off into the sunset, not just on a cruise or a middle-aged gap year, but a whole new way of living. Like the best-ever holiday without an end. Now they just had to persuade the others.

# CHAPTER TWO

Simon stared at the screen of his computer and surreptitiously pulled a packet of cigarettes out of his pocket. He was allowed to vape in the house, but it wasn't the same; he missed the ritual of flipping open the packet, the flick of the lighter. He glanced down at the pack and met the gaze of an ashen-faced hospital patient, the photo strategically placed above a reminder that smoking causes nine out of ten lung cancers.

He stuffed the pack back in his pocket and reached for his e-cig. Come to think of it, surely it was nearly time for lunch. Any excuse to get him away from his self-imposed confinement in the study where the only distraction came from watching passers-by in the street outside. A young woman with ripped jeans was pushing a buggy towards the park and a couple of builders wearing hi-vis vests were loitering outside the house opposite. Or maybe they were burglars; he'd heard that was the least conspicuous way to dress if you were thinking of breaking and entering. That would add a little drama to this suburban hell, to quote the Pet Shop Boys. He'd only realised how quiet the days could be since quitting his job and becoming a home bird. The lack of action was staggering.

He pressed save and left the room to hunt out Beth. He found her in their bed, fully clothed under the covers, laptop balanced on her knees.

'Why are you in bed – are you an invalid or something?'

She looked at him over her recently acquired half-moon reading glasses.

'No, I'm quite well, thank you. Just staying comfortable.'

'I'm surprised you can concentrate. I find I fall asleep in bed. I was just wondering about lunch.'

'Were you now? Can I remind you that I married you for better and for worse but never for lunch?'

She was still getting used to having him around in the daytime, he knew. It was a bit like waiting for the last guest to leave the party. You'd enjoyed their company, but enough is enough.

'That's as may be, but there's no point in both of us shuffling around the kitchen separately when we could sit down together in a civilised way. And I've just reached something of an impasse.'

'Ah, I thought that might be it. Book not going too well?'

'It's challenging. As I knew it would be, but that's fine. And better than being the bloody executive vice chairman.'

He had been CEO of his ad agency for eight years, before being given what they'd called 'a sideways promotion'. But in truth he'd been knocked off the top post into what he perceived as a non-job. A couple of months of that was enough to prompt his resignation, not entirely to Beth's delight.

She pushed the covers aside and got out of bed.

'Come on then, let's have some poached eggs. Anyway, National Divorce Day was last week so we've missed it for another year.'

'I didn't know there was such a thing.'

'First working Monday after the Christmas holidays. Family pressure, the strain of keeping up festive appearances; it's the most popular time for people to ring divorce lawyers, apparently.'

'They should just soldier on, don't you think? Still, what do I know? I'm lucky enough to have a wife who makes me lunch, so I know which side my bread's buttered. With Marmite, please, lightly toasted, with the eggs.'

He followed her down the stairs, grateful that he didn't have to lunch alone.

'One egg or two?' Beth asked, adding a dash of vinegar to the pan of water. She was wearing a tunic thing that skimmed over her substantial bottom. Her tabard, as he called it, more suitable for archery than loungewear.

'Two, please. I haven't yet reached the full masochistic depths of self-denial. Bad enough giving up drinking – can't believe we've still got another two weeks of abstain-uary left. I also can't believe that word – who comes up with these ghastly terms?'

'Don't be ratty, just because you're gagging for a pint.'

'Negative. A glass of bubbles, maybe.'

'We have to take the sensible long view: our bodies are temples, blah blah blah.'

'So bleak,' said Simon.

Beth cut the root off a radish and handed it to him.

'Here you go, a little calorie-free appetiser.'

He ate it without interest.

'I really thought, when I stopped working, it would be an exciting new beginning. That great feeling you get when you break up from school and you know you've got all that free time stretching ahead and you can do whatever you like.'

'And now you've got the rest of your life, never mind six weeks' annual leave.'

'But instead, everything feels so . . . reduced. My world has shrunk to watching people walking down the street.'

'And having lunch with your wife.'

'Well, yes, that too – an unexpected bonus. I wasn't counting on that when I threw in the towel.'

At the time of his resignation, Beth was still working as a TV producer. That was before she got herself into trouble with a social media post in support of a journalist caught up in a gender pay gap case. Her dashed-off tweet about older female presenters getting the boot in favour of younger, better-paid and often male celebs was meant to be a throwaway comment, until a national newspaper picked up on it. And that was when she was called in to see the big bosses.

'And yet here we both are, out on our ear – or should that be ears?' She presented him with his eggs on a mean square of toast. 'Eat it slowly, then you'll feel more full.'

They were on to coffee when Beth's phone rang.

'Miaow!' she said as she answered, smiling at Simon across the table.

'Oh, I can't guess who that is,' he said. 'It really is time you grew up, the pair of you.'

It was the way Beth and Nicola always greeted each other, a throwback to their starter pets when, as young marrieds, they had both acquired a kitten from the same litter. The kittens had turned into cats and were duly supplanted by children, but it still amused them.

'Can we meet for dinner tonight?' Beth was repeating. 'Yes, I think we can, let me just check with him indoors.'

She looked at Simon enquiringly.

'Spontaneity is my middle name,' said Simon. 'Anything to escape my lonely life in thrall to my muse.'

'That's a yes then,' said Beth. 'And yes to that gastro pub, although I don't think we use that term anymore. But you've intrigued me now. What is this project of which you speak? Fair enough, we'll find out tonight. Bye then, my pretty puss.'

'What's all that about then?' Simon asked after she'd hung up.

'No idea. Nicola says they've got an exciting proposition to discuss with us.'

'Not salsa dancing, I hope. Or hot yoga.'

Although he quite fancied the thought of salsa dancing with Nicola; it conjured up the thought of the flouncy skirt she'd worn during their travels across South America one long student summer a lifetime ago, when they were far too cool to do anything as naff as moving their bodies to a choreographed routine. They'd been a couple then, for a few months, before Dom came on the scene and Simon was kicked into touch. Luckily Beth had been around to offer comfort – and the rest was history.

'Maybe they want us to go to a swingers' club?' he said. 'That's the sort of thing people of our age get up to, isn't it, to keep the spark alive?'

'Gross! Can you imagine?' Beth pulled a face. 'Anyway, I don't think she was talking about a bit of titillation. Whatever they're thinking of, she said it was potentially life-changing.'

'Like an injury.'

'What?'

'That phrase always makes my blood run cold. An accident resulting in life-changing injuries.'

'You're cheerful.'

'That's my other middle name.'

Simon and Beth arrived first at the pub, allowing them time to study the menu, which had moved over to 'small plates' since their last visit.

'It's an absolute con,' said Simon. 'It makes it all sound reasonably priced but by the time you've factored in three tiny saucers each, you might as well order one normal-sized portion of honest food.'

Beth had accused him of becoming mean with money since he had stopped working, but he claimed he was just being careful.

They were already tucking into the bread and olives when Dom and Nicola sat down beside them. Simon clocked Nicola's denim-clad thighs with his usual pang of regret.

'Your hair looks fab as usual,' said Nicola as she embraced her old friend. 'Why are you always so devastatingly cutting edge?'

Beth tossed her sharp bob; she knew her hair was her finest asset. Dark and glossy, it always stayed in place. Strangers often accosted her in the street to compliment her on it.

'You old flatterer,' she said. 'So, what is this news you want to share?'

'Tell them, Dom,' said Nicola.

'I'm joining you all, in the ranks of old wasters,' said Dominic. 'No, that sounds too negative. I have decided it's time to move on to the next golden stage of life. I'm handing in my notice.'

'Good man,' said Simon, with genuine pleasure. Like every status-conscious man, he was always happy to hear of others stepping off the career ladder. It was reassuring when your friends joined you in the murky waters of being a nobody.

'Well done,' said Beth, 'you won't regret it. Simon will share with you the delights of being free to lunch with your wife every day.'

The women exchanged knowing glances.

'Which brings us directly to the point,' said Nicola. 'We don't want to become a bog-standard retired couple. We want to do something different.'

'Don't split up, please,' said Beth. 'How often have we agreed that it's much better to stick with the devil you know.'

'No, of course not,' said Nicola, with a possessive hand on Dom's knee.

'We want you to join us in a new way of communal living,' said Dominic.

'That sounds earnest,' said Simon. 'Or maybe it sounds kinky. Do explain.'

'We've thought about this really carefully – well, for twenty-four hours – and we know this is a completely fantastic idea,' she said. '*We* – that is, you two and a few others, though we haven't mentioned it to them yet. Anyway, we think we should all sell our houses and buy an enormous place in the country where we will live together happily ever after.'

Simon and Beth looked at her blankly.

'What, set up a commune?' asked Simon. 'Like a kibbutz? I thought that was a 1970s thing. Compiling washing-up rotas and taking it in turns to do the weeding. I don't think so!'

'No, no, not a commune,' said Nicola. 'We're not talking about a free-for-all, only a very select few. This will be like the best-ever house party that goes on for the rest of our lives. Think about it: what do we really enjoy? Being with our friends, isn't that right?'

'Yes, that's true,' said Beth. 'My very favourite thing is being with my friends.'

'And whenever we've been on holiday together, think about how sad we all are at the end, because we miss each other so much when we go back to our normal lives. Well, now we wouldn't have to.'

She watched the idea taking root.

'I can see the attraction,' said Simon. 'Always someone to take on for a game of backgammon. And watch the match with.'

'We'd need two telly lounges,' said Beth. 'Costume dramas vs gritty crime.'

'Try to get beyond the TV room,' said Dominic impatiently. 'Think of the library, the dining room, the massive terrace where we would sit out with our nightcaps enjoying stimulating conversation.'

'Who else are you thinking of?' Simon asked. 'I mean, you've got to choose carefully.'

'You're already hooked, I can tell,' said Nicola happily. 'Dougie and Mary, Leo, Will and Fizz, we thought.'

Simon nodded. 'Nobody there to hate. And where will it be, our mansion?'

'There's the thrill,' said Dominic. 'Once we know we're all in, we can begin the hunt.'

The dinner of small plates was fruitful. Over goat's cheese and cannellini beans, they enumerated all the things they wouldn't miss about London. The crowds, the moped muggers, the whey-faced office slaves on the tube – the people they'd been until recently.

'Trapped between their mortgages and their payslips,' said Nicola. 'Look at them all in here, drinking to forget how stressed they are. Whereas we know that all that really matters is family and friends. Love, in other words. And what's more, we're lucky enough to be able to do something about it.'

\*

On the street afterwards, they hugged their goodbyes in the rain. Soon they wouldn't have to do this, they said, they could be cosily hunkering down together around their shared fireplace, after another convivial dinner.

Once at a safe distance, Beth and Simon fell into step, avoiding the slushy puddles.

'So, now it's just us, what do you really think?' asked Beth.

'I think it's very exciting,' said Simon. 'For a start it would solve our mortgage problem. As you know, I'd hoped to hang around at work until they paid me off, but in the end I just couldn't stand it – I have my pride! We can sell the house, pay off the debt and have enough left over to plough into the new place.'

'That would be such a weight off my mind, too,' said Beth.

'And on a less prosaic note, it's completely thrilling!'

He jumped over a puddle with a Fred Astaire twirl.

'A complete change, a fresh new start – just the impetus I need to get properly going on my book.'

He was imagining his oak desk transposed into a grand study, overlooking a lily-covered pond. They could even get a floating duck house, like that MP had claimed on his expenses. He'd always fancied that; much better than gazing out onto a street lined with cars that were better than his. And then there was one very obvious attraction: he'd be living with Nicola. Maybe in a different wing – they'd talked about having independent quarters – but he would see her every day.

'Exactly,' said Beth. 'It's so tempting with the way the world's going to just escape and bury ourselves away with like-minded people. We can have our own piece of paradise and sod everyone else.'

'You charmer.'

'I know you feel the same. We've always agreed that hell is other people.'

'So, let's close the door and forget about them.'

'Apart from one person, of course.'

'I was waiting for that.'

'I know she's officially grown up and everything, but she still needs us.'

Beth and Simon had always agreed they only wanted one child. They weren't prepared to see their lives crumble into a morass of family-focused compromise, the way so many did. Although in retrospect, Beth wondered if Eva might have been a little more resilient if she'd had siblings to contend with. She was training to be a physician associate, on a post-graduate course that would propel her into a medical career where she would actually make a difference. (Unlike the less-worthy professions of her parents, was the unspoken comparison.) She lived in a flat they had indulgently bought for her, but called round regularly to share – in painstaking detail – the challenges of her study programme.

'She can visit,' said Simon. 'It's not like we're moving to Australia. And we can visit her too. When her lodger moves out, we can reserve the spare room in her flat. It is our names on the deeds, after all.'

Beth thought about life in a rural idyll, punctuated by trips up to town, lunch with her daughter, combined with appointments at her hairdresser's. She would become like his other clients – country ladies who came up for a trim after the rush hour and take in a matinee while they were about it, or tea at Fortnum & Mason. She wasn't sure about staying at their daughter's flat, though; it had been a long time since she'd shared a bathroom and she wouldn't want to cramp Eva's style. Not to mention the close exposure to Eva's boyfriend James, a surly City trader who stayed over when his punishing schedule allowed. If only Eva would look elsewhere; there must be plenty of other men around whose interests extended beyond the 'How to Spend It' section of the *Financial Times*.

'Don't worry about Eva, it will do her good to have you loosen the apron strings,' said Simon. 'My main worry is how to make sure we get the best rooms in whatever house we buy. No point in moving to a mansion and ending up in the serv-ants' quarters.'

'Well, that was easy,' said Dominic as he slipped into bed beside Nicola. 'Now we only need to get the others on board.'

'I think Beth is just delighted at the thought of diluting Simon,' said Nicola. 'She's found it quite a strain with them both at home all of a sudden.'

'Quite surprised she was given the push,' said Dominic. 'She was very highly regarded, I believe.'

'They got her on a technicality. Showing bias or some nonsense. You can't say what you think on social media anymore. But I can't believe they were trying to fire her over a tweet. I think really they were just scared she'd found out about the pay gap in her office.'

'Except in our new house of fun. Can't wait for our conversations where no subject is off limits. And when it dries up, wc'll have constant Netflix. I feel free already!'

'Wasting your days glued to the telly – don't think I signed up for that!'

'You can stay in the library. We can buy books by the yard and get a ladder to reach the ones on the top shelf, then you can lie on a chaise longue and devour them all.'

'We've still got to talk to the others. They might not be so keen.'

'I bet they will! We're all in the same boat, looking for a way to maximise the rest of our lives. Will has been like a rat in a cage, looking for something to do since the life coaching went south. He'll jump at it and I'm sure Temple-woman can be persuaded; she can do her holistic nonsense anywhere – bound to find clients in whichever gorgeous little corner of England we intend to make our very own.'

Temple-woman was their term for Will's second wife, or current wife, as he jokily referred to her. To be fair, if anyone of their acquaintance had a body worthy of temple status, it was

Fizz. She had youth on her side, for one thing, and a naturally slim physique. But the temple-body did involve an awful lot of consecration, with all evil substances barred from entry. They didn't quite understand what she did. It seemed to involve a lot of Instagramming pictures of green juice and her workout routines. How she had made a living out of that escaped them.

'I think Leo will love the idea, too,' said Nicola. 'He's been very down since David left and keeps complaining he's too old for the London dating scene. Listen to me! "The dating scene." That's the sort of thing my mum used to say.'

'All women turn into their mothers,' said Dominic. 'Or so my dad told me – one of his many little nuggets. Just as well yours was as beautiful as you are.'

'Dear Mum,' said Nicola, snuggling up to him. 'You know, I still miss her every day. And I find myself using her expressions all the time. It'll all be the same in a hundred years' time – that's one of my favourites. Such a comforting thought.'

After Dominic had dozed off, Nicola heard a key in the door – one of the children returning home. That would be the next challenge: persuading them in the kindest possible way that it was time – whisper it – for them to move out.

# CHAPTER THREE

Will knew that timing was everything when it came to persuading Fizz to move into an unspecified house in the country with him and his old friends. Experience had taught him that she was most receptive following her daily workout when the fresh sweat on her glowing skin reminded them both of how lucky he was to have her. Fizz, Wiz, Flick – he loved all her nicknames that spoke of the confidence of the upper classes whose private schools had taught them – above all – that they were breezier and luckier than ordinary people. Even their cars had silly names; it was very endearing.

Will knew that he blended into the 'comfortable' classes these days. A high-flying law career had given him polish and confidence, but he was fascinated that Fizz was born into the kind of security he had worked for years to achieve. Ever since he'd met his best friend, Dom, and the rest of his university friends, he realised his hunger to achieve would get him places. He had never taken success for granted, never had a safety net – but it had only spurred him on. He'd probably have been able to buy a country pile all by himself if it hadn't been for the unfortunate divorce settlement. Still, he'd rather have Fizz and no money than be living the high life with his first wife. Or at least that's what he'd thought until his midlife career change had hit the rocks. He knew he wasn't offering Fizz the kind of life she'd expected. He kept putting feelers out in the law world, but so far no bites. Perhaps this crazy scheme of Nicola's was the change he needed.

'You look energised,' he said, as she came into the kitchen with her yoga mat rolled under her arm. They'd had some fun on that mat in the past; not so much recently.

'Thanks,' she said, shaking her hair out of its ponytail and moving to the fridge to help herself from the smoothie jug. Liquidised vegetables were all she allowed herself in the mornings – she had to walk the walk as well as talk the talk of being a holistic health and yoga practitioner – but he had already taken the precaution of eating a full English.

'I love how your gym kit leaves so little to the imagination,' said Will. 'Every delicious contour of your body is exposed.'

Fizz frowned prettily, the lines merely a brief decoration to her smooth brow.

'Don't be a perv,' she said.

Will recalled that she had used that term about him during the hot early stage of their relationship. That first kiss behind the filing cabinet, when she had reached into the pocket of his lawyerly suit and discovered the extent of his interest. 'You perv,' she'd said, pulling away to look him teasingly in the face. 'You're supposed to be my boss. And you're old enough to be my father.' She had continued their embrace with such enthusiasm that he decided the 'perv' tag must be a compliment. He felt then, as he felt now, that he would sacrifice anything for the sensation of that first kiss.

Fizz had been temping at the office for a couple of months after completing her history of art degree. Even her choice of subject seemed exotic to Will. He could never have justified that to his parents. *If you must go to university, for heaven's sake do something useful so you can earn a living out of it*, was his father's advice. Fizz had already spent the obligatory year travelling the world in a pleasant, aimless vacuum, entrancing Will on their first meeting with tales of moonlit beach parties and yomping through mountains – the antithesis to his own structured existence as a hardworking husband and father.

'I thought I'd temp for a bit while I work out what I really want to do with my life,' she'd told him, with such beautiful insouciance that he knew there and then that he had to be with her. As it turned out, what she really wanted to do was become the second Mrs Hodgkins. It took a while for Will to dispose of the first Mrs Hodgkins, and a considerable emotional toll, especially when it came to his relationship with his son Sam, who was away at university at the time. The usual story, he wearily conceded, but he never regretted his decision. He and Fizz had recently celebrated their anniversary with a weekend at the Gritti Palace in Venice, staying in the Hemingway suite where Fizz had gazed out over the Grand Canal and conjured up a pleasing resemblance between their love affair and the legendary couplings of the great writer. It was a magical couple of days, and he knew it was the way Fizz believed their life should always be. The only downside was coming back to mundane reality. The seven-year itch, you could call it. They'd been together since she was twenty-five and now she was thirty-two, which she kept saying felt pretty old to her, though Will scoffed at the thought.

'I have something to discuss with you, actually,' said Will.

'Oh yes?'

'You know how we once flirted with the idea of moving to the country? You remember – free from pollutants, able to let our souls expand.'

Fizz looked up with interest, encouragingly.

'Yes, I do remember. But we couldn't afford anywhere I liked because you had to give all your money to your ex and pay for your son to move to the States.'

This wasn't going according to plan.

'Not all of it, to be fair. But yes, unfortunately I wasn't in the position to afford quite the kind of manor house you had in mind . . .'

'And now you are?' She was looking at him with more eagerness than she had for a while.

'Not exactly. But Dom has come up with a plan that I really think might work for us.'

'Dom? What's he got to do with us?'

'Apart from the fact that he's my best friend, you mean.'

'Is he going to give you some money?'

It was disappointing, Will thought, that she made so little effort to conceal her materialism. Or maybe he should see it as charming that she should be so direct and artless. He needed to put a positive spin on this tiny character flaw of hers.

'Better than that! He and Nicola have invited us to join them in a sort of . . . grand commune, you might call it. We're going to club together to buy an amazing house in the country. It will be so huge that we can divide it up into independent living quarters. Obviously I'll make sure we get the best rooms – I'm a lawyer, after all. We'll have a fantastic time and grow our own food – you remember, a bit like on *The Good Life* . . .'

He stopped himself. Of course she didn't remember; she wasn't even born when Felicity Kendal and Richard Briers charmed suburban dreamers everywhere with their TV sitcom about self-sufficiency.

'That is if you want to, of course,' he added, watching anxiously for her reaction. 'I thought it could offer some real opportunity for personal growth, for both of us . . . You could do your holistic stuff, I could even coach clients who want to follow the dream of quitting the rat race – it's what we always talked about.'

'Who else have Dom and Nicola invited? ' asked Fizz, studying him with her green flecked eyes. The miraculous eyes that had entranced him when he first introduced himself. *Hi, Will Hodgkins, senior partner, glad to have you on board.*

'Beth and Simon. And they're going to talk to a few others. Leo, I believe.'

'I love Leo. He's amazing for his age.'

'He's only my age, actually. But yes, everyone loves Leo.'

Fizz was nodding.

'I think it has possibilities. I could vlog it – set up my own YouTube channel to go with my Instagram. Moving into a rural shared space with a bunch of people twice my age. Defining a new way of simple living, crossing the generation divide – it's very zeitgeisty.'

'Not quite twice your age,' said Will indignantly. 'I'm a sprightly fifty-seven.'

'Very sprightly,' said Fizz. 'Don't worry, hon, I'm only teasing.'

The omens were undoubtedly good, Will thought, as he watched her peel off her tiger camo leggings. Even the suggestion of fresh country air seemed to be having the desired effect. Bring it on.

Fizz turned away from him and gazed out of the window, picturing herself in a bohemian Demelza Poldark dress, digging up beetroots that toned with the flame and garnet of her skirts. She'd have two million followers before she knew it;

van-loads of products would be delivered to the gates of the mansion in hope of gaining her endorsement. Fizz Fortescue (she'd kept her maiden name – it had more of a ring to it, she thought) escapes the rat race and defies the conventions of other millennials by opting for a simple life in the company of mature friends.

'Let's do it,' she said, turning back to Will. And, as if to remind herself that her husband wasn't that much older than her, she led him upstairs to the bedroom.

Leo took off his protective cotton gloves and rubbed his fingers appreciatively over the freshly gilded picture frame. He was an expert in all the refined arts of interior design but gilding was his absolute favourite. Separating the gossamer-thin sheets of gold leaf, then smoothing them onto the carved wood gave him enormous satisfaction as he turned a drab old thing into a shiny delight with all the flashy bling of its Georgian origins. It would hang very well in his drawing room, the ornate frame in daring contrast to the painting by a radical new artist, which he had recently bought at auction to replace the one that David had taken with him.

It had all been so sudden. Twenty years of happy cohabitation and then on Christmas Eve, David had just upped and gone. Leo had taken to his bed and told no one; the last thing he needed was an invitation to wear a paper hat and a brave face at someone else's festive lunch. After seven days, he'd risen from beneath the duvet – the thinnest he'd been in years; you couldn't beat heartbreak as an aid to weight loss – and decided he was through with self-pity.

*No point in dwelling on it*, he reminded himself again. There was only so much recrimination you could indulge in without feeling sick. He reached for the hand cream and smoothed it into his palms – it was surprising how the dust from sanding worked its way in despite the gloves – and thought about what to wear for his date later. Maybe the winter white coat with the mauve Paul Smith shirt beneath it and the vintage Prada scarf with silver filigree. Aidan didn't look like a snappy dresser from his profile photo; he was wearing the cop-out all-black uniform favoured by the unadventurous. Still, you never knew, and it was important to get out there and not sink into morose introspection.

He went upstairs to lay out his outfit on the bed, and had just discovered an infuriating stain on his cream trousers when his phone rang. He knew it wouldn't be David, but his reflex was still to hope it was.

'Nicola! I've had a total calamity. Can you believe it, I've just discovered a mark on my slacks, and can't decide whether it's oil or fruit-based, so no idea which product to apply, and I'm having to rethink my entire outfit for this evening.'

'Leo, you are speaking to the wrong person about this. When did I ever show any interest in laundry?'

'It gets worse: I'm meeting a man later. Can't think why – it's bound to be a disappointment. You don't know how lucky you are with your gorgeous husband and nothing to worry about.'

'What time are you going out? Can I come over first? I've got something to discuss with you.'

'Oh yes! Come right now and cheer up a lonely old queen. We can have cake. I'm still two kilos down on my ideal weight.'

Nicola jumped into her car for the short journey to Leo's house. She knew it was important to recruit him; he had the knack of lifting every occasion and would make all the difference to their party. And the timing was perfect for him: he was at a crossroads in his life now that ghastly David had gone. There was no way she could have moved in with him and his fusspot ways.

She had met Leo at university, where he was Beth's friend originally. Against a backdrop of a sea of grungy students, Leo stood out like a bird of paradise, wearing a heather mix jacket with a turquoise lining. He was a breath of fresh air compared to the medical students in her lectures who were so bowed down by the constant pressure of work that they had no time to be colourful – unless you counted the occasional drunken nights out when they'd let their hair down with bawdy sing-songs and unfunny practical jokes. Beth and Leo were both studying languages, and while it was obviously far more useful to learn to cure diseases of the body, Nicola couldn't help feeling jealous of the hours they were free to devote to Baudelaire and Flaubert. The idea that reading romance could count as work seemed deliciously decadent to someone whose daily diet was diagrams of body parts.

Leo led her into the kitchen and served her a slice of pomegranate and orange cake.

'I'm glad you've got your appetite back,' said Nicola. 'We can't have you fading away. And you look fab as always.'

Leo gave her a twirl in his carefully assembled outfit.

'Cooking is essential,' he said, 'but clothes are the real saviour of a broken heart. I honestly believe that fashion is the fight against death.'

'On that basis, you'll be immortal. And I'm doomed.'

'Oh, I don't know,' said Leo kindly. 'You have your own timeless style. Jeans and dirty blonde hair – it seems to work for you.'

He poured her a cup of earl grey from his vintage teapot. He'd had unmatched crockery years before it became fashionable, buying up odd pieces of Royal Doulton wherever he found them.

'So, what is it you want to talk about?'

'I want us to live together.'

Leo looked up in surprise.

'It's a bit late now! I know we used to talk about it at uni when you were getting sick of Simon. I wondered whether I should undergo a conversion programme in order to become your boyfriend. But then you produced Dom, luckily for both of us.'

'Don't panic, I'm not talking about sex. Something far more interesting.'

'Now you're showing your age. Do you remember when sex was our primary driving force?'

'Whereas maturity has brought in other priorities. Which is what I'm talking about.'

'Go on, I'm intrigued.'

'OK, so where do you see yourself living for the rest of your life?'

'Good God, I don't know. You sound like that intense woman who interviewed me the one time I applied for a proper job. "Where do you see yourself in five years' time?" she wanted to know. *Not in your shoes, dear, that's for sure.* It was at that moment I realised I was destined for a life of self-employment.'

'You're far too exotic for corporate life.'

'Weird, you mean.'

'That too,' said Nicola, patting his hand affectionately. 'Anyway, you're much better suited as an interior designer where you don't have to rein in your character and your weirdness is a plus. But seriously, have you thought about the next stage? I know it's early days with David leaving so recently, and you obviously need to adjust to that, but that's exactly why my plan is perfect for you.'

'I know you hated him,' said Leo. 'You don't need to pretend otherwise.'

'I didn't hate him! And I wouldn't dream of saying I told you so. But he was a bit of a shit.'

Leo remembered David's parting words as he stood by the front door with his overnight bag. 'It's no good,' he'd said. 'I can't pretend anymore; this isn't what I want.' Leo had remained rooted to the spot, listening in shocked silence, but he knew there was no point arguing. You can't help what you feel.

'You're right,' he said, 'he was a bit of a shit.'

'So, here's the big idea,' said Nicola, pushing aside her plate as she leaned in to deliver her pitch.

'You sell your house, we sell ours and so do our other carefully selected friends. We pool our resources and buy a country pile of unbelievable grandeur, so vast that we can all inhabit different wings. Then we live a merry life in a shared community and are happy all the rest of our days!'

Leo's face was a picture of horror.

'You needn't seem quite so appalled,' she said. 'You look as if you've had a stroke.'

Maybe he just needed time for the idea to sink in, so she waited a few seconds for him to respond.

'So come on,' she said, becoming impatient at his silence. 'First thoughts?'

Leo carefully replaced his teacup.

'Darling Nicola, where do I start? You know what a private person I am. Like Marlene Dietrich, I need to be alone. And you haven't even said who the other inmates are.'

'The usual suspects. You can probably guess. Beth and Simon, Dougie and Mary, Will and Fizz.'

'So I'm the token singleton.'

'You're not the token anything, just your fabulous self.'

'And how on earth does it work? Do we all bring our own furniture? Think of the style confusion!'

'We can work it out. Do as we please in our own rooms, then have some kind of overarching plan for the communal areas. You should be in charge of that, obviously, with your unrivalled eye. It would be a fantastic project for you. It could even be a sort of live portfolio for you – you could show your clients the kind of transformation they long to achieve in their own homes.'

She watched Leo as he tried to conjure up this new imaginary home.

'It would certainly be a challenge,' he said eventually, 'but I think I could get used to having those big het men around. Fizz is a funny little thing, I quite like her even though she's rather spoilt, and of course I adore Beth. Mary is the only person I've met who can outdo me when it comes to housework, so we'd have that in common . . . Do you know what, Nicola, I think it could be the most enormous fun!'

He leaped to his feet and pulled her out of chair, twirling her around the room.

'Will there be a ballroom?' he asked as they came to a standstill, shrieking with laughter. 'We absolutely must have a ballroom, and invite the county set. I'll be the polka master. Master interior decorator and lord of the dance!'

It was, he decided later in the deadening quiet of his lonely bedroom, the perfect antidote to his heartbreak. If David had decided that Leo wasn't what he wanted, then Leo should find something that *he* wanted, and this could well be it.

'I knew Dougie and Mary would be shoo-ins,' said Nicola, when she put the phone down. 'Mary said that since they stopped teaching, they no longer feel part of the university. "A couple of research fellows put out to seed", is how she described it. They're absolutely on for a new beginning. Dougie also said he's tired of living in their modernist box house; he now fancies living in a character home with a sense of history.'

'I always liked their house,' said Dominic. 'That development reeks of Sixties dreamers; you can almost smell the brown rice cooking.'

'Which is exactly why it's time for a change.'

Dougie and Mary lived in Highsett, a Span housing development in Cambridge that had won an architectural award in 1966. Nicola and Dominic met them thirty years ago on the day they moved into their Clapham house, when Mary appeared on the doorstep with a loaf of warm bread and a cup of salt to wish them luck. It turned out she lived next door with Dougie, both of them then studying for their PhDs in London. 'Our boffin neighbours', as Dominic referred to them. Or Walking Encyclopedia, which was his nickname for Dougie when he was getting on his nerves. For two years they enjoyed the particular friendships that can flourish between neighbours, in and out of each other's houses, until the 'boffins' upped sticks to continue their academic careers in Cambridge.

'Mary said yes straightaway,' said Nicola. 'Her only reservation was her mother, who lives in a home nearby. But then Dougie pointed out that her visits were mere exercises in guilt-reduction. Her mother hasn't a clue who she is, calls her Brian most of the time, and asks her if she's come to deliver the kippers. Plus Mary's sister will still be on hand if their mother does worsen.'

'Poor thing. Old age ain't pretty.'

'Which is exactly why we need to do this now – while we've got twenty or thirty years to enjoy it all before we all turn gaga. I'm so excited!'

'Me too,' said Dominic. 'Look, I've been doing some research. This one's in Hampshire.'

Nicola curled up beside him on the sofa to take a look at the imposing house displayed on his laptop. It boasted a long line of high Georgian windows and a crenellated roof worthy of the mad wife in *Jane Eyre*.

'Nice. Have you looked it up on Google Earth?'

'I'm on it.'

They watched together as the house came into focus, the marvels of modern technology showing the surrounding trees, the expansive gardens. Then, as they zoomed out, the factory and office block bang next door.

'It won't do,' said Nicola. 'The dream falls flat if you've got to look out on an industrial estate.'

'Snob,' said Dominic. 'I quite agree.'

# CHAPTER FOUR

Two weeks later, the hunt was properly underway. To Nicola's surprise – and delight – everybody had said yes, and it was with intense excitement that she launched the WhatsApp group Dreamy New Life. Images from primelocation.com were pinging in at all times of day and night, much to Dominic's concern. It was all very well for Mary to nurse her insomnia in Cambridge by conducting research in the small hours, but it didn't mean he should be woken up by her messages about the important Jacobean wood panelling in one house she'd spotted. Most fanciful was Leo's suggestion: an entire Scottish island complete with lighthouse – just think what they could do with that!

They'd thrashed out a rough budget, based on what they could afford. Estate agents had been called to see what their existing houses might be worth, sold or rented out, while Dougie – used to planning for a fairly lean academic retirement – had been giving them advice on what they could all unlock from their own pensions. Still, even with a magic number on paper, it was hard not to get carried away as they sent each other links to all sorts of once-grand stately homes, actual castles and a deconsecrated monastery with dungeons and cellars, accessible only by boat. Luckily, Dougie was there to bring them down to earth.

They settled on a shortlist of three properties: a manor house in Oxfordshire with its own deer park, a stately pile in Gloucestershire, formerly a nursing home – 'appropriate to our ageing needs,' as Leo pointed out – and a cluster of farm buildings in Herefordshire – an entire hamlet – which had the advantage and disadvantage of lodging them all under separate but neighbouring roofs. They agreed they should visit them all on one lightning tour and Will arranged to borrow a minivan for the purpose, letting it drop that he would be the best person to take the wheel as he had passed his advanced driving test.

'Who on earth bothers to take their advanced driving test?' Dominic wanted to know. 'That is the saddest thing I've ever heard.'

Mary and Dougie travelled down to London on a frosty Friday afternoon, staying overnight with Nicola and Dominic in anticipation of the early start, which found them all a little bleary as they gathered on the doorstep the following morning to await their chauffeur. Leo was last to arrive, in a taxi that drew up at the same time as the minivan.

'This is it, decision day!' said Will as he jumped out of the driver's seat to open the rear door for his passengers. Fizz remained sitting in the front, plugged into her earphones. Simon banged on her window and she looked up crossly.

'Age before beauty, Fizz,' he said. 'If you don't mind, I'll take the front seat. You can squeeze yourself into the back.'

She sulkily complied with his request, changing places with a face like thunder, which wasn't lost on Nicola. She did hope this wasn't all going to be a terrible disaster.

'I feel like I'm on a school bus,' said Simon, plumping himself into the prime seat. 'All we need are some signs on the rear window.'

'I shall go in the back with Fizz, as we are the bendiest,' said Leo.

'Bendiest and the hottest,' said Fizz, finally breaking into a smile as she placed a flirtatious hand on Leo's knee. 'I'm sure the others won't mind me saying.'

Beth shot Nicola a sour look, and Nicola winked back at her. They had privately discussed the likelihood of Temple-woman turning out to be a bit of a nightmare, but thought she was manageable. And in any group dynamic, it was useful to have one person who annoys everyone: it gives the others someone to bond against.

'Hands off, Leo, she's mine!' said Will, speaking into the microphone that was fitted over the driver's seat.

They set off in high spirits, Beth passing round a bag of sweets to confirm the impression of being on a school outing.

'Second childhood, get used to it,' she said. 'I can't wait for us all to be installed in our early retirement home. Remind me which one we're seeing first?'

'Langbourne Manor,' boomed Will through the microphone. 'Smallest of the three but comes with its own orangery and the village cricket pitch, not to mention the deer park. Can't argue with that.'

'Turn it down, old chap, we're not deaf!' said Simon.

'Not for me, thank you,' said Fizz, passing on the sweets. 'I've given up refined sugar for January, though I rarely take it anyway. Empty calories.'

After all their anticipation, the first visit was over very quickly. They'd tumbled out of the van, wide-eyed at the grand avenue of trees that flanked the drive, and staring up at the vast façade of the house. But their private dreams of what life could be like as lords and ladies of Langbourne Manor were promptly shattered. The charm of the house and the expansive park was eclipsed by its proximity to the M40, the roar of the traffic particularly noticeable in the bleak midwinter, without the insulating camouflage of summer leaves. They inspected the interior out of courtesy to the agent, but it was impossible to ignore the noise of thundering lorries that passed through the mullioned windows with no respect for historical authenticity.

'Can't believe we didn't pick up on that before,' grumbled Dougie. 'It should have been obvious from the map. It is entirely pointless to trade the peace of Highsett for the sound effects of living on a racetrack.'

'Never mind, onward and upward,' said Nicola, determined not to let the mood deteriorate. 'We still have the other two to see, and it will make the choice easier now we've ruled one out. I've got a good feeling about the next one. It's miles away from any motorway and it has so much space we could be really creative about how we adapt it.'

On arrival at house number two an hour later, they realised just how creative they would have to be to remove the nursing home atmosphere that permeated the dingy rooms, which were still kitted out with support rails and hospital-style bath equipment.

'It's not speaking to me,' said Leo, as they walked in silence through the dining room with its refectory-style table, scattered chairs and grim overhead lighting. 'Or rather, it is. It's reminding me that I'm headed for the quiet fastness of the grave and before I get there, I'm going to be wheeled round an institution in a bath chair.'

'That's the wrong way to think,' said Nicola. 'Imagine when it's stripped of all this geriatric equipment and decorated with our flair and multiple lighting sources. Think back to when this was a gracious home of a country lord. You must admit it's a potentially beautiful house. It was and it will be again.'

'It's got a good-sized lake at least,' said Simon, thinking of his duck house as he peered through the window at the large but rather bleak garden, where budgetary constraints had clearly prevailed over aesthetic sensibilities and resulted in a blank stretch of lawn. 'And it certainly ticks the boxes in terms of space.'

'And it's within budget,' Dougie chipped in.

'That's the problem, as I see it,' said Beth. 'It fulfils our technical requirements: substantial old house, big garden, rural location, an asking price that means we can afford at least some renovations. But there's no magic.'

'There was certainly no magic in that dreary high street we just drove through,' said Leo. 'I can't see myself wandering along there with my shopping basket. Not a vegetable in sight as far as I could see, never mind a delicatessen or artisan bakery.'

'This is *so* depressing,' said Fizz. 'There's no way I could live here. Imagine trying to get a good Insta shot in this place. Bleak.'

'I'm inclined to agree,' said Will, 'but I also think we're tired and hungry. How about we get some lunch in that pub we passed and gather our thoughts?'

'Good idea, I'm starving,' said Simon.

The pub was in the familiar style: a beamy old building on the through road, with a large car park and a sign outside announcing Sunday roasts.

'Glad it's not Sunday,' said Beth. 'I'm such a sucker for a roast dinner, I'd have been loading my plate with heaps of potatoes, then feeling bad about it.'

'I agree,' said Will. 'Toby Carveries are my guilty pleasure; it's like a really delicious version of school dinners, queuing up to ladle on the gravy.'

They settled down at two tables and Simon and Dougie went up to the bar, under the watchful gaze of two men seated there over their pints. Two couples at the next table were looking at the newcomers in a not very welcoming way.

'It's all a bit *American Werewolf in London*,' said Beth. 'Look how they've all gone quiet at the entrance of strangers. You know, that scene where they wander in off the moors and the whole pub falls silent.'

'Nonsense, you're just being paranoid,' said Will, giving a smile and a nod at the woman staring at him, which wasn't reciprocated.

Simon returned with a tray of beers and some menus.

'Dougie's getting a bottle of wine. I'd recommend the pies, they smell fantastic. But then pies always bring out my inner Billy Bunter.'

'So, what are our thoughts so far?' asked Will, once they had given their orders.

'I think it's safe to say we are still looking,' said Mary. 'Neither of the places we've seen today come anywhere near our expectations. Maybe we are being unrealistic, but I think it's important to trust your instincts on these things, and if you're not blown away on first sight, then it's a big no-no.'

'Agreed,' said Leo, pulling a face as he took a sip from his glass. 'And I can't be doing with this pub; we couldn't possibly have it as our local. The wine is shocking and I bet that everyone in here voted Leave.'

'Shhh,' said Nicola. 'Stop sounding like a member of the metropolitan elite.'

'Out and proud,' said Leo. 'There's no need to pretend.'

'There's still Herefordshire,' said Will. 'Third time's a charm, maybe.'

They all dozed off in the back seats on the final stage of their journey, heavy with the food and drink, although Will kept up his cheerful commentary through the microphone, inspired by road signs to places he had visited in his youth.

'No one's listening, Will,' Fizz informed him sleepily from the back seat. 'They're asleep and even if they weren't, they soon would be after listening to you banging on about your camping holiday in Worcestershire.'

'That's harsh, Fizz, but I forgive you. Nearly there, then you can wake them up.'

The agent was waiting for them when they drew up outside an attractive cluster of farm buildings.

'Good lord, I didn't realise there'd be so many of you,' she said, greeting them as they climbed out of the van. 'Which of you is Dominic?'

'I'm here,' he said, shaking her hand. 'As I explained on the phone, this is a group venture, so we need everyone's agreement and thought there was little point in sending an advance party.'

'I see, decision by committee,' she replied, seeing her chance of a sale withering as this odd gathering shook themselves down and looked around at the view across the valley. 'Multi-generational living is becoming quite the vogue,' she added, looking from Fizz to Dougie and frowning as she tried to work out where Leo fitted in.

'As you can see, it's a spectacular setting,' she said. 'No immediate neighbours, so you'd be very private. The vendor owns the entire hamlet; it's been in his family for years.'

'What beautiful scenery,' said Mary. 'It brings to mind "Piers Plowman". I could imagine it would be conducive to visions.'

'Piers who?' asked Fizz.

'It's a medieval narrative poem,' Dougie explained, 'conceived by William Langland in this very part of the world. It's an allegory about a vision—'

'Leave it out, Dougie,' said Simon. 'Nobody cares.'

'It's certainly bucolic,' said Beth. 'No risk of traffic noise ruining our meditation.'

The agent led them into the central farmhouse, which was surrounded by a number of barns and stable blocks.

'This is a good-sized house, but as I explained, there's lots of other accommodation arranged in the outbuildings, with opportunity for development. And three cottages just down the lane.'

Inside was less appealing; the house was rather dark with low ceilings and small windows designed to keep the heat in.

Leo ducked his head as they moved between the rooms.

'It's a bit nooky wooky,' he said. 'I'd be knocking myself out on these beams.'

'It's very charming,' said Nicola. 'But possibly more suitable for a loved-up cosy couple than a group of middle-aged friends who need their space.'

'There are plenty of rooms,' said the agent. 'Let me show you upstairs. And as I said, you could spread yourselves out in the other buildings – you might find it a relief to have a bit of distance between yourselves.'

She really couldn't imagine why this disparate group of people would want to live together; it certainly wasn't her idea of an enjoyable or manageable life.

By the time she'd walked them back to their vehicle, the agent knew this was a non-starter. She'd been in this game long enough to tell.

'I wasn't convinced by Herefordshire anyway,' said Leo, after they'd waved her off. 'Dangerously close to Wales and you know how they react to incomers. Quite likely to creep over the border and burn our house down.'

'That was years ago,' said Mary. 'You really need to move on from old prejudices. Besides, they've calmed down now they've got their language back.'

'It's not Wales here, don't be ridiculous,' said Nicola.

'All right, I stand corrected,' said Leo. 'But I couldn't cope with those low ceilings. Very oppressive, especially in winter. I'd be curling up in a ball and hibernating until spring time.'

'Like a furry little vole,' said Nicola.

'Actually, that's a common misconception,' said Dougie. 'Voles don't hibernate, they just dig deeper tunnels and carry on eating.'

'How do you know all that stuff?' asked Fizz. 'I can't believe all the facts you keep coming out with. You'd be great in a pub quiz.'

'Most of it serves little purpose,' said Dougie sadly. 'The older I get, the more I realise how pointless it is to endlessly acquire information.'

'And on that bleak note, let us begin the long drive home with our tails between our legs,' said Simon, opening the van door. 'Project hope dashed against the rocks. Someone else can take the front seat this time; I'll relegate myself to the middle row.'

Nicola slid onto the seat next to him and he felt the familiar shape of her thigh pressed against his. He remembered a long bus journey they had taken across Patagonia years ago. The memories of their time together had become more insistent since they'd taken on this new venture and he kept having to remind himself that these were very different circumstances.

'Any sweets left?' he asked.

Nicola rustled in her handbag and brought out the remains of the Minstrels.

'Take two,' she said. 'You know you want to.'

'Leave some for us,' said Dominic, stretching his hand back from the front seat. 'I'm keeping the driver company so I need to stay lively.'

They fell into a flat silence as the journey began. Even Will had lost the heart to deliver his chirpy commentary and the only sound was the windscreen wipers dealing with the rain that intensified as they reached the motorway.

'I've had a thought,' said Beth suddenly, leaning forward to grab the back of Dominic's seat. 'In fact, not so much a thought as a brilliant idea. Genius, actually.'

'Tooting your own horn again?' said Leo. 'Pray, do share.'

'OK, hear me out. We all agree that the houses we've seen today fell short of our ambitions.'

'Well short,' said Nicola.

'And that's because we're not being ambitious enough! We're not just standard retirees looking for a rural bolthole within striking distance of London – that's far too pedestrian. We need to move somewhere we can properly live out our fantasy of a grand new life, not just be content with mooching down to the local for pie and chips and going to the garden centre. Where's the glamour in that? You might as well stay in London where at least the shops are better. We need to go properly exotic. What we want is a château in France.'

Nobody replied for a while, then Simon spoke up.

'Ridiculous idea. I've always thought there's something not right about people who move abroad. What's wrong with their own country?'

'Nothing,' Beth replied. 'Well, quite a lot, actually. But you love France, I know you do.'

'Doesn't mean I want to live in the bloody place. Holidays are one thing, but turning into a tragic ex-pat is quite another.'

'What's tragic about it?'

'Do you need to ask? Boozed-up Brits abroad, bingeing on cheap wine and fags, and hanging out together without speaking a word of the local lingo. No thank you.' Simon grimaced.

'She's not talking about the costa del crime,' said Nicola. 'And anyway, between us we speak enough French to get by. Of course Leo and Beth studied it at university, so they can help us all remember our O-level French, and we've all managed a bit of pidgin French on holiday over the years.'

'Our au pair taught me French,' said Fizz. 'I've not used it since I did my last ski season.'

'And if Dougie and I can find our way around a medieval French manuscript, I'm sure we can manage a modern newspaper,' added Mary.

Nicola grinned. She was absorbing the idea slowly, and found she was ready to become very excited about it.

'That's a fantastic plan!' Will suddenly boomed through the microphone, making them all jump. 'Have you seen the kind of places you can get in France for the price of a Gloucestershire barn conversion? I've done some French property porn surfing in my time and I can tell you: palatial, magnifique, turrets, moats, the lot.'

'What about Brexit?' asked Simon.

'Brexit, schmexit. Plenty of Americans live in France without ever having been members of the EU – doesn't put them off. And plenty of Brits are living there now. Look at Nigel Lawson.'

'Nigel Lawson applied for French residency after campaigning for Brexit, the hypocrite,' said Leo. 'But I'm definitely up for France, as long it's not in his village. Finally I'd be living somewhere worthy of my ancestors—'

'How about the rest of you?' asked Nicola, before Leo could launch into his spiel about coming from a great and noble family now sadly fallen from glory. He'd watched one too many episodes of *Who Do You Think You Are?* and was convinced one day someone would find a regal branch of his family tree. He knew in his bones that he was royalty.

'Dom, what do you think?' Nicola continued. This whole scheme was their idea; it was important they stayed in charge.

'I'm all for it,' said Dominic. 'I agree with Beth: we may as well go full throttle on the escapist fantasy.'

'I agree,' said Mary. 'We'd be following in some very illustrious footsteps. Scott and Zelda, Ernest Hemingway, Oscar Wilde.'

'Peter Mayle,' said Beth.

'Oh no, not Provence,' said Leo. 'That would be just too corny.'

'And too far from home,' said Nicola. We need to be in driving distance for when we want to visit the kids.'

'And I need to get home to visit Mum, even though she doesn't know who I am now,' whispered Mary.

'Close to Paris would be marvellous,' said Dougie. 'We could take ourselves off for culture whenever we tired of *la vie sauvage*.'

'Fab fashion houses in Paris, too,' Leo said. 'I could rework my entire wardrobe. And I could get the best of both worlds in terms of my work – I could tempt over British clients who want a touch of French *brocante chic* in their homes, and sell my interior design skills to Parisians keen to get something a bit different. They can't all want pared-back Gallic style or formal Louis XV chairs with bendy legs – I bet a bit of English eccentricity will go down a storm in design circles.'

'Does anyone want to know what I think?' Fizz asked plaintively from the back seat.

'Of course, pumpkin,' said Will. He looked anxiously at her in the rear-view mirror.

'*Pumpkin!*' said Beth. 'What the actual fuck, Will?'

'Don't be bitter,' said Will with a smile. 'Just because Simon doesn't sweet-talk you anymore.'

'I think it's a brilliant idea,' said Fizz. 'It's been such hard work setting up my holistic health venture. This is just what I need to refresh it. To be honest, I was a bit depressed looking round the places we saw today. It all seemed too ordinary. Far more exciting to be in a foreign country. I've always loved travelling and it would bring an angle to the lifestyle YouTube channel I'm going to start. English girl in French château. I could present myself as a sort of modern-day princess, even a kind of Marie Antoinette figure – my viewers would love that. I could dress up in period costume like that woman does on her history programmes.'

'So, it looks like I'm outnumbered,' said Simon. 'I'm clearly the only person with any common sense on this bus. I think we should all take a step back and think about this seriously over the next few days before rushing like lemmings off a cliff just because Beth says we should.'

'Beth has always been an ideas person,' said Nicola. 'That's why we love her.'

'I know you'll come round,' Beth said to Simon, who was sitting next to her with his arms crossed in a petulant manner. 'One of the reasons you're so keen on this whole project is that you want a safe space to say what you want and make off-colour jokes without anyone reporting you. Well, firstly, the French won't understand you, and secondly, they're much less politically correct than over here. You can be as offensive as you like.'

*

Simon did come round, of course. It only took a couple of hours browsing through pictures of mouth-watering châteaux for him to imagine himself in the role of *seigneur*, striding onto his box-hedged terrace to smoke his post-prandial cigar as he gazed across the fountains of their Versaillles-worthy formal gardens. Not to mention the food. He sat back from the screen and conjured up the dinner he would soon be savouring. Escargots, côte de boeuf, a reblochon au lait cru and a tarte au citron with the finest, lightest crust you could imagine. In a magnificent chandelierlit dining room where he could express himself with no regard for the thought police, in the congenial company of his wife and dearest friends. And Nicola.

Au revoir, broken Britain, and bonjour, *la vie en rose*. The hunt was on.

# Part Two

# Spring

# CHAPTER FIVE

'Oh my God!' said Nicola, as she and Dom drove between the high iron gates and saw the enormous façade of the eighteenth-century château bathed in the spring sunshine. 'It's even more beautiful than I remember. And now it's ours. Pinch me or I'll think I'm dreaming.'

She experienced the same excitement she'd felt when they had their first sighting three months ago. Eight of them had piled into a minivan to come and view it – Fizz had opted to stay behind – united in their desire to secure this dream home before someone bought it from under their noses.

They had all been mesmerised by the picture-postcard châteaux they saw when they decided to switch their search to France. They'd trawled countless property websites. Clicking through pictures of monumentally vast houses in luxurious amounts of land, they'd fallen in love time and again. It was so easy to bring up another set of details and imagine their lives at each property they clicked on. Luckily, a glance at the asking price often brought them back down to earth. Some were too vast, others too dilapidated but always with tall windows framed by pastel shutters designed to melt every English heart. Above all, it was the sense of space that won them over, the realisation that you could lose yourself here, driving along country lanes without seeing another car. Not to mention the appeal of buying their food in darling little épiceries – the everyday pleasures of life were taken so much more seriously in France. They had been unanimous in their final choice, Château Lafarge in pastoral Normandy, a place where time stood still and you could inhabit the idyllic life you always wanted. It was a happy medium – not so tumbledown that it risked falling in on them, but with sufficient renovation needed that it fell within their budget – just.

They had rushed into it with such speed, there had been no time for a full-blown survey. Anyway, Nicola had reasoned, a survey would only tell them what they already knew. It needed a lot of work. But seeing it today, her doubts evaporated into the warm spring air. The château was magnificent. Well, it had magnificent potential, anyway. *And what could be more exciting than that?* she thought. A real project.

'May is more beautiful than February. And this time it's for real, it's *ours*,' said Dominic, remembering their animated discussion in the hotel de ville following their initial viewing. Snails in garlic butter, confit de canard and several carafes of red had impelled them to offer the asking price, to the evident surprise of the *notaire*, even though he knew the British could always be relied on to pay over the odds.

Now, in the sparkling spring sunshine, they couldn't have hoped for a more spectacular arrival. Nicola and Dom had come along as the advance guard and she was relishing this chance to see it before the rest of the gang descended. The apple trees were decked with blossom and three long rows of windows sparkled in welcome as they swept up the drive. The façade was anchored at each end by a turreted tower and the top of a third tower was just visible behind, reminding them of the other wing that extended out of sight, at a right angle to the main part of the house.

Nicola was dazzled by the size of the building, and focused her attention on the high window of the left tower, fancying she could see Rapunzel swinging her hair down for her courtly prince. The warmth from the fresh baguette she was carrying spread through her body as she was overcome by a wave of euphoria.

'It's unbelievable, isn't it? This amazing château is ours. We are going to have the most fantastic time, all of us. I'm so happy, I literally don't think I've even been happier!'

'Is that why you're crying?' Dominic asked.

Nicola wiped her eyes and hugged him.

'I know, I'm a big girl's blouse. Come on, let's go in!'

She jumped out of the car, followed by Dominic, and ran up the central steps to the iron-studded front door.

'I feel like Alice in Wonderland – this key is ridiculous,' she said, as she inserted it into the lock and pushed open the heavy door. 'It looks like something from a fairy tale. I should have it dangling from my waist, like a proper chatelaine.'

They stepped into the wood-panelled entrance hall, dominated by a staircase that reminded Nicola of *Gone with the Wind*. All she needed was a floor-sweeping velvet gown and she would be Scarlett O'Hara. Over the stairwell hung a theatrical chandelier, which had been negotiated as part of the fixtures and fittings. The vendor, Madame de Courcy, agreed it would be a crime to remove it. Doors on either side of the hall opened onto a succession of interconnecting rooms, like a labyrinth, according to Nicola, who made straight for the staircase and ran up the steps to the first floor, shouting at Dominic to follow her.

The scale of the place was dazzling. Before the move, they had sat down with the floorplans and carved out five separate apartments, in order to achieve their goal of maintaining independent living quarters while sharing the grand reception rooms – that was firmly in a distant and comfortable future, though. The present reality was more stark. They would have to muck in together until the work was done. One kitchen and two cranky old bathrooms would have to serve them all for now.

'At least we've got plenty of bedrooms to choose from in the short term,' said Nicola, pausing on the landing as she wondered which corridor to follow.

'Eighteen once we get them all habitable, wasn't it?' said Dominic. 'Not counting the attic rooms. Let's go this way, down the west wing. Didn't we agree to go for the one at the end? It's furthest from that excuse for a bathroom, but that could be an advantage, given the noisy plumbing.'

'West wing, get us!' said Nicola, glancing into each room they walked past to make sure they weren't missing out on a better option. Though in fairness, she'd be thrilled to have any of them, with their generous proportions and breathtaking views over the lake. Most of them were empty, but a couple were still furnished with heavy antique beds and wardrobes that Madame de Courcy had insisted must stay. 'They belong in my château; it is unthinkable to move them.' She was equally adamant about the dining table and a particularly ugly sideboard that Leo had taken against. Nicola told him they could get rid of it later; she didn't want to hurt the outgoing chatelaine's feelings.

'Here we are!' said Dominic, throwing open the final door. 'I can safely say we've made the right choice. Double aspect, look! We can see our beautiful garden from two angles. Or what will be our beautiful garden once you've worked your magic on the overgrown wilderness out there.'

There was one window looking out over the lake and another that offered a spectacular view westwards over the valley. Nicola walked slowly between the windows, feeling her way in.

'I'm never leaving this room,' she said. 'You can carry me out in a coffin.'

'Let's not be maudlin. Anyway, it will all change when we divide the house up the way we planned, but I agree we did well to secure the best room for the time being.'

'I know I wanted the tower room to start with but Leo was insistent and this is much bigger. Plus it's another flight of stairs to the Rapunzel turret.'

Dominic came up behind her and wrapped his arms around her as they gazed out together over the lake and the cows grazing peacefully beyond against a backdrop of rolling pasture punctuated by stately trees.

'We should christen it, really,' he said, slipping an exploratory hand into the waistband of her jeans.

'Much as I love these old floorboards, I'd rather wait for our bed,' said Nicola, opening the window. 'Isn't it great how the windows open inwards? The French are so sensible.'

'It's because of the shutters, they're on the outside.'

'I'm sure they're designed to lure British buyers – you must admit they were a factor. Let's have some coffee and some of that bread with proper butter,' said Nicola. 'Yet another reason to love the French. They don't hold truck with fads about low fat and counting calories, yet still live much longer than we do.'

She took his hand and led him back along the landing, then skipped down the stairs with a lightness she hadn't felt in years. It reminded her of when she was a child – the first day of the summer holidays, counting the stairs on her way down and wondering what excitement was in store as days of freedom and sunshine stretched ahead.

She stood in the middle of the hall so she could see the rooms leading off in both directions.

'I love these interconnecting rooms,' she said. 'They call them *salles en enfilade*, like a stately procession – they just go on and on. Let's see if we can remember where the kitchen is. You grab the coolbox and I'll take the rest.'

She picked up the basket of provisions that she'd left at the foot of the stairs and moved through to the *grand salon*, where three sets of French windows opened onto the terrace. A set of double doors on the far side led into the crystal ballroom – a sparkling chandelier gave the room its name – and from there it was through to the *petit salon* and then the dining room, with the baronial-sized table and huge matching sideboard.

These grand rooms formed the heart of the reception space and it was unanimously agreed that they should be reserved for shared use. There was plenty of scope in the east and west wings, as well as the south wing that ran behind, for them to create their own kitchens and living quarters, but the central core of the château should remain unchanged.

'It's massive,' said Dominic, trying not to think about the heating bill. 'Just as well there are plenty of us.'

'It's the beauty of our scheme,' said Nicola. 'Ideal proportions for a sharing community.'

She opened the door to the kitchen. It was, they all agreed, the weak spot. Whoever designed the house had not accorded too much space to the servants' working quarters, any more than he had to their attic bedrooms. He couldn't have known that this subsequent generation of chatelains would be so keen on performing their own domestic duties, with competitive zeal and designer cookware.

Nicola took out the kettle and cafetière she had thought to bring with her and placed them on the worn worktop. The empty shelves lining the walls were covered with grease and the old-fashioned cooker looked as if it had never been cleaned.

'Basic, but functional,' she said. 'And much more authentic than our fitted kitchen at home. It will be fine to tide us over until we get round to installing our separate flats. In fact, it will do us all good to live more simply; we're all so spoilt with our luxury appliances.'

Though as she filled the kettle from the stiff tap over the butler sink, she did suffer a pang of nostalgia for the smooth lines of the island unit of her London home, which would soon be subjected to the robust attentions of her children's flatmates. They hadn't found a buyer in the rushed few weeks since their offer on the château had been accepted, so agreed that Gus and Maddie would stay there for now and recruit some friends to pay rent. Dominic wanted to charge their own children as well but Nicola had put her foot down. She felt guilty enough about abandoning them as it was, without forcing them to pay for their parents' desertion. Gus's face had been a picture when they'd told him. 'You mean like a commune!' he'd said. 'A bunch of sad old hippies!' Maddie had been less outraged, seeing the potential for holidays and suggested they might like to install a swimming pool.

Dominic was relieved when he found out that they could buy into the French project without selling their house. He'd looked into a pension he'd largely ignored, the lucrative sort you were no longer offered, relating to a job he'd left twenty years ago. If they added that to Nicola's NHS pension and the rent on their old house, they figured they could get by. On the strength of that, he decided he could afford to cash in his main pension pot. 'Might as well blow it all on a share of a château,' he said. 'Become one of those feckless old people who become destitute thanks to the new pension freedoms.'

They carried their coffee out to the terrace and sat on the steps to enjoy the bread spread with butter miraculously studded with salt crystals.

'It's called a tartine, did you know that?' said Nicola. 'I always thought that meant a little tart, but in fact it's just bread and butter. I love how everything sounds better in French.'

'*Mon amour*,' said Dominic, working his lips into an exaggerated pout.

'Look at all the blossom,' said Nicola. 'Just wait until the apples come, we can gather them while wearing rustic smocks. You can take a large stick and knock them off the branches, like they do in films.'

'It beats brunch in London, wouldn't you say? Not an avocado-eating hipster in sight. Listen to the silence.'

'I don't know, the birds are pretty noisy. And there's a lot of rustling. Who knows what creatures are out there.'

'I'll protect you.'

He put his arm around her and watched the dragonflies skimming over the lake as he bit through the warm crust of the baguette.

'We could plant some water lilies,' he said, 'go the full Monet. Convert one of the huts into a studio and learn to paint. There are so many opportunities. Thank you for bringing me here, it's perfect. When you think I could still be in that office, worrying about things that don't matter.'

'Worrying is such a waste of time.'

She kissed him fondly, then noticed someone approaching them from the end of the terrace.

'Hang on, someone's here – who is that?'

'It's Madame de Courcy.'

They watched her slowly making her way over, pausing every few steps to rest on her cane. She was every inch the grand country lady, with her discreet tweed suit and white hair fastened in a chignon. The last time they'd seen her was at the *notaire*'s office, where the clerk had to bring in extra chairs for the large numbers of signatories to the sales agreement. It was most irregular, the *notaire* had sternly informed them. Never before had he sold a property to such a large group of people. He made them sound like a shifty, possibly criminal bunch. In contrast, he treated Madame de Courcy with the utmost reverence, letting them know that she was a person of great significance, with ancestral attachment to the region. *Unlike you lot*, was the unspoken implication.

'Please, don't get up,' she said as she drew nearer. 'What a charming scene you make: a couple in love on the terrace of their new home. I saw your car outside and wanted to present you with this.'

She handed over a pot planted with a single lily of the valley, the tiny white flowers almost plastic in their bell-shaped neatness, shrouded by dark green leaves.

'Thank you, how very thoughtful,' said Nicola, trying to switch to French and wondering if she'd got her accent right. She'd swapped her addiction to games on her phone for a serious Duolingo habit to try and get her French up to scratch. She wondered if the old lady had been watching out for their arrival; they certainly hadn't informed her of their moving-in date.

'It's *muguet*,' Madame de Courcy continued in her near-perfect English. 'We always offer it at the beginning of May to wish good luck. It was Charles IX who introduced the tradition, and we give it now to signify the happiness of a new beginning that comes with the spring.'

She sat down beside them with some difficulty.

'At my age it is hard to be quite so enthusiastic about each new year, but I am happy in my new *pavillon* down the road and so pleased that my real home has found good owners. There are some who think it is a betrayal to sell to *les rosbifs*, but I prefer you who will live here all the time to some Parisian who will only visit rarely. Smell it, you will love the scent, it is softer and less assertive than roses, which I find a little vulgar.'

Nicola obediently leaned forward to breathe in the scent, thinking how all flowers smelled the same to her. Maybe that would change now she was a country person.

'It's beautiful,' she said, 'and we are so thrilled with the house. Thank you for selling it to us.'

Madame de Courcy waved her hand dismissively at the mention of money.

'Nobody ever owns a château,' she said. 'It will go on through the centuries, and we are all mere custodians, safeguarding it for the next generation.'

'Like a fancy watch,' said Dominic.

Madame de Courcy looked confused.

'The advertisements for Patek Philippe watches,' Dominic explained. 'They show a handsome father handing over a watch to his son and the line is: *You never actually own a Patek Philippe. You merely look after it for the next generation.* Terribly smug.'

'What is smug?'

Her English was very good but she occasionally needed clarification.

'Pleased with himself. *Content de lui.*'

'I see. However, I think you will find the château is more complicated than a watch! If a watch breaks, you take it to the menders, but you'll soon discover the maintenance of Château Lafarge is an endless round of hard work – and expense – *oh là là!*'

Dominic noted the triumph in her voice. No doubt she was delighted to have fobbed them off with this damaged old ruin.

He and Nicola had spent many sleepless nights talking about how much they would need to spend to put it right. Dougie was the only sensible one; he'd suggested from the start that they should get a builder in before they made the offer, so they'd have a ballpark figure for how much the repairs might cost. Simon had shouted him down, said you might as well ask how long a piece of string is; the budget would be what they decided it would be, and they had all concurred. At this price, it was an absolute steal. They egged each other on because they didn't want any reason not to buy this house.

'I do hope everything is in good working order,' Madame de Courcy said, reading the alarm on Dominic's face. 'I think perhaps it is a little more dilapidated than you had hoped?'

*You hope*, he thought.

'We haven't had time yet to fully check everything,' said Nicola. 'After all, we only arrived an hour ago.'

'Of course, you are in the honeymoon period! *Noces de miel.* And the weather is kind; it is good you did not arrive in the winter. *Alors, ça!*'

She embarked on a detailed description of the hardships of the winter months, the draughty windows, the exact spots where they would be advised to place buckets on the attic floor in the event of heavy rains, the tendency of the septic tank to overflow, the likelihood of the electricity going down during storms, *because our* tempêtes *are legendary here, they are* magnifiques! Only last year they had a summer hailstorm, with stones of ice as big as tennis balls, which even smashed the windscreen of her car! What a relief to be in her newly built little house where she no longer lived in fear of the weather.

Eventually she stood up to take her leave.

'I thought she'd never go,' said Dominic as they waved her off. 'I feel completely depressed now. And notice she didn't mention any of those structural defects until we'd closed the deal, the wily old witch.'

'Oh, come on,' said Nicola, trying to put a brave face on it. 'She's only being friendly.'

'Friendly! Merchant of doom, more like.'

'You can't say we didn't anticipate all those problems; nothing really surprising there. And at least there are no termites or asbestos; we have certificates to prove it.'

'French law is weird. You can sell someone a crumbling pile of stones, just as long as it hasn't got termites! Never mind everything else that's wrong with it.'

Nicola sighed, unable to keep up her fake optimism.

'OK, I admit it. We should have had a survey. But we are where we are and it's good to have Madame de Courcy on side: she'll be useful if we need to know anything.'

'Sitting in her *pavillon*, counting her money. We shouldn't have offered the asking price. She must have taken us for naïve English dreamers, which we are, of course.'

'Yes, we are hopeless dreamers. But that's because we are living the dream, which can only be a good thing. It's funny that word *pavillon*, isn't it? It sounds really grand but it's not a decorative summer house at all, just a small Barratt home.'

'The kind of retirement home we should have looked at if we'd had any sense.'

'Stop it, we are castle-dwellers now and don't you forget it. And look, here comes our van! They've made good time, haven't they?'

They watched the lorry manoeuvring in the narrow lane in order to get through the gates, the access being better suited to a horse-drawn carriage than a heavy goods vehicle. Finally, the angle was achieved and the van crunched its way across the gravel drive towards them.

The driver stepped down and walked up to the front steps, throwing his arms in the air to show his appreciation. His name was Terry, he'd told them when he was packing them up in London, and he loved his job. Nothing better than helping people move on to their next place. Nicola had admired how delicately he had wrapped each glass, the finesse of the task at odds with the heavy lifting of furniture, which he undertook with equal efficiency.

'Well, this is a bit better than your standard terraced house, isn't it!' he said, shaking Dominic vigorously by the hand and giving Nicola a reassuring pat on the shoulder. 'I've done a few moves to France in my time, but I've never seen anything as grand as this. Fit for a king. You must be over the moon!'

He was joined by his colleagues, equally effusive in their appreciation as they stretched their legs after the long journey by wandering around the vast reception rooms. Nicola felt a rush of warmth towards them, grateful for the reminder that this was indeed a wonderful place rather than a flawed money pit.

'Cup of tea would go down well,' said Terry.

'Two with sugar, two without, I seem to remember,' said Nicola.

'That's it, love.'

Nicola left them to start unloading and went to put the kettle on, setting out a packet of Hobnobs (after all, they still needed a little taste of home!) alongside the chunky mugs of tea. When she returned with the tray, Dominic was directing operations, allocating their furniture to the relevant rooms. They had left most of it behind for the children and their tenants, but Dominic especially wanted to bring their bed – for sentimental reasons, he'd said. The few other pieces they had brought along for the sitting rooms appeared small and lost in their new, grand surroundings.

'That bookcase used to fill an entire wall in our study,' said Nicola, 'but here it looks tiny. I've told Leo he'll have carte blanche as interior designer. I'm sure he'll want to do away with all our stuff.'

'He'll have a fit when Beth and Simon's furniture arrives,' said Dominic, smiling at the thought of it. 'The entire contents of their house – all of it in questionable taste, as we've often discussed.'

'It doesn't matter, it's only temporary and at least we'll have somewhere to sit, even if it looks all wrong.'

'Leo may be in charge of the shared rooms, but I know exactly what I want in our bedroom. I'm going to get round the local auctions to find a heavy French armoire like that one we saw at Lots Road, do you remember? Big and carved and beautiful, but there was no way of getting it up our stairs. This place is made for it.'

'We should take one that's already here – didn't you notice there are at least three of them in the bedrooms? Make the most of what we have. There are plenty of other ways to spend our money.'

When the last boxes had been stacked in the hall, the removal men said their goodbyes.

'That will keep you fit,' said Terry, nodding at Dominic's racing bike, which was leaning against the wall, still wrapped in its protective polythene. 'Plenty of hills to negotiate round here.'

'I'm going for the yellow jersey,' said Dominic. 'They're big on cycling in France.'

'Just need a string of onions round your neck and you're sorted.'

'Thank you again,' said Nicola. 'Are you heading straight back?'

'No such luck,' said Terry. 'We're going down to the Dordogne now. Reverse procedure. The clients have decided they've had enough sunshine and foie gras and are moving back to England. Maybe that'll be you in a few years; we might just meet again!'

'Don't say that, we're here to stay!'

They watched the lorry renegotiate the gates and disappear down the lane, then closed the door to continue their familiarisation. *Like dogs*, Nicola thought, *sniffing our way around every corner*. They paraded through the crystal ballroom, the salons, the panelled library, all the bedrooms, imagining their friends settling in right away and thinking forward to when everyone would be permanently installed in their separate apartments. Leo would love the fairy-tale turret, and the warren of attic rooms would be ideal for visiting family.

'I already hate the idea of leaving this place,' said Nicola as they went down again to the sitting room. 'It would feel like failure to me, creeping back in defeat. Imagine how everyone would gloat.'

She stretched out on their old sofa, a survivor from the 1980s fad for Victoriana. Covered with a Colefax and Fowler fabric featuring sprays of roses, it had been covered up with a neutral throw and banished to the study in London when they'd succumbed to modernism. Even though it was a large three-seater, it was dwarfed by the proportions of their new sitting room. Or *le grand salon* as Dominic called it, puckering up his mouth in his new French pout that could start to get on Nicola's nerves, she thought, before reminding herself that they were both tired and it had been a long day. All around them were piles of cardboard boxes awaiting their attention.

'Surely *le soleil* is over the yardarm,' said Dominic, sinking into an armchair.

Nicola got to her feet.

'Most certainly. I'm not even going near those boxes; they can wait until tomorrow.'

She picked her way through more paraphernalia on her way through to the kitchen.

'I love how it takes so long to move from one room to another!' she shouted to Dominic. 'We'll be able to really lose ourselves here – so much space.'

She returned with a bottle of prosecco and two glasses.

'Here's to our final British supper, which is to say Italian wine, chicken tikka masala and New York cheesecake. No wonder we are confused as a nation. From tomorrow, it's French all the way! But I am glad I brought supplies for today; we've had enough excitement without having to think about shopping.'

She poured out the prosecco and Dominic sat up to make a toast.

'To Château Lafarge and all who sail in her,' he said, looking up at Nicola and thinking how marvellous she was. Fancy her remembering to bring food for tonight, along with everything else. He didn't know what he'd do without her.

'To the current custodians,' Nicola replied, taking a sip from her glass, then plumping up her hair in anticipation of a selfie. 'Let's send a photo to the others.'

She crouched down beside him and grinned at her phone, held out at arm's length.

'Do try to look a bit more natural,' she said, looking critically at the image. 'You always pull such gurning faces.'

Dominic tried to relax his features into a carefree smile.

'I can't help it if I'm not a little show pony like you.'

'That's better.'

She inspected the result, the two of them cuddled up in the armchair, against the backdrop of the grand windows, and edited the photo with a dramatic warm filter.

'Amazing,' she said, then added the caption *waiting for our chums* and sent it to the WhatsApp group she had renamed Chatelains.

Dominic drained his glass and wrapped his arm tightly around Nicola's waist. All was well. He was elated about this new life and his happiness was combined with a profound sense of relief. How foolish he'd been, all those years ago, to make such a stupid mistake. And how lucky he was that Nicola had never found out. Now he could put that sorry business firmly behind him and start again, properly this time.

'Shall we have a little lie-down before supper?' he asked, raising his eyebrow in what he hoped was a sexy French way. 'Make sure the bed has survived the move?'

# CHAPTER SIX

'*Allez, allez, allez, allez!*'

Beth's fist pumped the air as they drove past the Eurotunnel check-in and on to passport control, where long lines of cars were waiting.

'What are you, a French football hooligan?' said Simon, frowning at the sight of further delays ahead.

'Contradiction in terms – it's not the French fans who bring disgrace on their country, staggering around with beer cans.'

She turned to face Leo, who was folded up on the back seat, his long legs tucked decorously to one side.

'All right, my friend?'

'Yes. I'm just thinking about all my things packed up in that van. I hope they don't go missing. There are some important pieces in there; everything I need to get started on selling clients back home the dream of French country interiors. Plus, I've packed all my best outfits. I've got to look the part if I'm selling myself as an international interior designer now – rather than just part of the London crowd.'

'Don't worry,' said Simon, 'you can always borrow mine. Trousers could be a challenge, mind you – I doubt we're the same waist size but I can always give you a pair of tracksuit bottoms.'

He grinned affectionately at Leo in the rear-view mirror.

Leo pulled a face.

'Tracksuit bottoms! I've never worn a pair of those, and have no intention of starting now.'

He didn't look like he was moving to the country, dressed in a turquoise Prada mac and cream trousers.

'New beginnings,' Simon replied. 'It's time to try different things.'

'I can't tell you how excited I am,' said Beth. 'Nicola says they're preparing a special welcome feast. We're going to sit round that massive table tonight and every night. I honestly can't think of anything better. Which is just as well because there's no turning back for us since we've actually *sold* our house. Unlike you and the others, Leo – you've still got your fall-back options if it all goes tits-up!'

'It won't go tits-up. Why would it?' said Leo soothingly. Although he was secretly relieved that the inheritance from his late father meant he was able to buy his share of the château outright, with no immediate need to dispose of his London home. He tended to keep quiet about his trust fund; he knew he was fortunate to come from a wealthy background, with income from tenants on the family estate allowing him not to worry about money. Beth was particularly spiky about it – unfairly, in Leo's opinion. It wasn't *his* fault he was born into wealth – you can't help where you come from – and he was proud that his ancestors featured in the Domesday Book. He had rented out his house at below the market rate, to a young man he knew through work, chosen for his extreme carefulness and aesthetic sensibility. No risk of him scuffing the walls or trampling crumbs into the carpet.

'We have to make it work,' said Simon. 'I admit I was the last one to come round to the idea of moving to France but I honestly believe the only way to make a go of it is to properly burn your bridges.'

'Quite right, Simon,' said Beth, putting her hand on his knee. 'I finally feel properly relaxed for the first time since those bastards gave me the sack. It's a whole new chapter for us. Bring it on.'

The trauma of being fired, she realised, had been eating away at her in spite of her robust protestations. The idea that she, a staunch feminist all her life, had effectively been given the sack for sticking up for her sisters made her sick to her core. So much for solidarity.

Saying goodbye to Eva had been the hardest thing. Their daughter had taken the sale of her childhood home as a personal blow. Never mind the fact that she had her own flat, paid for by her parents; she seemed to expect that the family house should be maintained forever in case she fancied dropping by. On the day before completion, Eva had taken an emotional tour with Beth around all the rooms; it was like saying goodbye to her childhood, she said. It was a painful experience but Beth realised that a little distance might actually be good for the complicated mother–daughter bond that had dominated her thoughts too much since she had stopped working.

'We've chosen the wrong lane here,' said Simon, thumping his hands on the steering wheel. 'Look at that queue, we've obviously got the trainee border controller!' He was further outraged when, after showing their passports, they were pulled aside to have their car inspected.

'Do we look like drug smugglers?' he asked the uniformed woman who was leaning in to flick his steering wheel with what looked like a feather duster.

'Can you open your bonnet for me, please?' she replied.

'Sure,' he said, then whispered to Beth, 'Do you know how to open the bonnet? I'm not a bloody mechanic – I've no idea!'

Beth reached across his lap to pull a lever beneath the dashboard.

'You'll have to become a bit more savvy once we're left to our own devices in our rural wilderness,' she said.

They missed their scheduled departure and were put in a line to wait for the next one.

'So much for only one hour motorway-to-motorway,' said Simon.

'*What is this life if, full of care, we have no time to stop and stare,*' said Leo from the back seat. 'Heed the soothing words of William Henry Davies.'

'Exactly,' said Beth. 'That is the whole point of this new life. We have given ourselves the luxury of time.'

'Not much to stare at here, though,' said Simon, gazing out at the expanse of tarmac.

'There will be,' said Beth, 'just you wait.'

In the self-service restaurant aboard the *Normandie* ferry, Dougie and Mary were loading up their trays with full English breakfasts. They had opted for the long crossing from Portsmouth to Caen because it involved less driving. Neither of them were confident drivers and every car journey was a nervous collaborative exercise, with Mary reading the road signs and advising Dougie about when to change gear. She wished they had taken their tests when they were younger and more oblivious to the inherent danger of moving at speed in a powerful machine.

'Last time we'll have one of these for a while, I daresay,' said Dougie, carrying his fry-up as they sat down at a window seat offering a fine view of the Portsmouth docks as the ferry glided along the coast. 'It's a shame we didn't have time to inspect the historic dockyard. I've always wanted to visit HMS *Victory*.'

'We can take it in when we come home to visit,' said Mary. 'I can't believe you're having baked beans; it makes me quite nauseous just watching you.'

Dougie loaded a forkful into his mouth.

'They symbolise the British way of life. I can imagine I'm going to fight in the trenches, with only tins of beans and bully beef to sustain me. I certainly intend to visit the battlefields when we're there – it's a whole new area of study for me.'

'I don't expect we'll get bully beef for dinner,' said Mary. 'Nicola is a marvellous cook. I'm worried about letting the side down when it's my turn.'

'Just leave them to it, there are enough show-off cooks in the party, too many of them spoil the broth. You have other domestic skills.'

'Yes, though I must say I'm a little daunted at the thought of cleaning a place that size. The sheer scale of it! I'll be much happier once we're installed in our own quarters, with only our flat to worry about. As it is, there will be nine of us messing up that primitive kitchen. And just two bathrooms with mouldy old taps, then centuries of filth engrained everywhere through-out the thirty-two or however many rooms. It really requires a team of housemaids. Still, it's important to challenge yourself, don't you agree?'

Mary was a prominent medievalist – the author of many important papers – and the only thing that helped her switch off from her constant overthinking and academic analysis was the uplifting, soul-enriching task of cleaning. Their house in Highsett was too easy, she had come to believe; the straight lines and sim-ple design meant it was a doddle to keep in sparkling condi-tion. But the potential of Château Lafarge's high windows and infinite dark corners had kept her awake last night just thinking about it. She had bought a long-reach extendable ostrich feather duster especially to reach the cobwebs that she was sure would be waiting for her. Friends had sometimes gently suggested her housekeeping might be a borderline case of OCD, but she failed to understand how taking pleasure in a clean home could be considered a disorder.

'That is the joy of this experiment,' said Dougie. 'We all bring our particular talents to throw into the mix.'

Watching him tucking into his eggs, Mary wondered which particular talent he would bring to their new domestic arrangements. He was famously useless at anything practical, bless him, and his back problems ruled him out of any physical work. On the other hand, his agile mind – the mind she had fallen in love with – meant he was fascinating company; she just hoped the others continued to think so when they were exposed to him on a daily basis, as opposed to the occasional dinner party when his brilliance was invariably admired. He could be rather annoying, with his know-all ways; it wasn't necessarily what you wanted over breakfast. At least he was good with money. She wouldn't say he was mean, exactly, but he didn't like waste. And listening to Simon and Dominic discussing their extravagant plans for the renovation, she could see that his carefulness would be invaluable for keeping them all in check.

She had been flattered to be invited into this experiment, as Dougie insisted on calling it. Nicola was such a dear girl, only a couple of years younger than herself but it seemed like more. Mary had adored her since their first meeting when they became neighbours, but if it hadn't been for that coincidence, it was hard to imagine them becoming friends. Nicola and Beth, together with their dashing husbands, seemed to inhabit a more glamorous world and it came as a surprise to her and Dougie that they were considered suitable candidates. 'We're not very clubbable,' Dougie had pointed out, before being overruled by Nicola, who said that this wasn't a club, for who on earth would want that? Rather, it was *a country house weekend with no going-home date*, which sounded quite irresistible.

Dougie was nervous about how quickly they'd rushed into it. To buy a historical monument without undertaking a detailed survey was madness, it went against all his sensible instincts. But somehow, he'd been swept along by the group euphoria and it was too late now to sound the alarm bell. For years he had been carefully investing their salaries – their frugal lifestyle involved little spending – which meant they didn't need to sell the Cambridge house. They rented it out instead to a young couple with a baby. *That way, we have our escape clause*, he'd said, and Mary, too, was relieved that they had a way back if things didn't work out. She tried not to think about the baby crawling all over her floors and smearing food on the walls.

'I see this as an extended reading party,' said Dougie, waving his fork. 'I've decided to shelve my anxiety that the château is going to crumble into a heap of dust. Do you remember that summer we retreated to the Alps to work on our theses? The luxury to focus on our studies away from the outside world, the fruitfulness of sharing ideas with kindred spirits. Like when Mary Shelley was holed up with Percy and Lord Byron and had a nightmare that inspired her to write *Frankenstein*. Who knows what great works will emerge from our collective creativity when we are all assembled within those ancient and noble stones!'

'Nothing so melodramatic in my case,' said Mary, whose strengths were analytical rather than fantastical. 'I don't think Gothic fiction is my thing but I do intend to finally complete my paper on the broken leaf of the Magdalene manuscript of *The Hare and the Serpent*.'

'Ah yes, that old chestnut!'

It was something she had been working on for years. Only one manuscript of the thirteenth-century poem had survived and part of it was damaged, which had led to learned speculation on what the missing words could be. Mary was confident she was the best person to produce the definitive answer. In her darker moments, she did wonder what was the point. It was so long ago and, really, who cared? But that sort of thinking undermined the rich purpose of scholarship – it was better not to go there.

'They said there's a quiz in the Blue Note Bar, later,' she said. 'Shall we join in?'

'Definitely. I doubt there'll be much competition.'

Dougie's optimism proved to be unfounded. A few hours later, they suffered a bitter humiliation, coming second from the bottom after being trounced by some other passengers.

'It's hardly surprising,' Mary whispered to Dougie, as the com-pere led a round of applause for Steve and Kylie from Bridport. 'As we don't own a television, we can't expect to score well on *Love Island* contestants. And we've never pretended to know anything about sport.'

'Dumbed-down Britain,' said Dougie crossly. 'Why can't they have questions about normal things like history and geography? You got one right, though how on earth did you know the name of the winner of *I'm a Celebrity Get Me Out of Here!*?'

'I sometimes watch it on my laptop when my concentration's flagging,' said Mary. 'I like it when they have to eat insects.'

Dougie looked at her with admiration.

'You surprise me every day. It's just a shame you didn't extend your guilty viewing to include a few more trash programmes – we might have stood a chance!'

They spent the rest of the crossing reading in armchairs. Mary browsed the off-duty store with its seductive range of miniature perfume bottles and novelty shortbread tins. She bought a giant-sized Toblerone and a bottle of gin and returned to find Dougie standing by the window.

'We're arriving!' he said. 'It's farewell to perfidious Albion. I can smell liberty, equality and fraternity! Look, there it is, the shores of the glorious Hexagon await us. How absolutely thrilling!'

Mary watched with him as they drew closer to land and recalled when she had made this journey before. She was ten years old, a serious child, and her parents had brought her on an educational trip to the Normandy beaches to see where her father had taken part in the D-Day landings. In his careful, quiet manner, he had sat down with her on the sea wall at Arromanches and pointed out the remains of the harbour, the portable pontoons that he and his comrades had brought over from Britain to enable troops and their equipment to land where they were least expected. After that, they'd wandered through the cobbled lanes and he'd bought her a crepe, cooked in front of her on an enormous circular hot plate, then sprinkled with lemon and sugar and folded up in a paper serviette. Her father died of a stroke twenty years later and whenever Mary caught the smell of pancakes frying in butter, she thought of him.

'I'll drive this end,' she said as they made their way down to the car deck. 'Then you can look at the map.'

Ouistreham port had none of the historic grandeur of Portsmouth, just a few sailing boats moored up and a couple of lacklustre fairground roundabouts. As they drove through the sleepy town, they noticed small groups of tall young black men walking slowly together by the seaside, or sitting on a wall, or lying beneath the trees on the grass in the parkland on the outskirts of the town. Dreaming of somehow boarding a ship and escaping to a new life in Britain, though it seemed an impossible task in view of the heavy police presence guarding the port. *I am a migrant now, too*, thought Mary, *but with the great good fortune that I'm doing it by choice and not out of desperation.*

She would return soon to visit her mother, lost in her shrinking world at the nursing home. How fortunate Mary was that she could come and go like that.

Living in a group would be a massive change for her. She and Dougie had inhabited a companionable bubble *a deux* for over thirty years now, untroubled by intrusions from children or housemates. And now that comfortable equanimity was about to rocked. They were friends with the others, to a greater or lesser extent, had been on holiday with some of them, but there was a world of difference between two weeks in a villa and every single day for possibly the rest of your life.

Will and his young wife were the ones she had least knowledge of. She remembered the first time she met Will when they were invited to dinner at Nicola and Dom's next door in Clapham. Will had still been with his first wife and was a typical lawyer, they agreed afterwards, pushy and arrogant, straight out of Chaucer's *Canterbury Tales*. He'd had a sort of conversion since then, turning his back on his career, and seemed to still be searching for something to replace it. The young wife she barely knew at all. She could easily be one of the students who used to drift into Mary's lectures, dressed in gym clothes with full makeup and a distracted air. It was difficult to see what common ground they might share, but she was open to persuasion. More worrying was how Dougie would fit in with the other men. There was a macho swagger to Simon that was quite at odds with Dougie's fussy manner; she did hope there wouldn't be too many awkward moments.

'Turn left!' said Dougie. 'You were supposed to turn left there!'

He had the map spread out over his knees and was pointing back over his shoulder to the road they should have taken.

'You're meant to tell me beforehand, not after the event,' Mary said smoothly. 'But it doesn't matter. I'll do a U turn at this roundabout, we'll be there in no time. Are you excited?'

'Excitement is not appropriate to our age. Let's say I'm in a state of heightened anticipation.'

'Heightened anticipation. I couldn't have put it better myself.'

# CHAPTER SEVEN

'Good morning, mistress of the château.'

Dominic reached across the bed to nudge Nicola, who was still asleep.

She stirred into consciousness and couldn't remember where she was. Then she opened her eyes and saw the *toile de jouy* curtains decorated with hunting scenes, and burgundy-coloured horsemen cavorting across a cream background. The wallpaper had the identical pattern, reminding you, in case you had forgotten, that you were in an eighteenth-century country home of distinction.

'Hooray, we're here,' she said, turning towards him. 'Did you sleep all right?'

'In the end. I took to counting huntsmen in the dark. I reckon there are at least five hundred in this room, when you tot them all up.'

'Charming, aren't they? Really set the tone.'

'Especially the ones that are peeling off the damp walls.'

'Eeyore! We can stick them down again, or hang new wallpaper. I'm sure you can still buy it in the same style – you know how nothing changes in France, that's its great appeal. Maybe we should keep this room in its original state, as homage to the château as we found it, once we've redecorated.'

She jumped out of bed and went to open the curtains, releasing a cloud of dust that danced in the morning sun.

'Mary is going to love it; so much to keep her occupied with her feather duster.'

'What time are they arriving?'

'This afternoon sometime. Oh, just look at that view! We still haven't been round the walled garden. I've always wanted one of those – proper high stone walls with espaliered fruit trees. Get up, let's go and inspect it right away.'

Dominic admired her gamine silhouette outlined against the sunlight, her unruly blonde hair tumbling over her nightdress. What a fool he'd been, to even think about threatening what they had. Not for the first time, he thanked his lucky stars that she'd never had any inkling, that he'd managed to preserve their happiness.

'Come on then, let's take a tour,' he said.

'Better get dressed first in case Madame de Courcy shows up again.'

Their shoes were soaked by the time they'd walked through the long grass to the entrance of the walled garden. It was magical, with rows of vegetables gone to seed and the fan-trained fruit trees showing their pink blossom to maximum effect against the cream stone walls.

'I'm going to spend all my time in here,' said Nicola. 'We can become self-sufficient and I'll grow stuff to put in jars for the still room. I've always fancied a still room; even the name is the very epitome of peace. Look at the rhubarb!'

She broke some thin pink stalks off one of the crowns that were sprawling over the edge of a bed.

'That's tonight's pudding sorted – rhubarb fool made with crème fraiche. We should get to the shops right away. You know everything closes for lunch over here.'

The drive to the local town took them along a narrow lane that ran beside the river, shaded by trees and flanked by gently sloping pasture grazed by cream-coloured cows. A different experience to Nicola's former traffic-blighted route through busy streets to Sainsbury's.

'Supermarket first,' she said. 'Get the basics and then top up at the little shops, don't you think?'

They bypassed the centre of town and found a modest industrial estate on the outskirts with a DIY store and a garden machinery shop, with ride-on mowers parked enticingly in the forecourt.

'We should definitely get one of those,' said Dominic. 'I'll cut the grass while you bring on the vegetables.'

'I just love French supermarkets,' said Nicola as they pushed their trolley through the doors. 'It reminds me of being on holiday.'

She thought about the time when they'd taken the children to a villa in Provence – the blast of heat when they stepped out of the car before arriving in the air-conditioned delights of the hypermarket, loading up with bottles of rosé and tubs of strawberry ice cream.

They dawdled through the vegetables and Nicola seized upon a fat bunch of watercress and a russet and green lettuce. 'So different to the sad collection of leaves in plastic packets we're used to. And look, it's all grown locally.'

'We really should buy the cheese from the high street shop,' said Dom, 'but they might be closed by the time we get there, so let's get it here, just for today. There'll be plenty of time in the future to ingratiate ourselves with the local shopkeepers.'

They bought an orange Livarot cheese, its circular form finished with a band of raffia, then a wedge of Comté and a slab of hard sheep's cheese, along with a Papillon roquefort, chosen from four different varieties that were on display, all of them made with unpasteurised milk, because they knew, as all committed foodies do, that *au lait cru* is the must-have for flavour.

'It's not as if we have to worry about contaminating any unborn children,' said Nicola happily. 'There's an upside to our advancing years.'

The fish counter was a source of wonder, an unbelievable range of produce glistening on a bed of ice.

'Seafood to start with. Let's get oysters and those tiny grey shrimps, and some langoustines. Then a great big whole fish as a centrepiece. '

As the assistant weighed the shrimps, they pondered which fish to buy, eyeing up some whole salmon and sea bass.

'It's got to be this one,' said Dominic, pointing out a spectacularly ugly creature with spiny growths. 'Look at that face it's pulling, like a sulky old man.'

'Yes, the Saint Pierre,' said the assistant, nodding his approval. 'You will see the dark mark in the centre of his golden body – that is the mark of the thumb of Saint Peter, according to legend. He pulled a piece of gold from the fish's mouth.'

Dom was pleased he could just about understand what the fishmonger was saying – as long as he left room for a little creative licence.

'Better take two,' said Nicola. 'Everyone will be hungry after their journey.'

After loading up the car, they drove into town, where the high street was lined with medieval houses with walls that leaned at such alarming angles that you might worry about their stability, were it not for the fact that they had held firm for five centuries and were not about to give up now. It was the sight that had entranced them on their first visit and convinced them that this was where they should settle.

'I can't believe a tiny town like this can support four boulangeries,' said Dominic, as they strolled down the street, wondering which one to choose. *That was retirement for you*, he thought. *Such decisions could take up a disproportionate amount of time.*

'And four pharmacies. Look at the window display in this one – wheelchairs and equipment to help you get out of the bath. Let's hope we won't need that for a while ahead of us.'

'Alongside a poster showing you which mushrooms you shouldn't eat, otherwise you'll end up needing all the stuff in this shop. We townies have got a steep learning curve ahead of us.'

When they arrived back at the château, Will's sports car was already parked outside. Dominic jumped out of the car and rushed forward to greet him.

'Maaate!' he said, in an ironic imitation of how they had noticed young men liked to salute each other. 'You're early!' He embraced his friend in the awkward man hug they had recently adopted.

'Yeah, well, you snooze, you lose,' said Will, releasing his grip and holding Dom by the shoulders. 'We wanted to make sure we got the best room. Sorry, second best room – you made sure of that.'

'They are all fab, no worries there – and they'll be even better once the work's completed,' said Nicola. 'And anyway, it was all agreed, if you remember, precisely to avoid any unseemly jostling on moving-in day. Where's Fizz?'

'She's gone for a run – stretching her legs after the journey.'

'Of course she has,' said Dominic. 'You can stretch yours by helping us in with the shopping.'

'This is fantastic,' said Will, carrying a crate of beer through to the kitchen. 'Even better than I remember, though I guess the weather helps.'

'Exactly what we said: spring sunshine smiling on our great adventure. Let's crack open a couple of these and I'll give you the tour.'

The two men set off with their beer bottles to walk around the lake and discuss the feasibility of establishing a cricket pitch in one of the fields.

'There's no shortage of space,' said Will. 'It could be like in *The Go-Between*: our team of nobs at the château versus the strong-armed men of the village.'

'Not sure how that would play out,' said Dominic. 'For a start, we're not what you'd call nobs, plus we're all a bit past it. Although the French don't play cricket, so we'd have that advantage.'

'You're more of a nob that I am, that's for sure,' said Will. 'My old man would have found it hilarious that I've ended up living in a poncey château! But I'm serious about the cricket. I've brought my bat so we can practice every day before breakfast – the reassuring sound of leather on willow. This really is an excellent scheme we've taken on!'

Nicola was unpacking the crockery when Fizz returned from her run, the sweat glistening on the exposed flesh between her bra top and her matching purple leggings. *She's so young*, thought

Nicola with a rush of maternal concern. *Not much older than Maddie. I do hope she'll be all right.*

'Hello, Fizz, how lovely to have you here,' she said, as Fizz performed a series of acrobatic stretches in the kitchen doorway. 'How was your run?'

'Pretty good, actually.'

Fizz consulted the fitbit attached to her wrist.

'Ten thousand, seven hundred and fifty steps in thirty minutes – not bad at all.'

She approached Nicola and gave her a careful embrace, holding back her sweaty body at a polite distance while kissing her on both cheeks.

'This is such a cool place – I knew it would be from the pics, but it's just as great as Will said it was.'

Fizz was the only one of the group who hadn't yet seen their new home. She had opted out of the visits, telling Will to sort it out and she would wait until it was a definite thing. No point in getting her hopes up, she'd said, only to have them dashed. Will had told the others that he thought this showed unusual maturity and was touched by her faith in his judgement, though admitted in darker moments that maybe she hoped the scheme would be abandoned. He'd decided she had clearly gone cold on the idea when she couldn't be bothered to accompany him on the subsequent trip when they signed the papers.

But now Nicola wanted to take Fizz's enthusiasm at face value, yet couldn't help wondering how on earth she would find it, trapped here in the middle of nowhere with a load of semi-retirees almost twice her age. Albeit *young* retirees, she reminded herself, not exactly a group of old pensioners.

'I'm so glad you think so,' she said. 'We're going to have a great time. The others are getting here later, then we can let our hair down and have a proper party.'

Fizz gave an amused smile to suggest that it wouldn't exactly be her idea of a party, sitting around with a bunch of people twenty years older than her. She must be mad! *Crazy, moi!* And yet this challenge provided her with a real opportunity. She had been seriously concerned about leaving London to move into a quasi-retirement home in the depths of the French countryside. To be honest, she had even considered staying behind, leaving Will to get on with it and maybe visiting once a month. But then she began to think seriously about her vlogging idea. This could be her big chance. Plenty of vacuous people ten years younger than her were attracting two million followers with their boring tips on makeup; surely she could match that by doing something really different and interesting.

She'd come up with a great name for her YouTube channel. Mademoiselle Bovary. Like a younger, modern Madame Bovary – the *Mademoiselle* would let the viewers know that even though she was married, she'd kept her maiden name. In fact, she'd started out married life as Mrs Hodgkins but decided it was too depressing to have the same name as Will's hatchet-faced first wife, and anyway, Felicity Fortescue had a far more dashing ring to it. The vlogs were going to be fab. She would tap into the angsty alienation of the rural French housewife, it would go down a storm and she could really start to make a name for herself as an influencer and holistic lifestyle guru. It remained to be seen if she'd be taken for a reputation-ruining ride in a carriage by a feckless French aristocrat. Probably not, but never say never.

'I must have a shower,' Fizz said. 'Would you mind showing me our room?'

*As if I'm the front-of-house of a luxury hotel*, thought Nicola.

'Um, a shower could be a bit of a stretch,' she said, 'but there is a hand-held attachment over the bath. Come with me.'

Fizz followed her up the stairs and down the corridor, to the opposite wing from Nicola and Dominic's bedroom.

'You're in here,' she said, opening the door. 'Will was particularly keen on this room because of the bed – it's been in the house forever, apparently. Isn't it beautiful with all those carvings?'

Fizz ran her fingers over the engraved elm headboard, then walked across to the window.

'Fantastic view,' she said, banging on the glass then waving at Will outside in the garden. He raised his beer bottle to her in response, and blew her a kiss. *He's drinking already!* she thought. *I'll put a stop to that. Never in the daytime, that's our rule.*

'So, where's our bathroom?' she asked, looking around the large room for a door to the ensuite. 'All I can see is that funny little basin in the corner.'

'Isn't it adorable?' said Nicola. 'I love the taps. There are two bathrooms to choose from. Neither has a shower, as I explained, but they make up for it in period detail. Come with me and I'll show you.'

Fizz looked disgruntled but followed Nicola down the corridor.

'The first one is here,' said Nicola, opening the door to a room with a freestanding iron bath and a washstand with a basin dropped into a wooden cabinet.

'There's no loo,' said Fizz.

'Ah no, that's at the end of the corridor, in glorious isolation. A real old thunderbox, in the grandest country house tradition.'

'So, let's get this straight, we are all sharing one loo and two bathrooms?'

'For the time being, until we get the renovations underway. And there's another loo downstairs, of course.'

Fizz put her hands to her face.

'I had no idea it would be so primitive,' she said. 'I mean, it's all very well if you're at a festival for a couple of days . . .'

'You'll get used to it,' said Nicola briskly. 'You don't know you're born, you youngsters. I remember when I was growing up and we had a second bathroom put in – it was considered the height of decadence.'

'And I expect you had an outside loo in those days,' said Fizz, with an attempt at humour.

'Haha, we're not that old! It will be fine, you'll see. As you know, we have elaborate plans to upgrade in due course, but we all have to share until then. It's part of the fun.'

'If you say so,' said Fizz. 'I guess for the time being I'll just have to pretend I'm camping.'

She pulled a grumpy face, but already she was imagining Mademoiselle Bovary expressing her discomfort at these reduced circumstances. Living in a château but sharing a toilet with eight old people!

'That's the spirit. I'll leave you to it. Come down when you're ready for a spot of lunch.'

*It's true that the shared bathrooms aren't ideal*, Nicola thought as she went downstairs to leave Fizz to her ablutions, *but honestly, that shouldn't be the first thing you think about when coming to live in this magnificent historic house. If you were to take your chatelaine fantasy to its limits, you'd have one bath a year and cover everything up with powder and perfume. The modern obsession with personal hygiene was so anodyne – what happened to romance and big ideas in our lives?* Anyway, her medical training taught her you could be too clean for your own good, washing away your natural resistance to germs so you fell prey to the slightest bug. She couldn't be doing with it.

All the same, it was pretty galling to think how long they'd be living like this. A year, at least, by the time they'd agreed the plans and found their builders. She knew from experience that you could safely double your allocated schedule as well as your budget when it came to home renovations, even on a humbler scale than this enormous undertaking. It was safe to say they'd be queuing for the bathroom for many months to come while they waited to construct their dream apartments. At least they didn't have to get ready for work every day. They had only roughly marked out the plans but she had already decided how her bathroom would be: decorated with tangerine curtains and a couch draped with grey silks where she would recline and look at herself in a mirror held by a cherub as featured in Velazquez's *Toilet of Venus*. And certainly not shared with eight other people.

It was nine o'clock by the time they sat down around the dining table for the long-awaited inaugural dinner. The others had arrived earlier, followed by their removal vans.

'Just like a royal progress,' as Dougie had pointed out in delight. 'Consider me a Tudor monarch, with all my retinue, bleeding my noblemen dry as I call for weeks of ruinous hospitality!'

Continuing his theme at the table, he asked if they would be served swan from the lake, and where was the pig roasting on a spit?

'That's for another time,' said Nicola, coming through with a large platter of oysters, prised open with some difficulty by Dominic, and another of langoustines surrounded by grey shrimps.

Simon rose to his feet and beamed round at the assembled company. 'I'd like to propose a toast,' he said. 'It was a brave and possibly foolhardy decision to do this but I know we are all delighted that we took the plunge and here we are now in this magnificent château.'

'Hear, hear!' said Leo. 'And thank you for allowing me the tower room. I couldn't be more thrilled. I hope you've all noticed I've changed into my celebratory arrival outfit: Renaissance pink slacks as a tribute to the old stones of our dream home.'

He stood up and did a twirl, greeted by delighted applause.

'Thank you, Leo, for setting the sartorial bar so high,' Simon continued. 'From tomorrow, we will all be pitching in and doing our bit, but tonight's feast is all down to Nicola and I'd like to thank her for that. More importantly, I'd like to thank her for coming up with the wild idea in the first place. It's down to her that we find ourselves here and I just know it's going to be a riot. To Nicola!'

'Hang on,' said Dominic, irritated by Simon's over-affectionate tribute to *his* wife. 'I think you'll find that it was my idea to leave London. Bravely jacking in my job in search of a better life. Nicola only fine-tuned the idea.'

Beth was also annoyed by Simon's simpering puppy-dog look of love. His recent schoolboy crush on Nicola was embarrassing and inappropriate. It was over thirty-five years since they were – briefly – a couple, and she had thought they both looked back on it with nothing more than a slightly nostalgic cringe – like remembering a bad mullet hairdo or the awful Eighties clothes they wore at the time. But there was an edge to Simon's toast she hadn't detected before.

'If we're competing to claim credit, can I put my oar in?' she said. 'Cast your minds back to the great minivan tour of the home counties and ask yourself, who was it who suddenly delivered the genius idea of moving to France?'

'Yes, yes, it was you, clever clogs,' said Simon. 'It's always you because you're smarter than everybody else, I'm the first to admit it and I love you for it. I also admit that I was the stick-in-the-mud who thought France was an appalling idea. My bad, as usual. I offer my sincere and heartfelt apologies for being such a short-sighted old boor. Anyway, let's not argue and lose the beauty of the moment. Raise your glasses and let's toast all the geniuses who brought us here. To the *nouveaux châtelains* – please note and emulate my outstanding pronunciation!'

There followed much noisy clinking of glasses and Simon sank back into his seat, his eyes still on Nicola, who was flushed with the wine. Her complexion always took that rosy hue after a few glasses; it only enhanced her appeal and led his drink-fuddled thoughts straight back to the days when she used to be his girl.

He once envisaged them living under the same roof, assumed they would be together forever, although it was never discussed – it's not something you talk about when you're twenty. Then they went their separate ways. She had tried to be kind when she dumped him. It was in a pub in Camden, she was wearing a bright pink mohair jumper and big hair, the way they all had it in the Eighties, and he was spider-thin, dressed all in black with his signature Doc Martens, as you'd expect from the front man of a Stranglers-inspired student band. She told him what a great person he was, that it wasn't him, it was her, all the bloody clichés. But they'd both found new partners and miraculously maintained their friendship through the years. How bizarre, and completely amazing, that they were now cohabiting and would never have to say goodbye again. He didn't know why he had suddenly become so fixated on her, but last night he couldn't get to sleep for thinking about her and how it could have been.

She was leaning across the table now to speak to him.

'That's lovely of you to single me out, Simon,' she said, 'but as Dom and Beth say, I can't take all the credit. Maybe I had the germ of the idea but we all evolved it together – it's a proper group effort.'

'If it's a group effort then you're the team leader,' said Simon. 'I'd follow you anywhere, you know that. Where you lead, I follow.'

He leaned across to take her hand.

Beth, who was sitting next to Nicola, gave him a sharp look then grinned at her friend.

'Let's see if we're all still on speaking terms this time next year,' she said. 'We'd all like to think it was our idea, but success has many fathers, and failure is an orphan. If it all goes tits-up, the rest of us can agree it was indeed Nicola's fault.'

'Miserable cow,' said Nicola, pinching Beth's arm affection- ately. 'But I wouldn't have dreamed of doing it without you. You are my best friend and I can't think of a better way of living out the rest of my life than sharing it with you and all you other gorgeous people.'

'Christ, this is all a bit *Friends*,' said Dominic. 'Let's get the DVD and keep it playing on a loop so we can all act out the parts. I'll be Joey; Nicola is Rachel, obviously.'

'Obviously,' Simon agreed. 'She even looks like her.'

Beth raised an eyebrow at Dominic, who smiled back at her. They were both put out by Simon's wine-fuelled infatuation.

'I'll be Monica,' said Leo. 'She has such great hair. And I'll never forget that shade of purple summer dress.'

'What are you talking about?' Dougie asked.

'It's telly,' said Fizz. 'I don't know how you've managed to avoid it. It feels like it's been on repeat for the last twenty-five years.'

'I do wonder if we've missed out, not having a television,' said Mary. 'There are so many cultural references that are dead to us. Rather like being unfamiliar with the bible; imagine what a negative impact that would have on our appreciation of art and literature.'

'Nonsense, Mary,' said Dougie. 'You've just confessed to me about watching that jungle thingy. I bet there's all other kinds of rubbish you're looking at on your computer while pretending to work!'

'We can have a dedicated TV lounge in one of the salons,' said Dominic. 'Slump in our armchairs and turn into vegetables. Seriously, though, it's a great way to improve our French – total immersion in mindless quiz shows in another language.'

After dinner, they went through to the *grand salon,* which was now cluttered up with mismatched furniture from all their different homes. It made Leo flinch just to look at it all. Will sat down at his piano and ran his fingers over the familiar keys. It had been quite a performance, bringing it over at considerable cost, but worth it to have it here, guaranteeing evenings of entertainment.

'Any requests?' he asked.

'"La vie en rose",' said Mary. 'One of my favourites and so appropriate.'

They all joined in, singing along with varying levels of tunefulness, and worked their way through a repertoire of old French favourites, ending with Fizz rising up to give a solo rendition of 'Je ne regrette rien', with full emotional wobble, before sashaying up to Will to give him a passionate hug.

'Temple-woman's too young to have much to regret, I'd say,' Beth whispered to Nicola as they watched Will turn round on his stool to pull Fizz onto his lap. 'You can only really sing that song if you're a gnarly old woman who's been round the block a few times.'

'Sweet, though, isn't it?' said Nicola. 'Young love, at least on one side. And one old bloke redeemed by the love of a young thing. To be fair, she's an improvement on the first model.'

'Anyone would be an improvement on Marjorie. It's hard to think of anybody in this world who would not be an improvement on Marjorie.'

They giggled at the thought of Will's first wife. She was the games monitor type, always bossing people around and drawing up lists. Once she'd decided to marry Will, she'd made a token effort to get on with his friends, but you could tell she didn't like them. In fact, she'd made the mistake of telling Will she found them rather silly, which had worked its way back via Dom, dashing any chance of them warming to her.

'I don't regret anything really, though, do you?' said Nicola. 'Or maybe we have a self-editing defence mechanism that stops us dwelling on what might have been.'

'The only thing I regret right now is that we didn't do this sooner,' said Beth. 'I'm loving it already.'

Will stood up and led Fizz by the hand to sit on the modern-upholstered love seat – the only large piece he had brought along, apart from the piano – that was incongruously parked between two old school armchairs belonging to Dougie and Mary.

'Time for some ghost stories,' said Dominic, opening the drinks cabinet that he had taken great pride in arranging that afternoon. 'Luckily we found the brandy glasses earlier, so let's

try this calvados while we summon up the spirits of the château –
there must be plenty of people who died within these walls over
the centuries.'

'That's horrible,' said Fizz.

'I disagree,' said Dougie. 'There is comfort and continuity in
the knowledge that so many lives have come and gone; death is
just part of the circle. I've conducted some preliminary research
into the history of our new home and there is one story that you
will enjoy concerning Eloise St Claire, who was once mistress of
the house.'

Mary watched him anxiously. She did hope he didn't lose
them with an overly detailed account.

Dougie ploughed on with his story.

'Her husband returned early from the war to find her in the
arms of another man. It appears he killed the lover, then locked
her up in the tower for nineteen years until her dying day. Her
ghostly form can still be seen at night, around the tower after
midnight.'

Mercifully brief, Mary noted with relief.

'My tower!' screamed Leo. 'I wish you hadn't told me that, I
won't sleep a wink now.'

'Don't worry, Leo, it's all a load of baloney,' said Simon. 'Every
château has to have an invented ghost to bring in the punters.
We should open our home to tourists one day, once we're fully
renovated – we'll save it for then. Have a glass of this to calm
your nerves.'

He passed a glass of calvados to Leo and took one for himself.

'I could get used to this,' he said, holding up the glass. 'First nose, you sniff it thus, without moving, then second nose, you swirl around the glass to let the oxygen release further nuances of aroma. I'm getting apple and pear, walnut, even a little butterscotch . . .'

He knocked back the contents, then put the glass to his nose again. 'And then you get a whole new range of complex aromas from the empty glass – it's quite extraordinary.'

'Tell us another ghost story, Dougie,' said Fizz, snuggling up to Will. 'Much more fun than watching Simon sniffing empty glasses.'

'What about Agnes of Eltz?' said Mary. 'She is very much a woman for our time, even though she lived in the twelfth century. She grew up pretending to be a warrior with her brothers, and didn't care for the boring knight her parents had arranged for her to marry. One day he forced himself upon her and she responded by slapping his face. He swore he would seek vengeance for the humiliation and waited until the men of the house were out hunting, then stormed the castle, killing the guardsmen. Agnes put on her brother's armour to fight back and the knight killed her, not realising it was his betrothed. Her ghost still defends her castle, and he appears as a phantom horseman outside the gates, seeking forgiveness.'

'Good story,' said Fizz. 'I like the feisty warrior woman – very *Game of Thrones*.'

It would make a good item for a vlog, if she could find a suit of armour to dress up for the part, or maybe just a toy helmet to give the flavour.

She jumped up.

'We could play a great game of hide and seek here; it's such a creepy place.'

'We're not six years old!' Simon protested.

'You can be the seeker,' Fizz said, turning him around to face the wall. 'Close your eyes, count to a hundred, then come and find us. No peeking!'

Simon did as he was told while the others scattered, giggling, through the château.

The room was eerily still as he counted under his breath; he half expected a knight to leap out from behind a curtain, wielding a sword.

'Coming to find you, ready or not!' he shouted, then checked behind all the curtains of the *grand salon* – luckily, no phantom intruders lurked there. He moved into the small salon, the library, the study, still with no result. The silence was chilling.

'This is properly creepy,' he shouted up the staircase, mostly to reassure himself. 'I feel like I'm Jack Nicholson in *The Shining*!'

He was halfway up to the first-floor landing when he stopped dead in his tracks. Someone was turning the lock in the front door. It was impossible, everyone was inside, and besides, there was only one set of keys and they had been discussing over dinner how they needed to get copies cut. Maybe it was a ghost.

'Hello!' he called out, watching in disbelief as the door creaked open.

A small woman with a neat white bun appeared.

'*Bonjour, monsieur!* I hope I'm not disturbing you but I saw the lights were on, and wanted to offer you this.'

Madame de Courcy waved a bottle of calvados in his direction.

'But are you all alone?'

She looked into the deserted salon, noticing the empty glasses and coffee cups.

Simon came down the stairs to greet her.

'No, they're all around somewhere, I think – I know – just not sure where. We were playing a game . . .'

He did feel a fool. Madame de Courcy laughed in delight.

'Oh, you English! Playing *cache-cache* at your age, how completely charming. I am in awe of your *joie de vivre*. Welcome to my château, monsieur—'

'Simon, please.'

'Monsieur Simon, of course, I remember you from the signature, how could I forget? Such a pleasure to see you again.' She gave him a smouldering smile.

It was true what they said about French women, Simon thought. They never lose their gift for *la séduction*.

# CHAPTER EIGHT

The following morning, Dominic already had the coffee on when Simon ambled into the kitchen, looking the worse for wear.

'Morning!' said Dominic, handing him a cup. 'Did you sleep all right?'

He looked pretty rough, to be honest. Dominic only had to take one look at Simon, with his jowly face and heavy physique, to feel incredibly good about himself. He'd go out for a bike ride before breakfast; it was important to keep himself trim. And to remind Nicola what a catch he was. Simon's overt flirting with her didn't bother him in the slightest – he was hardly a threat! In fact, he found it flattering that his wife should still have that effect on her ex-boyfriend.

'Bit fitful, to be honest,' said Simon. 'I got off in the end but couldn't remember where I was when I woke up.'

He produced the bottle of calvados, which he had picked up on his way through from the salon.

'Too much of this last night didn't help! I'm going native, by the way, having a splash of it in my coffee. I understand it's what constitutes a Norman breakfast. Want some?'

*That's pretty hard-core*, thought Dominic. *To think Nicola might have ended up with this old reprobate, instead of me.* He liked a drink, and so did she, but they flattered themselves they kept within reasonable limits.

He shook his head.

'Bit early for me. And I think you'll find Normandy farmers only have their morning tipple after they've done a stint in the fields.'

'Hair of the dog, just this once. And it will help kick-start my creativity, that's my excuse.'

'Ah yes, Nicola mentioned you were writing a novel. Dare I ask how it's going?'

'It's taking its own sweet course – you can't rush these things.'

'Of course you can't. And moving house is a big distraction.'

'A welcome distraction, as they all are!'

Simon slumped down into a chair and poured a generous measure of calvados into his coffee cup.

'To be honest, Dom, it's probably a load of crap, this book of mine. Most days I just stare at what I've written and can't believe my own inanity. But you've got to have a go, haven't you?' He perked up. 'I've decided to introduce a French flavour, inspired by our new surroundings. There might even be a cameo role for Madame de Courcy!'

'Unbelievable, wasn't it? Letting herself into our house like that! At that time of night!'

'Her house, apparently. She definitely said, "Welcome to my château".'

'I'm afraid there's going to be a lot of that if we're not careful. We need to change the locks, it's obvious. Nicola says that would be very hurtful, but we can't have her breezing in whenever she feels like it.'

'That's Nicola for you,' said Simon. 'She's always been too kind for her own good.'

*Here we go again*, thought Dominic, *another compliment in praise of St Nicola, the dream girlfriend who got away*. He honestly didn't know how Beth put up with it.

'Is she up?' he asked. 'Beth's still out cold – I've never known anyone sleep like her; the house could fall down around her and she'd still be there, snoring away.'

'Nicola's outside, getting started on the vegetable garden. Plenty to do there.'

'Plenty to do everywhere.'

Simon took a sip of his fortified coffee and walked towards the window through which he could see Nicola pushing a loaded wheelbarrow towards the bonfire heap.

'Can't help feeling we should have a team of gardeners in place to do all that, don't you? A household staff of twenty or so, in the interest of authenticity. You can't imagine previous lords of the manor doing their own dirty work; they'd be off fighting wars or sucking up to the king or sitting on Rococo chairs with spindly legs, counting their money.'

'Or writing their novels?'

'Or writing their novels. Speaking of which, I must away. Thanks for the coffee, mate, see you at lunch!'

He clapped Dominic on the shoulder and sauntered off, leaving Dom to wonder whether it would become necessary to draw up a schedule of tasks to make sure that everyone was doing their share. A simple spreadsheet was all it would take; he'd get on it right away. Nothing officious, just a means of keeping the wheels turning, and dividing the work up evenly. More specifically, he wanted to ensure that Simon pulled his considerable weight, the old boozehound.

'Good morning, Dominic!'

Mary appeared in the kitchen doorway, wearing a pinny and rubber gloves and holding a gaudy extendable duster that looked like a stick of candyfloss.

'Hello, Mary. You look dressed for action.'

'I'm raring to go. I'm not much good at cooking – certainly not up to Nicola's standard – but I bring other talents. I'm going to start with the fireplaces.'

'That's great. I can see you are going to become the most popular housemate.'

He watched her bustling over to the sink. She was going to be worth ten of Simon when it came to mucking in; he wouldn't need to chase her up on the spreadsheet. Mind you, she'd have to double up for Dougie on the practical front, but Dom could see he'd be useful for keeping a tight rein on expenditure. And maybe conducting tours of the château if and when they eventually opened to the public, leading groups of tourists through the grand rooms and bludgeoning them with historical information.

Mary filled her bucket from the creaky old tap and tried not to notice the cracks in the butler sink. She didn't want to think about the germs that might be lurking there. The wooden work surfaces didn't look too bad – they would scrub up nicely – but the shelves beneath were another story. She pulled back the greasy little curtains that were strung on a plastic wire and crouched down to inspect what they concealed: crumbs, dead flies and what looked like mouse-droppings

'I've changed my mind,' she said. 'I'd better start in here. We can't think of unpacking the kitchenware until this is cleaned up – we could all be wiped out. I'm amazed that Madame de Courcy could live like this; she's so elegant. It doesn't make sense that she would keep a kitchen in this condition.'

'I get the impression she never came in here,' said Dominic, coming up behind her to have a closer look. 'She had an ancient maid whose eyesight was failing, which might explain it. What is *that*?'

Mary had pulled out the corpse of what appeared to be a large mouse – not the sort he knew from London, one with a longer, decorative coat that could have been straight from the pages of a children's book.

'I thought maybe it was a rat,' she said, 'except for that cute tail, which makes it look less threatening. I'm pretty sure it's a dormouse.'

She threw the animal into the bin and laughed at Dominic's appalled expression.

'Don't look so horrified, Dom, it's perfectly usual to find animals in the countryside. The trick is to make sure they stay outside.'

'I can't believe you're so calm about it – you're supposed to be the clean freak!'

'And I'm surprised you're so upset by it,' said Mary. 'We just need to put some traps down. We can use those humane ones that cage them in, then you won't have the trauma of running into dead rodents all round the house. Leave it to me, I'll happily act as chief vermin officer.'

'I'm grateful. It's not quite the job title I was after when I quit my office,' said Dom. 'I guess we were all looking for some kind of new role, some change of life when we said yes to moving here . . . but ratcatcher is not high up my list.'

Upstairs, Beth was sitting up in bed and waiting for the aspirin to take effect. The euphoria of the previous night had given way to a dull hangover and faint misgivings about what they had undertaken. The room was piled up with boxes of their clothes but it was unclear how many of them would be of any use out here in the sticks. Her Vivienne Westwood would be redundant; she was hardly going to dress up to pop out to buy a baguette. Not like in the office, where they used to comment on what everyone was wearing; it was all part of the fun and her young colleagues would often pass compliments on whatever clever top she had managed to find to disguise the increasing softness of her stomach.

Her phoned beeped with a message from Eva.

*Have you arrived, Mum? How is it? I had a nightmare day yesterday, really not sure I can take much more of this.*

How long would it be, Beth wondered, before she would be free from worrying about her child? She'd heard it said that you never are, it goes on for the rest of your life, and she suspected this was the case. A child is for life, not just for childhood, in the same way that a dog is not just for Christmas, though she crushed that blasphemous thought at once. Eva was the love of her life, along with Simon. Beth just wished she wasn't quite so whiny.

She summoned the energy to reply in her accustomed way, the jolly-her-along supportive mother, caring but robust.

*What's up? Remember I've got your back. Whatever it is, you can do it, you'll see x*

Though what she really wanted to say was: *Leave me alone until the pills have kicked in, I've got a bitch of a hangover and don't want to hear your tales of woe right now.* She took a photo through the window and sent it with positive noises about blue skies, apple blossom and *Downton Abbey* grandeur.

*God you're so lucky, I wish I had your life.*

Why would a young woman in her prime want the life of her old mum? Beth would never have had that thought at her age, but her daughter's generation seemed to be growing up in the shadow of everything the baby boomers had done, or maybe it was only Eva who believed that everybody had it better than her.

Beth switched off her phone. Fresh air was what she required. She heaved herself out of bed and pulled on her baggy jeans. It was time to join Nicola on the vegetable patch.

Her mood lifted as she made her way down the staircase. She knew she could never grow tired of this entrance hall; she felt her soul expand with the grandeur of it. She opened the front door to the sound of Mary's hoover whirring and stepped out into the spring sunshine. It had rained in the night and the grass was shining, the white apple blossom even more luminous than she remembered. She walked round to the back of the château, down towards the lake and on to the stone walls that enclosed a hidden garden. Nicola stood up, resting on her fork, to greet her friend.

'What have we got here?' asked Beth. 'Artichokes, I hope, and fennel. *Artichauts et fenouil* – you see, I've still got the vocab.'

'Nothing but weeds as far as I can tell. I thought I'd get some lettuces in as soon as possible.'

'You've wanted a walled garden forever, haven't you, and now your dream has come true. I love those trees pinned against the wall – they look so organised.'

'Espaliered, for easy picking. When we're in our bath chairs we will be able to reach up our wizened arms and pluck the low-hanging fruit. I want flowers, too. Look at these beautiful alchemillas.'

She led Beth towards a clump of lady's mantle, the fan-shaped leaves enclosing drops of water like pearls.

'That's a rare sight,' said Beth. 'An antidote to my morning-after-the-night-before *gueule de bois* – I love that expression, don't you? Wooden mouth.'

'We all overdid it last night,' said Nicola.

'And my headache was compounded by an anxious message from Eva this morning.'

'I know the feeling. You think you can scurry off to a foreign country and leave your troubles behind, then you realise they've come with you.'

'Yours too?'

'Gus is a bit sulky. You'd think they'd be delighted to have the place to themselves, but oh no. They're both missing the services I provided. Suddenly the fridge isn't full and the washing machine no longer magically turns itself on, it would seem.'

'Good to have a bit of distance, though,' said Beth. 'Come on, let's lose ourselves in honest toil.'

She picked up a spade and worked alongside Nicola, turning over the earth and plucking out the weeds.

'Pretty hard grind, isn't it?' said Beth, taking a pause after a shamefully short time.

She wedged her spade into the wet earth and leaned upon it, gazing back to count the windows of the château. Nigh on a hundred of them, surely, if you included the skylights. At that moment, she noticed a tractor entering the field. It was driving towards them and stopped just outside the gate of the walled garden. A figure in blue overalls climbed down from the seat and began to walk purposefully in their direction.

'Look, Nicola, we've got company!'

Nicola stopped what she was doing to check out the athletic-looking man who was hurrying towards them, lighting a cigarette on the way.

'He looks like he's stepped straight out of a moody French film,' said Beth as the figure drew nearer. 'I love his boiler-suit; there's something so iconic about that shade of indigo.'

'*Bonjour, mesdames*,' said the interloper, shaking their hands with immaculate formality. 'I have come to introduce myself. Jean-Louis, I am the farmer whose beasts you will have seen in your fields. I want to wish you welcome.'

It took Beth a moment to translate. Perhaps she was out of practice, perhaps it was his strong Norman accent, or perhaps it was because she was concentrating on looking rather than listening. He was in his forties, she guessed, tall and fair – it must be those Viking genes. He was looking at Nicola with frank admiration and Beth was amused to see she wasn't immune to his charms, the little coquette, flicking her hair back and smiling up at him.

'I hope you understand me?' he said. 'My English is negligible, so you will excuse me if I speak in French.'

He flicked his lighter to reignite the roll-up cigarette that appeared to have gone out.

'My friend here speaks it better than me,' Nicola said in her faltering French, 'but I'm trying to improve.'

'Bravo,' he said, his cigarette now glowing again. 'I have a *mini-pelle* that will make your work much easier; it will turn the soil with greater efficiency. Tomorrow I will bring it to you.'

'Thank you,' said Nicola, making the correct assumption that he was talking about a piece of machinery. 'That would be a great help. I'm Nicola, by the way, and this is Beth.'

This seemed to amuse him.

'Bett, like my *bêtes!*' he said, pointing to his cows in the field.

'No, my name is Beth. *Th*. With the tongue between the teeth, like this.' Beth gave an exaggerated demonstration.

He tried to follow her example, but the sound was unfamiliar to his French tongue. *Extraordinary*, thought Beth, *that the accident of being born in a different country should prevent you from being able to pronounce basic elements of a different language.* She thought of all the clunky pronunciations and fumbled mistranslations she had struggled with back when she was learning.

'And Nicolas for us is a man's name,' he said. 'I shall have to call you Nicolette.'

'Nicolette,' said Nicola. 'I like the sound of that.'

Beth could tell she also liked the sound of him generally. She knew her friend never had eyes for anyone but Dom, but she thought it would do no harm for Nicola to realise she could still turn heads. They weren't all over the hill yet.

'I am glad to continue my association with the château,' he went on. 'My family has been farming this land for three centuries. When Madame de Courcy told me she was selling, I feared that might be the end of our arrangement, but the *notaire* assured me that you wished to continue the tenancy, and for that I am profoundly obliged.'

He gave a courtly nod.

'We don't know one end of a tractor from the other,' said Nicola, 'and we have plenty to occupy us here with the buildings, so we're delighted you're taking care of the land.'

The friends had been pleased there was someone to tend the rolling fields around the château, and Dougie in particular had been relieved to see the rent – albeit barely more than peppercorn – would give some welcome contribution to their coffers.

Jean-Louis was watching Nicola intently as she spoke, and she seemed to be searching for the right words.

'It's such a – how do you say it in French? – attractive backdrop for us,' she added. 'The château seems to be at home in these hills. *Le château paraît bien chez soi ici!*'

He nodded his approval and Nicola was glad that he liked what she said; it was encouraging to think her language practice was yielding results.

'There is a bond between farmer and land. I feel I must respect the traditional landscape – I am not one of those destructive agriculturalists who go tearing out hedges and planting only one crop as far as the eye can see. To me that is an abomination.'

He looked quite fierce as he recounted the sins of other farmers. Nicola could see he was passionate about his profession and took great pride in his association with the château. They were lucky to have him, she thought.

He relit his cigarette.

'I must continue my work now, but I would like to invite you soon to take the aperitif in my house. With your husbands, of course.'

He shook hands with them both and took his leave.

'What on earth is a *mini-pelle*?' asked Nicola, once he was out of earshot. 'I'm glad you were here – I found his accent quite difficult.'

'He's obviously taken a shine to you. Did you notice how he managed to keep his roll-up attached to his lip while he was talking? Quite a feat. Anyway, let's crack on, it must be nearly lunchtime.'

Nicola watched Jean-Louis's retreating form, with his long legs and easy stride. It was comforting to have congenial neighbours. She looked forward to getting to know him.

Leo was setting the table for lunch, trying to take his mind off the leaking roof that had ruined his sleep. He'd already spoken to Dominic about it – it was impossible for him to carry on sleeping in that room; they needed to overhaul the roof right away. The rain dripping onto his bedroom floor woke him up in the middle of the night and forced him to go in search of a bucket, fumbling his way down two flights of stairs, searching for unfamiliar light switches until he reached the back kitchen. He was then driven mad by the rhythmic drumming of raindrops on the base of the plastic receptacle, and had to stuff a towel inside to soften the effect.

He thought of his immaculate London townhouse, now under the care of its new tenant. What if David showed up, realising he had made a colossal mistake? Leo pictured him letting himself in and calling out, 'Honey, I'm home!' the way he always did, only to find an intruder installed in their former love nest.

He pushed aside this unhelpful scenario. There had been no contact for five months and if David wanted to get in touch, he only had to pick up his phone. The age for tragic misunderstandings was over, now we had so many means of instant communication. The silence was definitive, a big fat 'I don't love you anymore'.

The table was completed now with nine place settings. Leo admired his handiwork and thought about what to serve. Such mass catering was foreign to him; he and David used to give occasional dinner parties but in the last months it had been a tragic dinner for one most nights. The warmth and inclusiveness of this new living arrangement was appealing, but he needed to ensure he didn't run to fat with all the tempting food on offer. God forbid he turn into Simon, though Dominic and Will were in good shape and Dougie was positively skinny, a bag of bones, really, rattling around inside his tweeds.

'Hi, Leo, can I give you a hand?'

Fizz came in, wearing a bohemian maxi dress in a swirling turquoise print.

'Your frock!' said Leo. 'I adore it, and teal is your perfect colour.'

'Thank you,' said Fizz. 'I thought a long dress was in keeping with our hippie commune and luckily they're back in fashion.'

'The best-dressed woman I ever knew told me her secret was never to throw anything anyway,' said Leo. 'Everything comes back in again, even those monstrous Eighties padded shoulders. They're massive in Shoreditch.'

'I needed to wear something colourful to cheer me up after the shock of seeing that horrible bathroom,' said Fizz. 'But I love your outfit too, Leo – you always look amazing.'

'That's kind of you but I look completely shattered this morning, wrecked by a sleepless night on account of it raining *inside* my room. Glad you like this little suitlet.'

'What's a suitlet?'

'A teeny, tiny suit – look!'

He held up his arms to show it off. 'I'm dreading the return of baggy clothes; never happier than in a very tight jacket.'

'And the cropped trousers are great with your bare ankles. Where did you get it?'

'Topman. I think I'm their only customer over fifty.'

'I can't imagine Will shopping there. What's for lunch?'

'Something light, that's as far as I've got.'

In the kitchen, they assembled a watercress and orange salad, topped with slices of radish.

'We can make toast from last night's bread; waste not, want not,' said Leo.

Fizz took out her phone to Instagram the result.

'Clean French salad,' she said.

'We've become terribly moralistic about food,' said Leo. 'Slow food, clean food, goody-goody food. Makes me long for a bit of fast and dirty.'

'Let's call them in, shall we?' said Fizz.

'I'm feeling too weak to shout out, but luckily I have just the thing.'

He picked up a Victorian brass bell.

'I unpacked it this morning. I bought it years ago but it was too noisy and unnecessary in a terraced house. You'd better ring it inside and out; I'm not sure where everybody is.'

Fizz's enthusiastic ringing brought everyone into the dining room.

'Saved by the bell,' said Simon, taking the seat at the head. 'I was just wondering if I had time for another two hundred words but luckily not.'

'Some of us have spent a more practical morning,' said Mary, slipping off her pinny. 'I'm sure I've already filled an entire hoover bag.'

'Cleanliness is close to godliness,' said Dougie. 'I've been unpacking my books in the library – we should have an eclectic collection between us. Thank goodness Madame de Courcy left those steps – I would never have reached the top shelves without them. I believe it was Jorge Luis Borges who said he always imagined that paradise will be a kind of library. My friends, we are in paradise!'

'The garden of Eden, in our case,' said Beth, kicking off her wellington boots. '*And* we met Adam, or Jean-Louis as he calls himself, aka our friendly farmer. I have to warn you, Dom, he couldn't take his eyes off Nicola. Or Nicorette, as he calls her, whereas I am the Beast. *Bête*, which also means stupid, I happen to know.'

'Nicolette, actually,' said Nicola. 'And that's nonsense, Beth, he was equally chivalrous to both of us.'

'I'd better lock you up in Leo's tower,' said Dominic. 'I can't have him tempting you away from me with his irresistible French charm.'

'No use,' said Beth, 'she'd just let down her hair and let her Gallic lover climb up to claim his prize.'

'We need to talk about my tower,' said Leo. 'It's a disaster, up there on the front line with only some broken old slates between me and the elements. It's all right for you lot on the floor below, you're protected from flooding by a corridor of servants' rooms above you!'

'I know, Leo,' said Dominic, 'I think we need to have an emergency meeting about it.'

Simon sighed, bored at the mention of dreary repair works.

'Here we are again,' he said in a Geordie accent. 'Day two in the *Big Brother* house and the housemates are sitting down to a frugal salad lunch.'

'What are you talking about?' asked Mary.

'It's telly,' said Simon. 'If you wasted as many hours on it as the rest of us, you'd get the allusion.'

'I might not have seen it but I know all about *Big Brother*,' said Dougie. 'It started out as a Dutch sociological experiment, but turned into a voyeuristic spectacle of couples writhing under infra-red lights.'

'Is this the starter?' asked Simon, changing the subject and staring at the meagre plate in front of him.

'No, it's your *main*,' said Leo. 'We can't have two full meals a day, it's not sustainable.'

'Do I look like someone who can manage on a few leaves? I have a large frame to support.'

'Fill up with toast,' said Beth, passing him the basket. 'Or better still, get your lazy arse in the kitchen and do the cooking yourself!'

'Plenty more toast in the kitchen,' said Fizz, 'but I'm just having one piece.'

'*Un toast*,' said Beth. 'I like how they say that.' She put on a French accent. 'I am having a toast, I am writing on a paper. Economical and precise.'

'Glad to have you as our self-appointed French language expert,' said Leo. 'Remember you're not the only one with a French degree.'

'Don't be waspish, I'm just sharing our knowledge. Anyway, we'll all be bilingual soon, it's only a matter of time.'

'Sorry I'm late, everyone,' said Will, walking briskly towards them. 'I've just been mopping up upstairs. We noticed some water running down our bedroom wall last night, so I went up to the top floor to inspect the damage in the guest bedrooms. I think the roof is worse than we thought!'

'It's top of my list,' said Dominic. 'Actually, I was going to raise this with you all later but we might as well discuss it now, while we're all assembled around the table.'

The seriousness in his voice made them all look up.

'The thing is . . .' He paused, unwilling to deliver his bad news, then started again. 'The thing is, I know we've drawn up some exciting plans for renovating this château, and believe me, no one is keener than me to get on with it, so we can live as we intended, in our luxury self-contained apartments, coming together in the shared spaces of our great salons. It will be fantastic, I promise you.'

'I sense a "but" coming on,' Simon interrupted.

'You're right, there's a "but". We all agreed, didn't we, that there was no point in having a survey before we signed the papers. Waste of money, waste of time, we already knew there was work to be done.'

'That's true,' said Nicola. 'It's not as if any of us was prepared to be the cautious, sensible one.'

Dougie raised his hand. 'If I can just interject here,' he said, 'you may recall at the time I declared it an act of unmitigated folly to buy a historical monument without undertaking a full structural survey.'

'Yes, you did,' said Beth. 'And you then said, "It's just as well we are a group of middle-aged people who are proud and ready to engage in an act of folly.'"

Dougie looked annoyed and Simon grinned.

'You didn't exactly try to talk us out of it, Dougie!' said Beth.

'So,' Dominic resumed, 'the question of whether we should have had a survey is a moot point. We are where we are.'

'I hate that expression,' said Simon. 'It's about as meaningless as "Brexit means Brexit."'

'Shut up, Simon,' said Beth.

'Judging from our experience last night, when a rainstorm persecuted Leo and practically flooded the top floor, my view is that we need to replace the roof before we think about any other alterations. There's no point in doing anything else until we've fixed that problem. Any internal decoration would be a complete waste of time.'

There was a disgruntled silence around the table.

'What about the bathrooms?' said Fizz. 'I honestly can't see myself sharing that horrid old tub for more than a couple of weeks.'

'All in the fullness of time,' said Will soothingly. 'We'll get there, you'll see.'

'I notice you say *replace* the roof, not *repair* the roof,' said Dougie. 'That sounds frightfully expensive.'

'Which is why it's great there's nine of us,' said Dominic briskly. 'Spread the load, remember the economy of scale. We bought this place for a song, knowing we'd have to allocate a substantial budget for repairs and renovation.'

'Define "substantial budget",' said Dougie.

'Yes, how much are we talking?' Simon asked. 'Disappointing use of funds. I was hoping to spend our chunk of the refurb money on more exciting projects, like converting one of the barns into a writing hut – that would suit me down to the ground.'

'I don't care what it costs, the roof has to be done,' said Leo, 'otherwise I'll never sleep when it's raining. I'll become a forlorn ghost, drifting through the deserted wings of the château, hurling myself off the ramparts . . .'

'Let's not talk about money just now,' said Nicola. 'We are supposed to be in the honeymoon phase and this is beginning to sound like a divorce settlement.'

'I quite agree,' said Beth. 'We need at least a couple of weeks of reckless enjoyment before we get practical. The early retire-ment party, whooping it up and reminding ourselves why we are here. Leo, can you cope for just another fortnight? We've got some partying to do before we turn into building bores, spending our evenings debating tiles and scaffolding.'

'The Sybaritic delights of the nouveau pensioners,' said Dougie. 'I can go along with that.'

'Oh look,' said Mary, pushing her chair back to get a better view out of the window, 'isn't that Madame de Courcy? What's she carrying?'

They all left their seats and crowded round the window to take a look. The old lady was walking away from them towards the gates, holding her stick in one hand and a small, gilt chair with curved legs in the other.

'Cheeky old bird!' said Dominic. 'That's the chair from the entrance hall, one of the pieces she made us buy, as it was "inseparable from the château"!'

'I have the evidence,' said Fizz, who had snapped her on her phone.

'Shall I run after her and arrest her for theft?' said Simon.

'No, leave her be,' said Nicola. 'I think we just have to accept as far as she is concerned, she is still mistress of the château.'

'That's ridiculous,' said Simon. 'The next thing you know, she'll be helping herself to the chandelier and all the light fittings. We'll be plunged into darkness because Madame La Chatelaine thinks she can just come in here and strip us of our assets.'

'If she really wants to remain a part of the château, she might like to contribute to our roof renovation fund,' said Dougie. 'Give back a portion of her sale money to ensure the continuity of the château – that's very much in tune with her noble arguments.'

'Good plan, Dougie,' said Simon. 'Why don't you run after her now and suggest it?'

'But on the other hand, I think I agree with Nicola,' said Dougie. 'We don't want any unpleasantness and what is a small gilt chair between friends?'

# CHAPTER NINE

'I don't know why Napoleon described the British as a nation of shopkeepers,' said Leo, looking with pleasure at the contents of his wide wicker basket. 'It's the French, surely, who excel at that. Can you imagine finding a range of shops like these in a small English town?'

It was two weeks since their arrival and he was on a shopping mission with Beth and Fizz. He had been sleeping better since putting himself on weather watch. Before going to bed each night, he checked the hourly forecast to see if it was going to rain. If so, he would decamp to his back-up bedroom, which he had identified as the only one on the attic floor that didn't suffer from the leaky roof.

This morning they had just stocked up on cheese at the fromagerie on the high street, encouraged by the knowledgeable owner who took delight in explaining the provenance of all her products. Her descriptions were so detailed that it took them half an hour to make their selection, and another fifteen minutes of conversation ensued when she learned that they were the new château dwellers and wanted to hear all about it.

'God, I thought we'd never get out of there,' said Fizz. 'Did you notice those people behind us in the queue, ears flapping when she was asking about what our relationship was? I thought she was really nosy, asking so many personal questions.'

'She was merely showing an interest, that's what people do in the country, unlike in the cold city where nobody cares,' said Leo. 'I thought she was charming, and you can see why she might presume Beth and I were your parents.'

He held his basket up to show her the cheeses, each lovingly wrapped in its own paper.

'Look at that beautiful display. My favourite is the oval-shaped soft sheep's cheese with a Japanese leaf running through the middle.'

'It certainly beats a slab of cheddar in plastic,' said Beth. 'Which reminds me of the last time we shared a fridge. Leo, do you remember?'

'In that horrible flat when we were students! We had a shelf each and had to write our name on our individual cartons of milk. Those big northern boys became very upset if we put anything in their allotted territory.'

'And we used to play kill-the-slug. Pouring salt over them as they crawled up the kitchen wall, then watching them dissolve.'

'How cruel!' said Fizz. 'And how could you have slugs inside the flat?'

'I think our student housing was probably a little lower budget than yours, Fizz,' said Beth. But she smiled all the same, remembering those early days when she'd first met Nicola and Leo. How Simon, then at Nicola's side, had always made a night out into a party; how they'd managed to have the best of times with no money, no jobs but the luxury of time on their side. Hopefully those days were coming back. But with fewer slugs this time around.

'It was quite horrid,' said Leo. 'We didn't like our flatmates so we never cooked together. We each used to open our own can of soup and eat it sitting on our individual beds.'

'Not like now, when we're enjoying the proper benefits of cooperative living and the sensuous delights of a luxurious table,' said Beth.

'True! A tragic single person like me could never justify buying a cheeseboard like this. It would just sit there, rotting away.'

'I'm not sure Dougie will approve when we present him with the bill,' said Beth.

'He'll be happy with our bargain wine boxes, though. Bogof bag-in-box. Sorry, *un acheté, un offert* – sounds much better in French.'

As a self-proclaimed miser, Dougie had been appointed keeper of the purse strings. They all chipped into the housekeeping fund with only a certain amount of misgiving about who was eating and drinking more. Dougie couldn't help noticing how quickly the wine was going down and insisted they move on to *les bags-in-box*. There was no poetry in wine boxes, he agreed, but it was so much cheaper, and at least there wasn't the shameful tally of bottles to dispose of every evening.

'Oh, look at those darling little tomatoes,' said Fizz, stopping by the artfully displayed boxes outside the greengrocer's. 'We must get some.' She stopped to take close-up photos of them, no doubt soon to be found on Instagram.

They followed her in and watched the shopkeeper weighing out two sprays of the smallest cherry tomatoes, arranged like orchid flowers on their stems.

'Shall we put the kids through college or shall we buy some tomatoes?' Beth whispered to Leo as she was handed the bill.

'They are especially for me,' said Fizz. 'Remember I don't drink so I deserve some other treats to balance it out. Dougie will think it's perfectly fair.'

'I agree,' said Beth, giving Fizz a supportive squeeze. 'Fizz, it's probably no surprise that I was a little bit concerned about how you and I would get along – I mean, I'm about as far away from being a health guru as you can be – but I owe you an apology. You're a breath of fresh air and I think we're going to get along a treat.'

'Me too,' said Fizz, high-fiving her. 'You're a great example of a sassy older woman, Beth. You've got a lot about you and I'm going to feature you heavily in my vlogging, if that's OK with you. *This* is what a fifty-something woman looks like, guys!'

Beth paused. Was that a compliment or a dig? She decided she'd better give Fizz the benefit of the doubt. 'Finally I'm getting the recognition I deserve,' said Beth. 'How many followers do you have?'

Fizz looked defensive.

'I don't like to talk numbers. It's mostly friends and family at the moment. But it's literally only just launched; you wait and see.'

'I have faith in you,' said Beth. 'And with me in a starring role, how can it fail?'

Leo was studying the receipts as he filed them into the house-keeping purse.

'Two hundred and sixteen euros all in,' he said. 'Not bad for that car full of food and these exquisite little treats. I don't think Dougie can argue with that.'

'Very reasonable,' said Beth. 'None of us want to fall into the trap of arguing about money. It's the most common cause of marriage breakdown and that's what we're in, isn't it? A sort of group marriage.'

'Not really!' said Fizz. 'That sounds so unappealing.'

'Sounds unappealing to me too,' said Leo, 'but we're not talking about the messy side of marriage, only the companion-ship.'

'That's even worse! Companions sounds like when old people pay carers to look after them.'

'Why do you think we invited you along?' said Beth. 'You'll be helping us all to the toilet before long.'

'Haha!' said Fizz, not quite hiding the grimace that flashed across her face. She gave her phone to Leo.

'Can you film me standing outside this shop? Give me that baguette, Beth, I want a real French flavour to this one. I need to ratchet up the envy, let everyone know I'm living the dream. Imagine my followers stuck at their desks, wishing they were me. All I'm missing is a string of onions – oh look, they sell them here! I'll pop back in afterwards and pay for it.'

She selected a smooth plait of red onions, miraculously knotted together.

'I thought you told your followers you were gluten-intolerant,' said Beth, handing her the bread. 'Won't it strike a false note?'

'I'm going to edit that out. Actually, I think I am gluten intolerant, but French bread is so good that I've decided to overlook my intolerance.'

'Very tolerant of you,' said Beth.

'It's bad enough being a vegetarian over here; I have to cut myself some slack somewhere.'

'Let's get some pictures first. Get you warmed up. Give me a pout,' said Leo, holding up her phone.

Fizz struck a provocative pose, throwing the string of onions around her neck and holding the baguette across the Breton-striped shirt she was wearing over cropped jeans and a pair of clogs. She could pout for England, thought Beth. She was the very epitome of millennial poutiness.

'Now, walk past the salad displays and wonder aloud about which lettuce you should choose,' said Leo, enjoying his role as director.

Fizz did as she was told, turning to the camera to point out the difference between roquette and mâche, batavia and *feuille de chêne.*

'Gorgeous,' said Leo, handing back her phone. 'That's going to double your number of followers immediately.'

They walked together along the street, peering in the shop windows.

'Can you imagine anyone actually buying anything in here?' said Fizz outside the optimistically named Mode de Femmes. The window display featured a drab pleated skirt and a swirly patterned jumper. 'You hear about French chic, but honestly.'

'I think it's Parisians who dress well, not necessarily the locals,' said Beth. 'You can really spot the city dwellers when they come down for the weekends.'

They had soon become attuned to the tell-tale sign on the number plates of cars belonging to fashionable second-homers – the number 75 inscribed on a blue panel on the right-hand side, letting everyone know they were from the capital.

'Their fashion, their number plates and their bad-tempered faces,' said Leo. 'I can quite see why the locals hate them. Unlike us, I must say. It feels like everyone we've met so far appreciates our enthusiasm for embracing the French country life.'

As if to prove his point, the local drunk stopped by to greet them, waving his half-empty bottle of rosé then shaking them all by the hand.

'Dear old Willy,' said Leo. 'You must admit he's got some class – a bottle of côtes de provence instead of a beer can.'

'Has he turned up on your Grindr search yet?' asked Fizz.

They were fascinated by Leo's forays into French dating. A regular after-dinner entertainment involved passing round his phone to offer opinions on the surprisingly high number of potential hook-ups in their local area. Leo hadn't yet met any of them in the flesh; said he was just window-shopping.

'I think our resident drunk is more old school, and definitely not gay.'

'He's got good hair, actually,' said Fizz. 'Certainly better than most of the women around here. What is it with the aubergine short back and sides they all go in for?'

'We can't all have your flowing tresses, Felicity,' said Leo.

They drove home, listening to Beth's 'French and Happy' playlist in honour of their new life, featuring the best of Edith Piaf and Sacha Distel. By the time they drove through the gates, they were all singing along to 'Chanson D'Amour'.

'I really like these old songs,' said Fizz. 'I do sometimes think I was born in the wrong age.'

'You're hanging with the right crowd then,' said Beth. Then, '*What the hell!*'

She slammed on the brakes, just in time to avoid the car being struck by a procession of roof slates crashing down on the driveway before them. A very tall ladder was leaning against the front of the château, with a man standing on top of it who appeared to have provoked the dramatic cascade.

Leo stepped out of the car and picked his way through the smashed slates towards the foot of the ladder. The noise brought Dominic and Dougie running out of the house, and by the time the builder reached the ground, he was surrounded by a circle of accusing faces.

He held up his hands in self-defence.

'*Desolé!* But it is as I thought. The roof is dead – you see for yourself, the tiles, you only have to touch one and they all come down, like a set of dominos . . .'

'I'm staying out of this,' Beth whispered to Fizz. 'Let's take in the shopping.'

She lifted two bags out of the boot, but Fizz instead took her phone from her pocket and started filming the intense conversation that was taking place about the roof.

'Got it!' she said, slipping her phone away. 'It's good to show a bit of conflict. Poor Mademoiselle Bovary, almost killed by falling roof tiles, and now the old men are coming to her rescue.'

'Mademoiselle Bovary – is that you?'

'Yes, do you like it?'

'I do! And what is my role in this – the old housekeeper?'

'More of a wise woman – you'll see.'

She helped Beth carry the shopping in, arranging the vegetables artfully in a ceramic bowl on the battered kitchen counter. Beth saw she had a missed call and a message from Eva.

'It looks like we're about to have our first visitor,' she said. 'Eva says she fancies a break and asks can she come over next week. That's lovely news for me; hope the rest of you don't mind?'

'Great, I can't wait to meet her,' said Fizz. 'It's not as if we don't have the space!'

Beth couldn't wait to show Eva the place. She paused as another crash came from the roof. She just hoped the château was still standing by the time she arrived.

In the orchard, Nicola pegged out the final pillow case and stood back to admire the long line of fresh laundry blowing in the breeze. A gust of wind filled the fitted sheet and lifted it, just the way that you saw on sailing ships, which presumably was why yachties referred to them as sheets. Taking pleasure in simple tasks was a great benefit of her new life; she was constantly delighted by the exoticism of performing chores in the great outdoors. No comparison to loading the tumble dryer in London, with its monotonous, energy-guzzling drone.

At the far end of the orchard, Will was engaged in his favourite activity: sitting on the tractor, plugged into his music, and mowing the grass to within an inch of its life. Nicola wanted a more laissez-faire approach, creating a wildflower meadow, but he wasn't having it.

'I'm thinking of you,' he said. 'You don't want to walk through wet grass to hang the washing out, and we have our cricket pitch to think of – we don't want the seeds from your wilderness blowing over and ruining our surface.' He had compromised by allowing her a modest patch in one corner of the orchard, where she had scattered a packet of bee-friendly poppy and cornflower seeds, anticipating the summer blooms that would nourish the honey bees and enable them to fill the hives they had unearthed from one of the barns.

Suddenly she heard an almighty crash coming from the direction of the château, and spun round to see what was happening. She couldn't make it out at all at this distance. Maybe Jean-Louis was doing something with his farm equipment; he always seemed to be heaving some piece of heavy machinery behind his tractor. She sat down on the upturned laundry basket and gazed back down over the valley, breathing in the air and admiring the early spring flowers that already decorated the meadow.

A few minutes later, she was disturbed by Simon striding across the field towards her.

'*The maid was in the garden, hanging out the clothes,*' he said, plonking himself down beside her on the laundry basket, out of breath from the brief walk. 'You look the very picture of nursery rhyme contentment.'

'Until the blackbird comes down and pecks off my nose.'

'A very pretty nose it is, too. Anyway, I've just come over to put your mind at rest. That crashing sound *was* our roof tumbling to the ground, but the good news is it didn't land on anybody's head and the builder says he can start work on it right away.'

Nicola looked at him in alarm.

'Imagine if one of us had been hit by falling debris – what a terrible thing that would have been!'

'*The Curse of the Château*. Maybe that could be the title of my next book.'

'You've got to finish this one first.'

'On that subject, I was looking at the chapel this morning and thinking what a fabulous writing den it could become. So much inspiration; history breathing through it. I'm thinking of moving my desk over there so I can see the land through the filter of the stained-glass window. It's just the spur I need to drive me on.'

'Are you sure you're really writing this book? You won't tell us what it's about, you always seem keen on any distraction, and I thought the best view for concentrating was supposed to be a blank wall.'

'If I wanted to stare at a blank wall, I could have stayed in London. I certainly wouldn't have agreed to move to a massive great château in a country estate. I'm maximising the opportunities, all of them. And enjoying the company. Especially yours.'

Nicola stood up; it was feeling a little too cosy with the two of them squeezed up together on the basket.

'Me too,' she said. 'I love having people around; it seems much more normal somehow than being in an isolated couple. Those bleak pairs of pensioners who sit silently opposite each other, that will never be us, thank goodness.'

'You couldn't be bleak if you tried.'

Nicola glared at him. She was starting to find his compliments very irksome. He'd never been like this back home. Why was he suddenly digging up their ancient history?

'Leave it out, Simon.'

'Leave what out? Expressing the fact that I'm enjoying your company?'

'You know what I mean. Sidling up to me with your flirtatious comments. It's creepy, as if my brother were hitting on me. And get up: I want to take that laundry basket back up to the house.'

Simon obediently stood up and she picked up the basket.

'That's harsh,' he said. 'You didn't used to think of me as your brother. What about that time in Buenos Aires, after we'd been to that bar? Don't you remember?'

'No, not really. Well, maybe I do, but that's safely filed away in the distant memory category. You can't carry on dredging it up, it's absurd.'

She started walking back to the house and Simon fell in step beside her.

'I'm being honest with you, that's all . . .'

Undeterred, he carried on talking.

'Since we moved here, I've found that I'm really thinking about what's important to me. Questioning my life choices, thinking I should have made more of an effort to win you back . . .'

Nicola stopped in her tracks and looked him sternly in the face.

'Stop it! I've had enough of this nonsense! You made excellent life choices – you married my favourite woman in the world and we've all been friends ever since! I would never have suggested we go into this venture together if I knew you were feeling this way. And I don't even think you are feeling this way. I think you're a bit bored and seeking distraction from the impossible task you've set yourself for writing your plotless novel, or whatever it is . . .'

'The definitive state-of-the-nation novel, actually. Although I've confused myself slightly by moving abroad. Can you write a state-of-the-nation novel when you're no longer living in the nation? Maybe I should set it in France – there's a thought. Become the new Michel Houellebecq.'

'It's clear to me you haven't written a word of it; every time you talk about it, there's a different story.'

'Thoughts. Feelings. Snatches of brilliance. That's the way to start, then structure it later.'

'As long as I'm not in it, featured as some kind of fantasy figure!'

'Any resemblance to persons living or dead is purely coincidental.'

'Good, make sure you keep it that way.'

When they turned the corner they saw Beth and Leo collecting the shattered roof tiles from the driveway and heaping them up against the wall. Beth waved at them cheerfully and Nicola felt a twinge of guilt, as if she was somehow complicit in Simon's infatuation. How dare he put her in this position, making her feel like she was somehow betraying her friend. It just wasn't fair!

'You missed the roofer,' said Beth. 'He touched one tile and the whole lot came tumbling down. It was pretty dramatic.'

Nicola gazed up at the roof; patches of it were clearly missing, revealing the structure beneath.

'We'll have to deal with that fairly urgently.'

She put down her basket and joined them in clearing up the mess.

'The roofer and Dom were in earnest conversation over a document, which I presume was his estimate,' said Beth. 'But I refuse to let that get me down on this glorious morning. I'm as happy as God in France, aren't you? Did you know that's a German expression? But I think we can adopt it.'

Simon sat down on a stone bench and watched them at work.

'Sounds like something Napoleon would have come up with,' he said. 'He seems to be responsible for most of France's cultural history. You can't make an omelette without breaking eggs – that's one of his. He's their version of Shakespeare, I suppose.'

'He had unusually small genitals, apparently,' said Beth. 'Only one and a half inches.'

'The things you know!' said Simon admiringly. 'That explains the Napoleon complex, I guess. Not that I would know what that feels like, as you know.'

'I know, I'm a very lucky woman,' Beth said sharply. 'Exciting news, by the way: Eva's coming to stay. She just texted me; I'm going to ring her back.'

'Can't live without us, clearly,' said Simon, pleased. 'They're releasing her from the apothecary's coven, then?'

'Physician's associate course, yes. They have a week's holiday. Though she says she'll have to do a lot of studying while she's here.'

'What about James?'

'No, he's working.'

'Good.'

'She said she needed a break; not sure if she means from him.'

'A permanent break would be the best idea. I don't know how she puts up with his endless descriptions of what he spent his last bonus on.'

'I agree, he wouldn't be my choice. He doesn't care about anything you can't put a price tag on, and that's certainly not Eva. Do you remember when he said she was crazy for wanting to work in the NHS when she could go into cosmetic medicine instead and make a killing out of Botox and fillers?'

'Bring back the hamsters, I say. I'd prefer any of them over him.'

Hamsters was the term Simon employed to refer to his daughter's previous boyfriends. So-called because they were cute and cuddly and didn't last long.

'That's great news,' said Nicola. 'Our inaugural visitor.'

Beth stood up from her pile of slates and stretched her back, hands on hips.

'Time for a coffee, I think. Shall we go in?'

'I'm going to get changed,' said Leo, heading for the staircase as they went through the door. 'I'm covered in ancient roof tile dust. I'll be down in a minute.'

On their way through to the kitchen, the others passed Dominic, who was sitting, grave-faced, at the dining table.

'Dom, what on earth happened?' asked Nicola. 'You're looking less than your usual cheery self.'

'Sorry, my cheerful hat just slipped.'

He pushed a letter across the table for them to see.

'It's the estimate from the roofer.'

Nicola looked through the detailed sheets until she arrived at the mind-boggling final figure.

'Blimey,' she said, passing it on to Beth and Simon, who read it in silence.

'I know. I'm thinking, how difficult can it be to hang a few tiles? Maybe we should try to fix it ourselves.'

'You are joking,' said Beth. 'Think about Nigel in *The Archers*. I can still hear his blood-curdling cry when he fell to his death. I agree that there is a lot we can manage – we've all done painting and decorating and Simon's a dab hand at tiling. But I draw the line at climbing up on that roof. Look at what happened just now, and he was a professional!'

'I'll second that,' said Simon. 'Very happy to be on bathroom-tiling duty but I don't have the physique for clambering over scaffolding. Plus I'm a coward with no head for heights.'

Dougie wandered in through the French windows, having been checking for fallen slates on the other side of the château.

'Not so much damage out the back; I've put them all in a pile. And I've just said goodbye to the roofer. He seems a jolly nice chap, actually . . .'

He stopped when he sensed the sombre mood in the room.

'What's going on here?' he said. 'You look like you've had some very bad news.'

'You could say that,' said Beth. 'But put it this way, Dougie: would you rather shimmy up a very tall ladder to repair the roof, or leave it to the professionals?'

'Ah. Well, I think there's only one answer to that question.'

'Dougie on the roof!' Fizz snorted at the idea. They were all pretty old but Dougie seemed oldest of all to her, with his fusty old tweeds.

'Take a look at this,' said Beth, passing him the offending document.

'Good Lord,' said Dougie, after reading through it twice. 'Do you think he's added an extra zero by mistake? Or maybe he's quoting in old francs.'

'I don't think so,' said Dominic. 'He seemed a very modern young man. With unfeasibly smooth hands, I thought, for a manual labourer. I assume he brings in a team of tougher specimens to actually do the work.'

'And who would be less likely to bring the whole thing crashing down?' said Simon. 'If you ask me, that young man was a bit cack-handed, unless he deliberately knocked the slates off to convince us we needed to hire him to do the job.'

'Roofers are quite hot in my experience,' said Leo. 'Fearless and agile, we can enjoy the spectacle. And you certainly won't catch me volunteering to go up there. I've no desire to go before my time and certainly don't fancy splattering to my death from a height of forty feet. Much as I've come to love the musical bedtime sound of water tinkling through my tower, we need to get this fixed.'

'But it's so much money!' said Dougie. 'In fact, it's our entire renovation budget! How on earth will we ever afford to pay for the rest of the work so we can have the private apartments we planned? We'll have to live forever in this ramshackle, student-like existence.'

'Not quite like my studenthood,' said Simon. 'Far better fed and watered here, I find.'

Leo was determined to push it through. He'd be a nervous wreck soon if they didn't mend that bloody roof.

'We need to consider this expenditure in the way that Dominic first presented it,' he said. 'Divide that sum by nine, and you'll find that it comes out at a very reasonable price. We should see it that we each own one ninth of the roof; it's quite a bargain. Not like one person having to pay for the lot. And anyway, without a sound roof, spending any other money indoors would be pointless.'

'An excellent analysis, well done,' said Beth. 'Let's just get it done. Then we can all sit down and discuss how we can fund the rest of the interior repairs and renovations afterwards – and at least we'll be able to do that secure in the knowledge the roof's not going to fall in on us.'

'Should we have a show of hands?' said Dominic. 'Will has already agreed.'

Beth, Simon, Nicola and Leo all raised their hands. Nicola realised she was holding her breath. Was this it? Their dream of château life falling at the first hurdle?

Dougie paused, but eventually put his hand up too.

'I suppose it has to be done, and you can take my vote on behalf of Mary, too. She's gone for a lie-down – the roof destruction was too much for her.'

'Good,' said Dominic, 'that's settled then. Now I'm going for a bike ride. I need to oxygenate my brain.'

# CHAPTER TEN

'It's not exactly *la vie en rose* 24/7, is it?' said Nicola, lying on their bed. 'You could have cut the atmosphere with a knife at lunch. I don't know what I was expecting, but I didn't anticipate that mass huffiness. I suppose I thought it would be like an extended holiday but I'd forgotten that after two weeks in a villa you usually all go home to your normal life.'

Lunch had been a subdued affair and after clearing the table, everyone had retreated to their rooms for a sulky siesta. The reality of blowing their whole repair budget on one thing – albeit a pretty essential thing – had taken the shine off the day.

Dominic was standing in front of the full-length mirror, turning sideways to admire the flatness of his stomach. These regular morning bike rides were definitely having the desired effect; he was slimmer than he'd been in years.

Nicola propped herself up on her elbow.

'Hello? Are you listening? Or too busy worshipping at the shrine of your own image?'

'Oh, come on, it's not that bad,' he said, working his waist by turning his torso from side to side. 'I guess there's nothing like a socking great repair bill to lower the mood, but at least it's all agreed.'

'I thought Dougie was being particularly miserable, as if we'd created the problem especially to wind him up.'

'Mmm, well that's Dougie for you. I did say from the start that of everyone, he'd be bottom of my list. It'll be fine, don't worry.'

He lay down next to her on the bed and started performing some leg lifts.

'I mean, we're all worried about money but he acts like he's the only one who has to foot the bill,' Nicola continued. 'And I bet they're getting a good whack for renting out their house.'

'As are we. Or we would be if you'd only agree to charge the kids a fair rent. Are you having second thoughts, then?' He was on to his stretches now, extending his leg across her in a possessive show of masculinity. 'Was this a really stupid idea of ours, to buy a monstrous money pit of a château with a group of friends you've decided you don't like anymore?'

'Of course I still like them!' said Nicola, pushing his leg away from her. 'And I really love this place. At least, I think I do. Although I read a ten-point guide the other day on how to buy a château in France. The first piece of advice was: "Don't do it".'

'Ha! A little late for us.'

'But no, I don't regret it. It's just tougher than I thought it would be.'

'How do you think the others are finding it?'

'All right, I think. Though you never quite know what people are really thinking, do you? They're probably all bitching right now behind closed doors! Leo's marvellous, though, isn't he? In spite of his sleep deprivation.'

'Yes, he's a sweetheart. The one who really gets on my tits is Simon. He's so bloody lazy! Though not too lazy to follow you down to the field this morning when you were hanging out the washing, I happened to notice.'

He looked across at her with a questioning smile.

Nicola frowned. Once again she was being made to feel bad about something that wasn't her fault.

'I know, he's being very annoying. I've had words with him, actually – told him to grow up!'

'I love it when you're stern.'

Dom cuddled up to Nicola. He did love her – who could fail to fall for her dynamism and energy? And he knew she was the glue that had kept the family together – raising the kids as well as doing endless hours at the surgery. But sometimes he allowed himself a simpler frisson when he looked at her. He had to admit it wasn't just her heart he loved her for. It felt good having a fanciable wife – not something you could say about every man his age. Except Will, of course, but in a way that didn't count as it was second time round. Will had been a good friend to him over the years; he'd always be grateful for the way he'd made him see sense. 'Think very carefully, mate,' he'd said. 'I don't think you really want this, do you?' Stern. Just like Nicola. Just what you need in moments of emotional weakness.

'I can't believe how much it costs to replace the roof,' Simon complained. 'You could buy an entire village for that price, and we could each have our own little house – much simpler.'

He and Beth were lying side by side on the bed, both tapping away on their phones.

'I can completely believe it; this place is massive,' said Beth. 'And who wants a little village house when you can have a fuck-off château?'

'With all the attendant expense. I knew this would happen.'

'And where we create our very own senior co-housing community.'

'Ugh, what a ghastly expression.'

'It's very zeitgeisty,' said Beth. 'It's taken off in the States; it'll be big in Britain next.'

'I presume you're referring to those horrible retirement villages where Barbara and Dwayne drive around in golf carts with personalised plates?'

'Not in our case, obviously. Although Will has his sit-on mower, I suppose.'

'Boys and their toys.'

'You're not regretting it, are you?' Beth turned to face him but Simon continued staring at his phone.

'No, I'm not regretting it.' The silence felt heavy though.

'I'm looking forward to seeing Eva next week,' said Beth. 'I hope she's all right; she did sound a bit down.'

'I'm glad she's not bringing that dork.'

'Me too. He's the only one of her boyfriends I've never cared for.'

'You were always too attached to his predecessors, I thought.'

'I know, it felt like a small death whenever they left our lives. Just as we were becoming fond of them, Eva decided they weren't the one and we're back to square one.'

'And you always got their names wrong. Like when you called Luke Max by mistake and told him you'd bought the special cheese he liked, and Eva gave you that thundering look because Max was history.'

'Nobody does a thundering look like Eva.'

'Wonder where she gets that from?' said Simon.

Beth frowned.

'Do you think we spoiled her? Made her too fussy so she can't tolerate any relationship that's not perfect?'

'Don't come out with that spoilt only-child routine again. One child is quite enough, and if we'd had more, we would only have spoiled them all.'

'I suppose. I must say I'm enjoying being spared the daily accounts of her dissatisfactions. Or at least I'm only receiving them remotely.' She rolled off the bed and walked to the window.

'It's the skies I love here – the way the colours change and then darken when the rain's coming, as if someone's turned down the dimmer switch. I can see Fizz coming back from a run – just in time, from the look of it. She's a funny little thing, isn't she? I thought I was going to hate Temple-woman, but in fact she's really grown on me. '

'Well, she's younger and prettier and nicer than you, so no wonder you thought you wouldn't like her.'

Beth looked at him with intense dislike.

'Jokes!' said Simon.

'I just said I do like her; clean your ears out. Though I do find it strange that she's chosen this life. Married to someone twice her age, then holed up here with a bunch of old people.'

'We're not old. I read that middle-age ends at fifty-eight, so we're mostly still in range.'

'Maybe she saw Will as a convenient meal ticket. It means she can swan around with her vlogging rather than join one of those faceless corporations that her contemporaries will have signed up for.'

'That's a cynical view. Maybe she just fell madly in love with him. Or maybe he's a legend in the sack.'

'It's true she doesn't look *mal baisée*.'

'What does that mean?' Simon asked.

'It literally means badly fucked, though it sounds much cruder in English. It's one of the great French insults.'

'Though, by extension, you might conclude the insult applies to the person's partner, if they have one.'

'Do you think I look *mal baisée*?'

Simon looked up at her warily. 'Is this a trick question? You know we don't talk about such things. We're British, after all.'

'I agree. The secret of a successful marriage is never to discuss it. Assuming we do have a successful marriage?'

Simon looked back at his phone.

'Now, is it time to go down for a drink, do you suppose?'

'Good run, darling?'

Will looked up from the armchair in their bedroom window, where he was swiping through Facebook photos on his iPad. His ex-wife had posted a picture of the table setting for her birthday dinner, featuring elaborate quantities of glasses and folded napkins and hand-written place names. What a relief not to be there! He knew exactly how it would be: Marjorie would garner compliments for her perfectly presented dinner, served by a 'girl' she had hired for the evening. She had tagged the guests, many of them his former colleagues from the law firm who had taken her side when he walked out on the marriage. He didn't miss them at all.

Fizz was peeling off her running gear, her lithe body exposed for his delight. As he did most days, he thanked his lucky stars for the gift of her, with her youthful energy and zest for life.

'It was good, and I finished just in time before the rain. What are you grinning at?'

'I'm grinning at you.'

'Grinning fool.'

She took a towel from the rail by the radiator.

'Come here, forget the shower.'

She looked at him as if he was mad.

'I mean it, let me smell you in all your sporting glory.'

She walked towards the chair and he pulled her onto his lap, burying his face in her armpit.

'*I'm coming home in three days, don't wash!* Did you know that Napoleon wrote that to Josephine?'

Fizz wriggled away from him.

'Everyone was dirty in those days; it must have been gross.'

'And he referred to her private parts as the Baron de Kepen.'

'Weirdo.'

'Certainly eccentric. I'm reading a marvellous biography of him – you can have it after me.'

'No thanks.'

'I thought you'd say that.'

How marvellous to have a wife who could see no point in reading about a long-dead French general. Marjorie would have devoured it and then discussed it with him ad nauseam, contradicting him on his memory of its contents in exhausting detail.

Fizz slipped off his lap and lifted her arm for an exploratory sniff.

'All right, just for you, I'll go for the French approach. No soap, just perfume. It's so painful having a shower here, anyway. Not even a shower, just a clanky old attachment. I'm sick of crouching in that knackered old bathtub. '

She sprayed herself from the bottle on the dressing table: Annick Goutal's Tenue de Soirée, a gift from Will, who correctly believed she would love the purple pompom that was attached to the stopper. It was inspired by romantic nights in Paris, he'd told her, and soon he would be taking her there for a weekend of unimaginable luxury, to make up for the rudimentary bathroom provisions of the château.

Will watched her as she slipped into a fluffy pink jumper and pair of jeans. She then picked up the bangle he had given her for her last birthday and fitted it over her wrist. It was a Cartier love bracelet and Fizz complained it was slightly too small, like a mini chastity belt. 'You're trying to suffocate me,' she had said when she tried it on for the first time, 'but I don't mind, it's beautiful.'

'Dressing for dinner, then,' Will said.

'If you've got it, you might as well wear it,' said Fizz, twirling her arm at him. 'Can you film me walking over to the window? I'm going to post it under the heading: Chatelaine Spring Dinnerwear. Very Mademoiselle Bovary, I thought: a young woman in a fresh pink jumper preparing to sit down to yet another dinner with a bunch of old crocks. I'm starting to get a decent following.'

'Only if you promise to take everything off afterwards,' said Will. 'There's still plenty of siesta time left before evening cocktails.'

'Mocktails for me,' said Fizz, then frowned. 'Will, can I ask you something? Do you think I've become more boring since I stopped drinking?'

'You could never be boring.'

'Thank you. It's just something Simon said. He claimed I used to be more fun before I gave up drinking and took up running.'

'You know how he likes to tease. I think he could benefit from following your example, to be honest.'

'And you don't find me boring in other ways? I often feel when I'm with you and the others, you all know so much more than me, you've all read load of books . . . I sometimes think I don't measure up.'

'You are fascinating to me in every sense.'

'Because I know you were bored with Marjorie before you met me, and I'd hate to think I was going the same way . . .'

'Stop right there! You are as far away from boring as it is possible to be. And as for what Simon says, he is a controversialist who loves to provoke a reaction. Take no notice.'

'That's true, and I don't really care what he thinks, he's such an old dinosaur. I'd be more worried if Leo thought that too.'

'As I say, ignore him. Simon takes great pleasure in finding people's sensitive spots and needling them. He does it to all of us. When I first met him, I admit, I thought he was a troublemaker – out to prove everyone has feet of clay. But I came to realise it comes from a good place. He never judged me or looked down on me for not coming from the kind of comfortable background he does – he's not as much of a snob as he likes to pretend. He prides himself on daring to say what everyone is thinking, but dares not say! Which doesn't mean he's always right, but it can make him very entertaining. And you've got to admit, he knows how to have a good time. Now, let's get this video done then I'll show you how you are the complete opposite to boring.'

In Dougie and Mary's room, the talk was of a more scholarly nature. Mary was reading aloud the first draft of her thesis to her perfect audience, who was listening with his eyes closed and his hands together, as if in prayer.

When she had finished she lay the papers down and looked expectantly for his response.

'It's marvellous, Mary, well done,' he said. 'And it benefits greatly from being delivered as the spoken word. It reminds me of when you borrowed a recording of *Beowulf* from the faculty library, delivered in the sonorous tones of a don whose name escapes me. We listened to it together and I knew then that I had found my soulmate.'

'It wasn't everyone's idea of a first date. Do you really think it's all right?'

'More than all right. A first-class piece of scholarship, I'd say.'

'I still need to work on the footnotes, but I admit I'm pleased with it. It's so conducive to quiet study here, don't you find?'

'Aside from the riotous dinners, I grant you. Almost a college atmosphere there; I'm always expecting the more riotous members to start throwing bread rolls at each other. Not to mention the attendant noise of the château crumbling around our ears – you can practically hear the flurry of golden sovereigns falling to the floor, our careful lifetime savings thrown away on shoring up a ruin.'

'It will all work out, I'm certain.'

'It would help the budget if some of the others didn't insist on eating and drinking their body weight every night. I'm not convinced by this shared kitty idea, when it so obviously disfavours the more abstemious among us.'

Mary picked up the feather duster, which she kept propped up in the corner, and started flicking it around.

'Darling, I promise you there is not a speck of dust in this room,' said Dougie.

'You know as well as I do that dust mites are invisible to the human eye.'

She brushed the duster over the top of the window poles.

Dougie started slowly clapping his hands.

'Why are you applauding?'

'Not your housework, exemplary though it is. I am awarding you first-class honours for an outstanding thesis. It takes me right back. I'll never forget the moment I walked into the room for my viva. All the dons lined up in their gowns. I thought I was being interviewed to decide whether to award me a first- or second-class degree. Then they all stood up and applauded and one of them shook me by the hand . . .' His eyes filled with tears at the memory. 'It was a congratulatory first, Mary. The finest moment in my career.'

Mary had heard the story many times.

'You're a clever old stick and you've had many glories since. That was only the beginning.'

'That's kind of you but you know it's not true. My star has been sinking for some years.'

'Which is why we are better off here, away from the academic microcosm. We can enjoy the joys of scholarship without the rivalries and unpleasantness of the system. We're both getting so much more work done here than back at Cambridge, aren't we? I think it's something about not having to look your rivals in the eye every day.'

'Not much rivalry here, to my relief.'

'Exactly. Simon's writing, a book of course, but it's not in our field.'

'Not in any field from what I can work out. He seems to change the premise on a daily basis.'

'It will be fascinating to see what he comes up with in the end.'

'You've inspired me, Mary. I'm going to write about the Great War, now we're in the territory. I know it has been extensively covered, but with a little persistence I hope I shall uncover an aspect that until now has been little explored. We'll start by touring the battlefields, if you'll accompany me?'

'I'd love to.'

'I see this new life of ours as a semi-retreat, don't you? I've always disliked the self-absorption of those going into complete retreat; utterly pretentious to lock yourself away in a cave and think only about yourself. But here we have the opportunity to live within a small community like modern monks. I'm so glad we took the plunge.'

'Me too. I particularly like not being hassled by people knocking at the door. Do you remember how we used to play dead to avoid the Jehovah's Witnesses?'

'Ha! Remember when you lay down on the floor after peeping through the eye-hole and seeing them standing on the doorstep. Didn't dare to move in case they looked through the window and saw you!'

'Imprisoned in my own home and wracked by guilt at my mean-spiritedness! Much easier to hide away here where we have thirty-two rooms to choose from. Speaking of which, I'm going downstairs now to have a quick clean of the kitchen.'

She kissed the top of his head.

'I'm so happy you like my thesis.'


In the turret room, Leo was listening to the whirring of the *sanibroyeur* in the bathroom below. It was a specialty of French plumbing, he had read – they liked to install them in unfeasible places, where the usual downpipe was not available – which required a macerator to chop everything up. Very often it went into overdrive and the sound of it was the background music of his otherwise enchanting haven at the top of the château. On rainy nights, when he escaped to the watertight attic room, he even missed its soothing rhythmic hum.

He flicked through the copy of yesterday's *Times* that he had bought earlier from the newsagent. The foreign papers were always a day late, which gave the impression that you were slightly out of kilter with news from Old Blighty, which he didn't mind. It reinforced the feeling of being in a safe bubble, at one remove from what was happening in the real world. He had also bought a copy of today's *Libération*, but French news did not seem so pertinent to him, even though this was now his adopted country.

*The Times* had a feature on nature, which he found hard to get too worked up about. Apparently, there were 400,000 plant species in the world, a fifth of them under threat of extinction. *But surely 320,000 was plenty to be going on with*? Leo thought he could name maybe a hundred, if he was lucky – he hoped that didn't mark him out as a climate-change denier. Rather than worrying about the world, he found it soothing to focus his attention on his immediate surroundings – it was the only sane response to the general madness out there.

Mind you, his immediate surroundings were not without their challenges. The château had turned out to be in a far worse state than they had hoped, which was going to be a terrible financial burden. And as Chief Aesthetic Officer, he felt compelled to bring some kind of harmony to the reception rooms in the short term, even though the overarching grand scheme would have to wait. But how on earth could you combine Simon and Beth's huge modern leather sofas with Will's rustic farmhouse buffet – a legacy from his divorce – and Mary's eighteenth-century Dutch burr walnut and marquetry inlaid coffee table, without making it look a complete shambles? He had visions of setting up a beautifully curated salon – one that potential clients would fall in love with and hire him on the spot to bring the same blend of Anglo-French style to their own homes. But he couldn't let paying customers see him with a leaky roof and his friends' furniture looking like the leftovers from a house clearance sale. Instead, he'd concentrated on putting only carefully cropped shots of the château on his website and hoped for the best.

It was easier, really, to make an impact outdoors. He had claimed a row in the vegetable garden for his own use to raise rare salad leaves, sourced from specialist seed suppliers. Mustard Red Giant, lamb's lettuce, nasturtium leaves, dandelion – whimsically named *pissenlit* in French, because of their diuretic effect. You eat with your eyes, and his goal was to present plates of salad as paintings, so sitting down to dinner became a similar experience to walking round an art gallery. In London, David had been in charge of the garden, and woe betide Leo if he meddled with the planting. Now he was free to do as he liked. The salad bed was his way of moving on, to use that terrible expression.

He was hoping this afternoon's date would be an arty type, in view of the venue he had suggested. One night, after being a little too liberal with the calvados, the friends had persuaded Leo it was time to take the plunge and they'd agreed this guy looked perfect for him. They were to meet at a Renaissance château museum, located in a village a few kilometres away, because Bertrand said he wanted to show him the fifteenth-century frescoes. He was a lover of history, looked about the same age as Leo and sounded more up his street than any of the others who had presented themselves on the app. No tattoos, for a start. The château museum was set within a moat, clad with glazed green tiles that were untypical of the region, a legacy of the former chatelain's Italian wife, who missed her native land and hired workmen to recreate the luminous beauty of her home city – or so it said on the website, anyway. *At least it will be an aesthetic delight, no matter how the love interest turns out to be*, Leo thought.

# CHAPTER ELEVEN

'You know what's the best cure for a broken heart?' said Beth the next morning. 'A bracing dose of sea air, to blow away the cobwebs of disappointment.'

She and Leo were taking early morning coffee on the terrace while the rest of the household were indulging in a *grasse matinée*, as Leo called it, enjoying the judgemental tone of the French term for a lie-in. A fat morning – that was enough to ensure you never had one again. Only Dougie had been up with the lark as he wanted to speak to the builders when they arrived with the scaffolding. He was amazed the others had slept through it, with all that clanking and shouting.

'I'm not exactly heartbroken,' said Leo. 'Just disappointed by Bertrand's utter lack of charisma.'

'That's the downside of internet dating: someone can sound the very soul of charisma on the screen, and then you meet them and find they have no spirit. I think that's the most important thing, don't you, to have spirit? That would be top of my list if I was on the hunt.'

'You're not on the hunt, though, are you? Is Simon behaving himself?'

He couldn't help noticing the friction between them.

'Simon is being Simon.'

'That sounds mysterious.'

'We're fine,' said Beth. She wasn't minded to share her marital problems with Leo. Today was to be a glorious trip to the seaside, she had decided. *Pack all your troubles in your old kit bag and smile, smile, smile.*

'Don't you agree it's the perfect weather for an outing? We haven't been to the beach yet. It's only an hour away and it will be beautifully quiet – out of season and midweek, what could be better? Escape all these builders coming in to do the roof too.'

'Yes, the sky is periwinkle blue. *Vinca minor*, excellent ground cover with sky blue flowers – I was reading about it earlier, now I'm embracing gardening. Look, here comes Nicola. I'm sure she'll love the idea, won't you, darling?'

Nicola took his outstretched hand as she stepped sleepily out to join them.

'What idea is that? I hate this invasion, don't you? I didn't think they'd be starting quite so soon with the scaffolding. It's like living in Big Ben.'

'I've got just the answer. An outing to the seaside,' said Beth. 'What do you say?'

'Oh yes!!!' Nicola said. 'That is exactly what we need!'

The others didn't take much persuading, although it was a couple of hours before they were ready to leave. Dougie and Dominic were very engrossed in supervising the scaffolders, while Leo kept changing his outfit and Mary had to be dragged away from her cleaning duties. Simon insisted on an hour of quiet concentration on his writing before throwing in the towel for the day.

'Write every day,' he said. 'It's the first rule of authorship, and I intend to be too wasted to do any later. You're driving us back, Beth.'

'It's like organising a party of children,' Beth complained. 'I supposed I'd better ask everyone if they've been to the toilet.'

'Don't say toilet,' said Leo with a shudder.

Finally, they were on their way, sweeping through the château gates in a convoy, Will leading the fleet in his vintage sports car with the roof down, Fizz beside him in a glamorous hat, tied under her chin with a floaty chiffon scarf.

'She looks better than most folk you see in open-top sports cars,' said Simon to Beth. 'Have you noticed it's only ever vintage people who drive vintage cars?'

'Will told me he's gone off his car,' said Leo, who was in his preferred place in the back seat, playing the fake son. 'Ever since he read a review of a French château hotel that began, "We came in our vintage cars". It was about a bunch of middle-aged Brits arriving in their show-off old Bentleys and sucking up to the aristocratic host. Will said he's worried the car might make him look like a bit of a tosser.'

'It's true that vintage cars are generally driven by tossers,' said Beth.

'He thinks he may get a Fiat 500 instead,' said Leo.

'That's a girl's car!' said Simon.

'Don't be such an old chauvinist pig!' said Beth. 'It's a sexy Italian man's car. Just because you're too fat to fit in one!'

'Come off it! When did you ever see a real man getting out of a pistachio green Fiat 500?'

'You're sounding terribly unreconstructed,' said Leo. 'I don't approve of this sexual stereotyping. Remember you're in the company of a member of an oppressed minority.'

'Nobody is less oppressed than you, you old queen,' said Beth.

'If anyone's an oppressed minority, it's the white, middle-aged heterosexual male,' said Simon, pulling a faux woe-is-me face. 'The tide has turned against us.'

'Drive on, you old mutton,' said Beth, opening her window to wave at Nicola in the car behind. Dougie and Mary were safely installed in Dominic and Nicola's car, always happy to take a back seat.

The route to the coast was a glorious drive through woods and fields. Will chose the smaller roads, so their approach to the sea was through narrow lanes beneath a canopy of sun-dappled trees, arriving at a harbour fringed with cottages and enticing restaurants with tables set out on the pavement. He parked alongside an MG Midget sports car, rather similar to his own, with British registration plates.

'They stopped making them in 1979,' he told Fizz, 'so that car is older than you.'

They sat on the wall, waiting for the others to catch them up.

'This is pretty nice,' said Fizz, looking down at the fishing boats moored beneath them. 'Salty air, seagulls, old fishing nets – exactly the place for Mademoiselle Bovary to let her hair down. Would you mind?' She took off her hat and shook out her hair, then passed Will her phone and posed in profile, chin cupped in her hand and with one foot resting on the wall to present an interesting triangular form.

As Will was focusing, an elderly man tapped him on the shoulder.

'Please, allow me,' he said, taking the phone and ushering Will towards the wall. 'I will make a beautiful picture of you and your daughter.'

The man's wife, wearing the local aubergine short-back-and-sides, nodded her approval as Will sat awkwardly next to Fizz.

'*Ouistiti!*' said the self-appointed photographer. 'Smile, please.'

'What a cheek,' said Fizz, after Will had thanked him and said goodbye. 'Your daughter!'

'Technically possible, I suppose.'

'But you look nowhere near your age, I've made sure of that. Oh look, here come the others. OAP outing, with their sexy young carer.'

Leo stepped out of the car and waved at them. He looked magnificently out of place in his powder blue suit and dove-grey lacy shirt. Fizz would definitely feature him on her YouTube channel – she'd get him talking to camera about his clothes.

'That's not fair,' said Will. 'It's only Dougie and Mary who look their age; the rest of us are in pretty good shape.'

Dominic and Nicola had parked further down and walked up to join them, hand-in-hand, followed by Dougie and Mary.

'Look at these restaurants, actually serving food at three o'clock in the afternoon,' said Nicola. 'You wouldn't find that inland; it's only when you reach the coast that the usual rules are thrown out the window.'

The rigidity of French dining hours was something they had remarked upon, because the culture shock of all-day dining had been firmly resisted in a country where everything revolved around meal times. Lunch at 12.30 and dinner at 7.30; anything else was an abomination, unless you were at the seaside where, it seemed, anything goes.

'Let's work up an appetite first,' said Dominic. 'Oh look, Will, someone's admiring your car.'

They turned to watch a tall, eccentric-looking figure with wild grey hair inspecting Will's car in great detail, bending down to peer inside at the dashboard.

'Does this belong to one of you?' he asked.

'Yes, it's mine,' said Will. 'And you're a fellow Englishman, from the sound of you.'

'There's a lot of us about! You know, the mayor here tried to ban the sale of any more houses to *les rosbifs*, claimed it was ruining the atmosphere. Not me, of course, I've been here for decades. I am the atmosphere of this town – he told me that himself!'

He was wearing a yellow jacket, a floral-patterned shirt and bright green trousers, the walking embodiment of the French idea of English style – bizarre and strident.

He held his hand out.

'Quentin, pleased to meet you.'

'You're the first Brit we've met since we moved here,' said Nicola as they introduced themselves.

'Well, I certainly won't be the last,' said Quentin. 'Normandy's crawling with them, most of them ghastly. Mind you, they probably say the same about me.'

He beamed at them.

'The reason I noticed your car, Will, is that I have something similar, right there.'

'Ah, it's your Midget.'

'Can't beat a classic car, especially if you don't use it much. I hardly go anywhere, have everything I need right here. I paint portraits – my studio's up there, you can come and take a look.'

'I'd love to,' said Beth, and Nicola and Fizz followed, leaving the others to explore the town.

They followed him away from the harbour, along the narrow, cobbled streets of the old town until they arrived at his shop front. A life-size full-length portrait of Quentin was displayed outside, easily recognisable.

They followed him into the cluttered interior. A work-in-progress featuring a woman holding a dog was propped up on an easel and other portraits were hanging on the walls. *Heightened realism*, Nicola thought. *Larger than life in their vibrancy*.

'They're very good,' she said. 'Have you always been a painter?'

'No! I trained as a thatcher and came over here in my early twenties to work on the roofs of French cottages. That's where the word comes from: *chaumière*, from *chaume*, which means thatch. Then I decided I was too old to be scrambling over houses, so taught myself to paint. Nothing like moving abroad to enable self-reinvention, as you'll all find. I couldn't go back to Britain now; I wouldn't fit in. My most recent wife didn't feel the same, though. She moved back last year.'

'Your most recent wife? How many have there been?' asked Nicola.

'Four, at last count, and several petitioners for number five. That's the great thing about being an artist – the women love it! I'm not in any hurry, though. The last thing I need is another divorcee with baggage and kids; I've had plenty of them to be going on with! Isn't that right, Sylvie?'

He addressed his last remark at a woman who had just wandered into the shop. Of uncertain age but definitely the other side of sixty, with long hair dyed black and frightening makeup, she had appearance of a ghoul, the spirit of the 1960s in her Brigitte Bardot faded denim.

'Oh yes, Quentin, we girls all love you, you're such a distinguished English gentleman!'

She kissed him on the cheek and wandered out again.

'There are so many like her in this town,' said Quentin. 'They move down from Paris, bless them, to embrace the bohemian life, wandering around thinking they're Marguerite Duras.'

They said their goodbyes, exchanging numbers and promising to be in touch, with the complicity of strangers in a strange land, and stepped back out onto the street.

'The self-proclaimed master of self-reinvention,' said Beth once they'd rendezvoused with the others. 'You've got to hand it to him, he's built himself a good life here. I could imagine living in this port. There seems a real community, people popping in all the time, not like us in our glorious isolation.'

'Bit of a chancer, if you ask me,' said Simon. 'All that eccentric English gentleman shtick. He's probably a suburbanite just like us, trying to make himself sound interesting.'

'That's harsh,' said Fizz. 'I thought he was charming, and I loved his portraits. I'd like Will to commission one for our bedroom – then you could look at me in duplicate, sweetie, in the flesh and on canvas. What do you think?'

'Good idea,' said Will. 'You know I can never see enough of you.'

'Leave it out, you nauseating lovebirds,' said Beth. 'Let's do some shopping. This is exactly my kind of place – all quirky little plate and candle shops.'

They meandered around the town with the slow pace of those with no particular objective. Dougie picked up a history of the

D-Day landings in a second-hand bookstore and Beth found a set of antique pottery mugs – truly authentic, she said, for serving cider. Mary bought a length of plasticised table cloth, decorated with flowers, to protect the dining table and Nicola found a pair of rubber purple clogs for gardening.

'That's enough knick-knacks,' said Dominic. 'It's time for what we came here for – a walk by the seaside.'

The cobbled lane led them down to a wide sandy beach, with expansive views across the ocean. The tide was low, the water far away beyond a stretch of wet sand, but a walkway of wooden boards was set out on the soft dry sand higher up, allowing visitors to stroll along the coast, admiring the sea and the handsome nineteenth-century villas with witches' hat turrets whose gardens opened directly onto the beach. A handful of people were flying kites and one or two hardy souls were braving the water.

'Come on!' said Beth, pulling off her shoes. 'Let's go for a paddle!'

She ran towards the sea and one by one, the others joined her, feeling the sand beneath their toes as they headed through the shallow pools left by the ebbing tide, down to the waves lapping at the shore.

'Never mind paddling, I'm going all the way!' said Dominic. 'Silly of us not to bring our swimming costumes, but here goes.'

He stripped down to his underpants, displaying his taut physique, to Leo's shrieks of delight.

'Calvin Kleins!' he said. 'You're a dead ringer for Freddie Ljunberg. I'll stay here – these slacks are dry-clean only.'

'We are so *lucky*!' said Dominic, as he caught up with the others on the water's edge. 'Three o'clock on a weekday afternoon and we could be stuck at our office desks, and instead we are here.'

He plunged into the water and broke into an energetic crawl against the icy flow.

'All you need is a knotted handkerchief on your head to be the perfect English holidaymaker,' said Will, from the safety of the shallows. You wouldn't catch him swimming in these temperatures.

'But that's just it, we're not holidaymakers, we are full-time French château dwellers,' Dominic shouted back. 'We're not counting down the days until we return to the grind – we are living the life!'

Nicola had stopped to gather some mother-of-pearl shells and looked up to watch them laughing at the water's edge. The cold January night when they came up with this idea seemed a lifetime ago; Dom's work stress had melted away and she was happy to see he was more carefree than he had been for years. Beyond that ocean, but not too far away, was the life they had left behind; the sense of escape was enhanced by the distance imposed by the English Channel. The French called it *la manche*, the sleeve that tapered into the narrow cuff of the Dover–Calais crossing. Yesterday's tension about the money and renovation and irritations within the group was blown away by the sea air.

She gave Dominic her scarf to dry himself off and they slowly retraced their steps along the boardwalk. A group of young people were playing beach volleyball on a thoughtfully provided pitch and some older men were engaged in a serious game of boules on a court laid out beside the grand casino, a monument to *fin de siècle* grandeur. A miniature white train drove past with a handful of passengers squeezed into the carriages as the driver pointed out the sights.

'Such a civilised nation; everything is arranged for enjoyment,' said Mary. 'You know, Monet spent his honeymoon here, painting beach scenes, and Flaubert fell in love for the first time with an older woman on this beach when he rescued her cape from the rising tide. It really has the feel of a seaside town arranged for everybody's pleasure.'

'Speaking of which, I'm looking forward to our very late lunch,' said Simon. 'We've shown incredible restraint. Do you realise this is the first time we've eaten out since we arrived?'

They strolled past the covered fish market with stalls displaying glistening fresh seafood that could be sampled on high stools and small tables set up on the pavement, then arrived at their destination: a renowned art deco brasserie with long communal tables lined up outside, protected from the elements by a maroon canopy and patio heaters emitting a welcoming glow.

'Never mind the planet, eh?' said Simon. 'As long as we can park our old arses on a nice warm seat.'

'Table for nine?' A business-like waiter ushered them to a table set with a white cloth and they shuffled into chairs pushed close enough for their arms to touch each other. He brought out two baskets of bread and a couple of carafes of chilled *macon villages*.

'You can't beat French waiters,' said Beth. 'They manage to be friendly and professional at the same time, with none of that fake matiness you get at home.'

'I'm going in to find the loos,' said Mary.

Inside the restaurant was a well-worn zinc bar and tightly packed tables. The atmosphere was of an archetypal French bistro, enhanced by black and white snapshots of music and movie stars dining at this famous establishment that lined the staircase up to the restrooms.

'You must take a look inside,' she said, returning to her seat. 'It's so cosy, like stepping back into the 1950s – you feel like you're on a film set.'

'Warmer, too, I bet,' said Simon, always mindful of his comfort.

'We're hardy Brits, remember,' said Dominic. 'We should really be wearing cap-sleeve T-shirts to reinforce the image.'

'It's lovely out here, and we can look out over the sea,' said Nicola. 'Just think, we can actually see the source of our dinner – it's so on-trend.'

'Never let it be said that we're not on-trend,' scoffed Dougie.

They started with crab and whelks, presented on a raised platter of crushed ice with metal implements designed to smash the shells and coax out the flesh.

'I'm not having any of those whelks,' said Leo. 'Ghastly things, like lumps of rubber. I'm sticking to the crab.'

Dougie was keeping an eye on the budget and made everyone order *moules frites*, turning down Simon's request for a Dover sole.

'I hate to lower the mood by mentioning the roof, but you'll all thank me when the bill comes.'

The waiter arrived with mussels piled up in large tureens, their soft orange centres contrasting against the purple-black carapaces. As the bowls filled up with discarded shells, he swept them away with quiet, practised ease.

Fizz dipped a skinny chip into the parsley-strewn wine broth that had puddled at the bottom of her plate.

'So much better than fish and chips. None of that oily batter and big fat soggy chips.'

'I must stop you there,' said Dominic. 'Your enthusiasm for all things French is blinding you to the fact that fish and chips is one of our country's finest achievements. Triple-cooked hand-cut chips, crunchy on the outside, light inside, then a moist flaky piece of cod encased in beer batter. I'm getting quite homesick just thinking about it.'

'Washed down by a couple of pints – none of the tiny half-measures you get here,' said Will.

'With a massive bowl of sticky toffee pudding to round it off,' said Simon.

'Pie and mash,' said Dougie wistfully, 'and pork pies – you can't get them here. Well, there is *paté en croute* but it's not the same.'

'Listen to you all!' said Beth. 'Going on about what you miss in the old country. You sound like a sad crew of expats of the very kind we were determined not to be! We are on a great escape and don't you forget it. One thing I really don't miss from home is people whingeing on all the time, worrying about the future of the country.'

'True, it's a relief not being assailed by the news every day,' said Dougie.

'I think you'll find people do whinge and worry here, too,' said Nicola. 'It's just that that we don't notice because we're in our little bubble.'

'What are you looking for, Leo?' asked Fizz, noticing he had turned around in his chair.

Leo turned back and showed her the image of a glowering young man on his phone's dating app.

'What do you think? He must be in here somewhere to be that close. Maybe he's inside.'

His phone was passed round the table so they could all appraise the photo.

'No, he's not for you,' said Simon. 'He looks bad-tempered. You deserve much better. And anyway, we can't abandon you here. You might find yourself imprisoned by a lunatic in a fisherman's cottage. We have a duty of care.'

'Thank you for caring,' said Leo. 'And anyway, I don't like his teeth.'

They paid the bill, supervised by Dougie with his calculator, and decided it was too soon to go home, so moved on to a bar of immense charm where they ordered carafes of rosé in anticipation of the summer ahead. Fizz and Will went back to Quentin's studio to discuss a commission for her portrait, and he joined them for *un verre*, which turned into several *verres* as they celebrated their new friendship.

'He's an all right bloke, actually,' said Simon in the end. 'Even something of a role model, I thought. Developing his creativity at a later stage of life, rather like me.'

It was getting dark by the time they rejoined their cars and began the drive home with Fizz, Nicola and Beth as the sober designated drivers. The brightly lit streets of the town gave way to broad roads, then narrow country lanes, until they drew in through the gates of the château. After the bustle of the seaside, the silent darkness of the château was striking, almost intimidating. Nicola went round switching on the lights and suggested a game of charades before they all turned in, wanting to prolong the jollity of the outing.

'Cup of herbal tea and parlour games, that's what we need,' she said.

'Forget the herbal tea,' said Beth, 'I'm pouring myself a large glass of wine after my evening of abstinence.'

'Not me,' said Fizz. 'I'm off to bed.' She turned to whisper in Will's ear, 'Don't be too long.' She gave him a playful kiss and waved good night to the others.

*Just one game*, thought Will, *and then I'll join her*. He didn't want to risk her being asleep by the time he went up.

Nicola put the kettle on while the others settled into teams and started to scribble down ideas, using the tin of pencils and scrap paper that were kept in a sideboard alongside other essentials for a middle-aged toy cupboard: packs of cards, Scrabble, chess, and other, shoutier games like Articulate and Linkee, which usually resulted in someone storming off in a huff.

Beth opened two bottles of red and distributed glasses among the more committed drinkers of the group: Simon, Dominic and Leo, who were on a roll by now and claimed they needed more than herbal tea to enhance their charade performances.

Mary went first, unfolding the title of *Fifty Shades of Grey*, which she knew to be a book and a film, though of course she hadn't read, let alone watched it. She flashed up both hands five times, hoping that once they got as far as fifty, they'd guess the rest and save her the indignity of acting out scenes of sexual submission.

'Fingers!'

'Help!'

'Gesticulate!'

'*Edward Scissorhands!*'

Mary shook her head. *How slow could they be?*

The game was interrupted by a piercing scream from upstairs.

'Eugh, yuck, that's disgusting!'

Fizz came rushing downstairs in her nightgown, whose transparent properties were not lost on any of them.

'I just flushed the loo and it's spilling out all over the floor. It's still churning out horrible sewage everywhere, it's creeping down the landing . . .'

'All hands to the pump!' said Dominic. 'Thank God for all those buckets!'

He led the assault on the back kitchen, seizing the mop and leading the charge up the staircase. Mary sat down, ashen-faced.

'Do you mind if I opt out of this?' she said. 'I clean because I never want to face something like this!'

'I'll stay with you,' said Fizz. 'There's no way I'm going up there until it's sorted.'

'Yes, of course,' said Beth, 'it doesn't need all of us. Leave it to those of us who've had kids. Once you've done dirty nappies, something kicks in which makes you immune to disgust.'

'On that basis, I'll exclude myself,' said Dougie, relieved to have an excuse.

'It's vomit that I can't stomach,' said Nicola, pulling on a pair of rubber gloves. 'I always left that to Dom. Everything else is manageable.'

She and Beth set off up the stairs to join the mopping-up operation.

'I suppose we're the sensitive ones,' said Leo, who had also remained in his seat. 'Our child-free status has made us unfit for dirty business, which is rather a blessing.'

'It's not a status we all chose,' said Mary.

Dougie moved towards her and put an arm round her shoulder.

'No, we didn't,' he said gently.

'Could you not have them?' asked Fizz.

Leo flinched at the directness of the question, but Mary didn't seem to mind.

'They never came along,' she said. 'I suppose we could have tried IVF but neither of us felt sufficiently strongly about it. Or rather, we didn't want to get into that painful cycle of raising your hopes, only to have them dashed.'

She remembered the relief on Dougie's face when she told him she didn't want to go through with it. If he had shown just a flicker of doubt or regret, she would have given it a go, of course she would.

'I'm not going to have children,' said Fizz. 'Far too many people in the world as it is.'

'That's a pragmatic response,' said Mary. 'But you're still young enough, you may change your mind. It was only when I reached the end of my fertile years that I started to feel regret. I do still think about what our children might have been like.'

'You'd only be worrying about them,' said Fizz. 'Look at Beth and Nicola – they're always fretting about theirs. Nicola told me the other day that part of the appeal of coming here was to get away from them. She didn't exactly put it like that, but she said she was glad to find herself more removed from their daily lives.'

'It hasn't worked then,' said Leo. 'I heard Nicola on the phone to Maddie the other day, something about the boyfriend's unsatisfactory behaviour. It seems to me that it's enough to have yourself to worry about, never mind feeling responsible for other lives.'

'On a more prosaic level, we have our plumbing to worry about,' said Dougie. 'On which note, I'm going outside to attend to my needs. I hope that by the time we get upstairs it will be safe to retire to our bedrooms.'

'True, it will be all the more bearable in the morning,' said Leo.

Eventually Beth delivered reassuring news from the mopping-up party that the coast was clear and Leo made his way upstairs to his tower room. He climbed into bed, thinking about what a beautiful day they had spent, and picked up *Sense and Sensibility* from his bedside table, for what better way to end it than with a little Jane Austen?

Just as Marianne was being scooped up by the dashing Mr Willoughby, his room was suddenly plunged into darkness.

They'd had floods and effluence, thought Leo – he should have known there would be more to come. He flicked the light switch in vain a couple of times then flopped back on his pillows in the dark. He thought of his bedroom in London. Crisp sheets, carefully positioned low lighting and an en-suite with no danger of flooding. Not for the first time, he wondered what on earth they had done.

# CHAPTER TWELVE

'Thank goodness the sun is shining,' said Nicola the next morning, as she brought a tray of coffee into the bedroom. 'I'm not sure I could have coped with no electricity, outdoor toilet facilities and the pouring rain.'

Dominic sat up in bed to take his cup.

'Have you been out already?'

'Yes, it took me right back to girl guide camp. I only went for one weekend, never again, the latrines were too much. I prefer our setting here – enough space for us all to find our own personal earth closet.'

'I must admit I opened the window to save going downstairs. Reminded me of a French exchange I did when I was thirteen. My *copain* Pierre used to piss out of the window every morning; his mum had a big argument with him about it, said he was turning the tree outside yellow.'

'Gross.'

'So this morning I thought, when in France . . .'

'When in France . . . you might as well turn into a horrible old man who pisses out of his bedroom window. Supposing someone happened to be taking a stroll?'

'Authentic medieval behaviour, true to the origins of our historic dream home.'

'Our dream home with no functioning toilets.'

She climbed in next to him, placing her cup of coffee on the bedside table. 'I thought it was very romantic, going to bed by candlelight. My phone has died now, too, so it's just like the olden days. I'm going to stay here for a bit and read my book before thinking about the septic tank and power failure.' She picked up her book and opened it with a sense of quiet satisfaction. 'Hopefully someone else will have dealt with it all by the time we get up.' The upside of shared ownership was that there was always the option to leave it to the others.

Dominic, too, had enjoyed the romance of guiding Nicola up the stairs by the light of the candle he had taken from the kitchen cupboard. He hadn't shared with her the memory of the last time that had happened. He had been on the point of doing so – 'Do you remember?' he had said, then stopped himself. It wasn't with Nicola, it was in a different house with a different person, and he was glad he had managed to hold himself in check. Just in the nick of time, again.

'Cheeky lie-in, good idea,' said Dominic, extending a hopeful hand in her direction beneath the sheets. 'Every morning is Sunday morning when you're a silver fox in early retirement. And no chance of the morality squad bursting in.'

One of his irritations about living with their adult children was the lack of privacy. You never knew when one of them would come charging in, with no thought about what they might be interrupting. Whereas they wouldn't dream of opening Maddie's or Gus's door for fear of what they would find.

'Maddie's forgiven John, by the way,' said Nicola. 'She texted last night to say she's thinking of moving in with him.'

'That was quick! Never crossed her mind to move out when we were there putting food on the table.'

'I'm pleased for her. It's what we wanted, isn't it, for them to grow up a bit?'

'It's rather sudden.'

'Not really, they've been going out for two years. If you remember, we moved in together after three months and that turned out all right.'

'More than all right.'

He snuggled up to her.

'Nothing would take me back to the UK now. Even with all the hassles, I feel we've found our place. And it finally does feel like our place, now that Madame de Courcy seems to have given up on letting herself in at random moments – maybe we don't need to change the locks after all.'

Nicola got out of bed and walked towards the window.

'I'll never get tired of this view.'

'Talk me through it,' said Dominic. 'Imagine I've lost my sight, fast forward a couple of decades to when I'm old and losing my faculties.'

'OK, so I can see the sun dancing on the surface of our extensive lake, the apple tree blossom falling onto the grass like confetti, the cream-coloured Charolais cows grazing with their calves, the dovecot rising up to remind us of our aristocratic heritage, the chapel calling us to prayer . . . Did I tell you Simon wanted to take it over as his writing retreat?'

'The master of displacement activity.'

'And there's Dougie walking across the field, carrying a spade. We can guess what he's been up to . . . And there is our neighbourly farmer who's just pitched up below our bedroom window – good job he wasn't there in your line of fire ten minutes ago. I'd better go down and see what he wants.'

She pulled on her jeans under Dominic's regretful gaze and went out onto the landing, which still carried the lingering smell of disinfectant, at odds with the grandeur of the staircase with its chandelier. She had the sudden impression of living in an institution. Madame de Courcy had told them the château once served as a rehabilitation centre for wounded soldiers; she could imagine herself as a sainted nurse administering to the lines of men on camp beds who gratefully kissed her shadow as she passed.

There was no sign of life. It was clear that everyone was taking the same approach to the plumbing and electric problems and remaining resolutely in their bedrooms. She slipped into her clogs and went out into the fresh morning air, skirting the wing of the château to the terrace where Jean-Louis was waiting in his trademark blue overalls, cigarette clamped between his lips. In a previous age, when smoking was desirable, he would have made a good subject for a tobacco advertisement, a farmer version of Marlboro man.

'Bonjour Nicolette,' he said. 'I hope I'm not disturbing you, but I was just speaking to your friend who told me about your little problem with the *fosse septique*.'

'It must have been Dougie you spoke to, I think he's the only one up. The rest of us are all trying to avoid it!'

'It can be easily fixed. I want to give you the number of my plumber, he is an honourable man and he will give you a friendly price when you say you know me.'

He took his phone from his overall pocket, a strangely modern accessory to his timeless image of a noble peasant.

'Here it is, do you want to note it down?'

'That's kind,' said Nicola, 'but I haven't got my phone on me, and anyway, it's out of battery. Did Dougie tell you we also had no electricity? Would you mind coming inside so I can write the number down – old school pen and paper!'

He followed her round to the front door and carefully removed his boots.

'I see your scaffolding is going up. It will be a great relief for you to have a new roof.'

'It certainly will,' said Nicola. 'Would you like a coffee? If you've got time, that is.'

'Thank you, that would be most agreeable.'

'It's my first time in this room,' said Jean-Louis, looking up at the ornate mouldings on the ceiling as they walked together through the *grand salon*. 'It is very magnificent.'

'Really? I thought you'd been grazing the land here forever?'

'That is true, but I have never stepped beyond the front door or the kitchen. Madame de Courcy is very *correcte*.'

'And we are very incorrect. I'll show you around if you like. We have thirty-two rooms, all of them fabulous.'

'Yes, I would like that very much. Now, you say you have a problem with your electrics? I can help you with that.'

When they reached the kitchen, he went through to the *arrière-cuisine* and turned his attention to the fuse box.

'You seem to know your way around,' said Nicola, watching him inspect the unit with an expert eye.

'Madame de Courcy would often call me in when she had a power failure, usually after a storm.'

He fiddled with something and the lights miraculously came back on.

'My hero!' said Nicola, and noticed Jean-Louis blushing with the pleased look that men have when they manage to fix something.

'I am sure Madame de Courcy has told you the installation is *non conforme*. You will have to completely rewire the château.'

'Let's not think about that now,' said Nicola. 'We'll get the roof done first, then rob a bank to pay an electrician.'

He looked alarmed, then relaxed into a smile.

'Of course, your famous English humour! *Monty Python*, *j'adore!*'

'Let's have a coffee to celebrate.'

She was aware of him watching her as she screwed together the elements of the coffee maker and placed it on the stove.

'Bialetti,' he said. 'I had an Italian girlfriend who used one. She had them in all sizes, lined up like Russian dolls, just like yours.'

'I love them,' said Nicola. 'We also have cafetières but I prefer these. They remind me of being on holiday; you always find them in Italian villas. What happened to your Italian girlfriend?'

'She went back to Palermo, said she could not tolerate the fog.'

'The fog!'

'You may not have seen it yet but it is a feature of our climate here in Normandy, especially in autumn; a beautiful grey mist that falls over the land like a cloak.'

Nicola liked the sound of the words as he said them: *brume*, *brouillard*, all delivered with that French 'r' that the English could never quite manage to pronounce.

'A bit of fog wouldn't put me off. What brought her to Normandy? Sorry, I'm being nosy, it's none of my business.'

'She came over for her studies and chose this region for the architecture, because she loved the Norman Byzantine buildings of Sicily and wanted to see what the Normans built in their homeland. But she was disappointed by our castles, she said she missed the Arab influence.'

'Ah. It sounds like you maybe weren't very compatible.'

She tried to imagine the connection between this man of the soil and a fog-hating Sicilian lover of Byzantine buildings.

'So now I live alone,' he said sadly. 'It is not *evident* to find somebody in my work; I am solitary much of my time.'

'I'm sure you'll meet somebody,' said Nicola. 'It's only a matter of time.'

'I don't just want somebody. I am very choosy.'

He looked at her appreciatively, as though she might very well be someone he would choose.

Nicola suddenly felt self-conscious and moved away to check the coffee on the stove.

'As you should be,' she said, with her back to him.

'And what about you?' he asked. 'Now that I have told you my story. What brings you to our beautiful land of fog and cider and camembert?'

She picked up the coffee pot and unscrewed the bottom portion, using a tea towel to protect her hand from the heat, then brought it to the table.

'A fresh start for us all,' she said, pouring the coffee into two bowls from the set that Madame de Courcy had left behind. 'We wanted to live together – somewhere big enough so we could all have our own space and at the same time enjoy each other's company, like a non-stop house party, if you like. And when we found this château, we knew it was the place for us.'

'You are brave. For me, I could not live in a house with so many people.'

'I love it, it's like an extended family, without the feelings of family obligation. We have some disagreements, of course, like in any family! But it was a good decision for us and we have no regrets – in spite of the complications. Like having no toilet!'

'My plumber will deal with that. And do you not have any children?'

'Yes, a girl and a boy. They're still in the UK. It gives them proper independence, being free of their parents.'

'Are they in boarding school? *En pension?*'

That always made her laugh, the French for boarding school, making children sound like little old retirees.

'Oh God, no, they're in their twenties now! We are the ones *en pension* – in the other sense of the word.'

'I cannot believe you have children in their twenties! You don't look old enough! And certainly not old enough to be *en retraite.*'

She couldn't believe it herself sometimes; in her head she still felt about thirty-five.

'Thank you for the compliment, but I should point out I took early retirement. I was a doctor.'

'*Un médecin!*'

She felt his admiration move up a notch. It didn't matter where you were, who you were with, everybody was impressed when you told them you were a doctor. Quite different in Flaubert's day – Fizz had inspired her to read it again – when Madame Bovary's poor chump of a doctor husband was perceived as a plodding nobody.

'Yes, so you know where to come in a medical emergency. Although I'm really looking forward to doing something different. I want to get my vegetable garden going – there's less to go wrong with a carrot than a person, and it's ultimately more rewarding.'

'True, it is the same with my cattle. It is always a small pain for me when I take them to the market, to know I have raised them just to send them to . . .'

He demonstrated a knife across his throat.

'But with my fruit and vegetables, there is no killing. It is peaceful.'

'Yes, it's very hippie. *Soixante-huitard.*'

'You know you sound exactly like Jane Birkin. Especially when you say that word. You know her song, "*Soixante-neuf, année erotique*"?'

'Hello, hello, what's going on here? All this dirty talk of Jane Birkin and her erotic year!'

Simon strode into the kitchen and nodded at Jean-Louis. Nicola scowled at him, annoyed that he had interrupted their conversation with his obnoxious remark.

'Any of that coffee going? Getting my courage up to go out there and dig my own cesspit.'

He illustrated his remark for Jean-Louis's benefit by putting his foot on an imaginary shovel.

'Yes, I heard about your *petit problème*, which is why I proposed to Nicolette that she call my plumber. Here.'

He passed his phone to Nicola, who jotted down the number. 'Monsieur Robinet!' she said delightedly. 'Mr Tap, the plumber – talk about nominative determinism.'

Jean-Louis said his goodbyes, shaking them both by the hand and leaving them together in the kitchen.

'Beth was right, he's certainly got the hots for you!' said Simon, with a probing smile.

'Oh, shut up,' said Nicola, cross with herself for blushing. 'He came in to pass on his plumber's number, that's all. I'll ring him right away. At least one of us is doing something about our massive stinky problem.'

Monsieur Robinet was as good as his name suggested, turning up in his van right away and taking care of the blockage.

'It is a problem of feminine hygiene products,' he explained to Nicola as he climbed back into his van. 'You must never place in your *cuvette* anything that is not lavatory paper, which assures you on the packaging that it is fit for the *fosse septique*.'

He waggled his forefinger at her in that condescending way that certain men seem to have been born with, particularly in France, she'd noticed. She forgave him, though – he wasn't to know that she was well past the age of feminine hygiene products, as were all the ladies of the house apart from Fizz. It was one of the few perks of their advancing years.

'Good news, everyone,' she announced to the reading party who were assembled in the library, buried in their books to insulate themselves from the unwelcome upset in the sanitation.

'Well, that's a relief,' said Beth, after hearing Nicola's explanation. 'Ah, *bonjour*, Madame de Courcy!'

Nicola turned round to find the old lady standing behind her.

'I just saw Jean-Louis on his way out,' she said by way of explanation. 'He told me about your difficulties, and I wanted to make sure everything is now functioning for you?'

'Yes, thank you,' Nicola replied, trying not to sound too impatient. 'It all seems OK for the time being.'

'But soon you must replace the septic tank – you know it is *non conforme*, and so are the electrics! You will be *mise en demeure*, blacklisted by the authorities, if you do not address these issues without delay!'

*For God's sake*, thought Nicola.

'Yes, Madame de Courcy,' she said, 'we are well aware that we are non-conformist. It's just a shame that we didn't find out before we signed the sales agreement!'

Madame de Courcy gave a charming little smile.

'But your *notaire* will have been informed! I think it is the case that none are so blind as those who will not see, and you wanted only to see the beauty of the château, and none of his faults!'

'I'll show you out,' said Nicola, extending her arm to invite the uninvited guest to go before her.

'Ah, while I am here, I hope you do not mind if I take that clock from the wall?'

She walked behind the chair where Mary was sitting and unhooked the timepiece.

'I thought I would have no place for it in my new home but now I find I do. Also, I am sending over somebody to collect the beehives from the barn. He has the key, you need not concern yourselves.'

*The cheek of the woman.* Nicola had had enough!

'Actually, we do need to concern ourselves,' she said. 'Those beehives were included in the sale, they belong to us now, and so does that clock. And while we're about it, could I ask you to give us back your key to the château? You are very welcome to visit us at any time. All we ask is that you knock at the door, rather than just let yourself in.'

Madame de Courcy looked at her with a new respect, then replaced the clock on the wall and obediently handed over the key. The little English blonde was not quite the pushover she first thought.

# CHAPTER THIRTEEN

'I can't remember the last time I had such an early start,' said Simon, closing his eyes and pushing back the driver's seat into a reclined position. 'The last time I left home before sunrise was back in my wage-slave days, en route to some meaningless meeting. Thank God those days are over; it feels completely unnatural.'

He and Beth were sharing a thermos of coffee at the ferry terminal at Le Havre, waiting for Eva to arrive off the night ferry. The weather had turned and the sky was a glowering grey with dull, relentless rain, which suited the austere architecture of the port, with its industrial refineries and severe 1950s apartment blocks.

'I rather like the concrete chic,' said Beth. 'I'd love to see inside one of the apartments. You know this was declared a World Heritage Site in 2005?'

'It's a bit hipster for me,' said Simon. 'Give me old stones any day.'

'We could leave the car and wait in the café,' Beth suggested.

'Doesn't look very appealing. I'd rather stay here and listen to the *Today* programme.'

They didn't listen much to Radio 4 at the château, but tuned in when they were driving.

'It's strange how quickly we've become acclimatised. All that UK domestic political stuff they cover seems so irrelevant now.'

'Thank the lord. Oh look, here she comes.'

Eva had spotted their car and was walking towards them, pulling a wheelie bag and looking cross underneath her umbrella. She was stylish as usual, in a black belted patent coat and chunky boots. She reminded Beth so much of her younger self.

Beth opened the car door and stepped out to embrace Eva in a warm rush of maternal affection.

'Hello, my darling, it's so lovely to see you. How was the journey?'

'Pretty bloody awful, actually,' said Eva, flopping into the back seat while Beth put her bag in the boot. 'Couldn't sleep at all in the cabin for the noise of the engine. It was like a prison cell – no windows.'

'Good to see you too, sweetheart,' said Simon with a grin.

'Hey, Dad. Sorry to be a grouch.' She leaned forward to give him a kiss. 'I'm here now, that's the main thing. What's with this weather, though? I thought the whole point of moving abroad was to have more sunshine. You should have gone further south.'

'It has been beautiful. Dominic was swimming in the sea the other day. You must have brought the weather with you.'

'You know me, I always carry my own little rain cloud.'

Her face broke into a smile.

'That's my girl,' said Simon. 'I always said your bad temper was just a front for the radiance within.'

'I'm not feeling at all radiant, as it happens,' said Eva. 'Which is why I needed to come over for a break.'

Beth listened to her outpourings of woe on the journey home with a weary feeling of familiarity. She had forgotten how draining it was, especially as there was nothing she could do to fix it. It boiled down to pressure of work and a sporadically unsatisfactory boyfriend. The only advice you could give was quit the course or change the boyfriend, neither of which Eva was prepared to countenance.

'Anyway, how are you guys doing?' asked Eva eventually.

'Great,' said Beth firmly. 'We're having the best time, give or take the odd hiccup. Sorting the house out, planting the garden, hanging around boulangeries, endless dinner parties – it's fab. Apart from the catastrophically damaged roof and the plumbing and electrics conking out, which is going to cost us a small fortune, but we don't talk about that.'

'You're so lucky,' said Eva. 'Although I'm not sure I'd want to live with so many people. Especially when one of them is Dad's ex. Don't you find that a bit weird?'

Beth shuffled in her seat.

'Not at all, it was a lifetime ago, as you know. Nicola's my best friend; it's perfectly natural for us to be together.'

Simon kept his eyes on the road.

'Here we are,' said Beth, as they swept in through the gates. 'Mum and Dad's new gaff. Not too shabby, is it?'

'It's amazing,' said Eva. 'It literally *is* a castle! It's even better than in the photos. You can imagine an entire court living here. Shame about the scaffolding spoiling the view.'

'That's how we see ourselves,' said Simon, 'mini-Versailles. I hate to break it to you but you're in the servants' quarters. I'll show you to your room.'

He picked up her bag and escorted her into the entrance hall.

'Everyone's still in bed, I'm afraid, so there's no welcome party, but you're allowed a glimpse of the grand rooms on your way through. There's the crystal ballroom, where you'll be joining us later for mah-jong and backgammon and other pastimes we early retirees engage in to while away the long afternoons. Beyond that lies the salon, then the dining room – the scene of many competitive dinners. On the other side of the staircase here we have the library, where your diligent father spends fruitful mornings writing his book and where those models of scholarship Dougie and Mary research their esoteric papers.'

'It reminds me of my college,' said Eva, as she followed him up the imposing staircase. 'You can feel the weight of history on your shoulders. Now, show me where I'm sleeping.'

'There's a service staircase at the end of the wing. We could have slipped up via the scullery, but I'm taking you this way for the full effect.'

He enjoyed seeing the place anew through his daughter's eyes. It was the whole point of having a grand home, surely, to see how it inspired and delighted your visitors. Once you were living there yourself, you became accustomed to its delights and barely noticed them.

'Here are the noble bedrooms, where your elders and betters lay their weary old heads,' he said, leading her down the corridor until they reached the door at the end. 'And here are the backstairs.'

The smaller spiral staircase that accessed the top floor was a much humbler affair. Eva could imagine the legions of maids whose footsteps had worn the treads, as they rose each morning to prepare the fires.

'You'll be relieved to know this is one of the few rooms that's not affected by the leaking roof, so you won't be woken by a puddle of water – we wouldn't do that to you, my girl. Here, this is you.'

He opened the door to reveal a simple room with a single iron bed and an old-fashioned washstand with an inset rose-patterned bowl and jug. Eva sat on the bed and swung her feet up, stretching out luxuriously.

'How incredibly quaint. Am I supposed to fill my own water jug with cold water to splash on my plain maid's face?'

'Never plain, you know that.'

She had his own striking dark features, with a touch of Beth's softness around the jaw.

Eva sat up and pulled her bag onto the bed, unloading a stack of medical textbooks.

'I've got all this studying to do while I'm here, so I won't be joining in all your fun and games, I'm afraid.'

'We'll keep you fed and watered; you'll be free to do whatever you need to do. I'm proud of you, Eva, you know that – training to do something properly useful, unlike the rest of us.'

'Apart from Nicola – she had a useful working life.'

'Yes, and it's handy to have a medic around in a houseful of future geriatrics.'

'I look forward to talking to her, actually, now we're in the same field.'

'She'd like that, and she is your godmother after all.'

'I only remembered when I was on the ferry that she used to be your girlfriend. I mean, I've always known, but she could have been my mum. How weird is that?'

'Ah, but you wouldn't be you if she was your mum.'

'True.'

Eva looked at him.

'Are you and Mum all right, now? I couldn't help noticing you were arguing a lot before you moved here.'

He saw the anxiety in her face and couldn't quite meet her gaze.

'Yes, of course we're all right. It took a bit of adjusting, with both of us stopping work and being under each other's feet all day, but that's to be expected. As you'll find out for yourself one day, when you're part of an old married couple like us.'

Old married couple – the term was a killer.

'I just can't imagine that, it's so far from where I am,' said Eva. 'Good, I'm glad you're getting along better – I know lots of couples find it tough when they retire. Suddenly they're stuck with each other all day long. And anyway, I don't want to cope with my parents divorcing – that would be another stressful thing to deal with in my stressful life.' She laughed.

'You millennials and your stress. I do find you all overthink things. Just get on with it, I say.'

'OK, Boomer! It was all right for your generation, you had it much easier – houses you could actually afford, pensions that kick in before the dementia does and you got to have real relationships, not just online ones.'

'Come on, Eva, don't give me that old trope! We're attacked from all sides, we baby boomers! Our parents telling us about "when I was your age", and banging on about the war, and now our own kids telling us we had all the breaks ... We are the put-upon sandwich generation, if you must know, abused from both ends!'

'You're not sandwiches; you and Mum both lost your parents before you had to worry about them. I know you both miss them but you can't deny the nest egg helped set you up. Anyway, if you are sandwiches, you're the tasty filling in the middle with no boring crusts, so either way you win.'

'Still the feisty one, I see!'

'Don't use that word, it's sexist. When did you ever hear a man described as feisty?'

Simon wondered, not for the first time, why she was so angry. She had been given every advantage: a first-class education, even a flat they'd bought for her outright. Everything on a plate. He really didn't get it.

'How's James?' he asked. 'Do the two of your ever find time for a little fun? Or is that off limits these days?'

'Is that "how's James" as in you hope he's on the way out? I know you don't like him.'

'It's not that I don't like him, I'm just not sure how much you like him, if I'm honest.'

'I like him very much, actually. It's just that we're going through a few issues at the moment. Which is why I'm here, partly.'

'Call me old-fashioned, but when you're in love with someone, you don't waste your time working through issues. You rejoice in that person and seize the moment.'

'Like you and Mum, you mean?'

'Well, yes. When we got together, we just decided that was it. When you know, you know, isn't that what they say?'

Although he really wasn't sure at all if he knew anymore.

'Very touching. And on that tender note, I'll ask you to leave me to my studies and my millennial self-absorption.'

She gave him a dazzling smile.

'Thanks for picking me up. I'm happy to be here, you know.'

Simon gave her a bear hug.

'You are great, you know that. I'm here for you, even if I am a terrible old un-woke dinosaur. I'm still your dad.'

'Those roofers are getting on well. I can't tell you how much pleasure it gives me to see them up there on the scaffolding,' said Nicola, looking up at them from the terrace where she and Dom were enjoying a morning coffee.

'Bloody noisy though,' said Dom. 'I can count at least six of them. Let's hope it's over before long. Tell you what, it's a beautiful morning, why don't we use it to move all that junk from the library into the barn, like we talked about.'

'Excellent plan.'

Their unwanted furniture and boxes of files had been stacked in the library since the day they moved in. They agreed there was no place in their grand new home for a knackered old armchair and a threadbare chaise longue, which Nicola had bought for a song in a junk shop with the intention of using her upholstery skills to make them good as new.

The question of what to do with everyone's furniture had been something of a bone of contention. Dominic and Nicola had not brought much with them – most of it was still in their

London house – and the same went for Dougie and Mary, although they did bring their favourite old armchairs. Leo had left pretty much everything behind, and Will and Fizz had brought only a piano and a pink upholstered love seat, which Leo detested.

Beth and Simon, on the other hand, with no bolthole left in London, had arrived with a huge cargo of flashy and cumbersome items, acquired over thirty years of slavish devotion to every furnishing fad. The waterbed they were allowed to keep hidden in their bedroom so it would not offend the eye. The sprawling crimson sofas were permitted for the time being, on the basis that they all needed somewhere to sit while they waited for Leo's design overhaul, but everything else of theirs – garish Indian paintings, a zebra print coffee table, a Wild West built-in bar and a stuffed badger – was stored in the largest barn. Leo had dictated that it could only be brought out for use in their private apartment, if they ever got that far.

However, one great advantage of the château was the opportunity to store all their possessions in the outbuildings. Even those housemates who had travelled light intended to bring more belongings over at some point, and each of them had been allocated a shed or barn. Here they would keep the stuff you would normally get rid of when moving house, or else pay exorbitant rates to pack into a warehouse where it would lie undisturbed until your death, when your children would throw it all away, wondering why you held on to such a load of old tat.

Dominic had earmarked a smaller outbuilding for their own use: a colombage wattle and daub building, with potential for conversion in the unlikely event of them ever needing more space. He and Nicola loaded up the car with the furniture – assisted by one of the roofers, who had gallantly climbed down to give them a hand – and drove it into the field, parking up beside the barn.

'Here we are,' said Dominic, pushing open the door. 'This is better than a rip-off Big Yellow self-storage unit off the M25.'

'Loads of room,' Nicola agreed, looking around at the dark space.

There were no windows, so the only light came through the large open door, which revealed a hayloft containing a few straw bales and what looked like an old mattress.

'You could imagine a horror film scenario here,' said Nicola. 'Someone locked up in chains and tortured by his captors.'

'Don't be gruesome. Let's bring the stuff in.'

'Look at the dovecot, isn't it just beautiful?' said Nicola. 'If there was one single thing that sold this place to me, it was that – I can just picture a flock of white doves flying out of it.'

The tall and gracious dovecot stood at the far end of the field, its circular walls lined with nesting holes for birds, now long departed. Madame de Courcy had explained that it was only the most noble aristocrats who were given the right to construct an independent *colombier* away from the house, in an early form of planning permission. Less esteemed families had to make do with a *pigeonnier* attached to the château, she'd said with a dismissive wave of the hand, as if this were beyond the pale. Nicola was proud of the way she had seen off the former mistress of the château. It was great to meet her occasionally, to share snippets of information like this, but they all felt more comfortable since she'd handed back the key.

Simon had wanted to convert the dovecot into a wine cellar, installing a cooling system and expanding the niches to convenient bottle-sized slots, which could be reached with a long ladder. He was shouted down on the basis that the château already had several underground cellars, with dark and damp conditions ideal for the purpose.

'The mice will probably get to this chair before we do,' said Nicola, as they heaved it out of the car. 'We should wrap it in a tarpaulin to keep them out.'

'Or put it on the bonfire. Do you really think you'll ever get around to it?'

'Of course I will! Think of the long winter nights – I'll need a project.'

'Hmm. Just the history box to go now. Let's do it.'

They trudged back to the car and carried out the battered cardboard box that had sat untouched for years in their attic, containing yellowing papers related to their past. Old bank statements and payslips, medical records, children's school reports, estate agent details of their previous homes – the stuff you hang on to for no good reason except as a sentimental record of your history. Yet somehow Nicola had felt she couldn't leave it behind. More precious were the birthday card from seven-year-old Maddie, with its large, slightly deranged letters declaring: 'Mummy, I love you so much', and a crude pottery vase that Gus had made for them. Best of all were shoeboxes of photographs from the pre-digital age. They couldn't resist looking through them.

'How cute we used to be,' said Nicola, picking out a snap of them in their early twenties posing beside some ruins on holiday in Turkey. She passed it to Dominic.

'I remember that denim skirt,' he said wistfully. 'So short it was barely there and with poppers down the front so you could just whip it off. I'm surprised you weren't arrested.'

He gave her bottom an affectionate squeeze.

'You were lovely then and you're lovely now. There are still a couple of stools in the boot, but don't worry, I can manage them on my own.'

He left her to her nostalgic browsing, studying their evolution through different fashions and haircuts, snapshots of Christmas parties and holidays, Dominic standing on the doorstep of their first house, looking thin and sexy in a pair of jeans. Then she noticed a metal file container hidden at the bottom of the box.

'I don't recognise this. Is it yours?' she shouted to Dominic, who was out of earshot.

She lifted it up. It was surprisingly heavy, like a safe box, and she had the mad hope that it might be stuffed with bank notes or priceless jewellery that would pay for the roof! Instead, when she opened the lid, she found only a collection of old manila envelopes, containing receipts rather than money. Lying on top was an exercise book bound in maroon leather. Curiosity got the better of her and she opened it up, recognising Dominic's spidery writing.

'It's your teenage diary, how hilarious!' she said to Dominic, who had returned, carrying one stool under each arm.

She flicked through the pages, seeing references to bands he had seen, clothes he had bought, and what appeared to be a star system attributed to Saturday night dates.

'Don't look at that, it's private!' said Dominic. He dropped the stools and snatched the metal box from her.

'Calm down, I won't. No risk of you finding my diaries – I burned them years ago. Far too embarrassing.'

Dominic scrabbled around in the box until he found what he was looking for – a small key on a piece of string. He took the diary from Nicola, put it back in the box and locked it, pocketing the key.

'Yours must be really embarrassing,' said Nicola. 'There's no shame in it, you were only a child. What does two stars stand for, by the way? Attributed to Kim, it seems.'

'Kids' stuff,' said Dominic with a guilty smile. 'You must be aware of the lustful ambitions of teenage boys. One star for each key stage.'

'Who was Kim?'

'My first girlfriend. I told you about her.'

'Oh yes, I remember. I once found a letter she sent you – she signed herself off "loadsaluv, Kim" with a heart over the "i".'

'You're so judgemental. Anyway, you shouldn't have been snooping. Just as well I've locked it all away. I can see I'm going to have to hide the key – don't want you sneaking out here and raking through my past.'

'Don't worry, I wouldn't dream of it. It was before you met me, in any case.'

'Exactly. Let's lock up and go back to the house. I'm desperate for a coffee.'

Dominic patted the pocket holding the key and breathed a sigh of relief. Once again, he'd managed to dodge a bullet. He must think of a place to hide it from Nicola, although she didn't seem overly curious. It would be safer to simply dispose of the evidence, just set fire to it, but he didn't want to do that. One day, far in the future when he was a sad old widower, he might want to revisit the contents of the box. It had been foolish – and a betrayal of Nicola and the kids, he knew – but it had been irresistible too. For a while it had made him feel young, but now it just felt like a cliché. One he planned never to repeat.

\*

Up in her servant's bedroom, Eva was bonding with Fizz, sitting side-by-side on the narrow bed, where Fizz was showing her her YouTube channel and the ever-increasing follower count on Instagram.

'That's amazing,' said Eva. 'The château looks incredible and so do you, drifting through the rooms in your beautiful outfits. You make me want to be you, which I guess is the goal, isn't it?'

'Thanks,' said Fizz. 'That's the idea. You need to make people dream of living your life, and I must admit I've made it look pretty dreamy. But I hope I'm also conveying a sense of loneliness and disconnection? That's what I was going for when I chose the name. Can you imagine being the daughter of Madame Bovary, trapped in the deep countryside with old people who don't get you?'

'Really? What's not to like about living in an isolated commune with people old enough to be your parents?'

She raised her eyebrows enquiringly and Fizz laughed.

'They're not quite old enough to be my parents, I have a few years on you.'

'Even so, it must feel quite odd, doesn't it?'

'Not that odd. I mean, I'm playing it up in the vlogs but I've always enjoyed being around older people. I'm married to one, for a start. And I don't find I have that much in common with people my own age, I guess because my life has always been so different since I've been with Will. My friends were all obsessing about their careers and relationships, and I was already settled down at twenty-five.'

'Smart move, if you ask me. You're the one living in a château without having to get a job, and I'm the one swotting away for bloody exams in the maid's room.'

'I don't think I'd be capable of sitting another exam. You quickly lose the habit.'

'What did you study?'

'I should have picked something I loved, like nutrition, or skipped university altogether and gone with my passion. I've always loved yoga, alternative health – you know the kind of thing. But my parents wanted me to go to uni, so I picked History of Art – very Kate Middleton, I know – the classic subject choice for a posh girl waiting to get married! I never really engaged with it, though. I travelled for a while afterwards, then took a job temping in a law office, which is where I met Will. Though I soon realised office work wasn't for me.'

'But Will was? For you, I mean.'

'Yes.'

'And it didn't bother you, breaking up his marriage?'

'Ooh, you're very direct!'

'I'm never afraid to ask; people can always refuse to answer. Feel free to tell me to mind my own business.'

'No, I don't mind. In fact, I didn't break up his marriage because it was already over, in everything but name.'

'They all say that!'

'That was his business, she wasn't my wife. And she was pretty awful from all accounts.'

'What about their son?'

'Sam? We get on reasonably well. He lives in the States now.'

'Do you want children?'

Fizz shook her head.

'Definitely not. I've never wanted them and I'm lucky that Will already has Sam, so he's not bothered. What about you?'

'Maybe one day, when I've run out of more interesting things to do. Not for years and years, though. I'm thinking of taking some time out to do some travelling, once I've got this qualification. Before I get sucked into the treadmill of work – not that you need to worry about that! My boyfriend was thinking of quitting his job to come with me, although we're going through a rough patch at the moment, so we'll have to see.'

'Oh really, do tell me about it. That's something I miss, talking to my friends about their relationships. Everyone here has been married for a million years, so it's not a topic of conversation. Apart from Leo, of course, who is full of gossip and surprises.'

'I love Leo.'

'Everyone loves Leo. He's the star of my next video, I just need to edit it. He's cooking tonight, by the way, so prepare yourself for a visual feast.'

*

Leo was preparing a *navarin d'agneau printanier*, a dish he had chosen partly for the pleasure of being able to walk into the butcher's and ask for a *navarin* for ten people, as though you could conjure up a whole dish simply by requesting the ingredients. It pleased him how precisely you were served in the food shops here. The butcher had put together the exact amount required of middle-neck and shoulder of lamb, then Leo had gone to the greengrocer's next door to select bunches of the tiniest baby turnips with smooth cream and purple skins, and some slender carrots that were almost cartoonish with their frothy green leaves, tied up with straw.

'Take a look at these veg,' he said to Beth, waving the bunches at her. 'So small and exquisite, they seem almost criminally under-aged. I'm doing springtime lamb, to celebrate our beginnings here. The first shoots of spring, hope, Easter, He is Risen, etc. For a starter we're having asparagus with wild garlic leaves and sweet violets, foraged by me in the woods this morning. What do you think?'

Beth admired the plates he had already arranged like works of art: asparagus spears aligned at the same angle in each case, with a border of long green garlic leaves and topped with three small purple violets.

'Masterful,' she said. 'It actually seems a shame to eat it. Are you sure those flowers are edible, though?'

'Yes, I checked, they feature in my book on cooking with flowers. Just you wait until the roses and lavender come in – our dining table's going to look like a florist's counter. The pansies will be ready soon, and Sweet Williams. I'll be incorporating them into my salads.'

'Do you find we think too much about food?' asked Beth. 'Eva has decided we're terribly decadent. She says we should eat to live, not live to eat.'

'What an appalling idea! In that case, we might as well be astronauts sucking dried food out of an aluminium tube. I think we are right to focus on pleasure at our time in life. Why on earth wouldn't you? And why move to France if you're not prepared to take advantage of her exceptional cuisine? Speaking of which, I must scrape these tiny potatoes. Have you ever seen anything smaller? They look like toy marbles.'

'Hey, Leo. Anything I can do to help?'

Eva had wandered into the kitchen and was looking around at the cramped work space.

'It's so small in here compared to the rest of the house!'

'It encourages intimacy,' said Leo. 'It's in here that we exchange our darkest secrets. You can wash these potatoes, if you don't mind.'

'Sure.'

Eva moved to the sink and filled the bowl with water.

Beth was pleased to see Eva showing willing; she couldn't remember the last time she'd volunteered to do anything around the house. Then she recalled her own mother saying that families always behave better when there's at least one person present with no blood connection. On that basis, they were on to a winner.

'Tonight, Eva, we are celebrating spring,' said Leo. 'I may even perform a dance later.'

'Round a maypole, you mean? With ribbons?'

'Certainly not! Can you imagine me wearing a smock and a beard like a Morris Dancer? I was thinking more Stravinsky's "Rite of Spring". I shall be the sacrificial maiden, chosen to dance myself to death.'

'Let's get dinner organised first,' said Beth. 'Perhaps a little *apéro* while we work – what do you think?'

By the time they were seated for dinner, the mood was jubilant.

'I know it's not November,' said Leo, 'and none of us are American, but let's pretend it's Thanksgiving and go around the table saying what we're most grateful for. I'll start by saying I'm grateful for that brand new roof that is being installed on our château by young men of astonishing hotness. And talking of fresh meat, I'd like to say I'm grateful for our first ever guest – in the lovely form of Eva. Just as we were at risk of running out of conversation, we find we are blessed by her arrival, and we hope she is just the first of what will be many visitors.'

'Thank you, Leo,' said Eva. 'It has been pointed out that my generation is defined by what we don't like, rather than what we do like. But I like being here very much and I'm so grateful to you all for taking my parents off my hands.'

'Hear hear!' said Dougie. 'We are grateful to you for letting us have them, and enabling us to embark on this marvellous adventure. I know I have the reputation for being a little on the stingy side . . .'

His confession was met with whoops and cheers.

'So I'm grateful to you all for encouraging me to loosen up my miserly habits . . . and become a reckless spendthrift in my old age! Thank you for forcing me to throw my life savings at the crumbling magnificence that is Château Lafarge!'

Simon stood up. 'Continuing my daughter's theme of knowing what we don't like, I'm thankful to be living in a country where you don't have to join in with everything. I don't want to join Instagram, I don't want to give £2 a month to Save the Hen, I don't want to superglue myself to the gates of Downing Street protesting about the modern world. I just want to write, to be completely selfish and just be left alone – present company excepted, of course!'

'Too negative!' said Beth. 'I'm grateful for having four patisseries in our local town with *millefeuilles* and *religieuses* and *tartes au citron* of such breathtaking quality that they move me to tears.'

'Oh, and one more thing,' said Simon, standing up again. 'I forgot to say I'm also grateful that mad old Madame de Courcy has been forced to abandon her night prowling, all thanks to Nicola and her courageous insistence that she hand back the key!'

Nicola nodded her acknowledgement. At least it wasn't as gushing as the last time Simon had proposed a toast to her.

'I'd like to move away from food and say I'm grateful for the other great French appetite – *l'amour*,' said Will. 'You have to be thankful to live in a country where love is celebrated, free from the shackles of puritanical shame.'

He looked adoringly at Fizz.

'I love their lingerie,' said Fizz. 'I'm grateful to know that I shall never again shop in Marks and Spencer, now I have worn a French bra. Oh, and I'm also thankful for our handsome farmer Jean-Louis for fixing the electrics and sorting out a plumber for the sewage crisis. I'm just hoping the plumber will return soon to create my beautiful bathroom!'

'For me it's the bookshops,' said Mary. 'Picking up a classic Gallimard edition, the plain cream cover decorated with only the title in a red font, is an intellectual's dream – the antidote to dumbing down. Your turn, Dominic!'

'I'm grateful for a second chance,' said Dominic, turning to Nicola. He hauled himself back, just in time. This was not the moment to confess! What was he thinking? 'I mean, for a retirement full of possibilities rather than being on the scrapheap, and that's thanks to you, Nicola.'

Nicola looked around the table, beaming with happiness.

'All right, I'm going to be really uncool now. I'm going to say that I'm incredibly grateful to you all for coming with us on this "journey".'

She made ironic speech mark gestures in the air.

'No . . . !' said Simon. 'You know we don't use that word! Being on a "journey" is a naff British thing; nobody in France talks about being on a voyage, unless they really are – on a boat or something.'

'But most of all,' Nicola continued, 'I'm thankful to be living here in our fairy-tale château with my very own Prince Charming. Dominic, my darling, that's you.'

She kissed him plumply on the lips and everybody cheered (apart from Simon), though the following morning it was generally agreed that it was probably only the drink talking. They would not usually tolerate that level of sentimentality, and normal service soon resumed.

# Part Three
# Summer

# CHAPTER FOURTEEN

'I think this is as good as it gets, don't you agree? I'll give anyone a hundred euros if they can spot a cloud in the sky.'

Beth set down her glass, lay back on the blanket and stared up at the blue sky through her oversized sunglasses. The spring days had lengthened into midsummer and for two weeks the château dwellers had been embracing a heatwave that might have proved troublesome if they'd actually had to do anything. Instead, they had luxuriously succumbed to the weather. Even cooking was too much of a chore, and lunch was invariably – like today – a picnic spread out across the lawn, under the shade of the apple trees. It was so easy to put together a *pique-nique* in France where local ingredients offered themselves up to make a delicious repast involving zero effort: fresh baguettes, a plate of charcuterie, a camembert that ran prettily across the plate, leaves from the vegetable gardens and a bowl of cherries, washed down by a glass of chilled rosé. What more could you possibly want?

'You look like a fly in those sunglasses,' said Simon, reaching across to tap on her lenses.

'Bzzz!' said Beth, rubbing her hands together in an insect-like way to complete the impression.

Bordering the lawn was a lavender hedge, alive with bees and butterflies. Will had been photographing them, identifying each species with a newcomer's zeal, and was preparing to set up the hives that Madame de Courcy had tried to take from their barns.

'Château Lafarge lavender honey,' he said, flopping down beside the others. 'It's bound to be a winner – we'll be selling it throughout the world.'

'All in due course,' said Beth lazily. 'Pour me another glass of wine, would you?'

Will reached across to take the bottle from the ice bucket and filled her glass, refreshing his own while he was about it.

'Go easy on that,' said Dominic, from his place on a neighbouring rug, where he'd been dozing with his head in Nicola's lap. 'Remember we've got cricket practice later.'

They had marked out the pitch, the grass assiduously maintained by Will on his mower, and were determined to make use of it, even though it would prove challenging to establish a single team in these parts, never mind finding some opponents so they could play a match. Dom thought they should invite a team from an English village – plenty of room to put them all up at the château – although in this heat, the idea was enough, there was no need to do anything about it quite yet. Adjacent to the cricket pitch was the croquet court, which Dougie had marked out with mathematical precision after unearthing a vintage set of hoops in the barn. It was his kind of sport, he said, one that did not involve working up a sweat.

'I'm up for a late-afternoon game of croquet, if anyone cares to join me,' he said, brushing the baguette crumbs from his trousers. Even in this blistering heat, he never wore shorts but stuck to his year-round uniform of long-sleeved shirt and pleated trousers; his only concession was to discard the jacket.

'I will,' said Nicola. 'Another hour of siesta and it will be time for some light exercise. I feel incredibly lazy, don't you? Especially when you look up there and see them hard at work.' She waved her hand in the direction of the château.

The builders were making fast progress with the new roof, determined to get it finished before the weather broke and made their task more challenging. Unusually for France, where a two-hour lunch break was considered normal, they had a simple *casse-croute* on the job, powering on noisily until dusk, which was part of the reason the château residents preferred to take their lunch at a safe distance from the work site.

'Oh look, here comes Fizz,' said Leo. 'Silly girl to be running in this heat, she could melt away!'

The others were facing the lake, but Leo was turned the other way, leaning against a tree and making pencil drawings in his sketchbook of the château rising up before him. He was reassured by the speed of the roof work; soon they would be able to move on to the wiring – lighting would be key in the refurbishment of the grand reception rooms. He knew exactly how it should be managed in order to show them to stunning advantage.

Fizz slowed her pace as she drew near, then lifted her leg against Leo's tree to perform the stretches they were all so familiar with by now.

'You put us to shame, Fizz,' said Beth, 'always prancing around like you do. We've saved you some lunch – it's under that muslin cloth, to keep the bees off!'

'I'm OK thanks,' said Fizz, casually pulling her ankle up behind her ear. 'I was just talking to one of the guys up there who asked if we were going to the fireworks tonight. First I've heard about it.'

'Of course!' said Nicola, sitting up and gently pushing Dom's head away. 'It's so easy to lose track of the days, but it's the thirteenth of July today, isn't it? Bastille Day tomorrow, the big *Fête Nationale.*'

'How many bank holidays do they actually have in this socialist paradise?' asked Simon. 'There were four of them in May alone, as I recall; it's a wonder they ever get any work done.'

'Says the man whose life is one everlasting holiday,' Beth retorted.

'After a long and hardworking career, you may recall.'

'It's the perfect season for fireworks,' said Nicola. 'A hot midsummer night is so much better than rainy November for standing around outside. There's also the *Bal des Sapeurs-Pompiers* – that's the fire brigade. We can pay two euros a head to go to the party at the fire station. Shall we?'

'Ooh yes!' said Leo.

'I want to go and vlog it,' said Fizz. 'Mademoiselle Bovary checks out the local talent. Will you come with me, Leo?'

Leo put down his sketchbook and clapped his hands in delight.

'Is the Pope Catholic? Or should that be, are firemen hot? Either way, the answer is yes.'

'I've got another idea, too,' said Fizz, stretching her arms over her head and arching her back. 'It came to me when I was running round the lake and saw you all sitting around having your picnic. Beth, you can help me with this one – I could do with your professional expertise.'

Beth pushed her sunglasses up.

'Oh yes, what for?'

'You know that Manet painting, *Le Déjeuner sur l'herbe*? I saw it in the Musée d'Orsay when I was on the Erasmus year of my course. It shows a naked woman and her scantily dressed friend casually having lunch outdoors on the grass in the company of two fully dressed men. It's so bold – the naked woman is staring right at you! Too scandalous to be shown at the Paris Salon so Manet exhibited it in the Salon des Refusés instead. Well, I was thinking, we could do a brilliant re-enactment of it here! I'll be the nude, Nicola can be the woman in the background, with Dom and Leo in Edwardian dress! Directed by Beth, of course. It would be so cool!'

Beth sat up, suddenly energised.

'I love that painting! I can see it right now: she's sitting by her discarded blue dress, with a basket of bread and fruit tumbling over the ground beside her . . . What's more, we have that trunk of old clothes that I found in the attic – they will be perfect! Let's do it right now!'

Four hours later, they were almost ready for the shoot. The *grand salon* was converted into a dressing room, with Leo and Dominic parading around in frock coats from the chest in the attic, which by happy circumstance fitted them to a tee. Nicola was wearing a gauzy vintage nightdress and sewing a black tassel on to a hat to complete Dom's outfit. Fizz had unpacked a blue dress and straw hat that she had last worn at a friend's wedding, and a basket found hanging from the rafters in the *arrière-cuisine* was deemed a perfect replica of Manet's original.

'The light is perfect now,' said Beth. 'We just need Will to come back with the goods.'

Will had been sent out to buy peaches and a round loaf of bread – and the more challenging task of finding two fake beards in a fancy dress shop.

'Here he comes,' said Leo, looking through the window, 'preceded by the satisfying crunch of wheels on gravel, one of my favourite noises.'

Will came in with a tray of lush peaches, a boule of bread, and a couple of elasticated black beards in cellophane wrapping.

'You won't believe how far I had to go to source those beards,' he said. 'Halfway to Paris! A massive warehouse full of fancy dress; it was a shame I had such a limited brief. Hope they're all right.'

Dom slipped his beard on, along with the tasselled hat.

'You look perfect,' said Fizz.

'Very dashing,' said Will. 'It's just a shame my brutal haircut ruled me out from appearing in this, but I can see why I fail as an Edwardian.'

'I don't like this at all,' said Leo, pulling his on with distaste. 'I've always loathed facial hair. Why are you coming at me with those scissors?'

Beth started snipping at his beard.

'Yours has to be more meagre than Dom's if we want to be authentic.'

'Let's get on with it, shall we?' said Dom. 'I'm sweltering in these clothes.'

They walked down to the spot near the lake where they had picnicked earlier. Beth spread the blue dress out on the grass, placing the hat on top of it and tipping over the basket of peaches and bread.

'You sit there, Dom. Hold the cane and stretch your leg out – that's it! Leo, you go there, facing him, lift your right knee – perfect. Now you, Nicola, get behind them and bend over as if you're looking for something, and hold your dress in with your left hand – great!'

Fizz stood next to Beth, watching the scene.

'And now for you, Mademoiselle Bovary,' said Beth, with a reassuring hand on her shoulder. 'When you're ready.'

Fizz shyly stepped out of her shorts and peeled off her vest.

'God, this is embarrassing,' she said. 'Can you all please look away?'

Everyone obediently averted their gaze as she slipped off her underwear and sat down beside the overspilling basket.

'That's better,' she said, 'now I feel like a professional. Actors are massive tarts, though, aren't they? It's bad enough just sitting in the nude in front of people, let alone having to pretend to have sex with them!'

'Look straight at me, Fizz,' said Beth, from behind her camera. She clicked away, pleased at the tableau she had created, enjoying the buzz of enacting a project.

'OK, it's a wrap!'

Fizz quickly stood up and put her clothes back on. Dominic threw his hat at Nicola and peeled off his beard and jacket in relief.

'Thank goodness that's over. Did you get what you need, Beth?'

Fizz joined Beth to look at the pictures.

'Well done, Beth,' she said, 'these are fantastic. I'm going to use that one, don't you think? I love how you've managed the lighting, so my body is pale against the dark of the landscape and the men's suits – well done!'

'Should I keep my jacket on for the *sapeurs-pompiers*, what do you think?' asked Leo, getting to his feet. 'I'll just freshen up, then it'll be time to go. Fireworks and dancing – what a giddy life we're leading!'

On the *place de la mairie*, Bastille Day fever was in full swing, with enthusiastic dancers of all ages jiving to the music of a live band, while the sounds of a rival party at the fire station could be heard down the street.

'Come on, Leo,' said Fizz, pulling him up from his seat, 'let's go and check out the *sapeurs-pompiers*' ball. See what's going on down there.'

They wandered off, leaving the others at a table on the terrace of the bar where they'd been enjoying a convivial evening, drinking and soaking up the atmosphere of the town. Dougie and Mary had stayed home at the château, as they were leaving in the morning on a visit to Mary's mother and wanted to have an early night.

Will signalled to the waiter to bring another bottle of rosé, now Fizz wasn't there to keep an eye on him. Even at this hour the cobblestones were still warm from the sun beneath Nicola's feet as she slipped off her flip-flops.

'Do you know what the French is for flip-flops?' she shouted in Dom's ear, struggling to be heard above the noise of the band.

He shrugged. '*Les flip-flops?*'

'Wrong. It's *les tongs*.'

'That sounds like it should mean thongs. Those tiny knickers you don't like wearing anymore.'

'No, those are called *les strings*.'

Simon leaned across to butt in.

'Enough of your dirty underwear talk – do either of you want to dance?'

Dom shook his head.

'I like many things about the French but one thing I don't understand is their fondness for dancing *le rock*,' he said. 'There's another Englishism! But we don't talk about dancing the rock, do we? We say rock and roll.'

'I love dancing *le rock*,' said Nicola. 'Simon and I joined the Dancing Le Rock society in our first term, didn't we, Simon?'

'And the rest is history,' said Simon. 'Come on then, let's show them how it's done.'

Nicola took his hand and followed him on to the dance floor, twisting and twirling with practised ease.

'It's like riding a bike,' Simon shouted, 'you never forget.'

He rested his hand on her hip as they moved together, then raised her hand in his to set her free on a dizzying spin. The crowd of dancers around them withdrew a little to give them space, impressed by these newcomers to the floor.

'Let's get more ambitious, shall we?' said Simon, fired up by all the attention. He was twenty-two again, showing off to the crowd as he partnered the liveliest girl at the party.

He took both her hands and she swooped between his legs, then he pulled her back up and threw her into the air.

Dom watched in admiration as Nicola ducked and swerved, light as a feather against Simon's solid frame – though he knew his stuff, too, no doubt about it.

Beth slipped into the seat beside him. 'Quite the couple,' she said, raising an eyebrow.

'Aren't they just,' said Dom. 'I'm more than happy to be the wallflower, aren't you?'

'Totally. I've never enjoyed dancing. Would much rather drink and watch. Cheers!'

She clinked glasses with him.

'Those photos you took earlier are terrific,' said Dom. 'It looks like a real pastiche – like when Picasso did his own versions of Velazquez's *Las meninas*.'

'Praise indeed! I didn't know you were a Picasso scholar. Anyway, it was Fizz's idea, I was merely the facilitator. But I enjoyed it; took me back to my working days.'

'Do you miss it? Working, I mean.'

'Sometimes. But the culture's changed, hasn't it? You have to be so careful what you say.'

Will leaned over and tapped Beth on the arm.

'Look, there's our friendly farmer, strutting his stuff. He's got all the moves!'

'Oh yes!' said Beth. 'His partner's good as well, isn't she? Look, they're going over to say hello.'

She watched as Jean-Louis and his partner, an auburn-haired woman in a fitted Fifties-style dress, crossed the dance floor to shake hands with Simon and Nicola. Simon didn't look over-joyed at the interruption, Beth noticed.

'Hilarious, isn't it, how they always shake hands?' said Dom. 'I thought we Brits were supposed to be the formal ones.'

'Pace too much for you?' asked Will, as Simon and Nicola returned to the table.

'Jean-Louis's a dark horse,' said Simon, wiping the sweat from his face. He sank into his chair and filled his glass to the brim. 'All that chat about how hard it is to meet women when you're toiling in the fields, and he turns up with a corker like that! Hats off to him, I say.'

He raised his glass in tribute, then emptied it in one go.

'A corker?' said Beth irritably. 'Who are you, Bertie Wooster?'

'I'm happy for him,' said Simon, 'and happy for us, too, if I'm honest. I'm not too keen on the way he hangs around you women. He could be seen as something of a threat with his Viking good looks and intense interest in our life at the château.'

'Actually, the woman he's with is his sister,' said Nicola. 'She lives in Toulouse but has come to visit for the *fêtes*. She's really nice. I've invited her in for a coffee tomorrow. Here they come now.'

She watched Jean-Louis introducing his sister Annick to the others and thought how charming he was, so attentive to his sister. He was dressed in a Hawaiian shirt he told her he'd bought for the only holiday he'd ever taken outside France, on a visit to Sicily with his ex-girlfriend. It was interesting to see, he said, but he preferred it here in Normandy.

'Now it is time for the *feux d'artifice*,' Jean-Louis said. 'It is a double celebration this year. The storming of the Bastille and your first year as our neighbours.'

It was well into the small hours when they finally stumbled home. Fizz drove Will back in the sports car but the others were well over the limit, so they all piled into Jean-Louis's Renault, with Nicola and Beth sitting on their husbands' laps. Jean-Louis assured them it was perfectly all right – he would be taking the back roads through the forest where there was no risk of the gendarmes arresting him for overloading his car.

'How many vehicles do you actually own?' Simon asked, as Jean-Louis drew up outside the château gates and they all spilled out in a giggling heap. 'I've seen you driving at least five or six, including the tractor. Do you know that song, "I've Never Seen a Farmer on a Bike?" It makes the point that even if you lot complain about never making any money, you always seem to have a fleet of expensive cars and trucks at your disposal!'

'But I also have a bike,' Jean-Louis replied, with impeccable logic. '*Bonne nuit, tout le monde.* I'm glad your first Bastille Day with us was such a success.'

Leo climbed unsteadily up his spiral staircase, thinking back over the day's events. A high summer picnic beside their very own lake, dressing up in Edwardian costumes, a competitive game of croquet where he narrowly beat Dougie, and then the fun of dancing with the wonderful Fizz at the *sapeurs-pompiers'* party. It was, he thought, the perfect day, and if he had slightly over-indulged on the Bandol, he knew from experience it was not sufficient to bring on a hangover.

He slipped into bed and thought how reassuring it was that even if there was a violent storm tonight, his part of the roof at least was completely sealed, and it wouldn't be long until the entire château was as watertight as it was when it was constructed hundreds of years ago, by men who presumably used wooden scaffolding – or did they have very long ladders . . . ?

He was just dropping off, musing happily about early forms of architectural construction, when his phone beeped. He reached sleepily across to see who it was. Then sat bolt upright.

*Guess who? I'm not sure I even have the right to send this message.*

It was David. After all these months.

Leo put his phone down; he wasn't ready for this.

Then picked it up to read what followed:

*I know you'll find my behaviour inexcusable, and I don't blame you. I needed space and time to think about what I really wanted, and I realise now that I made a huge mistake when I walked out on you. On us. On everything we had. I came by our house to tell you this in person and your tenant told me you'd moved to France? Sounds a bit extreme! Looks like you, too, are having a time of reflection and regrouping. But I'm sure you'll agree that we belong together. Come back, Leo, and let's just carry on where we left off. It's what I want and I'm sure it's what you do, too. Give your tenant notice, and we can be back in our home and forget this hiatus ever happened. Please. I love you. David*

Leo calmly scrolled up and read through the message again. And, in a moment of pure and undiluted happiness, he realised he no longer cared. For months he had been waiting for this – would have given anything to hear from David, for the slightest hope that there might be a chance to go back to how they were. He read the message one last time, then pressed delete. And fell into a long and blissful sleep.

'You'd have loved the firemen's ball, Will,' said Fizz, snuggling into his back in their large, carved bed. 'It was properly flirty, all the women with the firemen, but not in a creepy way, just good old-fashioned fun. Leo adored it, as I knew he would. I was going to post it, but I'll leave it until the morning – don't want to spoil my followers, they've already had our *Le Déjeuner sur l'herbe* today.'

'Put the light out,' said Will sleepily. 'I missed your restraining influence and wish I'd shown more self-control.'

Fizz reached across to turn off the light, and to check her phone before switching it into aeroplane mode – she was very disciplined about her uninterrupted sleep.

'Oh my God, Will!' She thumped him on the shoulder. 'It's gone completely mental, look!'

She passed her phone to him, and he stared blurrily at the screen.

'Very fetching, that photo of you with no clothes on, though I'm not sure about Dom in that fake beard. Pretty colours, too, with all the greenery and the dress and the fruit. What does it mean, all those numbers?'

Fizz was bouncing on the bed in her excitement.

'Come on, Will, don't talk like an old person. I thought you'd learned all about this during your life coach stuff! What it means is: *I've gone viral!*'

# CHAPTER FIFTEEN

'Remind me which feast day it is today?'

Dominic was lying in bed on a hot August morning; even at this early hour the air felt sticky, the covers thrown aside. Nicola had pulled open the shutters and he held his hand over his eyes against the blinding rays of the sun.

'Assumption,' said Nicola. 'When the Virgin Mary ended her earthly life and was assumed into heaven. And we have a party to prepare!'

They had chosen the public holiday to hold their house-warming garden lunch and mark the completion of the new roof. It made no difference to them in their life of leisure but they wanted those who were working to be able to attend. In the three months since they'd arrived, they'd made more new friends than they had in years – there was nothing like being dropped into a new environment for forcing you to make an effort – and wanted to invite them to what they billed as a typical English fete, with fun and games. 'And meat with jam?' one guest had asked, still scarred by the memory of lamb served with redcurrant jelly on his first and last visit to Britain.

'I'm so glad the weather has held,' said Nicola. 'I know we have the space to hold it indoors, but it's much more joyful outside. Get up, we've got work to do – you can't just lie there looking sexy in your boxers, even if you do.'

She went downstairs to find Dougie and Mary had already set the tables in a long line on the terrace, covered with chequered tablecloths on which Leo was arranging jam jars of freshly picked flowers at regular intervals.

'You're such a natural stylist,' said Fizz. 'That could be straight off the set of a French movie.'

'And so could you,' said Leo. 'That dress is perfect for our *fête champêtre*; you can't beat white linen.'

Their mutual appreciation was an ongoing source of amusement that reached its zenith with Leo's solo appearance on Mademoiselle Bovary. After the *Le Déjeuner sur l'herbe* post had boosted her following so dramatically, she decided to focus in on Leo, filming him sitting by the window of the crystal ballroom, reading a copy of *Madame Bovary*, wearing the pale blue and grey lacy outfit she so admired that he'd worn on their trip to the seaside. She then showed him parading through the grand rooms of the château, staring wistfully through the tall French windows over his beautiful country domain. Fizz's commentary, that here at last she had found her bae – a millennial trapped within the (incredibly young-looking) body of a fifty-eight year old – had clearly struck a chord. The post earned her a tsunami of likes. Judging from the comments, it was not only Leo's elegant appearance that they liked, it was his contrast with the other château residents, inadvertently featured in the background, looking very much their age. There had been some ruffled feathers, particularly from Dougie and Mary, about invasion of privacy, but it had blown over. Will was a little put out about her referring to Leo as her bae – surely that should be him? Fizz quickly pointed out that Will had no interest in discussing outfits with her, and anyway, it was only pretend, a bit of fun. Though with 20,000 followers and rising, she was hoping it would soon become something rather more lucrative than a bit of fun.

Will wasn't really complaining. He was happy to see her settling down and getting on so well with everyone – it had worked out far better than he'd hoped in that respect. He was enjoying spending time with his old friend Dominic, who had encouraged him to buy a bike and accompany him on vigorous rides through the lanes, providing quality bonding time as well as the chance to keep his weight down to a level acceptable to Fizz.

'Make way for the chef!'

Simon appeared, pushing a barbecue on wheels that he had unearthed from the pile of their possessions that had been hastily stored in an outbuilding on moving day.

'Can't believe we haven't bothered to get this out earlier, with this marvellous *canicule* going on. I love that word! *Canicule*, dog days of summer, *vague de chaleur* . . . It makes me feel hot and French just saying it.'

He whipped the cover off the barbecue and stared at it as if he'd never seen it before.

'It's been gathering dust in that barn the same way it sat virtually untouched for thirty years in our garage at home. I remember now why I never got it out; it means I have to do all the work.'

'You old Neanderthal,' said Mary. 'Why do you think it's a man's job? Are women too feeble to lift the tongs?'

'It's a primal thing, as you suggest. Dragging the carcass back from the hunt to toss it on the fire.'

'Simon, what are you wearing?'

Leo had looked up from his flower jars and was staring at Simon's Union Jack socks extending up his calves, leaving only his suntanned knees exposed beneath an enormous pair of khaki shorts.

'Do you like them? Thought I'd reflect the nationalistic theme of our lunch. '

'It's a bit Britain First,' said Leo. 'We don't want to give the wrong impression.'

'The locals will love them – they all vote Le Pen round here; madly jealous that we've succeeded in getting a Leave vote. I'm going to urge them to follow our example and take back control. That's a joke, by the way, Mary, you know my true feelings.'

'Did you buy those socks for yourself?' asked Mary.

'Ironic present from a colleague. And actually, I rather like them. Shall we go the whole hog and put an England flag up beside the lake?'

Nicola raised her eyebrows and went to join Beth in the kitchen, where she was mixing chicken pieces in a yoghurt marinade.

'Everything under control?' she asked. 'I'll get going on the salads.'

'I'm rather wishing we'd opted for a cold lunch,' said Beth. 'You can't go wrong with coronation chicken for feeding a crowd and it would have saved Simon from doing his swaggering act over the barbecue. He'll probably incinerate the meat like he did the last time when he managed to scorch the skin while the inside remained so pink it was inedible.'

'That's all right, it will just reinforce the French conviction that Brits can't cook. They'll go home happy. We could put Dom on barbecue duty if you think that's safer.'

'Definitely safer, but Simon won't hear it from me, you'll have to suggest it.'

'We could let him build the fire then encourage him to move aside when it comes to the cooking. He won't mind.'

'Simon never minds anything you suggest,' said Beth. 'Putty in your hands.'

There was an edge to her voice that Nicola hadn't heard in a long time.

'You know that's not true,' she said gently. 'Simon and I are ancient history. I thought we'd got over this?'

'Sorry, just getting a bit ratty with this bucket of raw chicken.'

'That's OK.'

'Although it is true that since we've moved here, he can't keep his eyes off you. Don't tell me you haven't noticed?'

Nicola had noticed, but she didn't think it helpful to say so.

'Nonsense, you two are solid as a rock. As are Dom and I. It's only fun and banter, you know what Simon's like.'

'It's not the fun and banter I'm talking about, it's the way he always makes a point of sitting next to you and looking at you with his stupid cow eyes when you leave the room.'

'Now you're being paranoid.' Nicola took hold of Beth's shoulders. 'Listen to me, there is nothing between us. It's probably just that I remind him of his youth or something. A bit like when you see an ancient photo of the old family pet and it takes you back to childhood.'

'Ha! I like the thought of you as an old dog.'

'Woof.'

'Miaow! Come here, pretty puss, and give me a hug.'

'That's more like it,' said Nicola, wrapping her arms round her. 'Gurlfriends! Now, enough sharing already, I've got kilos of carrots to grate.'

By one o'clock, the preparations were complete and Simon was cracking open a couple of bottles of Côtes de Provence.

'The greatest part of my education since moving to France has been an appreciation of rosé wine,' he said. 'Too many memories of overdoing Mateus rosé in the Seventies had left me scarred, but now I can't get enough of the stuff. Perfect for summer quaffing, and there's so much more of it on offer, have you noticed? Loads more shelves devoted to it in the supermarkets than to white wine.'

'It just looks right,' said Will, raising his glass. 'Youthful summer blush, just like my wife.'

He clinked his glass against her tumbler of Perrier. She looked ravishing in her strapless linen dress, exposing her sun-kissed shoulders. He couldn't wait to see her admired by their guests.

Dougie took a sip from his glass, then frowned and picked up the bottle to check the label.

'I thought so! This tastes far better than it should. Why on earth did you splash out on the *cru classé*? The ordinary one is perfectly good enough, especially for a party.'

'Chill, Dougie,' said Simon. 'These are just a little treat to get us started, a reward for the worker hosts. Plenty of plonk chilling for our *invités*, don't you worry.'

'Who do you think will be first?' Mary wondered.

'Looks like our first guest is already here: that draft-dodging hippie from the *brocante*,' said Dominic. 'Chris has form when it comes to filling his boots and he won't want to waste any drinking time.'

They turned to see Chris arriving, a tall dashing figure wearing a patchwork shirt and a pair of jeans that looked exactly the type that people used wear sitting in the bath to ensure a perfect shrink-to-fit.

'Hey guys,' he said, 'don't tell me I'm first!'

Chris's home and business were combined in a massive water-mill situated on the town's outskirts, each storey crammed with treasures, including the armoire that now stood in Nicola and Dominic's bedroom. They hardly needed to buy another one – there were plenty of them included in the sale of the château – but Dom had taken a particular shine to an eighteenth-century painted marriage cabinet; he said they must have it as a symbol of their revitalised marriage since they'd moved to the château. 'Not that it needs revitalising,' he'd said, before kissing her so passionately that Chris didn't know where to look and had to busy himself removing the price tag.

It had taken six strong men to heave the wardrobe up the stairs and since then Chris had become a regular visitor, regaling them with stories of his upbringing in Yellowstone Park in Wyoming where his father was a ranger. Like many Americans, he had travelled to Europe to avoid the draft and then found little reason to return. Dougie said Americans in France were the equivalent of survivors of the British Raj in India, staying on to grow old like the venerable settlers they were. It was an apposite comparison as Chris travelled to India every winter to load up a container with silk lampshades, elaborately engraved chests and painted doors that he sold to fanciful French home-owners looking to import exoticism to their country retreats.

Nicola handed him a glass of wine and he sat down to join them at the table.

'Do you need a hand with that fire?' he asked Simon, who was prodding at the smouldering charcoal.

'Would you mind?' said Simon. 'I had it going beautifully but it seems to be fizzling out.'

'Sure.'

Chris leaped to his feet and took up his place behind the barbecue, stoking it up with immediate results.

'That's a relief,' said Simon. 'Now I can enjoy myself. You're a natural, Chris, I can tell. All those years in the wilderness paying off.'

'I'm comfortable around fire. Seems to me the world is divided into those who can manage a fire and those that can't. I guess it's my natural element. What's yours?'

'I reckon I'm water,' said Simon. 'A fast-running stream.'

'Or a stagnant lake,' said Beth, giving him a filthy look. 'A breeding ground for toads and plankton.'

'I'm aether,' said Leo.

'That's not one of them!' said Nicola.

'Yes it is.' Mary nodded. 'Aristotle added it as a fifth element because he realised the stars could not be made of air, fire, water or earth.'

'I'm glad you have your resident scholar to clear that up,' said Chris. 'Oh good, here come some more guests. I was beginning to feel a little conspicuous.'

Madame de Courcy was approaching them slowly, looking around the garden as she paused to lean on her stick. She was a welcome guest at her former château, now she'd learned to limit her visits. Matching his pace to hers was Jean-Louis, who had discarded his overalls in favour of a pair of chinos and a sky-blue open-neck shirt.

'Your fancy man's looking good,' Beth said to Nicola. 'Didn't recognise him at first.'

'Ooh yes,' said Simon, 'he'll be singing sexy Jane Birkin duets with her in no time.'

'Shut up, you two,' said Nicola crossly. 'Take no notice of them, Chris, they're like a couple of kids.'

'That's the guy who grazes your land, right?' asked Chris. 'He came into the shop once with his girlfriend to buy a silver tea-pot. She was a cutie. Italian.'

'She's gone back to Italy now,' said Nicola.

'Leaving the coast clear,' said Simon mischievously. Jean-Louis was looking a little too handsome for his taste. He resented the way he was obviously so infatuated with Nicola. He needed to get to the back of the queue.

'And look, here come the kiddies!' said Leo, as a handful of blond children came into view, running towards the lake and chasing each other with whoops of delights. Their parents made their way, smiling, towards their hosts. Bernard was a carpenter, who designed and made finely crafted furniture that was displayed in his show rooms on the high street, its clean, modern lines contrasting with the ancient medieval beams above his shop window. Virginie was a whirlwind of energy. When she wasn't rushing up to Paris to work on fashion shoots, she was harvesting honey and making jam to fill artfully designed jars that were lined up for sale in Bernard's window. Leo couldn't get enough of them.

The usual double cheek-kissing ensued round the table – it was optional among Brits but compulsory with the French; nobody could sit down and relax until everyone present had been embraced. Dougie, in particular, found this an unnecessary and exhausting procedure, and he sat down with relief once it was over.

'We're so glad you could make it,' said Nicola to Virginie. 'And how delightful to have your children bringing the place to life. We've planned some games for after lunch that we hope they'll enjoy.'

Leo was deep in conversation with Madame de Courcy. She had developed a special relationship with him since discovering that he, like her, came from an old and distinguished family. 'As if they're the only ones with ancestors,' Beth whispered angrily to Nicola. 'Where do they think the rest of us sprang from? We all come from an "old" family, it's just that some of us don't have a family seat and noble heritage to boast about. Off with their heads, I say.'

'We own her family seat now,' said Nicola, 'and she's reduced to her humble *pavillon* down the road, so let her wallow in the past if it makes her happy. Leo's always pleased to find someone to discuss his family tree, so let them be.'

'Shoot me if I ever say I'm going to research my family tree,' said Beth. 'That's one middle-aged hobby I'll never get into.'

'You say that because you fear you're descended from a long line of housemaids, same as me. You'd change your tune if you thought you might be sprung from royalty.'

The rest of the guests arrived, a disparate crowd of friends they had made through the practical business of renovating the château – 'Aubergine hair!' Fizz said delightedly at the sight of Monsieur Robinet's wife – and others who had found them through various connections. A former colleague of Dougie's, who was at the Sorbonne and had a house nearby, turned up with his poet partner, Perpetua. And a couple of Parisian lawyers, who owned a neighbouring manor house and had made a point of befriending the new chatelains, insisting on talking to them in their bad English.

'I'm loving the mix of intellos and artisans,' said Simon. 'Can't wait to see how they deal with the egg and spoon race.'

The lunch was deemed a triumph, and once the plum clafoutis had been dispatched, Dominic stood up and banged his spoon on the table.

'I'd like to thank you all for coming today and for generally making us feel so welcome. There were those who thought we were mad to leave our homes to settle in a foreign land where we knew nobody. But we have proved them wrong and you have proved them wrong. We've had our challenges with the fabric of the château – though I'm sure you'll agree the new roof is a great improvement! – but we couldn't have asked for a better environment, nor for better neighbours. We lived in London for thirty years, where we barely got beyond nodding terms with the people who lived next door. Yet here we are, in this magical setting, in our home that we love, and in a community that we are proud to call our own. So, before I get too weepy, and before we move on to the after-lunch entertainment, I'd like to propose a toast. To our friends and neighbours, and to many more years of happiness together.'

'I thought you were going to start blubbing there,' said Nicola as he sat down following the warm reception of his words and mass clinking of glasses. 'The British stiff upper lip seems to have gone out the window.'

'Not sure it was ever that stiff,' said Dominic. He kissed her on the lips.

'It's worked out so well, hasn't it? I honestly couldn't be happier. Thank you, my darling.'

'Whoa, that's enough of that!' said Simon, getting to his feet at the other end of the table. 'Time to put an end to the cheesy stuff and get down to the important business. Some of you may have spotted a heap of sacks over there beside the lake. When I blow my whistle . . .' He produced it from his pocket and gave a demonstration. 'I want you all to run down there and climb into a sack. You must then run all the way round the lake as quickly as you can. When you get back to the starting point, you must climb out of the sack and pick up a spoon, like this, and an egg – from our own chickens, naturally – which you must balance on it, then do another circuit. Anyone whose egg smashes is disqualified. Are we clear?'

'Crazy English!' said the Parisian lawyer, clapping her hands in delight. 'We love your sense of humour. It's very Benny Hill!'

'Never mind Benny Hill, this is the fundament of our education system. We are who we are because at school we developed our moral fibre by taking part in the egg and spoon and sack race. They didn't teach you that at your *lycées*, did they? Now, let the games commence!'

He gave a flamboyant blow on his whistle and everyone pushed back their chairs and went racing down to the water.

'Competitive, I like it!' Simon shouted, following them down at a leisurely pace. The best thing about being the organiser was not having to take part. He watched the children leading the way, but Chris the draft dodger soon pushed into the lead, closely followed by Dominic, who was no slouch, with all that manic cycling he went in for. The children were less successful in the egg and spoon race, insufficiently coordinated to keep the eggs well balanced, whereas Nicola was steaming ahead. He watched her and compared her ungallantly with Beth, some distance behind. It was unacceptable to make comparisons, he knew it was wrong, but he couldn't help seeing what he saw and feeling what he felt.

The eventual winner was Chris, who was awarded a thirty-year-old trophy that Simon had found in one of his boxes in the barn, a legacy from his sportier days when he was quite a fast runner, impossible though that now seemed.

Then it was back to the tables for further refreshments and sedentary entertainments. Dougie's friend from the Sorbonne encouraged his partner to recite one of her poems, though its dark and existential tone was a bit of a dampener, then Dougie brought out his version of a pub quiz – far too highbrow – producing puzzled blank stares from the participating adults, while the children wisely returned to the lake, where they stripped off to take a dip until they were finally rounded up by Virginie, who decided it was time to go home.

'Please, do not let me break up the party,' she said. 'The rest of you must stay!' But the other guests all followed her lead, amid effusive thanks for the afternoon.

'Well, that was a riot,' said Beth, slumping down in a chair. 'Shall we have a party every week? They loved it!'

'I'm not sure my quiz was correctly pitched,' said Dougie. 'Next time I'll go for something more accessible – the songs of Johnny Hallyday, perhaps, or the A-roads of Calvados.'

'Well, it's nice to have company, but it's nice when they leave,' said Mary. 'I'm going to clean up the kitchen, then we can all sit back and relax.'

'Did we really get through all that bread?' asked Simon. 'I'm just thinking I could manage a light supper but they've cleaned us out, the little French *cochons*.'

'Can't believe you're hungry; I couldn't eat a thing after that,' said Mary.

'There's less of you to nourish, my dear,' said Simon, slapping his belly. 'This beast takes some filling.'

'I don't mind going out for some bread,' said Dominic.

'You're not driving,' said Nicola, 'not after all that rosé.'

'I'll go on my bike,' said Dominic. 'That's the great thing about cycling: you never get breathalysed. There should be at least one boulangerie open – the French don't allow the small matter of a bank holiday to come between them and their need for fresh bread. Want to come with me, Will?'

'No thanks,' said Will, 'I've had my daily exercise. I'd forgotten how tiring it is to shuffle along in a sack.'

Nicola watched Dominic walk briskly up to the house. It was a joy to see how energised he was, now that he was free of his office stress. It had been such a good idea to make this life change while they were young enough to enjoy it.

'Buy a brioche, if they have one,' she shouted after him. 'We can have it for breakfast.'

He turned to blow her a kiss.

'Will do, Marie-Antoinette!'

'Why's he calling you Marie-Antoinette?' asked Fizz. She had moved her chair into the sun, to avoid the lengthening shadows cast by the château.

'It's a reference to her famous words when she learned the peasants had no bread,' Nicola explained. 'When she said, "Let them eat cake," she really said, "Let them eat brioche", but that didn't translate into English.'

'Mmm, toasted brioche with apricot jam,' said Simon. 'Another reason to love the French.'

They cleared the tables at an easy pace, gossiping about the departed guests.

'I'm not a fan of children, as you know,' said Fizz. 'But I thought Virginie's were delightful. Did you notice how well behaved they were, sitting up at the table and eating their lunch properly? Not like British kids, who would have been wandering off and complaining about what they wouldn't eat.'

'That's how French children are,' said Beth. 'They are born with an innate respect for the table. You know they even teach them about food in nursery school? There's a compulsory *semaine du goût* when they blindfold the kids and make them identify the four flavours.'

'That sounds cruel,' said Leo.

'Only four?' said Fizz.

'Four principal flavours,' said Beth. 'Sweet, salty, acid and bitter.'

'I get the first three,' said Fizz, 'but what do they count as bitter?'

'I don't know. Coffee, maybe. Or chicory.'

'Four-year-olds drinking coffee?'

'I don't know the details, but you get the principle. Food is a serious subject that features on the educational curriculum.'

'Marvellous,' said Leo. 'It's also on our own curriculum for personal growth. Part of our ongoing adult education in the Château Lafarge school of culinary arts. My next goal is to master the perfect soufflé.'

'Good to see Dicky again,' said Dougie. 'He's suggested we visit them in Paris. We should go, Mary; it's only two hours on the train.'

Mary had her rubber gloves on and was wiping down the tables. She'd already stripped away the tablecloths and put them in the wash, but you needed to be thorough.

'I would like that,' she said. 'I thought Perpetua was charming and a very talented poet. She'd have to be a poet, wouldn't she, with a name like that? We should wait until it's cooled down, though; I don't fancy Paris in this heat.'

'Paris in August? *Absolument pas!*' said Dougie. 'How can you even think such a thing.'

'I'm going to see if the quails have laid any eggs,' said Nicola. 'There's something I never imagined myself saying a year ago. How much my life has changed, to think that collecting eggs has become my daily chore! Along with tending my roquette and mâche. I'll pick some leaves for a salad – a dainty supper to test our palate.'

'That's why it's stupid to say there are only four flavours,' said Fizz. 'What are eggs, for instance? They're none of those things.'

'Rocket leaves could count as bitter, I suppose,' said Nicola.

'I'll come with you,' said Beth.

*

The quails were housed in a miniature Norman-style colombage shed that Will had taken great delight in building, reviving his carpentry skills last tested at school and making the roof from slates he had reclaimed among those that had originally covered the château. Encouraged by his success, he was now planning a larger project, a studio for Fizz to eventually set up a health and beauty treatment centre. Nicola found a dozen eggs in the pen, which she placed carefully in her basket.

'Do you remember taking the kids to see *Chicken Run* at the cinema?' said Beth as Nicola closed the gate. 'Who'd have thought we'd one day have our own real-life version. Eva's planning another visit, did I tell you? She's taking a break from her tiresome boyfriend, which gives me hope.'

'How lovely. Maybe she could come at the same time as Maddie and Gus – plenty of space in the attic rooms and it would be fun for them to travel together. I do miss them, don't you? They drove me mad when we were all under one roof, but now it will be a real treat to see them.'

They wandered down to the walled garden, happily discussing plans for when the children came over. A trip to the coast, naturally; maybe they'd go over to Mont St Michel and breathe in the atmosphere of the island monastery.

The vegetable plot was lush with produce: runner beans hanging from their cane wigwams, comedy-size courgettes developing at such a pace it was hard to keep up with them, bright red tomatoes that smelled the way they never do in shops and *haricots beurre*, aptly named for their golden butter colour.

'Another bean salad, I guess,' said Beth. 'And some lamb's lettuce with chervil.'

'Death by beans. It's one glut after another, and let's not talk about the plums.'

They had been overwhelmed by the crop of *Quetsches d'Alsace*, small fruit that were falling all around them onto the grass, forming a purple carpet buzzing with bees gorging on their flesh. Nicola had made vats of jam, chutney and hoisin sauce, and the freezer was already packed with tarts, anticipating the winter evenings when they might be welcomed as the warm taste of summer, rather than greeted with groans complaining about plums again.

They walked back to the terrace with their laden baskets to find Fizz stretched out on a sun lounger with her phone, while Will was working on his design for her studio. The extra tables had been packed away and order restored.

'And then there were nine!' called Simon from the far end of the terrace. 'Far more manageable. I might as well set the table for whatever vegan delights you have unearthed for us. I'm guessing it involves plums.'

'And cunning ways with beans,' said Beth, 'just for you.'

'Glad to say there's still a good chunk of that wheel of brie left to help it down. Your husband's taking his time, Nicola. No sign of him or the bread.'

'I expect he's taken the long way round,' said Nicola. 'You know how he likes his exercise. Where are the others?'

'Mary's cleaning, obvs, and Leo and Doug have gone indoors to cool down. That's the miracle of old stone walls – keeping the heat out in summer, and holding it in for the winter.'

By the time they'd set out the cheese and salads, there was still no sign of Dominic.

'Straight to voicemail,' said Simon, putting his phone down.

'He may not have taken his phone,' said Nicola. 'I'll check if he left it upstairs.'

It was getting dark and she switched on the lights before making her way up the staircase and into their bedroom. Dom's phone was on his bedside table, showing two missed calls from Simon. She tried to shake off her uneasy feeling as she went down again and out on to the terrace where everyone had now gathered. They looked up at her expectantly as she approached.

'As I thought,' she said. 'He went out without it.'

'There was probably a really long queue at the boulangerie,' said Beth. 'There always is when it's a holiday. He'll be back in no time.'

'I'm sure you're right.'

'Game of cards while we wait?' suggested Dougie, pulling a pack out of his pocket. 'Nothing too challenging, just a quick round of Beggar My Neighbour.'

He dealt the cards and they started playing, pretending not to be listening out for Dominic's return.

'That sounds like a car,' said Will, putting down his cards.

They heard a car door slam and urgent footsteps on the gravel.

Jean-Louis was hurrying towards them. Nicola saw his sky-blue shirt first – he was still in his off-duty clothes, no tractor work for him today. Hopefully he'd have some news. Maybe he'd bumped into Dom and had a message for them as Dom had forgotten his phone, silly man. Her hopes faded as Jean-Louis approached; she could see his face was deadly serious.

*Please don't come near*, she thought. *I don't want to hear what you have come to tell me.*

'I am so sorry,' he said, then faltered.

*Don't say it*, thought Nicola. *This isn't happening.*

But Jean-Louis gathered himself and carried on.

'I was just driving to check on my cows and I saw a bicycle abandoned in the road, so I stopped my car to get out and take a look, and then I saw him lying there by the side of the road. He was so still, there was no movement, no sign of life . . .'

He was looking straight at Nicola with tears in his eyes.

*Stop it*, she thought. *Tell this news to the others. Let it be someone else. It can't be true.*

'I called the paramedics, of course, but I knew there was nothing to be done. I stayed with him until they came. I didn't have your number; I wanted to come and find you but

I thought no, I must stay with him, even though it was obvious to me . . .'

Later, when she thought back to this moment, Nicola could only remember the sky-blue shirt coming towards her, then the darkness closing in before she lost consciousness.

# CHAPTER SIXTEEN

'Here you are – drink this,' said Beth, sitting down next to Nicola and handing her a cup of tea. 'I know you don't want to, but you must.'

Nicola sat bolt upright on the sofa, holding Dominic's bike helmet, from which she refused to be parted. Through the blur of the hospital, the formalities, the terrible, terrible phone calls to her children, she had kept it beside her, as if it could somehow bring him back.

'He always wore it, he was such a stickler, he used to be furious with me for cycling off without one. I can smell him, Beth.'

She buried her face in the helmet, inhaling the musty smell of him, overlaid by the perfume of his shampoo, chosen by her to enhance the silver fox hair he was so proud of.

Beth put her arms around her friend – there was nothing she could do to take away the pain. It was twenty-four hours since Nicola's life had fallen apart and she hadn't moved from the sofa since getting back from the hospital. They had all taken it in turns to sit with her.

'Will has gone to pick up Gus and Maddie from the station,' she said gently.

'I should have gone with him.'

'It's better to meet them here. More private.'

'I've done a crap job of taking care of their father. It wouldn't have happened in London, would it? Not even with all that traffic, because he was on his guard, he would never have gone out without his bloody helmet. Instead of which, I let him get slack. Over-relaxed. I let him get too relaxed, Beth – it's my fault.'

Then, for the first time, she cried. Guttural, animal howls of grief.

'It's nobody's fault,' said Beth, stroking her hair. 'It was a freak accident, a pothole in the road.'

'I was so looking forward to showing the children around,' said Nicola through her tears. 'I could imagine their faces, picture them having their first dinner at that table, letting them hold the quails. I was going to send them up the ladder to pick the apples, take them to the seaside. Dom bought them kites, you know. He said, "I realise they're not kids anymore but you're never too old to fly a kite, if ever this heatwave stops and we get some breeze up."'

'I know,' said Beth, 'he was excited about them coming. You both were.'

'And now they're here and he's never going to see them. They're never going to see him again, and neither am I.'

Beth carried on stroking her hair. If only they could turn the clock back, if only they'd toasted some stale bread, if only he'd taken a different route, one without the pothole, if only they hadn't had that last bottle of rosé with lunch. 'If only': the nagging pain following every bereavement.

'That sounds like them now,' she said.

Maddie came in first, her heart-shaped face pinched beneath her blonde fringe. Beth was struck by her resemblance to her mother; it could be Nicola in the student union, anxiously waiting to take an exam. Gus followed her in, boyish in his T-shirt and jeans.

*They're too young to deal with this*, thought Beth.

Nicola opened her arms to her children and Beth quietly slipped away. They needed the space to be together, to grieve and to come to terms with their unfathomable loss.

# Part Four

## Autumn

# CHAPTER SEVENTEEN

'Season of mists and mellow fruitfulness,' boomed Simon. 'What do we have this evening, oh great market gardener?'

'As usual, whatever we didn't manage to sell off the stall,' said Nicola.

'Jerusalem artichokes,' said Beth, 'which I have combined with Chaource cheese to make the most marvellous soup, though I say it myself.'

'Aren't they terribly windy?' asked Leo. 'My father would never touch them; he said they were all you could get during the war and everyone suffered the most terrible side effects.'

'I doubt he tried them this way,' said Beth. 'I don't think there was much Chaource lying around in the Blitz.'

It was mid-October. Following the shocking end to the summer, they had all struggled to come to terms with how their idyll had been shattered. But life at the château was gradually settling into a reassuring routine. There were still balmy, bright days, but their lives focussed more indoors, closing the heavy velvet curtains against the dark nights, nurturing Nicola through her loss. She was grateful for their gentle administrations, helping her to get through the days, always on hand to offer comfort and support.

The funeral had been held in England because Nicola wanted her children to say goodbye to their father in the land where they grew up with him. She chose a woodland site on the outskirts of London: a light, natural building where the sun poured in through coloured windows and birdsong could be heard between the readings. Mourners stood in line to offer their condolences: family, friends, colleagues, people she hadn't seen in years, whose names she barely remembered but whose faces were full of pity.

After the funeral, her housemates returned to the château, but Nicola stayed on to be with her children. She slept in Maddie's old room, and when Dom's ashes were returned from the crematorium, she kept them on the chest, above the drawers where once she used to fold away her daughter's freshly laundered clothes. She'd wake up every morning, remember he wasn't there, and glance over to see him where she'd left him. There was some comfort in it.

For two weeks, she lived in a haze of indecision. Their new life at the château was a shared dream, one she and Dom had built together, and one that had just died. She should move back to London, to be near her children, now they only had each other. But as the immediate drama of tragedy faded into the day-to-day, she found she had little purpose in the city she once called home. Gus and Maddie had their own lives, which carried on – as she hoped they would – and she felt that her presence as sole surviving parent only served to remind them of what they had lost. Gus seemed relieved when she announced she was returning to France. She was an incongruous flatmate in her former home and while his young lodgers had been charming and solicitous, she knew it was time to go. Maddie had been more upset and urged her to come back soon. Nicola promised she would visit often – it was such a short distance – and Maddie should come over, with John this time, in happier circumstances.

On the ferry, she had stood on the deck so the wind blew through her hair, carrying away the worst of the hurt and encouraging her to start again. Beth and Leo were waiting for her at the port. They drove her along the familiar route and as she walked through the doors of the château to find the rest of her friends so warmly welcoming her, she knew she had come home. Mary had baked her a cake, a fallen Victoria sponge.

'I know I'm not a cook,' she said, 'but I just wanted to express how relieved we are that you're with us again.'

That made Nicola cry. 'I almost didn't come back,' she said, 'but I'm so glad I did. This is where I belong.'

Her first task was deciding what to do with Dominic's ashes. On her first night home at the château, the urn was placed on the mantelpiece in the crystal ballroom, where Will proposed a moving toast to his friend. Fizz suggested scattering them on the lake; Leo wanted to commission a life-size statue; Dougie proposed a Victorian-style headstone, engraved with weeping maidens. Nicola eventually settled on the idea of creating a rock garden in his memory, beside her vegetable plot within the high stone walls. That way, she would see him every day when she came to tend her crops. Granite boulders were assembled from around the grounds and Nicola trawled through the websites of specialist nurseries to compile a perfectly harmonious combination of exquisite alpines – African violets, Cape primroses, cyclamens, speedwell and gentians – which she carefully planted to form a perennial tribute to her beloved husband.

True to her practical nature, Nicola realised that keeping busy was the best way to cope, and spent most of her days hard at work in the garden. It was Jean-Louis's idea to develop this passion into a business. He regularly sold his apples at the local market and one day asked Nicola to come along to help him. She loved the bustling atmosphere, the sight of the boxes of *Belle de Boskop* and *Reine de Reinettes* emptying into their customers' baskets.

'You should join me in this market garden project,' Jean-Louis said. 'We can diversify. I have no time to grow vegetables, but you have the green hand – I have seen how your garden has flourished. With my apples and your salads, we can make a very good team.'

'We say green fingers not green hand,' she corrected him, but the idea was appealing.

Before long she was loading up her own crates of onions and lettuce and joining him twice a week at morning markets – one in their own town and the other fifteen kilometres away. She came to recognise their regular customers, who were intrigued to find an English woman manning the stall.

One elderly man with a twinkle in his eye always greeted her the same way, with a chivalrous, borderline lecherous flourish: '*A nous les petites anglaises!*'

'Why does he say that?' she asked Jean-Louis, who explained it was a reference to a film about French schoolboys on an educational trip to Kent that would have been released in her admirer's heyday. She found comfort in these moments of levity, a welcome release from the heavy numbness that was still her default mode.

After dinner – with the remarkably delicious soup – they took tea and games in the salon. The games had become a habit, an hour of companionable interaction before everyone disappeared to their own quarters. Nicola found it soothing to have something to focus on, rather than make conversation, which invariably brought her circling in to her own unhappiness. Tonight they were playing Articulate and Nicola was paired with Leo. She was trying to describe a ferret to him, but he was proving very obtuse.

'Put it down my trousers – whatever for?' he was asking.

'Come on, Leo,' said Will, 'everyone knows this!'

'Well, I don't. Nature is not my strong suit.'

'It's good to hear you laugh again,' said Mary, as they packed away the game. 'I think it works better if you store the cards like this – much tidier.'

Nicola let her rearrange the cards that she had carelessly thrown into the box.

'It's great to have you all here,' she said. 'I know we talked about the advantages of having friends on tap when we bought this place, but I never dreamed I'd have such urgent need of them.'

'You're doing so well,' said Mary. 'I'm going to fit in a couple of hours of study before bed. Have you got a good book to read? Very important in your condition.'

'I'm reading this thing that Fizz gave me, about a woman training a hawk in order to get over the death of her father. Can't say it's something that would cheer me up, but each to his own, I guess.'

'Your garden is your hawk, I suppose.'

'Yes, busyness is next to godliness. Or saves me from myself, or something.'

'Though you don't want to overdo the busyness. Remember Chaucer's "Sergeant of the Law's Tale": *And yet he seemed busier than he was* – a marvellous put-down of the self-important busy-busy culture that still infects us. You need to be kind to yourself, Nicola. Make sure you take plenty of rest.'

'I love my garden, it's so therapeutic. But I think perhaps I'm ready to give up on the goshawk. I'm going to read PG Wodehouse instead. Goodnight, Mary.'

Nicola climbed up the stairs, pleasantly tired after her morning at the market. She'd take it easier tomorrow: get up late, then have a sort through Dom's clothes and see about getting rid of some of them. She opened the door of the armoire they'd bought from Chris, remembering with a smile how he'd fallen in love with it. There were his shirts hanging in a neat line, the donkey jacket he'd cherished for many years, the Norwegian fisherman's sweater ready for the winter he wouldn't see.

It was too late to look at this now. She undressed and slipped into bed. The nights were the worst, everyone said so. The bed was too big without Dom. It was difficult getting to sleep without his warm presence beside her, and the small hours waking were such a cliché, but very vexing. She picked up a book from the pile next to 'her' side of the bed, in the hope that *Carry On, Jeeves* would see her through till morning.

Jean-Louis had told her that October was the best month in Normandy and Nicola could see what he meant when she woke and pulled back the curtains. A soft grey blanket of fog was lying across the valley and above it the sun was breaking through, pale yellow against the milky blue sky.

After giving up on PG Wodehouse, she had remembered Leo's advice and read a little Jane Austen, which had done the trick and she had slept right through. In her peaceful, rested state she could now contemplate the view across the russet-tinged trees with pleasure and gratitude.

Dominic's wardrobe was less intimidating in the sunlight. She pulled out his clothes and laid them out on the bed in a business-like manner. The obvious way to dispose of them would be to take them to a charity shop, but she hadn't seen any since the move to France, although she wasn't sure why; there were plenty of *depots-ventes* where you could buy incomplete sets of crockery and broken pieces of furniture. It must just be clothes that were deemed unworthy of selling on. Dom had been a big fan of charity shops; he often used to joke he was wearing a dead man's suit when he put on one of his second-hand bargains. Now it was someone else's turn to wear the dead man's suits, assuming Nicola could find a charity shop to take them.

She picked up a pair of jeans and started rooting through the pockets, the way she had done so many times when preparing a load of washing. Dom was by no means an unreconstructed patriarch, but she'd always taken care of the washing; he once joked that he wouldn't know how to turn the machine on if anything happened to her.

Tucked deep into a back pocket was a small key. She pulled it out and inspected it, but didn't recognise it. Possibly it belonged to an old bike padlock. Yet the jeans had clearly been worn quite recently and she had already thrown away the bike keys, which had been returned to her in the hospital, in a transparent plastic bag alongside his other personal effects: the trainers, the wallet containing a photo of her, his wedding ring. It occurred to her when they handed it over that there were only two eventualities that would result in such a transaction: death or prison release.

Then she remembered. He was wearing the jeans when they were moving stuff into the barn, and this was the key to the box of diaries that he was so keen to keep from her. Well, it was too late now, he no longer had the authority to prevent her snooping. It was like the moral dilemma facing relatives of deceased artists. Would they want their private letters shared for posterity or should they all go up in a pile of smoke? She took the unilateral decision that she should read them, and that she should do so right now.

Simon had stepped outside for a smoke and she passed him on her way out.

'Where are you off to?' he asked.

'I'm just going through Dom's things and want to check out some papers in the barn.'

'Don't make yourself too sad. Do you want me to come with you? I could serve as your filing clerk.'

'No, I'll be all right, but thanks for the offer.'

'Anytime.'

He took hold of her shoulder and addressed her in an unusually earnest manner.

'You know I'm here for you, don't you? We're all here for you.'

She laughed. 'Piss off, Simon – sincerity doesn't suit you. But seriously, thank you. I know you are, and I'm touched. I really am.'

She set off at a brisk pace, following the lavender hedge where some confused bees were looking for long-gone pollen in a half-hearted way. The last thing she wanted was company, witnesses to her delving into her late husband's diaries and tales of his teenage conquests.

A perfectly formed spider's web was suspended on the gate to the field, shimmering with drops from last night's rain, and Nicola stopped to admire it. There was not a breath of wind and although it was chilly, she could feel that the sun would be coming through later, bringing a couple of hours of warmth when you could imagine yourself back to the summer, back to the balmy days when she still had him.

She shook off that unhelpful thought and opened the barn door. Everything was exactly as they had left it, the chaise longue and armchair still uncovered – they'd never got round to protecting them with a tarpaulin. She went to the cardboard box and delved down through the photos until she found the metal box at the bottom. She heaved it out and tried the key – open sesame! There was the diary, exactly as she remembered. Dom's previous life, before he met her, laid out in hand-scrawled pages in an exercise book.

Did teenagers today keep diaries? She had no idea. Gus and Maddie never did to her knowledge – you'd have to hack into their online messages to uncover their most secret thoughts, private exchanges and photos, now evaporated into the ether of iCloud storage.

Reading through Dom's diaries now, she remembered why she chose to destroy her own. It wasn't a case of getting rid of evidence, it was embarrassment at the banality of the entries. The self-importance of adolescents, placing themselves squarely at the centre of the universe, interpreting every pedestrian exchange with their friends as a matter of extreme significance. She smiled as she noted his scoring system, as though each romantic encounter was a football match with goals achieved and nil-nil draws.

*So much for that*, she thought as she closed the book. *Nothing there I didn't know.* She put it aside and lifted out some photos, enjoying a leisurely trip down memory lane. How lucky she was to have had him for thirty-five years; she should focus on that rather than dwelling on her loss. The self-help books she had flicked through all advised gratitude for the gift of a departed loved one.

As she was putting everything away, she noticed that there were some brown envelopes tucked at the bottom of the metal box. She should look through them in case there was anything useful; her recent experience of red tape had made her realise the importance of keeping records, and there might be something here. The first contained payslips from Dom's student holiday jobs at a garage and a garden centre, written references to Whom It May Concern, vouching for his excellent character and capacity for hard work – she couldn't argue with that. Then she slid out the contents of the second envelope. A collection of letters, with his name handwritten on the thick cream envelopes, sent to his office, not their home address. She opened one up and inside found three sheets of flamboyant writing on the kind of stationery you don't use for business purposes.

*My darling Dom,*

it began.

*I know things are difficult for you right now, but I wanted to let you know that I completely understand and that I will wait for you.*

Nicola stared at it in disbelief. Her instinct was to screw up and throw away this utter nonsense, but she carried on.

*You talk of loyalty to your family and I love you for that. You are a good man. But you cannot let your past dictate your future and you know you agree with me that I am your future, as you are mine. You will never be happy if you deny yourself the opportunity that fate has thrown in our path. We must be together, and together we will overcome the obstacles.*

What on earth was this about? It had to all be nonsense. Or was it the scribblings of a crazed stalker who'd become obsessed with Dom? She checked the date at the top of the letter – it was several years ago, but she didn't recall him mentioning anything like this. Although there was that secretary at the office they used to laugh about, who obviously had a crush on him, but why would she actually post a letter when she could just drop it on his desk?

Confused, she flicked through the rest of the envelopes. There were loads of them, at least twenty-five. The date stamps showed most were posted twelve years ago, then some more recently, ten and eleven years ago – they covered a couple of years, it wasn't just a one-off.

She slipped another letter out of its envelope. The same careful handwriting – it wasn't dashed off in a hurry. It spoke of a weekend in Castel Gandolfo, their precious hours together in the shadow of the Pope's summer palace. There were too many accurate details for this to be the work of a crazed stalker. Like how happy Dom had been to find his favourite Tuscan fennel sausage to take on their picnic. How on earth would she know that was his favourite?

'It's not true,' she said out loud. 'It can't be true; it must be a mistake.'

She devoured the rest of the letter, then gorged on all the others, like a compulsive eater who can't stop, even though she knows it's bad for her. Then she read them all again. There were two possibilities. These letters were fabrications, or they were genuine. But if they were fabrications, why would Dom have kept them all these years under lock and key? Why would he have been in such a panic when she found them here and he thought she was going to read them?

She scrunched up the letters and threw them across the barn.

'You bastard,' she said. 'You sneaky, lying bastard. You sneaky dead bastard, who's not even around to hear what I've got to say to you. How could you!'

Then her methodical side kicked in and she picked up the scattered letters and laid them out in date order. The evidence, m'lud, set out in black and white. Or rather, purple and cream. She'd always mistrusted people who used coloured ink and fussy stationery, as if what they had to say was too good for normal methods or so trite it needed to be dressed up in fancy clothing, and now she knew why. What an absolute bloody cow.

It had all begun twelve years ago, apparently.

*I can't put in words how much I enjoyed last night. I've no idea how I'm going to get through the next week until we do it again. Once is never enough with a man like you. Take care, my Dom. Your Flora xxx*

*My Dom.* How dare she! Twelve years ago, when Gus and Maddie were at peak vulnerability in early adolescence. When Nicola was working flat out at the surgery and Dominic started travelling more for business. Or at least he said it was for business; probably it was a pretext for nights away with Flora. Stupid name. Flora and Fauna. Flora margarine.

As she pieced the timeframe together, Nicola drew the arc of the relationship with what she could glean from the one-sided letters. The heady early days – where did they meet? Infuriatingly there was no way of finding out. Then a full year of regular meetings, trysts in hotels, the weekend in Castel Gandolfo and a trip to Bologna, which provoked a lengthy recollection of the best tortellini she had ever tasted – along with other pleasures of the flesh, no doubt – and finally, the ultimatum, when Dom had evidently decided not to leave Nicola. That was big of him.

*You promised me, you said it would just take a little time to find the right moment to tell her, and now you tell me after two wasted years that there is no right moment.*

Was he seriously planning to walk out on her? Or was this just a bit of fun, which Flora had taken too seriously? *Why aren't you here?* she thought again angrily. *Why can't you explain and apologise to me?* It seemed that Flora's husband had left her shortly before the affair and that she had wasted no time in searching out a replacement. Revenge adultery, you might call it.

Nicola thought back and tried to remember if there was any sign, any way she might have known that he was cheating on her, but nothing came to her. They'd had their ups and downs, like everyone else, but it all merged together in her head, the long flow of married life, getting on with it, united in the pleasures that drew you together in the first place, then sharing your pride in the children as they miraculously evolved under your lazy watch. Benign neglect, it worked for them – they used to laugh at other people's helicopter parenting, overseeing every detail of their child's life in the hope of producing a cloned but better version of themselves.

'You still here?'

Simon appeared at the barn door.

'I've come to tell you that lunch is ready. You've been ages – what are you up to? Is that your filing spread out all over the floor?'

'Is it lunchtime already? I had no idea.'

She turned to face him.

'Good God, what's up?' he said. 'You look terrible. Like you've seen a ghost.'

'I have, in a way.'

'What a conniving little shit,' said Beth. 'I know you shouldn't speak ill of the dead, but really.'

She put the letter down and picked up another from the pile that had been passed around the table.

'She has lovely handwriting,' said Fizz, 'all in beautiful purple ink.'

'Darling, you're missing the point here,' said Beth. 'Nicola has just discovered the most massive betrayal and there you are admiring the Other Woman's style.'

'I'm not admiring her, I'm just saying she has lovely hand-writing.'

'So that makes it OK?'

'Steady on, Beth,' said Will. 'It was just an observation.'

He was uncomfortably aware that this was what he and Fizz had done, only viewed from the other side. Added to that, he was the only person in the room who knew anything about this. As Dom's confidant, he had lent a sympathetic ear at the time, just as Dom had supported him later, when he left Marjorie for Fizz. He remembered telling Dom that his marriage was over and how he saw just a flash of envy, a glimpse of Dom thinking: *That could have been me.*

'It's so distressing for you, Nicola,' said Mary. 'But can you be sure it really happened? All you have is a collection of letters and they could have been the work of a fantasist.'

Nicola shook her head.

'It's the detail that gives it away. I might have thought that if it was just a couple of generic letters, but everything rings true. How he always insisted on hot milk in his coffee and couldn't bear runny eggs. He even gave her a book that I know he enjoyed because I remember us talking about it – in fact, he probably gave her my copy, the bastard.'

'And yet he always appeared to be the most devoted hus-band,' said Mary. 'What's more, he's not here to defend him-self. There's no evidence of him writing letters to her, for instance.'

'I've always wondered how that works,' said Leo. 'Who keeps a copy of a handwritten letter they've sent? Only someone anticipating that their grateful public will want to read them once they're dead.'

'We are that grateful public,' said Simon, 'poring over the juicy details.'

'It's not funny, Simon,' Beth snapped at him. Why did he always have to make a cheap joke out of everything? Couldn't he see how inappropriate it was?

'I don't mind, Beth,' said Nicola. 'You've got to laugh, haven't you? And it's a relief being able to share this with all of you. Group therapy. I'd be going mad if I was shut up on my own thinking about it. What I really want to know is where he met her. She doesn't sound like she was a colleague.'

'Pity you don't know her surname, then we could google her,' said Fizz. 'That's how I found out who my ex was seeing: she was a Miss England finalist.'

'And not nearly as pretty as you,' said Will. 'Or as smart.'

'Flora's quite an unusual name,' said Leo.

'There was a mother at school called Flora,' said Beth. 'Do you remember her, Nicola? She had a son in the same class as Eva and Gus? We weren't that keen on her, thought she was a bit stuck-up, but then her husband ran off with the nanny and we felt sorry for her.'

'Oh my God,' said Nicola. 'It's her! Of course it's her. It was when Dom was going through one of his community-minded phases and was helping out with the lighting at the school play, and she was in charge of costumes. After rehearsals, all the helper parents went out to dinner together, or that's what he said.'

'Cosy dinner for two, more like.'

'I remember now, him talking about how hard it was for her, being left in the lurch. And no nanny, obviously. The perfect middle-class tragedy.'

'We were right to hate her,' said Beth. 'Scheming to put you through what she went through; how very unsisterly.'

'And then she moved schools a couple of years later and we never saw her again. I had no idea; what a fool I was. It just never occurred to me that Dom would do something like that. This is so much to take in . . .'

She put her hand to her temple; her head was throbbing.

'I suppose you never really know somebody, do you?'

'That's true enough,' said Mary. 'We come into this world alone, and we die alone.'

Beth frowned at her.

'So here I am,' said Nicola, 'grieving my sainted husband, who turns out not to be sainted at all.'

'We all make mistakes,' said Fizz. 'It doesn't mean he was a horrible person. Look at Will, he's not a horrible person and he fell in love with me even though he was already married. But Nicola's a thousand times nicer than Marjorie, so it wasn't really the same . . .'

'Please don't muddy the water, Fizz,' said Beth. 'We are here for Nicola and it is clear that Dominic did a bad thing, though that doesn't make him a bad person. Hate the sin and love the sinner.'

'It's all becoming a bit biblical,' said Nicola. 'I'm going to have a lie-down. Thank you all for being so lovely.'

Upstairs, Dominic's clothes were still scattered over the bed. Nicola pushed them onto the floor and slipped under the duvet. She closed her eyes and thought about this morning's discovery. Did she hate him? No. Did it make his loss a little easier to bear? No. A couple of years wasn't long in the total scheme of things, when she thought of the duration of their marriage. And he had chosen her and the kids – he had seen sense. But all that time of duplicity, of him coming up with excuses and cover stories. The months where she was being weighed up against some other woman, while Dom tried to make his mind up, all while she was blissfully unaware. She was furious that he wasn't there so she could have this out with him, scream at him and demand that he explain himself. Her feelings about him were so mixed up now with confusion and anger, she was already nostalgic for the straightforward sorrow that had been snatched away from her by the simple act of opening an envelope.

She was just dropping off when there was a knock at the door. 'Come in.'

Simon entered and closed the door softly, then came to sit on the edge of the bed.

'Are you all right?' he asked. 'I was worried about you down there.'

She looked at him sitting there with his blocky silhouette and hope in his eyes, so unlike Dominic with his trim physique and fastidious habits. Not that they did him any good; it all came down to fate in the end. As a doctor, she understood why so many doctors drink and smoke. Chance and genes so often determined your moment of death, not your lifestyle habits.

'Yes, I'm all right,' she replied. 'I hope you weren't hoping to make it all right.'

'I can't believe he treated you like that. I would never have cheated on you, you do know that?'

'Never say never, Simon. Who knows how things might have played out? You might have turned out to be a cheat, just like Dominic.'

'I never would.' He put an arm around her shoulders.

'Isn't that what you're trying to do now? Creeping in here behind your wife's back to tell me how you would never have cheated on me? Get real! You and me, it's ancient history, there's no point in harking back. You are a very lucky man to have such a brilliant wife. I couldn't have chosen better myself.'

'I know.'

He stared down at the floor, unable to look her in the eyes.

'But she's not you,' he said.

Nicola pushed away his arm and forced him to face her.

'Don't be an idiot, Simon. Don't do what Dom clearly did – risk throwing something good and real away for the sake of some flight of fancy. Love isn't in those letters that woman sent Dom. Love isn't you putting a rose-coloured filter on whatever we had when we were young. Love is coming through in the end and treasuring what you have. Before you lose it.'

She could see from his face that her words were sinking in, that he was acknowledging the truth of what she said.

'You're right,' he said eventually. 'I'm sorry, I really am. I'm going to try to make things better with Beth.'

Watching him leave the room, Nicola thought he might actually mean it.

# CHAPTER EIGHTEEN

'Let's get this fire going,' said Will, looking at Nicola curled up on the sofa. 'Warmth and comfort is what you need.'

He expertly constructed a loose pile of kindling, topped with a log that he had cut to size earlier. Using his chainsaw had become his favourite thing: the roar of the engine, the sense of a knife slicing through butter – it made him appreciate the joy of simple tasks. So much more rewarding than combing through the arcane intricacies of a legal document. He didn't miss that life at all.

Nicola looked up from her phone.

'Will, can I ask you something?'

'Ask away. There you go, that will be a roaring blaze in no time.'

'Did you know about Flora? You were Dom's best friend and if he confided in anyone, it would have been you. I'm just wondering if he ever said anything.'

Will carried on staring at the fire, playing for time, considering his options.

'He did mention it, yes. I thought about telling you yesterday but wasn't sure there was any point.'

He moved to sit next to her on the sofa.

'I'm sorry, Nicola, maybe I should have said something. But he swore me to secrecy and it was a long time ago and you were so happy together recently.'

It was true then. Any glimmer of hope that Flora was a deranged fantasist, the hope that had kept her awake last night, could now be put to rest.

'I see.'

'He just fell into it, Nicola. I told him he was an idiot but she did all the chasing and he was flattered to start with, and then it all became unmanageable and he wished he'd never got involved.'

'He did get involved, though. And then it became "unmanageable". I do like your choice of phrase, as though this was a business problem to be resolved.'

She thumped her fist on the sofa between them.

'I so wish he was here, so I could give him a piece of my mind!'

'He never stopped loving you, Nicola, you know that. But people are programmed that way: if something is offered up on a plate, we find it hard to say no.'

'Don't give me that stereotypical claptrap!'

'I'm not excusing him, I'm just trying to explain. I know it myself: you find yourself on a hamster wheel, churning around, stuck in the routine of work and home, same old, same old. And then you find you can have this whole other secret life. It's not real, it's a fantasy, but you feel that anything is possible, that you can be . . . an expanded version of yourself, I suppose.'

'So I kept him in a hamster cage, did I? Like a child with a pet? I was a hamster too, you know, running between the surgery and the kids. It didn't mean I took a fancy man on the side! I wouldn't have had the time, apart from anything else.'

'If it's any consolation, he had a horrible time when he broke up with her.'

'Diddums. Good, I'm glad his little heart was broken.'

'She threatened to tell you; he begged her not to. In the end, she did the decent thing. I think she realised that the whole episode was a reaction to her husband walking out on her. And that she was at risk of behaving as badly as the woman who broke up her own marriage. I say woman – more of a girl, really.'

'But it wasn't the nanny who behaved badly, it was the sleazebag husband who abused his position of authority! Why do people always blame the woman? It makes me sick.'

'He was so relieved when she decided to move away. He said he felt he'd been given his life back. He could write off the whole torrid two years. Couldn't believe how lucky he was.'

Nicola thought about when that would have been, based on the timeline of the letters that was imprinted on her mind. It was the year he booked an extravagant villa in Provence that belonged to a racing driver – way beyond their usual budget.

Gus and Maddie couldn't get enough of the infinity pool and Dominic had insisted on taking over all the cooking while she lay on a sun-lounger, working her way through a pile of books. They agreed it was the best holiday they'd ever had. It was also the best sex they'd ever had. With the benefit of hindsight, it was make-up sex, though she obviously didn't know that at the time.

'Was it Dom's . . .' She searched for the word. 'Dom's escapade that gave you the idea of leaving Marjorie?' she asked.

'Whoa! I thought we were talking about Dom.'

'But you were still with her then, weren't you?'

'Yes. And unlike Dom, I wasn't happily married. My fault – I should never have married her. But as I said, men are easily led.'

'Poor little victims, dragged up the aisle and then dragged into infidelity by scheming women.'

'That's not what I meant. But Marjorie and I married straight out of university, far too young. She was drawing up her wedding list at John Lewis in our final year – what kind of twenty-one-year-old does that? You should be experimenting with drugs at that age, not looking at saucepan sets. I've since read that you only discover who you are at the age of twenty-three. Before that you're not a real person, just an evolving child.'

'Fizz was twenty-five when you met, wasn't she? Twenty-seven when you got hitched? Just about fully formed then.'

'Touché,' said Will uncomfortably. 'I fell in love with her, pure and simple. My marriage was already beyond repair – nothing like you and Dom, you were such a great couple. Oh no, don't cry.'

He awkwardly put his arm around her, feeling that he was somehow complicit in Dominic's misbehaviour, though he was merely the confidant. He was glad he'd told her, though, it was a weight off his chest.

'We were great together, weren't we?' said Nicola through her tears. 'That's what's kept me going through the last few weeks. I kept saying, *Be grateful for what we had.* I had this golden image of us as the ultimate happy couple, but not in a boring way. A happy couple living a dream life with our gorgeous friends. And then yesterday it all fell apart.'

'That's a welcome sight on a cold afternoon,' said Mary, coming in with her jigsaw case. 'Nothing cosier than settling down with a puzzle in front of a log fire. Oh, poor Nicola . . .'

'No, I'm all right, just coming to terms with the idea of myself as the widow of a flawed man.'

'We're all flawed, dear,' said Mary, 'though after your discovery of those letters, I'd quite understand if you felt rather less inclined to commit sati.'

'What's sati?'

'The old Hindu practice of a widow throwing herself on her husband's funeral pyre. Now banned, I'm happy to say.'

Leo came in with a book and settled beside Nicola and Will on the sofa.

'Hello, my darling girl,' he said, kissing her on the cheek. 'Would it be inappropriate to say that grief rather suits you? It's brought out your cheekbones a treat.'

'When were you ever appropriate?' said Nicola, managing a wan smile.

'I'm steadying my nerves before my hair appointment,' said Leo. 'I'm going to that place on the *grande rue*, though nothing very grand about it, if we're honest, and I'm terrified I'm going to come out with an aubergine short back and sides.'

'You'd rock that look,' said Nicola. 'You can get away with anything with your genes.'

'How's the jigsaw progressing?' Leo asked Mary, who had set her board up on the coffee table and was peering at a piece of sky through her reading glasses.

'Rather difficult because there's so much blue – always problematic with a seaside horizon.'

'You don't worry about it being the most colossal waste of time?'

'Not at all! It's relaxing and brings the satisfaction of seeing the completed picture when you've finished. And no more pointless than doing a crossword. Or Sudoku. Now that really is a waste of time and I've often seen you doing them.'

'Keeping my mind active,' said Leo. 'Have you ever neared completion of a jigsaw, only to find the final piece is missing? That happened to me the last time I did one; it filled me with despair. I heard a man on the radio talking about his volunteer work – he completed every jigsaw donated to his local charity shop so if there were pieces missing, they could throw it away. '

'I don't mind, the pleasure lies in performing the task, and if you find some pieces missing, it is a good lesson in accepting that life is imperfect.'

'The jigsaw philosopher,' said Nicola as her phone started ringing. 'Oh, it's Maddie.'

She took the call and could hear straightaway that all was not well.

'Hello, darling, are you all right? No. What is it? Just a minute.' She stood up and covered the phone with her hand. 'I'll take this upstairs,' she said to the others. 'She sounds a bit upset.'

In the privacy of her bedroom, Nicola listened to what Maddie had to say. Between sobs, she managed to convey the vital information: that John had broken up with her.

'Oh, sweet Maddie, I'm so sorry. Are you sure? It's not just a lovers' tiff?'

'No, it's not a lovers' tiff, Mum. Stop making it sound so trivial! He broke up with me, don't you understand?'

'All right, sorry, I am listening.'

'So I'm moving out of his place. I'm going back home. Gus has been sweet about it . . . but, please, Mum, can you come back? Just for a while. Please?'

For a moment, Nicola forgot her own grief and anger. That fierce maternal urge to protect and comfort overrode everything else. She had marvelled with Dom about how when you're a parent, no matter what kind of pain your child is going through, you would far rather it was happening to you. It's the price you pay for that primal love, to wish their pain was yours.

'Of course I will. I'll see you tomorrow.'

# CHAPTER NINETEEN

'I hope everything will be well with your daughter,' said Jean-Louis, leaning forward over the steering wheel to get a better view of the road through the morning fog, which was slowly dissipating as the sun came through.

He had insisted on driving her to the station when she rang to let him know her plans.

'I think she is a strong person and only needs to see you for a short while. I hope so, because I need you here. I mean, for the markets.'

'Beth will take my place, she'll be great – completely up to speed on the vegetables and she's looking forward to working off the stall. She says her favourite toy as a child was a cash register and she can't wait to play with a grown-up version.'

'I like Bett, but I prefer you.'

A car pulled out suddenly in front of them and Jean-Louis slammed on his brakes and sounded his horn.

'*Oh la vache!*'

'That's such a weird expression,' said Nicola. 'Oh, the cow! Why do you say that?'

He looked across at her.

'I don't know, it's just something we say.'

'Keep your eyes on the road.'

'Did you see the car he was driving? It's a *sans permis*, with a very small engine and maximum speed of forty-five kilometres an hour. You can drive one without having a licence, which means they are usually driven by people who should not be allowed on the road.'

'Sounds dangerous.'

'Mostly it is old people, but also it is drunks who have had their licence confiscated. But what can you do? In the country-side, everyone must have wheels or they are condemned to the life of a hermit.'

The sun had risen by the time he pulled into the taxi rank in front of the station, where there were fewer passengers than Nicola expected; it seemed the French did not embrace com-muting with the same zeal as the British.

'Promise me you are coming back – the château needs you,' said Jean-Louis, as he took her suitcase out of the boot. He watched her until she was on the platform and when she turned round, he waved and she waved back.

It was less than two hours to Paris and as she stepped off the train at the Gare Saint Lazare, Nicola felt lonely and out of place. The station was buzzing with purposeful men and women dressed in grey and black; she remembered how she and Dominic had remarked upon it on their last visit, how averse Parisians were to colour. They had stayed in an apartment on the Ile Saint Louis for their tenth wedding anniversary, a converted *chambre de bonne* at the top of seven flights of stairs. 'No wonder they are all so thin,' Dominic had said, 'dealing with that every time they pop out for a baguette.' The room was cheap and bohemian, and they spent the weekend like students, drinking wine out of tumblers, wandering the streets and sitting down at unpretentious bistros whenever they were hungry. Not a single museum, they were proud to say; they had enough of that in London, shepherding the children around at weekends, good parents that they were.

As she stood in the taxi queue, running through her memories, Nicola was struck by the cold realisation that she was now a widow. A *veuve*, like Veuve Cliquot champagne, the widow spider, spending her widow's mite on a Eurostar trip to London. Last time, returning for Dom's funeral, she had booked the ferry with Gus and Maddie because it was cheaper, but now she was alone, she could take the train like a self-indulgent single person, with only herself to think about.

It was a short ride to the Gare du Nord, along narrow streets flanked by beige buildings of uniform height with high windows and those large doors that looked ancient but sprang open with contemporary edge when you entered an electronic code on a keypad. They had visited a French friend for dinner on their first trip to Paris and failed to ask for the code, resulting in a long wait on the doorstep in the pre-mobile phone age.

Nicola took the glass lift at the Gare du Nord, elevating her above the commuter platforms to the rarefied level of the Eurostar terminal. She recalled the tunnel opening, the Queen and President Mitterrand cutting the red, white and blue ribbons in Calais before hopping into the royal Rolls Royce and taking *le shuttle* back to England. Happier days, before political spats and nationalist rhetoric reappeared to dissolve the *entente cordiale*.

She settled into her comfortable seat, opposite a middle-aged couple. The woman with Surrey blonde hair wore a fur-trimmed pink jerkin and her companion was in red trousers and a green striped shirt – there was more colour between them than in the whole of Paris. Nicola noticed they were holding hands and decided they were almost certainly not married to each other. Which inevitably led her thoughts back to Dominic and Flora. It was the standard corny destination for *un dirty weekend* – what were the chances? She'd never know now whether their stay on the Ile Saint Louis was the last time Dominic went to Paris or whether he'd created more recent memories without her.

'Thank you for coming, Mum,' said Maddie. She had surprised Nicola by opening the front door when she heard the key in the lock.

'I thought you'd be at work,' said Nicola, putting her keys in her pocket and hugging her daughter tightly. She stepped back to study her face. She looked peaky, no doubt about it.

'I took the day off; I couldn't face it. They were quite nice about it – staff care is high on their priority list.'

Like most of her graduate friends, Maddie described herself as a consultant. Not a medical consultant, as Nicola had to explain to her doctor friends; she was a management consultant, but the 'management' was quietly dropped these days, the way that 'merchant bankers' had morphed into 'bankers'. Nicola had no idea what Maddie's job entailed, but she was fiercely proud of the determination she put into it.

'So, let's put the kettle on and you can tell your old mother all about it,' she said, slipping out of her coat and settling down on the familiar sofa. How often she had sat in this very position, waiting for Dom to come home from work. She could imagine him right now, bouncing through the door.

She watched Maddie making the tea and they chatted about the journey – small talk before getting down to business.

Then Maddie brought two cups over to the sofa and set them on the coffee table. She flopped down beside Nicola and folded herself into her mother's shape, leaning into her side the way she used to when she was a little girl, when she would close her eyes and wait for Mummy to make everything all right.

'It was completely out of the blue,' she said. 'John was lovely when Dad died, really caring. I was so grateful to have him there looking after me and knowing we'd be together through everything. Then last week, he just came home one evening and I was serving up a tofu katsu and he went all formal on me. Said it was all too soon, he felt he was turning into his father, it was like being a middle-aged couple, when we're only in our twenties. He said – and this really upset me – obviously he loved me but he wasn't ready to settle down, it was just him, it had nothing to do with me. Which is bollocks, of course. What he really meant is he doesn't want to settle down with me.'

Nicola felt a stab of indignation as she saw Maddie's lip trembling. How could anyone not want to settle down with her daughter? She was about to deliver a stinging list of John's faults – to reassure Maddie that she was better off without him – but then thought better of it. She'd done just that when her sister split up with her long-term boyfriend and then they'd ended up getting back together and married. It had been awkward ever since.

'Are you sure he wasn't just having a wobble? Sounds like an early midlife crisis to me.'

'Midlife crisis? He's only twenty-nine!'

'I had you when I was twenty-nine, it didn't feel very young to me, but then your generation do things differently.'

'It was his idea for us to live together; I was quite happy as we were, but then you said you were moving away so it seemed the logical next step for us to cohabit. Though that makes it sound like a cold decision, which it wasn't. I love him, Mum, and I thought he loved me.'

Her lip was trembling again.

'I'm sure he does,' said Nicola soothingly. 'He's always seemed very devoted. Like when he brought that fresh ginger and lemon over when you had the flu – that's the sort of attention I appreciate, never mind champagne and flowers.'

'He's never bought me flowers.'

Nicola couldn't help putting this down as a black mark, in spite of what she'd just said.

'Remind me how long you've been together,' she asked. 'Two years?'

'Two years since we had the "exclusive" chat. I know you laugh when I call it that. And we'd been dating for a few months before that.'

'Call me old-fashioned, but I do struggle with modern dating etiquette.'

'You are old-fashioned. Pretty much all my friends met their partners on Tinder. We went to a wedding last month where the groom said in his speech that it was love at first swipe and none of the old people knew what he was talking about.'

'That's quite funny; I would have understood it.'

'It was a great wedding, we all got completely wrecked on shots and the bride passed out during the karaoke.'

'Very romantic.'

'It was, actually. Then John started talking about what kind of day we should have when we eventually get round to it, trying to decide whether to go full English countryside or Tuscan hilltop village. He wanted two best men or possibly three, and thought

I should have at least six bridesmaids because you might as well go the whole hog, no half measures . . .'

Her eyes were sparkling as she described the scene to her mother, conjuring up the wedding fantasies that she and John had been spinning between them. Then her face grew serious again.

'And now he's dumped me. What do you make of that?'

'I think dump is a . . . let's say it's an unhelpful turn of phrase,' said Nicola carefully.

Maddie was looking away from her mother now, unwilling to meet her gaze.

'And there's something else I have to tell you,' she said, addressing the wall behind Nicola's shoulder. 'I didn't want to talk about it over the phone.'

They say a mother always knows and Nicola anticipated the words before Maddie delivered them. She thought of how she'd known the terrible news Jean-Louis had to deliver before he opened his mouth. She had the same sense of foreknowledge now. Some things were too big to be contained by words.

'I'm pregnant.'

Maddie was upstairs sleeping, giving them both time to gather their thoughts. Nicola had been in this position on a professional basis countless times: a distressed young woman in her consulting room seeking her advice on how to proceed following a positive test. This time it was personal, but she couldn't even let herself have an opinion until she'd heard Maddie's wishes. She could only say to Maddie what she always said: *It's your decision; only you can know what you want.*

The house seemed smaller to Nicola than she remembered; her sense of scale had evolved since moving to the château. This wasn't her first return visit to the family home, but on the last occasion she had been so dazed by Dominic's death that she hadn't noticed anything. Now she moved around the kitchen, refamiliarising herself with the cupboards and noticing some new acquisitions – a Nespresso machine and a NutriBullet mixer that Gus's vegetarian flatmate Alex had installed. The spice cupboard was well stocked as ever and she set about preparing a chicken curry for supper.

'There you are,' she said, as Maddie entered the room. 'I'm putting a curry together for us. Gus says he'll join us later. Does he know, by the way?'

Maddie nodded.

'I told him yesterday. He was sweet. Kept referring to himself as Uncle Gus, though I told him that was inappropriate at this stage.'

'Yes, it's very early days – luckily, you still have plenty of time. And what about John – does he know?'

Nicola had been wondering whether the unexpected pregnancy was behind John's sudden vanishing act.

'No. I'd only just done the test and then, when he said he thought we should break up, there was no way I was going to tell him. If he thought we were moving too fast already, can you imagine how he'd feel about a baby?'

'That's right. It's better to decide on your own. A woman's body is hers and hers alone.'

Maddie looked at her blankly.

'What do you mean, decide?'

Nicola put down the knife she was chopping onions with. This was not what she expected.

'I mean, decide what you want to do about the pregnancy,' she said gently.

Maddie looked appalled.

'What I want to do about it?' she repeated. 'You mean, you want me to consider an abortion?'

'I want you to think about your position, that's all. I'm just giving you the same advice I've given to countless patients . . .'

'I'm not your patient, I'm your bloody daughter! And I'm carrying your potential grandchild, in case you haven't registered!'

*Her grandchild*. Nicola suddenly realised that a huge part of her would love Maddie to have the baby. New life in the family after death. But she couldn't let herself say that – she must remain true to her medical code of conduct.

'Mum, I'm having this baby! She was conceived in love, and whatever happens, there's no way I'm going to get rid of her – or him. I've always wanted children, and just because John's being a jerk doesn't mean I'm going to throw the baby out with the bathwater! This child is a gift – don't you see that?'

*Oh God*, thought Nicola, *she really means it.*

'It's all right, darling, I can see you've made your mind up, don't upset yourself.'

'You think that's a bad decision – don't you? I can tell! You're a weird kind of grandma who doesn't even want her first grandchild to be born.'

'Now you're being over-emotional, Maddie, which is quite normal with the hormones. You know as well as I do, it's only a collection of cells at this point . . .'

'Trust you, you're a doctor!'

'Yes, I'm a doctor, and once you've calmed down, you'll know I'm telling you the truth. Whatever you decide is fine by me, but right now we are merely talking about a clump of cells.'

'We are all just clumps of cells, only bigger!'

'And with organs and fully formed brains . . . But anyway, let's stop this conversation.'

'What conversation is that, or can I guess?' said Gus, coming into the room. He'd grown a man bun and beard since starting his PhD, and Nicola found it suited him. He gave her a hug.

'Lovely to see you, Mum. Or should that be Granny?'

He looked over her shoulder at Maddie.

'I presume you've shared the news?'

'Mum thinks I should get rid of it.'

'Maddie!' said Nicola. 'I didn't say that. I didn't mean that at all.'

'But she's agreed it's my decision. So whether she likes it or not, she's going to be a grandmother.'

It was really happening. Nicola was suddenly overwhelmed by the enormity of it all.

'We are a grandmother,' she said weakly.

'What do you mean? Who is "we"?' asked Maddie.

'It's what Margaret Thatcher told reporters outside Downing Street after the birth of her grandchild. Roundly mocked because of the royal "we"'.

She was to be given a grandchild. What an extraordinary blessing to come out of all the turmoil and grief of the last few months.

'Come here, both of you!'

And she put her arms around her children and cried tears of joy.


'I honestly thought you'd want an abortion,' said Nicola. 'That's why you thought I was being so cold – I had to remain rational and keep my feelings at bay.'

The three of them were sitting around the remains of the chicken curry, then Gus stood up to clear the table.

'To be honest, I did think about it briefly,' said Maddie. 'It would certainly have been the easier solution. But I soon realised it was out of the question.'

'And now I can allow myself to become properly excited,' said Nicola. 'At last, here's something for us all to celebrate. It's just so sad your dad will never see the baby . . .'

She would have loved him to be here for this, could imagine his face lighting up with pleasure when he heard the news.

'I suppose I should start knitting,' she said brightly. 'The last time I picked up my needles was when I was pregnant myself. I made a beautiful white shawl, which I took to the hospital, then forgot to bring home – that was hundreds of hours of my life I never got back.'

'Crafts are very in,' said Maddie. 'My friend Lizzie goes to a patchworking evening class.'

'When will you tell John?'

'Not yet.'

'If he hadn't already done a runner, this would seal the deal, I reckon,' said Gus cheerfully.

'Gus!' Nicola reprimanded him.

'I wish Dad was here,' said Maddie. 'I miss him so much. He would have been very excited. Do you remember he once said he'd give twenty thousand pounds to whichever one of us produced the first grandchild? But I suppose that was before you spent every last penny on the château!'

'I don't think he was serious,' said Nicola. 'He was just feeling broody after a colleague brought her baby into the office.'

'He was a great father,' said Maddie. 'What about that treehouse he built us in the garden – do you remember, Gus? With a rope ladder? If he was still here, he could build another one for the baby.'

'Oh yeah, I can really see a baby climbing up a rope ladder,' said Gus.

'When the baby's older, I mean.'

'Mum,' said Maddie. 'It must be horrid for you being without Dad. He was pretty much the perfect husband. I know I'm biased but he obviously was.'

'We were very happy together,' said Nicola, in two minds about whether she should share her recent findings. She decided against it for now, unwilling to burst the bubble of the children's adoration. That could wait for another day.

'I miss him terribly, of course, and it's been difficult to adapt, but that's where I'm lucky. Instead of rattling around on my own, I'm surrounded by friends, and they've all been so kind. And I'm keeping busy with the market gardening.'

'A fine hobby for an old woman,' said Gus. 'You were always happy to get your hands dirty. I used to love picking strawberries with you.'

'Less of the "old woman", please! And it's not just a hobby. We're making money out of it.'

'Do you all get involved?' asked Gus. 'I can't see Dougie down on his hands and knees.'

'Beth and me, mostly. Then I go to the markets in the van with Jean-Louis.'

'The hot farmer?' asked Maddie.

'He's the farmer, yes. I'm not sure I'd describe him as hot.'

'He looks smoking in the photos you showed us! Or maybe that's just in comparison with your housemates – sorry, your château mates.'

'They are all lovely,' said Nicola. 'I am lucky – they don't mind if I'm a mess right now, they're not trying to heal me or wave a magic wand. They're just there when I need them. Anyway, let's talk about you, Maddie. It's the logistics you have to think about. Where will you live and who will look after the baby when you go back to work?' She corrected herself. 'If you go back to work.'

Maddie was full of surprises but Nicola did hope she wasn't thinking of giving up her job she'd worked so hard for.

'Of course I'll go back to work after maternity, Mum. I want this baby so much, but if I'm going to do it alone, I need to support us both. And I'll stay living here, if that's OK with you? Gus's flatmate is moving out anyway, so there'll be a spare room for the baby.'

'I see. Good, I'm glad you're not giving up on your career, though I've never quite got to grips with what exactly that entails. So, who will be pushing the pram around the streets when you're back at your desk?'

Maddie looked at her expectantly.

'Is there a crèche at work? A nice nursery nearby?' Nicola asked. 'Or maybe you could find a childminder. I had a lovely woman near here when you were a baby.'

'I was thinking of having someone live-in, actually,' said Maddie.

'You mean an aupair? No good for a baby, they're not supposed to work full-time, but it's useful once you get to school age. Or do you mean an actual nanny? They're very expensive, darling.'

'I was thinking more in terms of a family member, actually.'

Maddie took a deep breath.

'Mum, I wanted to ask if you would move back here and help me with the baby. It makes perfect sense: you're on your own now and you'd have such a close relationship with your grandchild. It would be incredibly bonding for you to spend every day together, and we'd have each other. It's the ideal solution, don't you agree?'

'Wow, you're going to be a grandmother! I didn't see that coming.'

Nicola was on the phone to Beth, snuggled up in bed in what used to be Gus's room. He had promoted himself to the master bedroom when they moved away and Maddie was now back in her old room, such were the musical chairs of their new family arrangement.

'Neither did I. And there's more: Maddie wants me to move back and be her nanny!'

'What? I hope you've told her it's out of the question!'

'I've told her I'd think about it.'

'Nicola!'

'What could I say? She's feeling vulnerable, as you can imagine. A single mother in the making – I'm not going to turn my back on her, am I?'

'There's a difference between turning your back on her and saying you're not going to chuck in your own life to make hers easier.'

'Harsh.'

'Clear-sighted. You'd be stuck in your old house with a baby all day. Remember how boring that was? And no end in sight, not like when we were on maternity leave. Anyway, we need you here, you can't just walk out on us.'

'It would only be for a while, until she's made other arrangements.'

'You mean for eleven years, until they go to secondary school and you'll be pushing seventy.'

'Don't!'

'Chatting with the other nannies and young mums at the school gate, or maybe they'd invite you along to their coffee mornings so you can sing "The Wheels on the Bus".'

'Oh God, I'd forgotten about all that.'

'While your vegetables go to rot in your beautiful garden here and we set an empty place for you at the table.'

'Now you're blackmailing me.'

'I'm just reminding you that your home is here now. I'm delighted for you about the baby, but it doesn't mean you have to turn into Mary Poppins.'

'How are things at the château?'

'Oh, horrible. Apples on the trees are glowing in the autumn sun, the Michaelmas daisies are the perfect shade of mauve against the white of the Japanese anemones, and the immaculate new roof means we are protected from all vagaries of the weather. Last night Leo made us a faultless *soufflé suissesse* from Michel Roux's Le Gavroche cookbook.'

'Did he take it out of the oven halfway through, then add cream and grated cheese?'

'Of course, I told you it was faultless.'

'I do miss you all.'

'And we miss you. Hurry back.'

# CHAPTER TWENTY

Maddie returned to work the following day, and was gone before Nicola came downstairs to find Gus eating a bowl of porridge to the sound of unfamiliar music.

'Hey, Mum,' he said, looking up from his phone.

'Do you mind if I turn it down?' asked Nicola. 'It reminds me of when we'd come back from a weekend away to find the radio tuned to an alien station. It used to drive Dad mad when he came down to make the coffee.'

'Because he couldn't start his day without listening to people arguing on Radio 4. I find the opposite; give me music any time.'

'Did Maddie get off all right?'

'I didn't see her, but I guess so.'

'What do you make of all this, Gus?'

'The baby? Great news, now I'm over the shock.'

'Me too. And how do you feel about having them living here?'

Gus sat back in his chair.

'I'm really happy about it. I know it sounds a bit circle of life cliché, but we were so cut up about Dad . . . and now we'll have a whole new person to take his place, if you see what I mean. Not that anyone could take his place.'

Nicola put her hand on his shoulder.

'He was so proud of you.'

Gus looked up at her.

'Was he, though? I always thought he disapproved of me going back to do a PhD. Perpetual student, blah blah blah, time to get on in the real world. Though he complained enough about his own real world job, you'd think he'd be glad I'd be spared all that for a couple more years.'

'He was probably a little envious – it coincided with his peak dissatisfaction at work. But he was glad to see you using your brain and doing something you love rather than that soul-destroying job you had, moving wealthy people's money around. As I say, he was very proud of you.'

'I'm glad he stopped working when he did. At least he had a few months of fun with you and the hippies before he died.'

'We're not hippies!'

'Rich old hippies.'

He grinned.

'Anyway, I'm sure you'll be glad to put that adventure behind you, now you have more pressing concerns.'

Nicola could see that Maddie had won him over. They were both presenting it as a fait accompli.

'Gus, you have to understand, the château is my home now.'

'This is your home! Now that Dad's gone, we are all you have. Surely you want to be with us?'

His words provoked a surprisingly strong reaction in Nicola. She loved her children, but the idea of them being all she had was dispiriting. As if she should put on her widow's weeds and quietly pack her own life away in a neat cardboard box.

'Of course I want to be with you, but not all the time! I'm thinking of you as well – it would drive you mad having me here now you're used to having the place to yourself. One of our motivations for moving away was the hope that it would let you grow up and be more independent.'

'Grow up! I'm perfectly grown up, thank you, and Maddie is so grown up that she's having a baby, which is about the most adult thing you can do. We thought you'd be thrilled that we wanted you here – lots of my friends can't stand their parents and do everything to avoid them. You should be flattered.'

'I am flattered. I'm just not sure I want us all to live together. And I'm certainly not sure I want to spend my days ferrying my grandchild to soft play centres, however much I love them, and I know I will love them to bits.'

'Think about Dad. What would he want you to do? Take care of his grandchild or rattle around like a spare part in a big house in France? You've said yourself that keeping busy is what has kept you sane since he died. This way you can keep busy and be close to us. Your poor orphaned children.'

'You're not orphans, you have me.'

'Exactly. Dad was such a role model for me, Mum; you had the perfect marriage. I hope one day I'll be as lucky.'

Should she tell him now?

'We had a happy marriage, Gus, but it wasn't perfect.'

'You'd shout at each other from time to time, but who doesn't?'

'It was more than that. There's something I need to tell you.'


Gardening as therapy, Nicola knew all about that. Tending her rows of vegetables in the château garden had been her source of strength and comfort in the months since Dominic's death, giving her space to grieve, in the knowledge that outside the garden walls, her friends were waiting for her.

Now she was about to put the same energy into the neglected rear garden in London. Gus had done a pretty good job of keeping the house in order, but the beds outside had been allowed to run riot; dead flowers were falling over the path and weeds were asserting their dominance over the once carefully maintained ground cover.

Nicola opened the door of the shed, which used to be an outside privy, and took out the old garden fork that someone had given them as a wedding present. Dominic's gardening gloves were hanging next to hers, moulded to the shape of his hands, reminding her of the death cast her aunt had made of her uncle that had spooked her as a child. She ran her fingers over the gloves and thought how he would never meet his grandchild, he would never show them how to plant a bulb, or help them to write the name of a flower on an old lolly stick and push it into the dark soil.

Gus had been indignant on her behalf when she told him about Flora. 'What a complete idiot!' he'd said. He remembered Flora from the school gates because her son was known as the class bully, yet he always went off meekly with his mother, hand in hand after lessons when he thought no one was watching. 'If I'd known, I would have duffed him in for you, Mum,' he said, as though they were in a revenge drama and the sins of the mother must be visited on the son. But he was unwilling for the memory of his father to be tarnished by what he regarded as a one-off aberration. 'He chose you, Mum. If he'd really loved her, he would have left. Plenty of my friends' fathers did; then they all got double Christmas presents. I used to be really jealous.'

She felt better, having told him. It put Dom's affair in perspective and somehow reduced her shame on his behalf.

The wheelbarrow was soon overflowing with uprooted bindweed and nettles, and she pushed it down the path to unload on the compost heap at the bottom of the garden.

'Hello, Nicola.'

She turned round to find John standing on the path behind her.

'Gus let me in. He told me you were out here.'

He looked sheepish. His blond hair was unbrushed and he stood with his hands in his pockets, as though waiting for her to express her disapproval.

'John, I wasn't expecting to see you!'

'I was hoping to find Maddie here. I suppose she's told you . . .'

'Yes, she told me.'

*And yet you're here*, she thought, with a glimmer of hope.

'She's not taking my calls, so I came over.'

'I'm pleased to see you, John, and I was just thinking it's getting cold out here. Let's go inside for a cup of tea, shall we?'

He followed her into the house, where she put the kettle on and took a good look at him as he slipped his coat off his athletic shoulders and sat up at the counter. He didn't have the air of a cad and a bounder; he had the look of a good person who knows he has just made a big mistake.

'You're looking well, Nicola,' he said politely.

'Better than you,' she said, taking in his red-ringed eyes. 'And I'm probably looking better than last time we met.'

'It was a very moving funeral. Maddie and I thought you were incredibly brave to give that reading.'

'It's all a blur but I'm glad I managed it.'

'Awful. Such a shock.'

He took his head in his hands.

'Oh Nicola, I've really messed up . . .'

*It's going to be all right*, Nicola realised, as she watched him preparing to pour his heart out. She so hoped that Maddie would agree to take him back. They'd be together again and she, Nicola, would be free. Then she chastised herself for her selfish reaction.

'She was devastated when Dominic died,' said John. 'And I was being very supportive, I really was. Making tasty suppers to be sure she was eating properly, holding her when she couldn't stop crying, taking care of everything so she didn't have to worry . . .'

'I know you were, she told me how good you'd been.'

'And then, just as she was starting to come to terms with it, being more her usual self, I had this awful reaction. I felt I'd become the dumping ground for all the misery she had been through, and that she wasn't interested in me at all. No sense of me as a person. I was just a comfy old sofa whose only role was to prop her up. She said I was her rock, but who wants to be a useless great lump of rock? I'm not a bloody rock, I'm her boyfriend. I *was* her boyfriend. I just wanted us to be the way we were. And then I said some terrible things and we argued and I said: "if that's the way you feel, we should just call it a day because I can't be doing with all this, I'm too young; it's not like we're some old married couple who are stuck together because they don't know what else to do with their lives." Then she just stood up and said she was leaving. The last thing she wanted was for me to feel like she'd trapped me into co-dependence. So she packed her bags and came back here.'

'And rang me because she was so devastated.'

'I didn't know that.'

*There's a lot you don't know*, thought Nicola. She empathised with Maddie's reluctance to tell John she was pregnant. Pride and hurt would have pushed her to behave the same way as her daughter.

'And now?' she asked.

'I want her to come back. Of course I do. I love her, Nicola. I can't imagine my life without her.'

He reached down into the bag at his feet and produced a bunch of pink tulips.

'Look, I even bought her some flowers. She complained I never bought her any, even though I explained that flowers only fade and die, which makes them an unsatisfactory present in general and a particularly unsatisfactory token of love.'

'They're beautiful,' said Nicola. 'Let's put them in some water and wait until Maddie comes back.'

When she saw Maddie walking up the front door steps, Nicola slipped away upstairs, leaving John to confront her on his own. This wasn't the moment to be third-wheeling. From the safety of Maddie's old bedroom, she could hear the murmuring of their voices below, then the sound of the front door opening and closing. At least it wasn't being slammed. She went out onto the landing to look downstairs to check if one or both of them had left the house.

Maddie swung round from where she was standing in the hall and stared accusingly at her mother.

'Have you been listening in? You're such a snoop!'

'Of course not! That's why I went upstairs, to get out of your way.'

Nicola came down and followed Maddie into the sitting room, waiting for her to say something.

'Honestly, he seems to think he can win me back with a bunch of garage flowers!'

She sat down on the sofa and crossed her arms defiantly.

'That's nice, though. You said he never bought you flowers.'

'No, but he could have chosen some decent ones. Not the sort an indifferent husband lazily picks up at the garage on his way home – that's exactly the sort of relationship he was so keen not to be involved in.'

'Hmm. I love pink tulips, personally.'

'Anyway, he says he wants me back, but I don't believe him.'

'He seemed pretty genuine to me, earlier. He told me he'd made a colossal mistake.'

'Yes, but why would he say those hurtful things if he didn't mean them? Say I do go back – what's to stop him doing it again? And this time it'll be me and the baby – I have to think of that now, don't I, Mum? I have to give the baby a stable environment, I can't just carry on as we were, treading on eggshells, waiting until John decides he's not ready for this after all . . .'

Nicola sat beside her and held her as she started crying.

'Did you tell him about the baby?'

Maddie shook her head.

'No. I need to get my head straight first. Obviously he'll need to know at some point. But for now, I just want things to be calm. I need to stay here, Mum. I can't go running back to John and then drop this on him.'

Nicola nodded.

'I can understand that. You know, of course, that I'll support you. I'll come over for the birth, and then you and the baby can come stay at the château for the rest of your maternity leave. Wouldn't that be a lovely way to spend the summer? With or without John, depending on how things work out.'

It was an appealing thought, to have her infant grandchild staying with them all at the château. Infinitely more appealing than returning to London to work as her daughter's nanny. She did hope that Maddie wouldn't wait too long before she told John he was going to be a father.

As it turned out, Maddie had no say in the matter. A few minutes later, there was a ring at the doorbell and Nicola was not at all surprised to find John standing on the doorstep. He nodded at Nicola and barged into the sitting room, where Maddie was curled up on the sofa.

'You're pregnant! Why didn't you tell me?'

Later that evening, Nicola called Beth to give her the welcome news.

'I can't tell you how happy that makes me,' said Beth. 'We've all been on tenterhooks waiting for your decision; it's been like a second bereavement.'

'Beth! You can hardly compare the possibility of me leaving the château to Dom's death.'

'All right, not quite the same. Talk me through it, then. Did he go on bended knee to ask her back?'

'Pretty much, but she wasn't having it at first. Sent him away with a flea in his ear and didn't tell him about the baby.'

'But he knows now?'

'Yes! On his way out, he bumped into Gus on the street, who shook him by the hand and said congratulations! John asked him what he meant, then Gus realised he'd massively put his foot in it and tried to backtrack. Too late, though – John made him tell him and came back banging on the door.'

'And is he pleased?'

'Delighted! I think all Maddie's anxieties melted away when she saw how thrilled he was at the news. I'd made a discreet withdrawal to my bedroom, but they came up to see me afterwards, stars in their eyes. He'd already decided he really wanted them to stay together and this is the logical next step, isn't it? Might as well get on with it.'

'Quite.'

'Maddie was more outraged than Gus about the Flora news. We talked about it after John left. She was pressing me about whether I suspected, could I remember any times when I might have had an inkling, when Dom was acting suspiciously. Then I did think back to how he used to go off on his bike at weekends, saying he was going to the gym, but his gym kit always came back clean.'

'He was getting his exercise elsewhere.'

'Thanks for reminding me.'

'Sorry.'

'Anyway, it was hard for her to have Dom fall off his pedestal. She's always been such a daddy's girl, and now he turns out to be less of paragon than she thought. But there's a silver lining. I think she sees John by comparison as a model of future fatherhood.'

'Even though he did ditch her when she was pregnant.'

'He didn't know she was, that's the point. But I'm glad he came back before he knew, which means he did it because he wants to, not because he feels obliged.'

'A happy result. When are you back?'

'I've booked my train – I get in at 6.15 tomorrow evening.'

'Hooray.'

'I'm excited! Does that sound ridiculous? It's the first time I've really looked forward to anything since Dom died. Apart from the baby, obviously, but that's ages away.'

The bedroom door opened and Maddie popped her head round.

'Who are you talking to?' she asked.

'Beth. Do you want a word?'

She handed Maddie her phone and watched her radiant face as she chatted about her plans.

'You too, Beth,' Maddie was saying, 'and look after Mum for us, won't you? Yes, will do, bye.'

She handed the phone back to her mother.

'I'm staying here tonight,' she said, 'to make the most of you before you go. And I've decided you're right, after all, about not being my nanny. A woman at work was talking about it today – she's about your age. She moved her mother-in-law into their basement to help with the children – they've now grown up, of course, but the mother-in-law is still there.'

'Exactly. I'm not sure how happy John would be to have me hanging around into my dotage.'

'He loves you, actually. But separate houses are probably best. And we can bring mung bean to see you. I can just see the baby playing in the fields, learning to crawl in the ballroom . . .'

'Mung bean?'

'That's how big it is right now. Soon it'll be peanut-sized.'

# CHAPTER TWENTY-ONE

Beth and Leo were standing on the platform when Nicola stepped off the train. They were holding up a hand-painted sign that read *WELCOME HOME, NICOLA*.

'God, you're embarrassing,' said Nicola, as she embraced them. 'What are we, the Waltons?'

'We're expressing our joy at your return,' said Leo. 'Beth told us about your ghastly plan to desert us to become Maddie's skivvy. What a terrible idea! Congratulations anyway – does this mean I become a grand-fairy godfather?'

'It does indeed. I don't know if they're thinking of having a christening but you would certainly be first choice godparent. Handsome, clever and rich. And no children of your own to share the inheritance.'

'I hope it's a boy then I can give him frocks.'

Leo took charge of Nicola's bag and they escorted her to the car park where Simon was waiting behind the wheel. He jumped out to greet Nicola.

'Happy to have you back. I am your obedient chauffeur. Beth said I didn't need to come but I insisted because I know she can't bear to be without me these days.'

Simon and Beth exchanged a flirtatious look. *Thank goodness for that*, thought Nicola. *It looks like they're back on track.*

The drive home through the countryside was beautiful, with calm expanses of autumn-coloured trees illuminated by the sun setting over the valley. The sense of wide open spaces offered a welcome contrast to the frenzy of Nicola's journey from London, and when the car crunched to a halt on the gravel, she felt a deep sense of peace she hadn't known in months.

The others were already on to the aperitifs, gathered around the fire in a warm circle. Nicola embraced them in turn, so happy to be back among her friends.

'You missed the event of the year,' said Will, after kissing her cheek. 'We found a wasps' nest in the outbuilding where our furniture is stored and the *sapeurs-pompiers* came over to remove it.'

'It was a magnificent sight,' said Leo. 'They changed into these sexy white boiler-suits and matching helmets with mesh veils, then went charging into the barn. Brave and medically trained – what a dream. I recognised one of them from the Bastille ball. He gave me his number, but he's not my type.'

'I can't believe we didn't notice it before,' said Will. 'That's the thing about having thirty-two rooms, you never know what you'll find.'

'Unfortunately we had to pay because it was more than a hundred metres from the house,' said Dougie. 'Any closer and it would have been free. They also warned us they'd be round at Christmas to sell us a calendar.'

'I can't wait for that,' said Leo. 'We'll have to invite them in for a hot toddy.'

'The nest was the most perfect shape,' said Fizz. 'I featured it in my latest vlog – peak hits! The most popular one since the thing I did on Mary and her dusting techniques; you've no idea how fashionable cleaning has become. I'm keeping the wasps' nest as a sculpture, to be installed in the studio that Will's building for me.'

'Congratulations, grandma,' said Mary. 'The inaugural grandchild of the château – we'll have to create a nursery for when they visit.'

Mary tried not to think of the attendant mess, though she was relaxing on that front; you had to when it came to old houses. After one sleepless night contemplating all the hands that had touched the stair rail, she had reached the conclusion that history was all about human traces. There was only so much you could remove with a cloth.

'Steady on, it's only a mung bean at the moment,' said Nicola. 'Let's not count our chickens.'

'Nothing will go wrong,' said Beth. 'You've used up all your bad luck this year. There's a casserole in the oven – *boeuf en daube*. Did I tell you we have a guest for dinner? I invited Jean-Louis. I came to know him much better on our trip to the market. It's amazing the confidences that are exchanged when you're sitting beside someone in a van, looking out of the window together.'

She gave Nicola a meaningful look.

'He was so pleased to hear you were coming back today, so I invited him.'

As if on cue, there was a ring at the door.

Nicola was surprised how pleased she was to hear this news, and when Jean-Louis came into the room, she realised how much she had missed him. Maddie's dramas had put a halt on her own life but now she couldn't wait to get back into her routine here. Especially her market trips with Jean-Louis – he would want to know every detail about the past week. It was quite a habit they had developed recently, to share their intimate thoughts and feelings, the way you do with close friends. How handsome he looked tonight, dressed in country casual style, a check shirt beneath a dark red waistcoat, his blond hair brushed more tidily than usual. He worked his way round the room with French formality, shaking the men by the hand and kissing the women on both cheeks. Nicola noticed he left her till last and she felt herself blushing when he turned to her.

'Thank you for coming back,' he said quietly. 'I was afraid that the draw of your family would prove too strong, that you would be disinclined to leave them to return to the life of a "country bumpkin" – you see, I remember the words you taught me.'

'Very good,' said Nicola. 'You're making excellent progress.'

'I have the best teacher.'

'I know I made the right decision. My children have their lives, and I have mine.'

'Yes, your life is here now, with me. And your friends, of course.'

Simon sidled over with a kir royale, which he offered to Jean-Louis.

'Not interrupting anything, am I? I'm glad you're here, Jean-Louis – I finally have someone to smoke with. Shall we take this outside?'

'He's a really nice man, isn't he?' said Beth as they cleared the table. 'And I love the way he introduces us to fresh French expressions. *Esprit d'escalier* – that was new on me. Thinking of clever things you wish you'd said at a party when you're on your way out.'

'And *partouze,* which sounds so much more elegant than having an orgy,' said Nicola.

'Typical French, think they know all about sex,' said Simon. 'Same way they claim to be experts on wine, when in reality they know nothing, they just keep banging on about *terroir.* If you grow grapes just over the border from the designated area for champagne, you can't call your wine champagne – how ridiculous is that?'

'I was intrigued by what he said about his ninety-year-old aunt,' said Fizz. 'That she kept herself young by making sure she had an orgasm every day.'

'Oh please,' said Simon, 'don't make me gag.'

'Ageist,' said Fizz. 'And anyway, you'll be ninety yourself soon enough.'

'He knows about football, too,' said Will. 'I liked his comparison between footballers and race horses. How they both need to be rested before a big match, then saying that footballers were like horses but with smaller teeth. Really quite droll.'

'You needn't sound so surprised. The French have an excellent sense of humour,' said Beth. 'We Brits don't have the monopoly on jokes, however funny we think we are.'

'I'm going up now,' said Nicola. 'I'm exhausted by the shock of exposure to city life, not to mention the journey. Thank you all for a wonderful dinner.'

'And a wonderful dinner guest?' Beth asked cheekily.

'Yes, it's a good idea to be on friendly terms with the farmer who's grazing our land.'

'He's particularly keen on being on friendly terms with you.'

Nicola ignored Beth's knowing smirk and retired to her room, appreciating its generous proportions after her nights in London. The carrier bags of Dominic's clothes were stacked in the corner where she had left them; slowly she was reducing his presence in the room, but she knew he'd always be with her.

She was unpacking her case when there was a knock at the door and she sighed when Simon came in.

'This isn't what you think,' he said, softly closing the door behind him.

'What do you think I think?' Nicola replied with a raised eyebrow. 'That you're going to pounce?'

'Pouncing is not my style, as you well know!'

'Or declare your undying?'

He looked uncomfortable.

'That's what I want to talk about. I couldn't say anything downstairs in front of everyone but I wanted to apologise. I was out of order, saying what I did the other day. Beth and I . . . well, we're getting on much better now, and I don't know what I was thinking. So please, forgive me and forget I ever said anything.'

'Oh no, Simon!' said Nicola, her face falling. 'I thought you meant it. I thought you were serious when you implied we should be together . . . Now Dom's gone I was counting on it and hoping you'd be the one to tell Beth . . .'

She let him suffer for a few seconds, then relented.

'Joke!'

'You're horrible! But seriously, Nicola, I want to apologise . . .'

'When are you ever serious?'

'I thought I was – about you. It was absurd, I know that now. I'd created a fantasy bubble and put the pair of us inside it, old fool that I am. So, in all seriousness, I want to say sorry. Not just for the other night but for all my inappropriate behaviour over the past few months. Losing Dom has been awful for you, I know – but it was a wake-up call for me too. If Beth died, I'd be lost, and I've been taking her for granted and getting lost in silly memories of what's long past. I've had it all out with Beth, she's forgiven me and I hope you will too.'

'Thank God that's out of the way,' said Nicola. 'Promise me you'll never do it again, you dewy-eyed idiot, thinking you can go back to our youth. Come here and give me a man hug.'

She felt relief surge through her as he gave her a proper bear hug, the kind of hug you give to a friend, not to someone you're trying it on with.

On his way out, Simon put his head back round the door.

'Jean-Louis's a really good bloke, you know. We had quite a heart-to-heart over our cigars; he's obviously quite smitten by you. I realise it's early days with poor Dom not gone more than a couple of months, but still . . .'

'Goodnight, Simon,' said Nicola. 'Sleep tight.'


'Why is he flashing his lights at us?' Nicola asked Jean-Louis on the way to market the following day. 'The car before did the same thing, and the one before that.'

'It's to warn us that there is a police checkpoint coming up. It is the one example of solidarity that unites the entire population. We may not have much of the Revolution spirit left, but everyone will warn their fellow citizen to slow down in case they are stopped by the police and fined.'

'Fraternity indeed – what a fine tradition.'

They drove on in silence for a while, then Jean-Louis said, 'I meant to ask you earlier but I did not find the moment. I would like . . . I mean, would you like . . . to have lunch with me, after the market? I have a little café in mind, not far from the square.'

He stared ahead nervously, waiting for her response.

Nicola, equally nervous, turned away to look out of her window. This wasn't a casual suggestion, she knew that. He was asking her out. On a date. And she knew she had feelings for him – she couldn't deny it. She turned to look at him as she gave her reply.

'Yes, I would. Thank you.'

His face relaxed.

'Maybe I should have asked earlier, because your friends will be expecting you home.'

'It's all right, I'm a free agent, I don't need an exit pass. We do our own thing for lunch, anyway; it's only at dinner that we all sit down together. We haven't yet adopted the French habit of three courses at noon!'

'Maybe not three courses, but I think it is better for the digestion to eat a proper *repas* at lunchtime. I do not care for the Anglo-Saxon habit of eating sandwiches at random times of the day, grazing like cows. And your junk food – pizzas and burgers – we have them more and more over here now, making us fat like you Anglo-Saxons!'

'Anglo-Saxons! You make us sound like ancient peasants in mud huts.'

'But it is the generic name, more economical than saying English, British, American, Australian . . . You see how heavy that becomes. Anglo-Saxon is succinct and accurate.'

'Fair point. I'll cook an Anglo-Saxon menu next time you come for dinner.'

'Eggs and bacon, with *haricots blancs*, which I know you call baked beans and ruin by adding sugar to the tomato sauce. Or fish and chips?'

'Definitely not egg and bacon, never for dinner. And not fish and chips – that's not something for cooking at home. I'm thinking more steak and Guinness pie, then apple crumble and custard.'

'We certainly have many apples.'

'We do.'

It was a busy morning at the market, confirming Nicola's observation that autumn was the finest season in the foodie's calendar, when the cooler evenings and the wealth of harvest crops inclined everyone to stay indoors and devote themselves to the pleasures of the palate.

She left Jean-Louis packing up while she went to buy some Vacherin Mont D'Or cheese from a neighbouring stall, now at its peak of perfection, as the stall-holder assured her.

'It is made only from the milk of two breeds of mountain cow whose diet is natural hay,' he explained, providing the kind of back story to which Nicola had become accustomed. She loved how food was taken so seriously here – the antithesis to a quick rush around the supermarket, picking up plastic packets.

She then moved on to choose mushrooms from an organic greengrocer, deciding on a box of *cèpes*, their fat white stems still carrying the soil from which they had recently been pulled.

There were mushrooms growing in the fields at the château, but it was agreed they'd be ill advised to eat them. Dougie had bought a copy of *Le Grand Guide Larousse des Champignons* from a second-hand bookshop, but for every photograph of an edible species, there was a matching picture of an almost identical poisonous specimen, dramatically captioned with a skull and crossbones. There were some risks that weren't worth taking.

When the last crate had been loaded into the van, Jean-Louis led Nicola up a side street until they arrived at a small bistro. They settled into a table in the window and Jean-Louis ordered a carafe of red wine while they looked through the menus.

'I'll have whatever you're having,' said Nicola, closing the menu.

'Good, I shall order their specialities: *andouillette* and *tripes à la mode de Caen*. Then you will see why we take lunch so seriously.'

He raised his glass to her, almost shyly, she thought.

'*Santé*. Thank you for accepting to have lunch with me.'

Nicola clinked glasses with him.

'Pleasure. Thanks for saving me from the Anglo-Saxon curse of the sandwich.'

'A sandwich is no good after a morning's work like we have just undertaken. Maybe it is acceptable for someone who is only sitting in an office.'

He shrugged as if such an activity was unthinkable.

'I am hungry, actually.'

Her taste buds were awakened by the delicious smells that were emitted from the kitchen every time a waiter came bursting through the swing doors.

They talked of the market, laughed about the customer who wanted to know precisely when the Alexander apples had been harvested, as he could only eat an apple that was directly from a tree, otherwise it would have lost its crunch.

'You have your colour back,' Jean-Louis said approvingly. 'Even though you still have your summer tan, I could see you were pale beneath – it was to be expected. But now I see once again the roses in your cheeks.'

'Oh really?' said Nicola. She was embarrassed.

'A real English rose – you say that, I think?'

'We do, though I never think of myself as one. An English rose to me is a young girl in a cotton-sprigged dress wearing an Alice band and long plaits, with a shy and modest manner.'

'I don't like the sound of that. I prefer my version, which is you.'

They were interrupted by the arrival of the *andouillette*, presented with a flourish by the waiter.

'*Bon appétit*,' he said, and judging on what Nicola could see on the plate in front of her, this sounded like a challenge rather than a pleasantry. The sausage looked like a large penis, but Nicola dismissed this childish thought and cut into it.

The smell assailed her first; she'd heard that *andouillettes* carry the whiff of the farmyard, but that was being too polite. It smelled of death and old people, but mostly it smelled of . . . well, shit.

'It's very robust, do you agree?' asked Jean-Louis, enthusiastically shovelling in a mouthful.

Then she peered at the contents, now exposed in gory cross-section. As a committed meat-eater, she was relaxed about eating all parts of an animal; indeed, it seemed contradictory to say you'll eat a leg but not a cheek, like being a fussy cannibal.

But this was different. Inside the animal-gut casing – again, she was fine about that – were what appeared to be writhing white worms attempting to escape.

She felt faint and pushed the plate to one side.

'I'm sorry,' she said. 'I'm the least fussy eater in the world and I'm all in favour of nose-to-tail butchery to avoid waste, but I can't do that. I never thought I'd be defeated by a sausage.'

Jean-Louis grinned at her.

'Do you mind?' he said, helping himself to the discarded delicacy and scraping it onto his own plate. 'We don't want to offend the chef; I come very often to this restaurant.'

The tripe proved less troublesome and though Nicola wasn't mad about the rubbery texture, she adored the rich brown gravy, wiping the bowl with a piece of bread to extract every last drop.

They agreed that dessert would be a step too far, so Jean-Louis called for the bill, which Nicola insisted on splitting, and they stepped out into the fresh air.

'There is somewhere I want to take you,' said Jean-Louis. 'I know you will love it, with your green hand – sorry, I mean green fingers. Do you have time?'

'Yes, I have time, that is the benefit of retirement,' said Nicola, then wished she hadn't. She didn't mean to remind him of their age difference. He was mid-forties, she guessed – hardly toyboy territory, but at least a decade younger than her.

He drove her out of town, in the opposite direction from the château, following the river path towards the surrounding hills.

'Oh look, there's Chris's place,' said Nicola, pointing out the watermill sitting imposingly by the side of the road. It had formerly been a cheese factory and was far too large for its present use, several storeys high with windows – many of them broken – glittering in the afternoon sun. Parked in front was a collection of gypsy caravans and, oddly, a red London double-decker bus.

'The American who came to your party?'

'That's the one. Do you want to call in and have a look around?'

'No, I can see no benefit in acquiring old objects – and you have a château full of them already. Why does he have a bus in his garden?'

'His business partner is a landscape designer; I can only assume he has a home-sick Brit as a client.'

They drove on further into the hills, then Jean-Louis parked up on the outskirts of a sleepy village. Every village in Normandy was sleepy, Nicola had noticed. It didn't matter where you went, you rarely saw anybody walking the streets; no sign of life apart from wood smoke rising up from the chimneys of the houses, the only suggestion that they might, after all, be inhabited.

'I have brought you to the source of the river,' said Jean-Louis, leading her to an educational panel that was mounted close to a thoughtfully provided picnic table on a well-tended expanse of grass.

'It recounts the origins of the wealth of our region,' Jean-Louis explained. 'The mills were built mostly in the nineteenth century, when the textile industry expanded, though we had a lace and wool tradition centuries before that.'

Nicola dutifully studied the panel. It had fascinating black and white photos of workers filing into work at the mills. Their clothes were of another age but the landscape remained largely unchanged.

'But that is not what I brought you to see. I have a more practical objective. Let's walk by the water. You see it is far smaller here at the source – a fast, shallow stream ideal for growing one of my favourite local products.'

They walked a little way upstream, and he pointed at the river where an abundance of green weed was floating on the surface.

'Watercress,' said Jean-Louis. 'Let's find a stick and we can fish it out. I know how much you like foraging.'

He found a couple of branches fallen from a nearby tree and handed one to Nicola.

'Mind you don't fall in!' he said, grabbing her arm as she slipped down the muddy bank. They dredged up enough to fill two carrier bags that Jean-Louis produced from his pocket.

'It will make a fine soup,' he said, 'but my favourite recipe involves *Coquilles St Jacques* with a watercress emulsion and topped with caviar. I'd like to make it for you. Will you allow me?'

'That sounds better than *andouillette*.'

'It is more refined,' he said. 'More suitable for someone with your sensibilities.'

And then he drew her close and put his arms around her.

*It's too soon*, thought Nicola, but she didn't pull away. The pain of the past few months were a lifetime away; she only existed now, in this moment. And she liked him very much.

'I have wanted to do that since the first time I saw you,' said Jean-Louis. 'But I do not want to impose myself. I can wait; I am a patient man.'

Nicola remained calmly within his embrace. As long as she didn't respond, it wouldn't feel like she was cheating on Dom. Though obviously he had already muddied that water. Her calmness was coupled with something else – a sense of freedom and the knowledge that there was something exciting around the corner. It was too soon at the moment, but one day she could envisage being ready to take the next step.

They walked back to the car, hand in hand, and he opened the passenger door for her. They drove back in intimate silence, happily united in an unspoken agreement.

'You dark horse, I can't believe it! That was definitely not just two friends having lunch together,' said Beth, lying stretched out beside Nicola on Dom's side of the bed. 'That was a date. And a very nice date by the sound of things!'

Nicola had decided not to tell anyone, but the urge to share was too strong, and she wanted confirmation that she wasn't making a horribly embarrassing mistake by even contemplating the thought of getting involved.

'It wasn't really a date. We split the bill.'

'Hello! It shows how long you've been off the dating circuit. I think you'll find that modern women pay their own way these days, even on first dates.'

'Don't remind me how unmodern I am. I'm acutely aware of the age difference . . .'

'Age is a just a number, we've always agreed. And why the hell not? He's a lovely man who clearly adores you.'

'Most people would say it's too soon.'

'I'm not most people. Anyway, what is a decent period? Two years? Five years? Maybe make it ten so you wait until you're really decrepit.'

'Two months does sound scandalous.'

'Rubbish, you haven't actually done anything yet, not even been on a date – or so you claim. Anyway, I know someone who got together with her best friend's husband just two weeks after the friend's death! I said *good on her*, you know how quickly handsome widowers get snapped up – you have to get in early.'

'Jean-Louis isn't a widower.'

'Apparently not. You don't know much about him, though, do you?'

'There you go – you do think it's too soon!'

'That's not what I'm saying.'

'We're not going to rush it. And I'm certainly not telling the children yet.'

'Oh, they'll be furious, whenever you tell them,' said Beth. 'There's nothing you can do about that. I was forty-two when Dad announced he'd met someone, and it still cut like a knife, even though my mum had been dead for eight years.'

'We all want to believe our parents were each other's one and only. Although at least that myth has been put to rest in the case of me and Dom.'

'Which brings me to my next point. Children. Barring a mercy intervention by an Italian doctor, you're not going to provide Jean-Louis with a bonny brace of babies.'

Nicola shook her head.

'He doesn't want them, he already told me. He actually mentioned it in a general chat, quite soon after we met – said he wouldn't want to become a father now he was in his forties.

And when I said yesterday I was concerned about the age difference, he told me straight out that it was immaterial.' She put on a French accent. '*You know, Nicolette, I am not looking for someone to bear me children, I want only you.*'

'How adorable! You can be his Brigitte Macron! I love her and her stilletos. What a role model.'

'I'm never wearing heels again, not even for him.'

'Quite right. You need to hang on to your knees for as long as possible. Anyway, he evidently prefers you in wellies – more suited to his purpose.'

'So you don't think I'm acting like a deranged widow?'

'More like a love-sick teenager, I'd say.'

Beth squeezed her friend's hand.

'It does feel exciting,' said Nicola, 'but it's very sudden. I never thought I'd have these feelings again. I was with Dom for ages and never looked at anyone else when we were together. I always thought he felt the same – shows how wrong I was there ... Anyway, let's not go through all that again. The point is, I love the way I'm feeling right now, but I've no idea how it's going to pan out. I can't wait to see him again tomorrow but I can't look any further ahead than that.'

Beth looked at her in wonderment.

'You're really smitten, aren't you?'

Nicola nodded. 'I really am.'

'Look, none of us know what the future holds,' said Beth. 'If there's one wise thing I've learned it's that you must live for today. Especially at our age. Oops, sorry, there I go again.'

'That's how I feel! It brought it home to me, being back in London with Maddie and Gus. I'm thrilled about the baby, but I don't want to spend the rest of my days looking after a grandchild. Not every day, I mean. I'd love to have proper time with the baby – maybe even lovely French holidays when they're older – but I want to be granny babysitter, not granny nanny. I relish the freedom to spend the days as I choose. That's why we bought this place, isn't it? So we could live a different way, enjoying the everyday pleasures.'

'Exactly. And you've just added the possibility of a young lover to your list of everyday pleasures.'

'He's not my lover! As I say, we're taking things slowly.'

'Slowly, slowly, catchee monkey.'

'Where do you get these expressions?'

'Just be happy, Nicola. That's all I want for you. It's what we all want for you. You know things are much better now between me and Simon?'

'He told me. I'm so relieved.'

'There were moments when I thought it wasn't going to work out. We were already having problems back in London, with both of us out of work and hanging around the house all day. I worried that coming here was just pushing it away and seeking distraction. Then he was being so embarrassing, following you around like a drippy teenager – it was humiliating for me, too.'

'I know, it was horrid for you.'

'But he really does seem to have come to his senses. I do love him, you know, even though he's a total arse.'

'He's your total arse.'

'You mean, I'm welcome to him.'

They laughed.

'I'm so pleased you've sorted things out,' said Nicola, 'and not just for your sake. I'm being selfish here but I can't see how I would have got through the past few weeks without you. Can you imagine how I would have coped if you'd decided to walk out of the château? With or without your Arse.'

'Ah, you're lovely,' said Beth, giving her a warm hug. 'Don't worry, we're here to stay. Both of us.'

# Part Five

# Winter Again

# CHAPTER TWENTY-TWO

The nights had drawn in, the days were at their shortest and a blast of winter weather ruled out any hope of working in the garden. Instead, the chatelains were preparing for their first Christmas in their new home. It was the unspoken understanding that this would be a painful time for Nicola; everyone wanted to make it as good as it could be for her. Maddie and Gus would soon be arriving, under happier circumstances than their last visit, driving over with John and Eva.

In the library, before the crackling fire, Mary was taking a break from cleaning and was bent over her jigsaw, while Nicola was stretching a newly made fabric cover over her old chaise longue. She had used one of the rolls of fabric that Leo had discovered in the attic, to his intense delight. Nicola had chosen a burgundy patterned velvet for her project, while Leo had already used the vintage silver tulle to great effect in the crystal ballroom, transforming it into a winter wonderland in readiness for their Christmas celebrations.

'Isn't that just the most insanely beautiful sight?' said Leo, as he came into the room.

'Thank you, Leo,' said Nicola, sitting back to admire her handiwork. 'I'm pretty pleased with it myself.'

'I mean that view,' said Leo, standing by the window. 'A pristine white carpet running down to the frozen lake, thick snow balancing on the branches of the trees – it's like living in a Christmas card. Your chaise is gorgeous, too, Nicola, don't get me wrong.'

'I really understand hibernation for the first time,' said Nicola. 'It's like being woodland creatures. Everything we need is here; we can just stay warm and safe until spring comes.'

Their winter preparations had been immaculate. Logs were piled high in the woodshed, the pantry was stuffed with kilner jars of orchard fruits and a new chest freezer had been installed in the *arrière cuisine* to store the glut of vegetables that would see them through until next year's crop.

Mary looked up from her jigsaw board.

'Has someone just arrived? I can hear an engine running.'

Jean-Louis appeared at the library door, in his heavy outdoor clothing. He looked adoringly at Nicola, who reacted by pointing to the chaise, splendid in its new cover.

'Look, Jean-Louis, all my own work. Are you impressed?'

He walked over to inspect it, touching her hand lightly as he approached. She squeezed it in response.

'I am very impressed. I see you are a *femme de l'interieur* as well as being an accomplished gardener. But it is Leo I am here for.' He turned to face him. 'I have those branches you asked me for. Shall I bring them in?'

'Ooh, heaven, yes, please!' said Leo. 'If you could put them in the crystal ballroom, I'm going to deck them with silver paint and snow-white decorations. It's bringing the outside in, you see, breaking down the boundaries between exterior and interior.'

He followed Jean-Louis to the front door.

'I'd love to help you, but my shoes . . .'

He looked down at his velvet loafers.

'Don't worry, Leo, I can manage.'

Jean-Louis retraced his footsteps through the snow to his tractor and returned, dragging three apple branches behind him. He shook off the excess snow before carrying the branches into the crystal ballroom. Leo had already put in place old wine casks, cut in half, in which he planned to arrange them.

'That's perfect, Jean-Louis,' he said. 'You see how well the mistletoe works?'

Each branch had been invaded by a perfectly round clump of mistletoe, adding variety of form and texture.

Jean-Louis nodded. 'I can see there is an aesthetic advantage to it, though I confess at first I could not understand why you wanted to bring these parasites into the château. For me, the logical place for branches infested with mistletoe is the bonfire!'

'Sacrilege!' said Leo. 'Don't you share our tradition?'

He held one of the branches over his head and turned his cheek towards Jean-Louis, tapping it with his finger.

'*Bien sûr,*' said Jean-Louis, placing a hearty kiss on Leo's cheek, '*on s'embrasse sous le gui,* we kiss beneath the mistletoe, but we only need a tiny bunch, the rest is for the fire.'

Nicola came into the ballroom.

'Oh, am I interrupting something?'

She walked towards them and both men opened their arms to draw her in between them. She kissed them both in turn on the cheek.

'It's a Norse tradition,' said Jean-Louis, 'I know it from my ancestry. The goddess Frigg's son Baldr was killed by an arrow made of mistletoe. She wept tears onto the arrow, which turned into white berries that she used on his wounds to bring him back to life! Frigg then blessed the mistletoe and promised a kiss to all who passed beneath it.'

'What a charming story,' said Leo. 'I always thought it was to do with the Druids and infertility, but I prefer the Norse version. And now we have our own trees of hope growing in the château, bringing love and healing to everyone here.'

'I must go and clear away next door,' said Nicola, breaking away from them. Her first Christmas without Dom. There would be so many other firsts: his birthday, hers, their wedding anniversary, the anniversary of their arrival at the château. At each milestone, she would remember the two of them together at the same point last year.

If only she'd been there beside him on the roadside, maybe she, too, might have wept tears that turned into white berries to bring him back to life.

In her bedroom, Beth was wrapping her final present. It was for Nicola, a rare edition of Baudelaire's *Les Fleurs du Mal* that she had bought on a recent trip to Paris with Simon. It was a delightful weekend – they'd stayed in a small hotel on the Left Bank and browsed the book stalls lining the Seine, feeling grateful that they had each other. Dominic's sudden death had heightened their awareness of their mortality, and the folly of wasting the time that was left to them in argument and conflict.

'It's what Dom would have wanted,' Simon said, as he cuddled up to her in bed, and Beth laughed at his use of the cliché. It was one of their in-jokes that whenever someone died, those who were left behind defined their every action as 'what he would have wanted'.

Beth wrote her message on the card, which carried an image of the famous Angel of Grief sculpture, showing a winged creature draped over a tomb and weeping in despair.

*When it rains, it pours, but soon the sun shines again. Better days are ahead and here is a gorgeous volume of decadent poems to build on your massive French language skills that have already come on so far. Love and luck to you, my dearest friend. Beth*

She left it lying on top of the present while she went to find the envelope in the chest of drawers. Simon came in and picked it up.

'That's a bit maudlin, isn't it? Hardly going to put her in the festive spirit.' He read the message inside. 'Nice words, though.'

'That's what we do as friends. We don't pretend everything's all right all the time. This Christmas is going to be horrible for Nicola. The point is we acknowledge pain and look forward to a brighter future.'

'You're so right, as always.'

He put his arms round her and kissed her.

'Speaking of fine words, dare I ask? Have you read it yet?'

'Have I read what?'

She looked at him teasingly. As part of their rapprochement, Simon had asked her if she would like to read his book. 'When I say my book,' he'd added, 'obviously I mean the bit of the book that I've already written, not the whole thing. God no, that's years away.' He wanted her honest opinion, he said. He didn't care if she didn't like it. 'Just tell me what you really think of it.'

'As a matter of fact, I have,' she said now. 'I galloped through it this morning. You're lucky I'm a professionally paced reader . . .'

'And? Come on, Beth, stop tormenting me.'

'I thought it was . . .'

She deadpanned, her face displaying no emotion.

'. . . brilliant!'

'You did?' He broke into a smile. 'I'm so glad. You're sure you're not just saying that?'

'I love it! And not just because it's the story of a man who almost ruins his marriage by chasing a woman from his past.'

'Mmmm.'

'And then luckily sees the error of his ways just in time to haul himself back from the abyss! Or at least, I assume that's what will happen – you haven't got that far yet.'

'No, no, but you're on the right lines. I hope the plot isn't too obvious . . .'

'It won't be to your other readers, but it is to me because I recognise the story.'

'Well, they do say write what you know . . .'

'And may I say how flattered I am by my portrayal! I never knew you thought those things about me.'

Simon looked flustered. 'You know me, I'm a bit of an emotional cripple . . .'

'Although there were a few details I could have done without . . . in the annoying habit category. I admit I recognised myself there.'

'In the interests of authenticity, I drew on my own experience.'

'Breaking eggs into my hands to separate the yolks from the whites, which you find so unhygienic.'

'You've got to admit that's a bit gross.'

'And clearing my throat before speaking as though I'm about to deliver a speech.'

'There are plenty of endearing details in there, as well! You know I heard somewhere that every writer has a compost heap, made up of every experience they've ever had. It all rots away unnoticed, then it matures into source material. And as most of my experiences are with you, it stands to reason you feature so prominently in my book.' He kneeled down before her, like a fake knight. 'Beth, you are my compost heap.'

She threw back her head and laughed. 'That's the nicest thing anybody's ever said to me.'

On Christmas Eve, the young guests were making themselves useful in the kitchen. They'd arrived late the previous night. Eva, Maddie and Gus had piled into John's car after work and headed straight for the Eurotunnel. Maddie shared the driving along the dark motorways, untroubled by the snow until the final stretch down country roads, when John had to use his chains after a wheel became stuck. It was a good job he was so sensible, they agreed – he was proper father material, keeping snow chains in the boot of his car.

It was the second visit for most of them, but John's first. Nicola's eyes had filled with tears as she welcomed them in out of the darkness, remembering the last time they had come through that door, in such different circumstances. High summer, blistering heat, numbed with grief.

'What's this we're listening to?' asked Dougie, frowning at the potato he was peeling. He held the peeler in a way that suggested he'd never seen one before, which was entirely possible. 'It doesn't sound familiar.'

'It's "Christmas in the Dogghouse", Dougie,' said Gus, expertly slicing carrots into *batonnets*. 'Do you like it? It's by Snoop Dogg.'

Dougie shook his head in wonderment. 'Extraordinary, this new music. And the names!'

'It's not new, this is ancient,' said Maddie. 'It's a song from our childhood! I'll be playing this to our baby when it's old enough, as a nostalgic throwback to Christmases past.'

'We've come a long way from Nat King Cole's "Chestnuts Roasting on an Open Fire",' said Dougie.

'Speaking of which, who wants to do the worst job in the world?' said Nicola, moving a hot saucepan of chestnuts from the gas ring onto the crowded table. The kitchen was cleaner than when they moved in, but still basic: an old range cooker, with a chaotic variety of pans hanging from a string attached across the ceiling. They had become accustomed to it, though, and were increasingly of the opinion that nothing needed changing.

'Someone needs to peel the skins off while they're still warm.'

'I will,' said John.

'Good boy,' said Nicola. 'What a very suitable young man you are to be fathering my grandchild.' She kissed the top of his head and exchanged a happy smile with Maddie. Everything was going to be all right after all. She was sure of it now.

Next door, Leo and Fizz were putting the finishing touches to the dining-room décor. In contrast to the white and silver of the crystal ballroom, with its ghostly mistletoed trees and sparkling frost effect, the dining room was designed in rich greens and crimson – a dark forest glade offering warm shelter.

'I love the way the reds play against the bronze and green velvet curtains,' said Fizz. 'Fancy us finding them packed away upstairs.'

'Madame de Courcy told me she'd put them away one spring in order to hang those horrid thin drapes, then forgot all about them. We should keep them up, assuming she doesn't reclaim them this evening! This décor is how I want this room to be permanently. The trees in the crystal ballroom are obviously just a bit of seasonal fun, but what we've done in here is for keeps.'

He stepped away from the table to admire the room. Taking his inspiration from the legendary French designer Jacques Garcia, he had focussed on his signature rich colours; the red was dominant and different shades of green harmonising. But he had added lighter touches of his own.

'We don't want to look like we're stuck in the 1990s,' he said to Fizz. 'This is maximalism revisited for the modern age.'

'That looks pretty cool,' said Eva, coming towards them. She had risen late, missing breakfast, and was wearing her Christmas jumper, featuring reindeer and snowmen.

'Certainly cooler than me,' she said, twirling around so they could admire her tasteless sweater from all angles. 'I'm taking a style break for the holidays. Note the necklace – that's my other naff seasonal accessory.'

Around her neck was a thin necklace of narrow multicoloured lightbulbs, which flashed on and off.

'I love it,' said Fizz. 'It's so retro kitsch.'

'I should put you on the top of one of my Christmas trees,' said Leo. 'You'd sit nicely above the mistletoe.'

'I saw those branches on my way through – they look fantastic! But don't we have a proper old-fashioned Christmas tree as well?'

'Not this year,' said Leo. 'We wanted to make it a little different.'

'But I want everything to always be the same,' Eva complained, putting on a cross face. 'I'm the classic spoilt only child and I decree that Nothing Must Change!'

'Everything has changed for Nicola,' said Leo.

'Of course, poor thing,' said Eva, softening. 'She looks so much better, though. I haven't seen her since the funeral.'

'She's doing very well,' said Leo. 'We're all looking after her.'

'I'm sure you are,' said Eva. 'Hey, Fizz, what about you and your massive profile! I can't go on YouTube without falling over your stuff. It's brilliant!'

'Thanks, Eva,' said Fizz. 'It's keeping me entertained and I'm really building up a following now – it seems there's a lot of people out there who are keen to embrace their inner Mademoiselle Bovary. Your mum has been a brilliant help, by the way. She was instrumental in getting that *Le Déjeuner sur l'herbe* photo done, which is when it really kicked off.'

'She loved it, she told me. I'm glad to see her and Dad getting on so much better – it warms the cockles of my hard little heart to see it.'

'There's nothing hard about your heart,' said Fizz. 'Come with me, let's go next door by the fire and you can tell me all about your love life. I'm starved of all that chat out here in the rural wilderness with only old people to talk to.'

Eva laughed. 'You love it here among your old people, I can tell you do!'

Some hours later, Gus and Maddie were put in charge of laying the table, setting out cutlery and multiple glasses as instructed by Leo, taking care not to disrupt the complicated central decorations involving holly, iridescent shot-silk ribbons, antique glass baubles and more candles than anybody would have thought possible.

'I guess there's safety in numbers,' said Gus to Maddie, flicking through the scarlet place cards, which Mary had inscribed with gold ink in her meticulous Gothic script. 'With sixteen of us for dinner, there's not much chance of Mum brooding quietly in a corner.'

'I thought we'd be doing the big celebration tomorrow,' said Maddie. 'As far as I'm concerned, Christmas Eve is for wrapping up presents and watching telly. Oh, and drawing up the cooking timetable. Do you remember Dad's lists?'

'How could I not!'

Dominic had always loved Christmas, and got deeply involved in its organisation. Every year he would bring out his notebook, containing a detailed history of the cooking methods employed

over the decades. The weight of the turkey, the oven tempera-
ture, roasting times, whether or not it was covered in foil, and
the family's verdict. The notebook as a piece of Christmas ritual
was as precious as the worn old stockings they used to hang out
at the end of their beds.

'Oh, Maddie, it's so awful, isn't it?' Gus put down the place
cards and turned to her. 'Knowing we'll never see him again.
Most of the time, you know, I just get on with it, and then suddenly it hits me.'

'I know.'

She put her arm around his shoulder, then pulled herself back
into brisk mode.

'Anyway, it is what it is. This year, you can forget the turkey
and Dad's notes. It's goose. And it's not even on Christmas Day,
it's a day early! But on reflection, I think it's great, don't you?
Apparently in France they always celebrate it on Christmas Eve,
and it's better to go along with that than being stuck in our rut,
wishing Dad was with us.'

'I guess. You know she's invited the farmer – what's his name?'

'Jean-Louis,' said Maddie, picking his personalised name card
from the pile and placing it in its allocated position. She noticed
he would be sitting next to her. 'She talks about him a lot,' she
added. 'Do you think there's something going on there?'

Gus looked horrified.

'Don't be obscene – Dad's barely cold in his grave! And he's
much younger than Mum. Anyway, there are other infiltrators.

The former owner, Madame de Courcy, for one – she'll be sitting on my right. Mum said to make sure she doesn't put the cutlery in her bag – she's known to be a little light-fingered, apparently.'

'That's the landed gentry for you – tight as anything,' said Maddie. 'Look at Leo. He's the first to admit he experiences physical pain whenever he has to spend money.'

'Madame de Courcy's nephew is also coming. He's visiting her from Paris,' said Gus. 'Beth told me the old lady was thrilled to be invited. Back in her old home, with other people doing the cooking and paying for the heating.'

'I rest my case – she sounds like a right old Scrooge,' said Maddie. 'The other guest is Chris, the hippie who sold them that weird wardrobe. Now largely emptied of Dad's clothes – I think Mum couldn't wait to get rid of them after the Painful Discovery.'

She and Gus had talked a lot about the revelation of their father's affair, and agreed there was little to add. 'We'll never know the full story,' Gus had said. 'Dad's dead and that's the real tragedy. The rest doesn't matter.'

'That's one topic that will be off limits this evening,' he said. 'There, the table looks wonderful. I think we've earned a glass of champagne, don't you? Sorry, I mean sparkling elderflower in your case.'

The *réveillon de noel* was the pinnacle of their culinary year, a succession of riches reflecting the serious food culture of their adopted homeland. Blinis with caviar and smoked salmon, oysters, foie gras on *pain d'epices* with his glass of sauternes (they suspended their conscience for the night), goose, cheese, and finally, the *bûche de noel*, a rich chocolate moussey log that was so much better than Christmas pudding – according to John, who managed three helpings. A token doll's-sized Christmas pudding had also been offered, together with mince pies, which the French guests were obliged to sample. Madame de Courcy, her nephew Max and Jean-Louis were of one opinion here, leaving their bowls untouched after sampling half a spoonful.

Jean-Louis was the last guest to leave, and by the time Nicola returned from showing him out, the others had left the table and were sprawled around the crystal ballroom, Leo claiming he would never eat again, while Simon wondered if he could just manage another tiny spoon of runny Vacherin cheese to help down his calvados digestif.

'You took your time,' Simon teased her. 'Did you walk him home?'

'We were just chatting,' said Nicola casually, sitting down next to Maddie on the sofa, beneath the silvery apple branch.

Maddie turned to her mother.

'He's lovely,' she whispered, so nobody else could hear. 'We had such a great conversation over dinner. I was glad you put him next to me. I'm assuming that was deliberate?'

Nicola was lost for words. To her embarrassment, she realised she was blushing. On the doorstep with Jean-Louis, she had suddenly seen the way forward for them, the perfect solution for their future. It wasn't a question of her leaving her friends at the château to move in with him – that was unthinkable. Nor could she expect him to move in with her; he belonged on the farm – that was obvious. Instead, they would keep both their homes, and visit each other in an ongoing series of date nights. A fulfilling courtship that would continue for the rest of their lives; it was incredibly romantic. She hadn't said anything to him about it, and she certainly didn't want to discuss it now with Maddie. Luckily, they were distracted by Dougie rising to his feet in front of the fireplace.

'Can I have your attention, please. Now that it's just us, Mary and I have something to tell you. First of all, though, congratulations to the chefs. Beth and Nicola, you've done us proud. What a dream team you are!'

'Thanks, Dougie,' said Beth, who was cuddled up with Simon on the controversial pink love seat that Leo hadn't yet managed to relegate to the barn. 'Though I must admit it just goes to prove what we already know about the French – they can't cook! They don't need to – the reputation for fine food comes from the ingredients. All we had to do was put the birds in the oven! The rest of it we just unpacked.'

'So what's your news, Dougie?' said Will. 'Is it that we've overspent the Christmas budget, in which case, we already know it!'

'No, nothing like that. Well, not entirely unrelated.'

'Tell us!' Simon heckled.

'Very well,' said Dougie, glancing over at Mary. 'You may recall that in the summer, before . . . before the accident . . .' He overcame his awkwardness. ' . . . before the accident, Mary and I took a trip home, to see her mother and so on. What we didn't tell you at the time was that we had decided to put our house on the market, which we did. And now, the good news is, we have a buyer! Contracts were exchanged last week, and so you see, we will have a welcome cash injection for our renovations.'

'Good man!' said Will. 'It also means there's no going back for you now!'

'I admit we weren't entirely sure at the beginning,' said Mary. 'We wanted to keep the house as an insurance policy. But we couldn't bear to leave the château now – it's our home. And you lot are our family.'

She was becoming a little weepy, and Fizz jumped up to give her a hug.

'Nice of you to hand over all your money, Dougie,' said Simon with a grin.

'It will be reflected in the accounts and apportioning of ownership, of course,' said Dougie, 'but it means we now have the liquidity to put all our plans into action.'

'Well done,' said Leo. 'And it looks like I'm in the money as well. Madame de Courcy's nephew adored what I've done in the dining room. Turns out he owns a chain of restaurants in Paris and wants to refurbish them, using me as their designer!'

'This calls for more champagne,' said Simon, downing his calvados and standing up to head for the cellar. 'Happy Christmas, everyone! Will, you need to get your arse onto that piano stool – it's time for a good old singalong.'

After all the noise and celebration, the château was restored to quietness in the early, dead days of January. The snow melted and the house guests departed, leaving the residents to clear away the decorations and think about the future. The plans for the apartments were resurrected and Will – who had declared himself clerk of works – drew up a shortlist of builders recommended by their roofer. It was finally happening. They would each have their own suite of rooms – at last, Fizz could have her bathroom – while keeping the grand reception rooms for shared use, as originally intended.

One afternoon, they were all gathered round the dining table, poring over the plans, when Jean-Louis appeared on the doorstep with a large cardboard cake box.

Nicola smiled as she opened the door to him.

'How did I know it would be you?' she said.

'Telepathy – you know we have our understanding . . . May I come in?'

They went through to the dining room, where Beth's eyes lit up at the sight of the cake box.

'Jean-Louis, you read my mind,' she said. 'I was just thinking I could manage a sweet finish. I'll go and put the kettle on!'

Jean-Louis placed the box on the table and opened it to take out a well risen puff pastry pie, along with two golden cardboard crowns.

'This is a *galette des rois*. We always serve it today, the sixth of January, for the feast of epiphany. Inside there is a frangipane almond filling, and also a *fève*, a china charm you must take care not to swallow. Whoever finds the *fève* in their tart can wear the crown – they are the king or queen, and they must choose a partner to wear the other crown.'

The tart was delicious, with the marzipan still faintly warm from the boulangerie oven. Nicola had noticed the *galettes des rois*, of varying sizes, lined up in the windows of the town's bakeries. She'd never bought one, as she knew they contained marzipan, which made her think of fruit cakes from her childhood, with their thick hard layer of bright yellow, chemical-tasting gunge that she would peel off and discard before eating the icing. This *galette* was something else, though. The French had reclaimed marzipan.

Fizz found the *fève*, so wore the crown, giving the other one to Will. It was a childish custom, thought Nicola, and allowed herself to imagine one day in the future, when her grandchild might be sitting here, eyes shining as they found the charm and claimed their crown.

After tea, Nicola asked Jean-Louis if he had time to take a walk with her. She had barely been out for the last few days, the weather had been so unpleasant, and she pulled on a hat and scarf, along with the fake fur coat she kept hanging in the hall. Dom used to call it her rock chick coat.

The sky was watery grey, but it wasn't raining. They fell into step and headed down to the lake, kicking through the dirty slush, which was all that remained of the Christmas snow. Nicola led the way to the corner of the field where they'd installed a swing seat that she'd spotted at Chris's shop. It had a bed-sized wooden base suspended from its frame, with antique heavy iron chains – part of Chris's recent shipment from India. During the summer, they kept cushions on the seat, but today Nicola sat on the hard wooden surface as it was. Jean-Louis sat down beside her, and pushed the ground with his foot, so the seat swung backwards and forwards in a gentle rocking motion.

Nicola spoke first.

'Do you know, it's exactly a year since we first came up with this idea. To move to a big house in the country – I mean, the French château thing came later.'

'It has been a year of enormous change for you,' Jean-Louis said simply.

'Yes.'

'You could not have envisaged what was to follow.'

'No.'

She turned to him. 'Jean-Louis, I can't change what has happened, but I can choose what happens next.'

He looked at her enquiringly.

'I'm ready,' she said.

His face lit up in delight but Nicola held up her hand.

'I don't want us to live together.'

His face fell.

'I will stay at the château and you will live in your house,' she continued. 'But we will visit each other. On a very regular basis. I want to be with you, Jean-Louis – that's all I want.'

And with that, finally Jean-Louis leaned in for the kiss he had been waiting for since the first time he saw her.

# EPILOGUE:
## EIGHT MONTHS LATER

'He's *magnifique!*' Beth said to Simon, as the mayor stood up, his tricolour sash straining over his impressive stomach.

They were crammed into the local *mairie*, a tiny room in a stone cottage with standing room only at the back. The door was open so the crowds outside could watch the action.

'Ladies and gentlemen, you are welcome to this international celebration,' the mayor boomed in his rich baritone. 'Never in my tenure as mayor of this village have I had the honour to unite two young people from the land of our friends across the channel. And may I say, I commend their choice. As we know, France is the land of love, and what more auspicious start to a marriage than to have it formalised here, in this beautiful part of God's own country.'

'I thought England was God's own country?' Dougie whispered to Mary.

'Or Kerala. Or New Zealand. Or Wales. The idea is widely adopted.'

Nicola was sitting on the front row, with a prime view of Maddie looking like a proper English rose in her sprigged muslin dress. John stood proudly beside her, wearing a blue and yellow tie to match his EU-emblazoned socks.

They fell silent under the mayor's disapproving frown and sat through the monotonous repetition of formalities, phrased in the tortuous bureaucratic language the French excelled in.

'And now, let the *fête* commence!' said the mayor. He pressed the play button on an ancient CD player, and the mournful strains of 'God Save the Queen' filled the room, followed by the rousing sound of the 'Marseillaise'. Both anthems were greeted with tumultuous applause.

The happy couple filed out first, all radiant smiles. Maddie paused to gather up her daughter, Lily, who was cradled in Fizz's lap near the entrance, ready for a quick exit if necessary.

'What an extraordinary occasion,' said Simon to Will amid the jostling of photographers outside. 'I'm going to have a French country wedding scene in my book – it's simply irresistible.'

He looked at Nicola posing beside Maddie and to his relief felt nothing more than warm friendship.

It was a short drive back to the château; the cars formed a procession, all honking their horns in celebration, in the local tradition. A marquee decorated with Michaelmas daisies was set out in the field – an unnecessary precaution, as it turned out, under the September sun, but Maddie had been adamant there was no way she would let it rain on her parade. They formed a receiving line, with Nicola standing between John's parents, who could not look more English – Geraldine with her wobbly mother-of-the groom fascinator and Geoffrey in the morning suit he insisted on wearing despite the informality of the occasion. 'I've got the damned thing; may as well get some use out of it,' he'd declared, showing the same aversion to unnecessary expenditure as his son, which Nicola admitted was a good thing now they had a family to consider.

It was six months since Maddie and John had made the move to France, following an idyllic Easter visit when they had been so reluctant to return to London that they decided they wouldn't. In that time, John had leaped into father-provider mode and converted the barn – the scene of Nicola's discovery of Dom's secret lover, now referred to as the Flora Letters – into an idyllic love nest for the young family. Will and Simon had worked alongside him, but his real partner in the project was Jean-Louis, the pair of them presenting a fine blond duo in their matching blue boiler-suits.

Lily came into the world under the gentle care of nuns who ran the nearby maternity clinic. They defied Maddie's NCT indoctrination about breastfeeding by taking the baby away at night so the new mother could sleep, and bringing her back for her morning feed. Nicola had to give them credit for that – Maddie's milk did not dry up as a result of a few hours respite and it seemed a far more sensible approach than the evangelical zeal of the breast-or-bust militants.

'It's funny how you and Maddie and the baby ended up living together after all,' said Beth, after seeking Nicola out among the marquee full of champagne drinkers. 'In spite of all your protestations.'

'Completely different circumstances,' said Nicola. 'Separate roofs, for a start, and as you know, it won't be forever. Just a gap year, and then they'll be bored with us and desperate to get back to the real world. They'll need to – they won't find work here – but they'll always have the barn for holidays. In fact, they've told us we can rent it out as a holiday let when they're not here – bring in some extra income for our château fund. It's such a delight to have them here and to know they'll always have the place to come back to.'

Fizz wandered up to them, a glass of fizzy water in her hand, her bump clearly visible beneath her billowing kaftan.

'Here she comes, Mrs I-Don't-Want-Children,' Beth teased her. 'At least you don't have to suffer the agony of giving up drinking, as you already had.'

'It's a woman's right to change her mind,' said Fizz. 'I'm getting some lessons in from Maddie, but I'm definitely not going to use disposable nappies – they're an ecological disaster.'

'Always the moral high ground,' said Beth as Fizz walked off to have her fecundity admired by a couple of John's aunts. 'I do love her, though. And you'll have her baby to dandle on your knee just as Lily disappears back to London. Though I must say I'm glad they're moving into the other barn. Far more peaceful for the rest of us.'

Shifting circumstances meant they had rethought their plans for separate apartments within the château. With Will and Fizz converting a barn for themselves, there would only be six of them in the château, and they had become so used to sharing the space, there was little appetite for breaking it up. So instead, they'd used Will and Mary's money to renovate the kitchen and put in three new bathrooms, which was just perfect.

Simon came to join them, balancing three canapes in his hand.

'I'm glad to be back in the land of decent food,' he said, slipping his arm round Beth's waist. 'You wouldn't believe what they served up last week; thought I was back in the 1970s. I kept expecting them to dish up Goblin meat puddings and Angel Delight.'

He had just returned from a residential writing course at a damp house set deep in the Welsh countryside.

'Apart from the food, how did you find it?' Nicola asked. 'Has it reignited your muse?'

'Pretty good, actually, even if it did feel like a massive self-help session at times. Mostly good people – I touted the château to them as a venue for a writers' retreat, which could be a nice little earner for us. There were a couple of tossers, as you'd expect.

Most notably the ex-adman – you'd have loved hearing him on the first day when we had to introduce ourselves. "I'm not exactly a beginner," he told us. "Last year I self-published a fable."'

Beth and Nicola snorted in delight.

'Are you discussing the fables of La Fontaine?' asked Jean-Louis, arriving with a bottle of champagne to top up their glasses.

'I don't know, did he self-publish them?' asked Simon, but Jean-Louis had turned his attention to Nicola.

'*Cherie*, you look *ravissante* today,' he murmured. 'I'm loving this *fête*, but I cannot wait until everyone has left and we can escape upstairs.'

'Hey, put her down!' said Gus, slapping Jean-Louis affectionately on the back. 'You don't want to upset your ready-made family.'

Jean-Louis lowered his head in mock apology.

'Excuse me, *mon fiston*, but your mother is a very beautiful woman.'

'So she is,' Gus agreed. 'And on that topic, I'm just going to have a word with that equally beautiful cousin of John's. I honestly can't believe she's related to him.'

Nicola smiled as she watched him exercising his charm on a pretty girl with a nose ring and a grapevine tattoo arranged aesthetically up her arm.

'Are you happy with the day?' asked Jean-Louis. 'I think it is a big success.'

'I'm happy with everything,'

'And you still don't want us to present ourselves before *monsieur le maire*?'

He gestured towards the mayor, who was in full anecdote before a crowd of admirers.

'Quite sure. We are perfect as we are. Why would we want to become an old married couple when we can keep up a lifetime of loving courtship. We have the château when we are feeling sociable, and your house when we want to be alone.'

'*Je suis d'accord*,' said Jean-Louis, as Bruno Mars's 'The Way You Are' started playing through the sound system.

He offered her his arm.

'Shall we dance?'